The Last Alicorn

- Tales of the Always Night, Part 1 -

ANDREW HINDLE

Copyright © 2020 Andrew Hindle

All rights reserved.

ISBN: 9798554225642
Imprint: Independently published

FOR THE NEXT GENERATION

For Lily and Ruby, Elsa and Lucas, Freja and Viggo.

Don't listen to us. This world is yours now.

CONTENTS

About *Tales of the Always Night*	i

Part One: The Bet
- Prologue — 2
- Galana Fen (Crewmember #1) — 6
- A Wayward Student — 11
- Basil Hartigan (Crewmember #2) — 15
- The ACS *Conch* — 21
- Devlin Scrutarius (Crewmember #3) — 27
- Into the Grey — 31
- Doctor Bonjamin Bont (Crewmember #4) — 35
- The *Chalice* — 43
- Wicked Mary (Crewmember #5) — 48
- Declivitorion-On-The-Rim — 57
- Chillybin (Crewmember #6) — 67
- Departure for Parts Unknown, and Adventure — 71

Part Two: Here There Be Space Dragons
- The Demon of Azabol — 78
- The Moon The Burned — 94
- The Star That Sang — 106
- The Man-Apes — 113
- The Ship of Sharks — 126
- The Star Serpent — 138
- The Planet of the Cancer — 151
- The Golden Idol — 163

Part Three: The Last Alicorn
- The Fantastical Cakes of Zoogo Zaroy — 178
- The Fang o' God — 191
- The Riddlespawn — 206
- The Blind Time Traveller — 227
- The Sirens of Gozonaar — 247
- The Star That Sang (Reprise) — 260
- The Perils of High Elonath — 272
- The Last Alicorn — 286

ABOUT *TALES OF THE ALWAYS NIGHT*

The story of the ACS *Conch* and its legendary circumnavigation of the galaxy was never a matter of Fleet record, and it certainly never got an AstroCorps mission log. Over the centuries, it became more folk tale than history. By the Thirty-Ninth Century YM, only fragments remained.

Loës Artikon, at one time a respectable historian, is responsible for assembling the most complete collection of *Conch* stories and lore, and destroying Artikon's own reputation utterly in the process. Loës Artikon is remembered, if at all, as an author of the most preposterous fantastical claptrap who was laughed out of the halls of over a hundred universities for attempting to pass such unbelievable rubbish off as *fact*.

In the unlikely event you have read Artikon's original collection of Xidh *theria*, or one of the popular interpretations to have been published as adventure stories under the title *Tales of the Always Night*, the story you are about to read will not strike a familiar chord. There are overlaps, of course, but the benefit of a folk tale is the sheer number of liberties that can be taken with characters and events.

The story you are about to read is the story of what really happened to the crew of the ACS *Conch* on their famous voyage.

This story owes a great deal to the work of Loës Artikon, which was in fact earnest and above intellectual reproach. The author hopes Artikon's memory might find some measure of vindication, perhaps even acceptance, as a result of this tale seeing the light of day.

Or, alternatively, he will join Artikon in obscurity and ridicule.

Either way.

The author would like to add a further special thanks to his firstborn, Elsa Hindle, for loaning him her imagination throughout the process of writing and reading this story. Without her, some of the wildest pieces of truth – Captain Pelsworthy of the Boze, the Nyif Nyif, perhaps even the Last Alicorn itself – may have remained untold by a cowardly storyteller, and dismissed as the desperate embellishments of a fallen historian.

PART ONE: THE BET

PROLOGUE

If anyone had told Fellandra ten hours ago that she would spend her duty shift carrying Ogre luggage from one end of a Worldship to the other, she would have laughed. That was before she found out it was really a thing that was going to happen, that Ogre luggage really existed, and how *massive* it could be. And some of it smelled … well, exactly like you'd expect Ogre luggage to smell, if she was being honest.

Fortunately, most of it went on a set of mechanised trolleys. Unfortunately, the flagship *Enna Midzis* was far bigger than Fellandra thought a starship needed to be. She'd thought it was about the right size, until she'd had to carry Ogre luggage from one end of it to the other.

She found the Captain in the aft viewing gallery, gazing down at the alien world spread out below them. It took Fellandra a few seconds to wrestle the trolley-train to a halt and put down the two additional cases she was carrying, all of which she did as quietly and politely as she could. The gallery was otherwise deserted.

She thought she heard the Captain murmur something. *You're still beautiful.* Something like that. Fellandra assumed the Captain was talking about the Earth, or possibly *to* it. It was a Captain thing. Captains had high-pressure and high-responsibility jobs, they were expected to do dramatic little monologues sometimes. Everyone maintained the polite fiction that they were recording an audio log or keeping a journal or something.

And the Earth *was* beautiful, she supposed. It was a mess, but it was a beautiful mess. The trick was to be far away enough that you couldn't see the horde of angry monkeys that lived down there.

" … we are not going *anywhere*," the Captain murmured a little more loudly.

"Captain Char?" Fellandra spoke up, worried that the Captain might think she was listening in on her Captain-monologue and judging her.

The Captain turned and regarded Fellandra solemnly, taking in her harried appearance, her stained uniform, the teetering caravan of boxes. "Yes?"

"The – the – our visitors' ... our new crewmates' luggage, Captain," Fellandra said. She gestured to the boxes, just in case the Captain thought she was talking about herself.

Captain Char frowned. "The humans had luggage at the feast venue?" she asked.

"No, the – the Ogres," Fellandra replied.

Captain Char's ears flicked in surprise. "The *Ogres* had luggage?" she looked down at the little blue figurine she was holding in one hand. It looked like a souvenir, Fellandra thought. And a pretty tacky one at that. When you went to an alien world and made contact, you should get a nicer present, even if things went badly. And things had really gone quite badly. "I thought – aside from the pack they had with them ... "

"This all came up on a separate transport, Captain," Fellandra explained. "Apparently there was a bunch of stuff they simply couldn't live without," the Captain was walking back along the train of carrier trolleys now, staring. She stopped at one battered, bulky metal object, gazed at it, then turned to look at Fellandra. "I believe that is called an *air hockey table*, Captain."

"I see."

"I was thinking, nobody seemed sure, perhaps you could direct me to the Ogres' living quarters and I could deliver this to them?" Fellandra said hopefully. Most of her hopefulness was reserved for wishing the living quarters wouldn't turn out to be back at the other end of the ship.

The Captain had returned to her study of the luggage. Now she aimed another polite stare in Fellandra's direction. "The Ogres are gone," she said, and pointed out of the viewing window, into space. "They left just now."

"Oh."

"Yes."

"When will they be back?"

"They're not coming back," the Captain replied.

"Oh," Fellandra repeated. She joined the Captain in looking at the mass of junk. "What happens when they want to play air hockey?"

"I would assume at that point they will remember that they had a bunch of luggage that included an air hockey table," the Captain said, "and they will either come back for it, or go on without it."

"Oh."

"It rather depends on how literally they can't live without it."

Fellandra waited, but it didn't seem as though the Captain had any more advice or orders to give concerning the luggage. "Perhaps we should place it in storage, Captain," she suggested, "in case they ask about it."

"Good idea."

"Only … " one of the largest boxes, a towering black metal thing with a row of holes along the top, gave a timely *boom* and shook the trolley it was sitting on. Something inside the box went *aaarghahhumpgrnk*. "Only that box," Fellandra said weakly, "is … occupied."

"*Occupied?*" the Captain finally got surprised enough to do more than flick her ears. "It's not an Ogre, is it?" Fellandra shook her head, and Captain Char lowered her voice. "Is it a human?"

"No, Captain," Fellandra said, and handed her a pad. It would be a lie to say it was a complete list of all the junk the *Enna Midzis* had taken on board from the world below, but the main stuff was there.

The Captain read the list. Her eyes widened and her ears went up. She looked from the pad to the crate, then back at the pad.

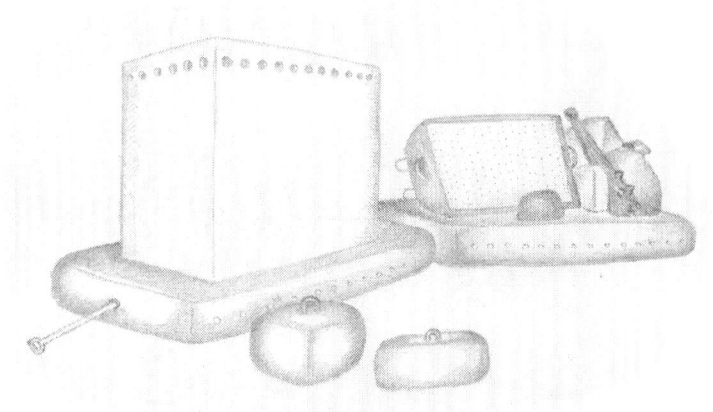

"Seriously?" she said.

Fellandra nodded. "The inspectors actually opened the box at the dock, Captain," she told her. "I saw it myself. It … " she gestured at her grubby uniform. "It was difficult to get it back in there."

"How are we supposed to – what do they eat?" the Captain demanded.

"So far, Captain," Fellandra replied positively, "it seems like pretty much everything."

Captain Char shook her head and sighed. "Alright," she said, "I suppose we're pet-sitting. Leave that trolley here. I'll allocate some deck space and resources to this. You can take the rest to secure storage."

"Yes, Captain. Would you like me to take … what is that?" she pointed at the little ornament in Captain Char's hand.

"It's … Mygon," the Captain said vaguely, then visibly shook herself out of her daze. "No," she went on, "I was asked to give this to one of the other Captains. Just store the rest of it and we will deal with it later."

Relieved, Fellandra unhitched the trolley in question and reconnected the others. The crate gave another *boom* and a low *hnaaarghblort* as she picked up the cases and trundled the rest of the luggage away, leaving Captain Char standing and staring at the box with a look of clear shock on her face.

Things like this were the reason Captains got to do monologues.

GALANA FEN (CREWMEMBER #1)

About four thousand years later.

The last thing Galana's mentor said to her before she went into the grand hall and got in a bet with the Fleet Ambassador was *I pulled a lot of strings to get you into this thing. Don't do anything embarrassing.*

It wasn't her fault some people had a stupid idea of what was embarrassing and what wasn't. Surely, standing and smiling while the snooty old dork in the ridiculous suit waffled on about the superiority of the Molran species would have been *more* embarrassing. Listening to his disgusting, insulting speech and *not* voicing some kind of objection would have been more embarrassing.

And besides, it wasn't as if she'd *heckled* the guy. All she did was ask a couple of questions about some things the ambassador said that were clearly at odds with what Galana had been taught at the Academy, the Fleet Edutorium, and in the course of her entire life. She'd been trying to figure out if she'd maybe missed something really important, that they only told to Molren over the age of three thousand. Because the only other explanation she could think of was that Ambassador Kotan was the most ignorant and obnoxious dimwit she had ever encountered. And that *definitely* would have been an embarrassing thing for her to say out loud. Wouldn't it?

After the speech and the short round of questions and answers, she found herself trapped in a conversation with Kotan and a flock of his closest admirers.

"So," the Ambassador said, speaking to Galana but *looking* at the glass of fruit wine in his upper right hand instead. "You are the little human rights activist who was asking all the clever questions. Is your class studying Müllick this year?"

"I'm glad you thought they were clever questions, Ambassador," Galana replied as nicely as she felt Stana Kotan deserved. "Since there didn't seem to be any humans invited here tonight – or any member of *any* of the Six Species races other than Molren – I thought it was only fair that someone ask a few of the questions they might."

"I couldn't agree more," Kotan smiled widely. "In fact, considering *how many questions* humans ask, I should thank you for letting us off so lightly."

"I have more questions if you'd like, Ambassador," Galana offered.

Some of the Ambassador's followers chuckled at this, but stopped when their master didn't join in. It was very sad. Galana wondered if any of *them* had been warned not to be embarrassing before coming along to the event.

"Humans," Kotan declared, "are a primitive species. They have their charm, and they have their uses, but like the Fergunak they need *constant* control and guidance."

"Yes, you already said so in your speech," Galana said. "It just seems strange to me that … well, we're all so pleased to be part of this amazing union, this interstellar civilisation. The Six Species has been our official identity for a *thousand years*. And yet a lot of the Molran Fleet seems to think it's all a big misunderstanding that will be cleared up soon."

"Oh my dear child," Kotan chuckled. "Has nobody told you? The Six Species is a publicity stunt. It's a joke to those who know better, and a sweet inspirational lie to those who do not. The Six Species has never *actually* been more than just the Two Species," he raised his two left hands, palms up, moving first one and then the other. "The Molren, and the aki'Drednanth. Aside from those two pillars there are our four charity cases, our little fixer-upper species. Our *improvement projects*.

"The Blaren. As finished as they're ever likely to get, their cultures reduced to a colourful decoration. Their sole purpose is as a warning. *Behave, be a good citizen, contribute to the wellbeing of the Fleet … and if you can't do that, we'll toss you out and replace you with someone who can.*

"The Bonshooni. Those poor, misbegotten souls who slept in storage while civilisation went on without them, only to be dragged out and forced to live in a galaxy they don't understand and never will. It would have been a greater kindness to let them remain in their Fleet pods and never wake, as some of the Blaren believe. But in their own way, they still serve a purpose.

"The Fergunak. Need I say more? They're part of our union because we're afraid of being *eaten* the second we turn our backs on them."

"And the humans," Kotan clucked sadly and shook his head. "If we'd invited *one* human to this event, all the others would have been offended. If we'd invited *more* than one, they would have been screeching and throwing poop at each other by now."

To be honest, Galana had more or less stopped listening to him after he'd said *my dear child*. It was true that, at a hundred and seventeen years of age she *was* little more than a child … but if she'd learned one thing over and over again in the course of her life it was that being old didn't make you right, it just made you more certain. She returned her attention to the Ambassador as he concluded his little performance.

"Oh, I don't think they'd be throwing poop at *each other*," she said sweetly. She wasn't sure she'd be able to smile at the pompous fool, but found it was easy when she saw her words wipe the smug smirk off his face.

"By all means go on believing in the intelligence and nobility of the lower species, and see how far it gets you," Kotan said stiffly, and now he finally stopped looking at his wine glass and gave a meaningful look – not at Galana's face, but at the tips of her ear-ribs. And the pearly spines that were a clear marker of her youth. "Like I say … it's only natural to be an idealistic dreamer when you're young."

"Apparently *some* old people are still idealistic," Galana replied, "unless you think AstroCorps is a publicity stunt as well."

"*AstroCorps?*" Ambassador Kotan snorted. "The Six Species' answer to the Molran Fleet? They're not a publicity stunt. They're a *catastrophe*. A bunch of those charity cases I just mentioned, flying around and making pew-pew noises under the supervision of Molren too incompetent to gain a Fleet position."

"I'll try not to hold that description against you," Galana said. "I've graduated from the AstroCorps Academy. I was one of the first Molren to do so."

"Hold it against me all you like," Kotan replied. "AstroCorps will never be granted full authority without my voice on the Fleet Council of Captains. *The Six Species* is not ready. It isn't ready at a thousand years of age, it won't be ready at five thousand, and it may *never* be ready."

"What if I were to ask you," Galana was surprised to find herself saying, "if there was anything that might change your mind about that? Your mind, *and* your voice," she added, when Kotan started to shake his head. Something made him hesitate, and study her curiously. Finally, she noted with satisfaction, looking her in the eyes rather than the ears. "Are you a betting man, Ambassador?"

"A *betting* man?" he said in some surprise. "What foolishness is this?"

Galana shrugged. "You seem very certain there is no way the Six Species can prove itself. No way AstroCorps can stand with the Fleet as its equal. I am telling you *you are wrong*," Kotan's little cluster of admirers tightened their nostrils and flared their ears and muttered angrily at this, but Galana waited for the Ambassador to respond. His response, after all, was the only one that mattered in this conversation.

"I see," he said eventually. "You are expecting me to … *bet* … with you, perhaps by setting your AstroCorps people a task that would normally go to the Fleet?"

"Something like that."

"If you succeed, I suppose, you expect me to admit that the Six Species is more than just a publicity stunt, and throw my support behind this ridiculous dream," Galana, who hadn't actually thought this far ahead in the conversation, opened her mouth but the Ambassador continued. "Your AstroCorps crew, let us say, will complete a standard Fleet tour of the boundaries of Six Species space. The *outer* boundaries. The map is very big and very empty, my child. A lot of things could wait out there in the dark. Without the Fleet to hold your hands - "

"No," she once again surprised herself by saying. "No, I intend to show you that the Six Species is a reality, that it is greater than the sum of its parts, and that its potential is greater than its *poor ancestor* the Molran Fleet could ever aspire to. And to do *that*, the challenge has to be greater than one the Fleet would face. I will show you that Molran, aki'Drednanth, Blaran, Bonshoon, Fergunakil and human can act as one unified culture. I will take a crew, Ambassador Kotan, and I will circumnavigate the galaxy."

Kotan's flock were staring now, silent and open-mouthed. But the Ambassador, annoyingly, was smirking again.

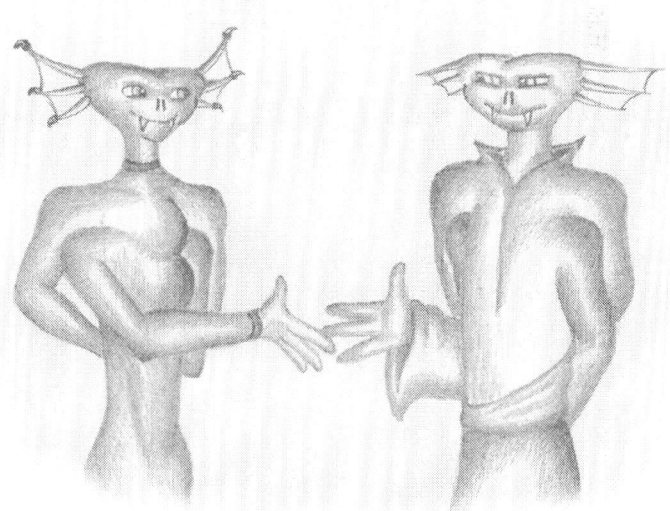

"So be it," he said. "We will meet in twenty months at Declivitorion-On-The-Rim, which will be your starting point. You have until then to put together your crew. We will meet *back* there again when you return – *if* you return – whereupon I will offer you my full and public apology and throw my full support behind AstroCorps and the Six Species. If you lose ... " he smiled and looked into his wine. "Well, chances are you will be dead. If you make it back alive but without completing the circuit, then you will be relegated to the Blaran species for the remainder of your natural life. I will lend my voice to the Five Species damage control initiative as planned, and we will stand back and watch while the Wild Empire of the humans finally bites itself to death. Let the rushing monkeys finish exterminating themselves. Oh, and because you seem *so* sure of the power of unity … " he raised his eyes once again, and his smile widened. "Your crew will be six. One member of each species, and no more."

Ambassador, I spoke without thinking and I am sorry if I offended you in my enthusiasm, Galana tried to say. Instead she found herself spitting on her lower right palm and extending her hand to the staring Kotan. She also became aware that a large part of the hall had fallen silent and were watching intently.

"It's a human thing," she said quietly, "I suggest you just go with it."

Ambassador Kotan stared a moment longer.

"Better than poop, I suppose," he muttered, then spat on his own hand and slapped it to hers. "You poor foolish child," he said loudly, "you have a bet."

A WAYWARD STUDENT

The first difficulty she faced was with her mentor, Parakta Tar.

"I really should blame myself for this," the elderly Molran woman said wearily. They were sitting in her quarters on the Worldship *Porticon*, enjoying cups of spicy *hoco* soup. Although more accurately Parakta had *offered* soup, and the cups were now standing forgotten on the table between them while the old scholar ranted at her wayward student. "When I told you not to do anything embarrassing, I should have made it clear this included jeopardising the cultural stability of the entire Six Species."

Galana spoke up when Parakta stopped to take a breath. "Smacking a Fleet nitwit hard enough for his head to drop out of his arse for twelve seconds hardly counts as jeopardising the cultural stability of the entire Six Species," she said, "especially since he doesn't actually believe in the Six Species in the first place. And it *was* only twelve seconds."

"That was apparently eleven seconds more than you needed to get yourself in trouble," Parakta retorted. "*Flying around the galaxy* ... no Fleet vessels will be available to you. Not any Fleet-connected *AstroCorps* vessels either, or Fleet-connected officers - "

"That's the exact *point* of this, Parakta."

"You're talking about ignoring ninety-nine percent of the Six Species' most experienced and talented spacefaring minds. *And* their ships."

"And *that*," Galana said, "is precisely the sort of misconception I mean to correct."

Parakta shook her head. "Galana Fen, you are the second-most impossible student I have taught in my three thousand, nine hundred and sixty-three years as a mentor."

"And the *most* impossible has been in prison for thirty-five years," Galana said with a smile. This was familiar ground.

"Thirty-six."

"You're not really angry. You've wanted to smack Kotan for years already."

"A law-abiding Molran of the Fleet does not *smack* other Molren," Parakta said. Galana could tell she was trying to maintain sternness, and on the brink of failing. "Apparently *AstroCorps* Molren are a different breed."

"I happen to believe this is an easy win for the Six Species," Galana told her seriously. "The mission is simple enough. Longer than a normal tour, but not *long*. And we get more out of Stana Kotan and his followers on the Fleet Council of Captains than a lifetime of speeches and political dealings would give us."

"An *easy win*?" Parakta exclaimed. "*Not long*? You didn't explain yet, how were you planning on getting around the galaxy without a ship? You going to swim?" Galana must have looked blank, because her mentor sighed. "I have taught you nothing."

"I admit it's going to be difficult to convince AstroCorps High Command to sign off on the mission," she said, "but I've got plenty of friends in high places on Aquilar."

"Your friends on the humans' capital world would happily sign off on you flying into Hell and tweaking the Devil's nose if it made the Fleet look silly," Parakta said, "but they don't have any *ships* you can do it with."

"They have dozens of ships," Galana frowned.

Parakta shook her head. "They – I'm sorry, *you* – rely on the Fleet. You've built a lot of *almost*-ships, but your friends on Aquilar have none to spare for you. They'd be signing away a resource they can't afford to lose, with slim chance of ever seeing it again, for a reward they won't understand," she sighed. "No. I'll talk to the Ambassador, clear this up. You were carried away with your enthusiasm - "

"No!"

Parakta sighed again. "Look. The galaxy is *huge*. The section of it that we've marked out as Six Species space is big enough, and it's the only part we're even *slightly* familiar with. And it's still almost completely unknown after four thousand years of exploration."

"Parakta - "

"The line from Margan's Leap to Declivitorion-On-The-Rim was mapped by the Fleet on our way to Earth," Parakta went on relentlessly. "*Nothing much else*. We just drew a box around this volume and whacked 'here there be dragons' on the rest."

"That doesn't mean - "

Parakta wasn't one to be stopped in the middle of a bombardment. "If you go out past the edge of Six Species space, you're at risk from the Cancer in the Core," she warned.

"We're not going into the Core," Galana objected. "We're not going anywhere *near* the Core. We're going around the outside."

"That's even worse. *Nobody* knows what's out there."

"We'll be in soft-space, at relative speed," Galana added. "Moving faster than light. Not even in reality for most of the journey."

"You're not in reality *now*."

"Cheap shot."

"You'll be in soft-space for *most* of it. Not *all*. Doing this like the Fleet means stopping, collecting information, making contact with dumblers. Otherwise you might as well just fly around Declivitorion-On-The-Rim at relative speed for fifty years and tell everyone you went around the galaxy. And even if you don't drop out of soft-space in front of something that swats you like a fly, you'll be skinswitched the second you get back."

"Only if I fail - "

"*Even if you don't*," Parakta snapped. "Leaving Six Species space puts our entire civilisation at risk. It breaks a founding rule of the Fleet."

"AstroCorps isn't the Fleet."

Parakta raised her ears. "So you think violating Six Species space borders is *okay* for AstroCorps?"

"I think if the Six Species charter has that much importance, I'll welcome any punishment that comes from defying it," Galana said. "And if it doesn't, then what am I worried about?"

Parakta clearly recognised that her bombardment was only hardening her student's shields. "Alright," she gave up, "I assume you'll be talking to Chilly first," she saw the look in Galana's eyes, and slumped even further in her seat. "You're not going to go to her first," she sighed. "You're going to go to her *last*."

"If I go to Chillybin first, everything we achieve will be because the aki'Drednanth wanted to do it," Galana said. "She has to be one of the six, but she can't be signed up before we even have a ship."

Parakta straightened, picked up her long-abandoned cup of *hoco* soup, and sipped. "*Discounting* the ninety-nine percent of experienced spacefarers connected to the Molran Fleet, then," she said, "you're looking at the ragged collection of Wild Empire freebooters who signed the charter in the hopes it would earn them something."

"And cynical social commentary aside … ?" Galana twirled her lower left hand.

"I can only think of one person crazy enough to join you," Parakta replied. "Basil Hartigan. *Captain* Basil Hartigan," she added warningly. "Don't think for a second that you'll be permitted to actually *command* this mad mission of yours."

"I don't care who gets to sit in the chair with the buttons, as long as they're Academy qualified," Galana said. Parakta made a face and tipped a hand back and forth. "Qualified-*ish*," she adjusted.

"I don't know if I'd go so far as to say qualified-*ish*," Parakta said sourly.

"Does he have a *ship*?"

Parakta paused for far too long, but finally nodded. "Yes. He has a ship."

BASIL HARTIGAN (CREWMEMBER #2)

Hartigan lived on the planet Grand Boënnia, which was handy because it was the planet around which the *Porticon* was currently orbiting. And with a little under two years to get all the way to the outer edge of Six Species space and their starting point, Galana really didn't have time for detours.

She descended into Dominion Central spaceport on a crowded AstroCorps shuttle, feeling a certain satisfaction as she sat among her fellow Corpsfolk and looked out of the window into the gloom. Satisfaction and excitement. They were descending into the night-side of the planet, through a solid rainstorm, and the entire landmass that was the heart of the Grand Boënne Dominion seemed to be covered in fog, but it was still exciting.

Galana Fen had been born and raised on the *Porticon*. Most of her species was spaceborne, living on the great Worldships of the Fleet. Few of them settled on planets. Didn't see the point of them. She'd done some of her Academy training in various parts of Grand Boënnia, but there weren't many things a planet could throw at you that couldn't be done artificially, and *controllably*, on a Worldship. Even fog and rain if you were into that sort of thing, and the Grand Boënne clearly were.

But she had to admit, there was a certain feeling to being on a planet.

Grand Boënnia was a funny, soggy little place. It was hard not to think of its oddity as a human thing, because it was mostly humans that lived there. The island nation capital of the Grand Boënne Dominion was a typical example. It wasn't the most sensible or convenient spot for the centre of a planetary government, it was just the place the first human ship had landed. Dominion Central spaceport was in fact built on the very spot, according to the tourist brochures.

The Grand Boënne thought of themselves as the custodians of an ancient and planet-spanning civilisation. A lot of the humans from other cultures found this attitude a bit grating. Galana, who had *friends* older than the Grand Boënne Dominion, thought it was adorable.

The shuttle made a shaky landing at the spaceport and Galana, hefting a rounded beige carrying case in each lower hand, trotted through the driving rain to a land skimmer that had been arranged for her. Its driver, looking extremely uncomfortable in a dark skimmer patrolman's uniform several sizes too small for him, was none other than Captain Basil Hartigan himself.

"Welcome to Grand Boënnia, Commander," he proclaimed as she loaded her cases into the back of the vehicle and climbed in alongside them. "I am Buck Spunko. My friends call me Nuts, don't y'know. Where would I be taking you this fine evening?"

It seemed, for some reason, Hartigan was pretending to be somebody else and was unaware that she had received his full details while she was still in orbit. Including a picture of him: a confident and cheerful-looking male with a perhaps over-decorative crest of thick black fur on his head. No, not fur. *Hair*, the humans called it. He had more ... *hair* ... between his nose and his mouth, black and styled in a similar fashion to the stuff on the top of his skull. There was no possible way it was hygienic. Still, it was all very exotic and alien to Galana, who was as hairless as all Molren.

She wondered what Hartigan was attempting to do. Humans, she'd learned at the Academy, often had trouble telling Molren apart, so it was possible he was assuming she would have the same difficulty with humans and was playing a little joke on her. Humans liked jokes.

"AstroCorps mission control and launch pads, thank you Nuts," she said. "May I call you Nuts?" Hartigan smirked behind his lip-fur – *his moustache*, she corrected herself – and nodded. Still smiling, he gripped the steering rods and sent the skimmer speeding across the wet paving. "I am actually a Captain, platinum class," she informed him, "but you were correct – I am filling the position of second officer for this mission so will be using my Commander credentials. I understand the man you are taking me to meet is a gold-stripe Captain? Martigan, Blartigan?"

"Hartigan," Hartigan said quickly, then added, "I, uh, I believe. And he's full gold class. Last I heard."

"My information must be out of date," she said mildly.

Basil Hartigan was thirty-three years old. As far as Galana was concerned, he was an infant. When Galana had been thirty, she'd wanted to sneak down into the *Porticon*'s hold and get into a sleeper pod and sleep until the Fleet found the gates of space. But you had to make allowances for the fact that he was a human. They lived *such* a short time.

In human terms, Hartigan was the equivalent of an eight- or nine-hundred-year-old Molran. By no means a revered elder, but at least a solidly accepted *adult*. Thirty-three was still impressively young to be a full gold class Captain. He may have cut some corners by owning his own ship, but AstroCorps didn't cut *important* corners. They didn't let any old pirate earn stripes.

"I understand you're down here with a perfectly *daft* plan to fly around the galaxy," Hartigan said.

"It is a perfectly simple and well-formulated plan to fly around the galaxy actually, but yes," she replied. "I'm hoping it will help to solidify AstroCorps as a valid and respected part of the Six Species - "

"AstroCorps has already been a thing for fifty-odd years," Hartigan said. "We don't actually *need* Kotan and the Fleet nobs to sign off on it."

"That is technically true," Galana replied, "but the reality is that we do need the Fleet's approval before we can hope to expand beyond Aquilar and central star systems like the Grand Boënne Dominion. And that means getting the support of … Fleet nobs … like Stana Kotan," she paused. "Interesting that you've heard of him, Nuts. Being a skimmer patrolman must give you plenty of opportunities to listen to rumours and news from the officers you drive around."

"Oh goodness me, yes," Hartigan said with evident relief, "lots of rumours, oh my. For example, I *heard* that this whole thing started with a bet. You *bet* the Ambassador that an AstroCorps crew could do this. And he fell for it. Do you really think he'll honour his side of the bargain?"

"Enough people heard him that he won't really have a choice," Galana said.

Hartigan laughed, and reached up to play the fingers of one hand along his moustache, smoothing it unnecessarily. "Not very *Molranny* behaviour, what? Making bets, laying wagers, gallivanting off around the galaxy?"

"I wasn't planning on *gallivanting*," Galana said, "but that depends on Captain Hartigan, I suppose. Can you tell me about him? Any rumours you might have heard? Is he a known gallivanter?"

Hartigan grinned over his shoulder at her as he swung the skimmer into a lane of fast-moving traffic headed to the big ship pads. "Plenty of rumours," he said. "It's sorting out the truth from the tall tales that's the challenge."

"I've heard he's quite the tactician," she said idly, "for a human of less than a hundred years."

By now Hartigan was having obvious difficulty remembering he was meant to be 'Nuts' Spunko. "He has his moments," he said with a big smile. "For a monkey."

"It is my hope that by the time we finish this mission, my kind will no longer think of the Sixth Species as a pack of wild primates we have to put up with," Galana said. "Perhaps humans will even stop referring to *themselves* that way."

"But humans *are* primates," Hartigan said cheerfully.

"What else can you tell me about Captain Hartigan?" she asked. "I've heard he is as eccentric as he is brilliant."

"That rather depends on how brilliant you think he is," Hartigan said, stroking his moustache again. Galana wondered if he was going to do so on a regular basis for the duration of their mission.

"I heard he got one of his earliest crews killed," she said, wondering how far she could push the man. "There is no official record, but the rumour is that he was trying to fly into the galactic Core."

"Not *into* the Core, just *through* it," Hartigan said, his voice hardening. "And that wasn't what *got them killed*. According to the rumours *I* heard."

"I'm relieved to hear it," Galana said. "I'm sure he will do his best to keep his crew alive this time. As will I," she paused again, letting Hartigan drive stiff-backed into the landing compound. "I have heard a very strange story about Captain Hartigan," she said eventually. "Something he's searching for, out in space. A creature."

"Mm," Hartigan said, still sounding offended. "The Last Alicorn."

"Yes," Galana said. "That was it. Can you explain this to me, Nuts? I'm afraid it was something I completely missed during my time at the Academy."

This was not entirely true – all the classic Fleet myths, back to the First Feast when the Fleet had made contact with humanity, were reasonably well-known to her. And she had read the additional notes on her way to the surface. But Hartigan immediately brightened up and immersed himself back in the role of Buck 'Nuts' Spunko, skimmer patrolman.

"Oh, of course. It's really more of a story the old space-dogs tell each other, don't y'know. Not sure how much truth there is to it, but Hartigan definitely believes it. *Oodles* of proof, but nobody will listen to him. An Alicorn, y'see, is a mythical being. Like an Elf or a Pinian or a Vahoon. But, like all of them, the story has a bit of truth behind it, what?"

"An Alicorn, to my understanding, is an animal similar to a horse," Galana said. "It has a single horn on its head, but it also has wings, distinguishing it from the mythical unicorn."

"Quite right," Hartigan said, sounding surprised. "You know your fabulous beasts of legend and folklore. The whole thing is the most *appalling* claptrap, of course ... "

"Biology and history more than mythology, and hardly claptrap," Galana disagreed. "The Alicorn, whatever else it may have been, was an item of registered Fleet cargo leaving Earth. That is a fact. Whether it was a real creature, and whether there is anything left of it after thousands of years, is quite another matter."

"You don't *believe* it," Hartigan said, slowing the skimmer and turning to stare at her.

"Please watch the road, patrolman Spunko," she said firmly. "As to *believing* it ... no, I don't believe it. I don't *not* believe it, either. There is not enough information for that. Perhaps Captain Hartigan and I will find more information on this mission."

"Seriously?"

"According to what I have read, Captain Hartigan still means to find the Last Alicorn," Galana said. "The *story* is that it ended up on the far side of the galaxy. The *story* is that he was trying to get there by the shortest route, and that was why he was planning on flying through the Core. That didn't work, but my mission might offer him another chance."

"The long way 'round," Hartigan said with a chuckle.

"*Very* long, for a human," Galana agreed. She'd calculated that it was likely to take them a minimum of fifty years to circumnavigate the galaxy. And that was with barely any stops. Which was no good at all, since a proper tour required stopovers and exploration. It was bad for humans' and Fergunak's health to spend too long at relative speed anyway.

Fifty years was more than half a Fergunakil's life. And while it was only about a third of a *human's* life, it would arguably be the best third of Hartigan's. He would leave Grand Boënnia at the peak of his strength and health, and would be lucky to return as an old man.

The greatest challenge Kotan had set her, she reflected, was getting the shorter-lived aliens around the galaxy and home within their lifetimes.

"Worth it, though," Hartigan said, as though reading her thoughts. He glanced back at Galana again as the skimmer turned in and began speeding along between landing berths. The AstroCorps ships of Grand Boënnia, all shapes and sizes but most of them huge in comparison to the little ground vehicle, loomed above them on either side. "So. Where's your uniform, Commander?"

"Where's yours, Captain?" Galana shot back.

Hartigan stared at her in silence for a moment, then he laughed. "When did you figure it out?" he asked, then laughed again. "You knew the whole bally time."

"Yes, Captain Hartigan," she replied. "Or may I still call you Nuts?"

"Wow. So even when you were asking about my crew, you knew *then*? I say, that was brutal," he chuckled, sounding appreciative rather than angry. "And how did you manage to say 'patrolman Spunko' with a straight face?"

"I'm a Molran," Galana replied calmly. "Saying things with a straight face is my superpower."

The skimmer pulled up in front of the ACS *Conch*.

THE ACS *CONCH*

Galana stood in the rain next to the manically grinning human, looking up at the ship with what must have been a doubtful expression on her face.

In that moment, in the dark and foggy Grand Boënne night, she had a disturbingly vivid glimpse of the future.

It wasn't anything in particular. It wasn't a prophecy or a vision. It didn't tell her anything specific or useful about what was to come. But she knew that this scene – Hartigan and Fen, human and Molran standing together, her looking dubious and him grinning like a madman – was playing itself out for the first time, and would play out again many, *many* times before they were done.

She didn't know whether their mission would succeed. But she knew at least one member of the crew was going to have a good time.

"Well?" Hartigan asked.

"It's a very nice ship," Galana said. "Where is the rest of it?"

The AstroCorps Starship *Conch* was a long, slender needle of a ship, all sweeping curves and dynamic fins. It had jets and thrusters but no sign of any proper engines, let alone machinery for faster-than-light movement. There were a couple of big gleaming fixtures with armour plating that Galana didn't recognise, but they weren't propulsion or guns. She couldn't see any weapons placements at all, for that matter. The vessel looked just about big enough to carry six crewmembers, although the Fergunakil would be a challenge.

Big enough to *carry* them, but not for anyone to live in for more than a month, let alone fifty years.

"Up in high orbit," Hartigan answered, still grinning. "This is just the command deck and the computer core, detaches and acts as a landing shuttle, don't y'know. We call her the *Nella*," his smile faded slightly, but remained … fond? Nostalgic? Galana wasn't good at alien facial expressions. "Named for my wife."

"Lolita Nella Hartigan," Galana said.

"Ah," Hartigan nodded. "In the file, what?"

"Yes."

"Her parents were keen on the *idea* of ancient literature but not big on the actual *reading* part of it," Hartigan said. "She ... preferred to use her second name."

"I regret that we did not have the opportunity to meet," Galana said. Hartigan glanced at her. "Her death was mentioned in your file too," she reminded him.

"Ah," he repeated, a little humour returning to his voice. "The whole 'getting my crew killed' thing."

"I apologise for my earlier wording," Galana said. "It was intended to provoke a response from patrolman Buck Spunko, in continuation of the joke I assumed you were playing. It was poor judgement on my part - "

"No no, it's alright," Hartigan said, and turned to look up at her frankly. "I think you judged it perfectly. You're ... not like other Molren."

Galana lifted her ears and glanced down at him. He was, she estimated, above average size for a human of the Grand Boënne Dominion, but that still left him a head and one set of shoulders shorter than she was, even with his dark hair styled up the way it was. "How many other Molren do you know?"

"Well, that's kind of the thing," he replied. "Up until now, I thought I only knew one."

"Indeed."

"You know, because you're all kind of same-y."

"I get it. Very clever."

Hartigan waved a hand. "Shall we go? Or do you want to enjoy the *bracing* Grand Boënne dampness a while longer?"

"We have no time to waste," Galana said, and pulled her cases from the skimmer. "Why did you not just dock with the *Porticon* when we exchanged mission data?"

"Oh, I've been down here for a couple of weeks, taking care of some things," Hartigan said vaguely. "Please, allow me to take your - " he stopped as Galana set one of the cases on the wet pavement for him, and he struggled to lift it two-handed for a few seconds before giving up with a chuckle. "Well that just weighs a bally ton there, doesn't it?"

"It's mostly research equipment and data cubes," she said, lifting the case in her lower left hand again. "I appreciate the offer, though."

"Anytime," at a touch of a device Hartigan was wearing around his wrist, a boarding ramp extended from the *Nella*'s undercarriage. "Anyway," he went on, "we had political reasons for not docking."

"Oh?"

"My – well, he *was* my Executive Officer, if you can call us a Captain and XO when it's just the two of us footling around in space," Hartigan explained, "but I guess you're the XO now, so that's the end of it. You'll want to sort that whole mess out, by the way."

Galana frowned at the human. He returned her look blandly, before starting towards the ramp. She followed, carrying her cases. Behind them, the skimmer closed up and rolled away slowly on autodrive. "What do you mean?" she asked. She hadn't anticipated having to replace an existing crew. According to Hartigan's file, he was flying alone.

"He's going to want something to do," Hartigan replied. "He'll be our Blaran crewmember, after all, and since they're not allowed to be officers on proper AstroCorps missions … "

Ah. Galana nodded to herself. *Right*. "I had not secured a Blaran crewmember for the mission yet," she admitted, "so this is a stroke of luck."

"Isn't it just, by jingo," Hartigan agreed cheerfully.

"I assume he is Academy qualified with a non-Corps rating - " she said.

Hartigan, who had stopped at the top of the ramp to welcome her aboard with an extravagant bow, waved a dismissive hand. "Yes yes, he's got all that and a bag of krunklets. *Centuries* of experience, and doesn't get all bent out of shape about not being allowed to wear the stripes, either. But docking with a Worldship is a bridge too far, if you follow."

Galana didn't follow, not really, but she accepted that Blaren – descended from the same root as her own species, but culturally very different – had a … *special* relationship with the Fleet. And now, sadly, with AstroCorps as well. "I hope this mission will help us all to understand one another better," she said, "and work together more effectively in the future."

"I can see we're going to have *brilliant* speech-making contests," Hartigan remarked. "The months in soft-space will just fly by."

The *Nella* was positively luxurious for a shuttle, and powered up smoothly and quietly even as the ramp sealed behind them.

"Good morning, Basil," the ship's computer said in a warm voice that Galana guessed was a synthesised human female. "Good morning, Commander Fen. Welcome aboard."

"Thank you," Galana said politely. It never hurt to be courteous with ship computer systems. Some of them had feelings. "Machine mind?" she inquired.

"No," Hartigan said, "the *Conch* doesn't link up with the big machines. It's an … independent system. SynEsDyne prototype, one of their last. You saw the big armoured extensions on the hull out there?" Galana nodded. "Those are the synaptic difference engines. When the *Conch* is separated, the computer comes with us. When we're connected with the main vessel, she integrates the rest of the systems. But she doesn't play well with other artificial brains."

"That might be an advantage in unknown interstellar territory," Galana allowed.

"It's certainly an advantage when flying with a Fergie," Hartigan led the way forward onto the spacious command deck. "You may not need to sleep, but I do."

Galana looked around, and nodded in approval. There were stations for Captain, Executive Officer, and four other posts that would be customisable for tactical, communications, sciences and engineering control. There was no separate helm but she guessed that the Captain would insist on piloting. It was a good setup.

The *Nella* sliced up through the clouds effortlessly, and by the time Galana had familiarised herself with the XO station they had cleared Grand Boënnia Orbital Control and were speeding through the black towards the ship. By the time she'd run through the basics and performed a couple of test commands – with the surprisingly helpful computer's assistance – they were there.

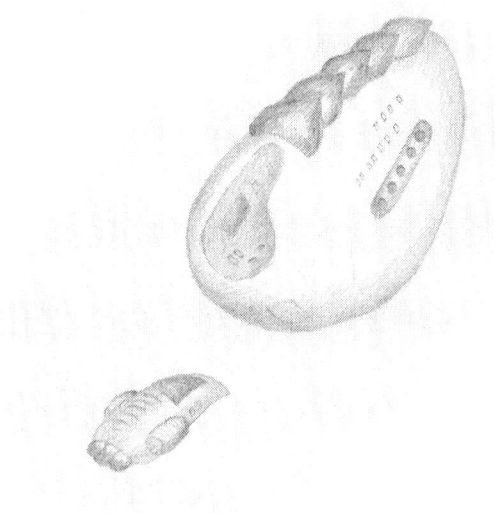

"Seven decks," Hartigan proudly listed the starship's features as they approached. "Detachable command and landing shuttle, as you've seen. Quin-torus cumulative relative field generator," at this, he gestured at the five heavy arcs of armour plating the *Conch*'s back like overlapping scales. "Fully-integrated nutrient and OxyGen crystal core chambers. High-yield webscoop power plant and twin Nova-Bridnak energy cells. Megadyne albedo shielding. Modular rail cannon and pulse turrets designed by none other than AstroCorps Special Weapons Division."

AstroCorps SWD, Galana thought with a little shiver. It was a part of AstroCorps she could have lived without, but the sad fact was you couldn't have a spacefaring military without weapons. Special Weapons Division was new, even by AstroCorps standards, but they'd already earned a dark reputation. And a grim nickname.

The officers and mentors at the Academy called them the Monsters.

"And of course," Hartigan was concluding, "plenty of hold space ready to be converted into a big old Fergie tank."

"She's a better ship than I could have dared hope," Galana said sincerely. Hartigan glanced back at her and she added, "I'm not being snide. AstroCorps can't field a long-range armed and armoured research vessel of this quality from their own yards. I would never have gotten a warship, and I don't know that it would be a good idea to take a *warship* around the galaxy anyway. The *Conch* is ... quite perfect, Captain."

"I rather think so," Hartigan agreed.

"One does one's best," the computer added modestly.

"Oh, and she does this simply *brilliant* thing when she translates dumbler-talk," Hartigan went on enthusiastically. "Instead of just giving the direct boring old translation in her own voice, she can give them special voices that sound like the aliens'd sound if they were speaking Grand Bo. It's jolly good, she hasn't been wrong yet. We met these blighters, what were they called, old girl?"

"The Smeeb," the *Conch* supplied.

"Right, the Smeeb," Hartigan laughed and tapped at the controls, sending the *Nella* curving smoothly around to connect with the sleek bulk of the starship. "Funny little devils ... she gave them this flabbidy blabbidy sort of way of talking, it was very good."

"Flabbidy blabbidy," Galana said doubtfully.

"A complex equation based on their palate and jaw movements and vocalising organs," the computer explained, "lung capacity, the nitrogen content in the air of the Smeeb homeworld - "

"They were bally hilarious," Hartigan asserted. "The point is, a couple of them ended up learning to *speak* Grand Bo, and you know how they sounded?"

"Flabbidy and/or blabbidy?" Galana guessed. Hartigan snapped his fingers and pointed at her in grinning confirmation. "So ... your Blaran XO," she changed the subject. "He's just been sitting up here in orbit, guarding the drive and life support and – and weapons segments of the *Conch*?"

"Yes, let's say that's what he's been doing," Hartigan said easily.

"What is his name?" Galana hadn't been able to find any information on the command systems, which to be fair weren't officially signed over to her as Executive Officer yet. "I should familiarise myself with his files, if we are to work together."

"Scrutarius," Hartigan replied with a stroke of his moustache. "I should *imagine* there's a file."

"Scrutarius?" Galana felt her ears drop. "Not … you don't mean *Devlin* Scrutarius?"

Hartigan beamed. "You've heard of him!" he exclaimed. "Oh, he'll be *so* pleased."

DEVLIN SCRUTARIUS (CREWMEMBER #3)

The ACS *Conch* was as stylish and well-designed on the inside as she was on the outside, a fact Galana wasn't really in a position to appreciate as she followed Hartigan off the bridge and out through a rear access hatch that had become the main entrance to the command deck now the ship was reassembled.

"Devlin Scrutarius is a *criminal*," she said with quiet intensity. "And I don't just mean that in the usual sourcat all-Blaren-are-criminals way. His family is one of the founding dynasties of the Fleet Separatists. Five Species traitors – now *Six* Species traitors. And Devlin himself is wanted for crimes against the Fleet, the Wild Empire, a dozen specific Worldships, the Grand Boënne Dominion … "

"All true," Hartigan said merrily. "And yet, he attended the Academy and graduated with honours, and is qualified to serve in any non-Corps capacity on a starship of - "

"He joined AstroCorps to take advantage of a legal loophole allowing him to escape the police of Wynstone," Galana said, "after trading Fleet-controlled nanomanufacturing technology to the Scarta Majaal and then *stealing a Wynstonian Colossus* … "

"Come now, that was five hundred years before AstroCorps was even founded."

"The criminal investigation has been very complicated."

"I imagine it has," Hartigan said. "The *loophole*, though, as you call it, was upheld at the highest level and his credentials are impeccable. And he has no marks against his name according to AstroCorps, although obviously if we happened to be flying anywhere remotely close to Wynstone – which we're not – we'd have to assist the police … " he stopped at the elevator doors that marked the end of the corridor. "So," he said, "I suppose the question you have to ask is, despite all your high and noble cocktail-party speechifying, do you actually believe we are beholden to our stern mummies and daddies of the Molran Fleet and responsible for things that happened hundreds of years before you or I or *AstroCorps* was born?"

"We are beholden to the laws of the Six Species. Hartigan – Captain – *Nuts*," she said in exasperation as the elevator doors opened and an AstroCorps-uniformed Blaran joined them in the corridor.

Of the three of them, Devlin Scrutarius was the only one in full AstroCorps uniform, or as close to full as a Blaran could get. The gleaming silver one-piece jumpsuit with its white piping and matching silver-and-white cap looked a little silly in Galana's opinion, but she hadn't been consulted about the style.

You could never tell what you were going to get, with Blaren. They were born more or less identical to Molren – four arms, two legs, flexible webbed ears, wide mouths with elongated eye teeth – and would grow up to be more or less identical too, left to their own devices. The problem was that most of them *didn't* leave it at that. Some of them coloured their skin in outlandish colours or patterns. Some of them augmented themselves with armour plating or spikes or horns or wings or finger-guns. Some of them gave themselves extra arms, extra legs, extra eyes, poison-tipped tails … there were as many different alterations, it sometimes seemed to Galana, as there were Blaren to show them off.

Some tribes or crews of Blaren sported the same kinds of decorations. Others were unique. As far as Galana could tell – only the man's head and his four hands weren't covered by the uniform – Devlin Scrutarius was completely un-augmented. He looked just like a Molran somewhere around seven hundred years of age.

He'd exited the elevator in time to hear her last exclamation. "Don't tell me Basil pulled the old Buck Spunko trick on you," he said with a roll of his eyes.

"Crewmember Scrutarius, I presume," Galana said, hating the stiffness in her voice. *AstroCorps doesn't let any old pirate earn stripes*, she reminded herself forcefully. *Even conditional non-Corps stripes.*

"I prefer the old-school title *Able Belowdecksman Scrutarius*, myself," he said cheerfully, and clipped off a smart salute. "Commander Fen."

"And she turned the tables on me, incidentally," Hartigan said. "Saw through the old Buck Spunko routine right from the start and just strung me along like a bally fool."

"I'd expect nothing less," Scrutarius said, and closed one eye briefly at Galana. This was a human gesture, she recognised – a wink, implying conspiracy and mischief. "We haven't flown with a Molran officer before," he told her. "I'm looking forward to seeing which of you cracks first."

"The *Conch* is pretty new," Hartigan agreed. "Just commissioned a year or so back, don't y'know. Never would've happened without Devlin. He worked in an unofficial capacity on the design and implementation."

"He means I messed around with the engines and borrowed some controlled components and cut through some red tape," Scrutarius explained. "I know the ins and outs of the standard drive, the relative drive, the gravity plates and OxyGen systems, as well as the engines in general. If it breaks I can fix it. If it burns out I can replace it. If it goes missing and all we have to use in its place is a weird blobby green piece of technology from a derelict alien vessel that looks more like it was grown than built, I can darn well hook it up and swear at it until it works."

Galana exchanged a glance with Captain Hartigan.

"How would you feel about a non-Corps Chief Engineer?" Hartigan asked her.

"Conflicted," Galana replied. She looked at the smiling, crisp-uniformed member of the criminal nobility standing in front of her. *AstroCorps doesn't let any old pirate earn stripes*, she repeated to herself. *AstroCorps doesn't let …* "But there are allowances for it in AstroCorps regulations," she went on, "for crews this small. We will all need to fill several roles."

"It will be my pleasure," Scrutarius said grandly. "Filling several roles is my specialty."

"On our return to Six Species space, you will submit to the authorities and answer for your crimes."

Hartigan put a hand over his face in despair. "Damn it, Fen … "

"No, she's right, I should face *justice*," Scrutarius said, still smiling. "I agree to the terms. When we get back, I will hand myself over to the Fleet, or the Aquilarans, or the Wynstones, or whichever authoritarian lynch mob you think has the best claim on my tattered hide," he turned from Galana to Hartigan. "We're ready to fly, Captain," he cleared his throat – another human mannerism that Molren and Blaren and Bonshooni generally didn't use – and added, "I got hold of those new Bridnak cells we were talking about, Baz."

"Ah, *excellent*," Hartigan declared. "That ought to keep us in the grey for a few years, what?"

"How does one *get hold* of new power cells?" Galana asked. "I did not notice them on the requisitions order."

"Did you notice *me* on the requisitions order?" Scrutarius asked.

"No," Galana said.

The Blaran smiled. "That's alright then."

"What does that even *mean* - "

"Ooh, and she has a file on you, Dev," Hartigan added eagerly.

"*Do* you?" Scrutarius's smile widened. "You simply *must* tell me *all* about it. In the meantime, we're ready to fly."

"Righto," Hartigan clapped his hands heartily and grinned up at the two towering Molranoids. "Just as soon as we know where we're going."

INTO THE GREY

It was almost six months' travel to the strange settlement called The Warm. Almost a third of the twenty months they had to reach the starting line, but at least they were heading in the right direction.

All of that time, the *Conch* hung in silence. If you went back to the rear of the ship, where the engines were feeding energy directly into the relative field, you could hear the deep hum of the power plant. But that was all. Of course, usually you couldn't hear anything that might have been going on outside the ship anyway, because that was how space worked. But at subluminal speeds, flying through the real universe, at least the normal drive rumbled away under the floorplates.

Relative speed wasn't the real universe. It was *unreality*, a grey void that went on forever and in which no laws of physics applied. There were laws of *unphysics*, but they were generally too big and weird to bother with a tiny little starship that was just passing through.

Back in reality, *relatively* speaking, they were moving at ten thousand times the speed of light. The thing was, when you moved that fast, the real universe would stop you from doing it so you had to go into soft-space instead.

The engines practically shut down, aside from the whisper going into the relative field, and the trickle that fed the systems providing their food, water and air. The utter nothingness outside seemed to press in, smothering the little bubble of reality they were riding in.

Galana had found it became disturbing after about a month, but didn't get much worse after that. Blaren began getting a little edgy, began looking for ways to distract themselves from the nothingness. Humans did the same, and even more quickly … but worse than that, they withdrew into themselves. They became listless, depressed. They seemed to absorb the grey into their own bodies, into their messy little brains. Six months was longer than Galana would have liked – she'd learned that four-month stretches were the longest humans should endure – but Hartigan insisted it was fine.

"The computer keeps me entertained," he assured her.

Fortunately, they didn't need to depend entirely on the *Conch*'s computer to keep Hartigan from sliding into the glooms. They had a project. It gave Molran, human and Blaran a chance to work together, learn one another's habits and strengths, and pretend the grey wasn't out there. Even more importantly, it was necessary for the mission.

Together, they expanded and reinforced the *Conch*'s spacious lower cargo hold into a huge buttressed cavern. Ready to be filled with water for their Fergunakil crewmate. Once it was completed it would house not only the Fergie, but also a self-sustaining farm of live food, a life-support system linked to the ship's crystal core chambers, and a *mass* of computer and system interfaces. Heavily protected from the main ship controls, of course. You didn't want to let a Fergie play with your computer.

Galana had no more idea who their Fergie team member was going to be than she'd had about the Blaran. Captain Hartigan, however, seemed optimistic that there was a perfect Fergunakil out there for them, and that 'the cosmos would provide'. This was good enough for Galana, at least until they got closer to the edge of the galaxy and the cosmos began to run empty. And Hartigan had, she was forced to admit, been right about Scrutarius. Criminal the Blaran might be, but he was also an excellent engineer and his knowledge and respect for AstroCorps protocols seemed boundless.

"So tell us about this Bonshoon we're going to be trusting our lives with," Hartigan asked.

They were taking their evening meal together in the Captain's quarters. By unanimous agreement, and as usual for AstroCorps crews, they'd adopted a timetable that was built around the human's need to sleep. For the ten hours in twenty-four that Hartigan needed to dedicate to a combination of relaxation and complete unconsciousness, the ship was placed in 'night mode' and tasks were suspended. Galana and Scrutarius, who didn't need to sleep, worked a lighter shift or took their own lull breaks to rest and pursue their own personal interests during this time.

It was an easy routine to slip into, but it never got easier to know when the human was going to be asleep, or tired before sleeping, or for some unfathomable reason tired *after* sleeping.

"Her name is Bont," Galana said.

"Bont the Bonsh?" Devlin asked in amusement.

"*Bonjamin* Bont the Bonsh," Galana replied, "if you enjoy alliteration. She is also a biologist, although she's technically a *xeno*biologist so that spoils it."

"We could call her a bug biologist," Scrutarius suggested. "Xenobiology is mostly bugs, right?"

"There are hardly any bugs," Galana said. "I don't know where this idea that all aliens are bugs has come from. None of the Six Species are *bugs*. Only three known dumbler species are insect-like. Why does everyone assume 'alien' means 'big gross bug'?"

"Popular culture," Captain Hartigan said promptly. "I have an interactive game on my entertainment system that's all about big gross alien bugs and how to shoot them. I mean, if my day-to-day life as an AstroCorps Captain had more bugs in it, I probably wouldn't need to seek out entertainment like that."

"*Bonjamin Bont the Bonsh bug biologist*," Scrutarius said with relish.

"Bont is one of the best … doctors I have ever worked with," Galana attempted to herd the other two back to the point.

"And yet you paused before saying 'doctors' just now," Hartigan noted.

"She's a xenobiologist," Galana repeated, "specialising in dumbler and theoretical medical science," 'dumbler' was the term the Six Species used to refer to new species they met – species that didn't necessarily know anything about the cosmos beyond their home planets' skies. Galana picked up a spicy ration wafer and continued. "As part of her studies, she took Molranoid medical courses and aki'Drednanth, human and Fergunakil extensions," she took a measured risk. "Those are considered veterinary courses by the Fleet, but they are very - "

"Hang about, I'm going to be treated by a *vet*?" Hartigan said. As Galana had guessed, he sounded more delighted than insulted by this. "An *animal doctor*?"

"We're all animals, Basil," Scrutarius pointed out. "What would you call a human doctor who was trained to do operations on other species?"

"I wouldn't call her a bally *vet* if I wanted those other species to agree to get operated on by her," Hartigan declared.

"She is more than capable of treating all the members of our crew, and applying her knowledge to alien species we encounter on our journey," Galana said. She took a bite of the wafer. The rations were a byproduct of the OxyGen system that gave the ship air, but aside from the fact that they were a minor biotechnological miracle, they weren't particularly exciting. The spiced ones, at least, had a bit of a kick. They reminded Galana of home, the *Porticon*, and her mentor's *hoco* soup.

"Is that why she's at The Warm?" Scrutarius interrupted her musings. "Studying alien biology?"

"I don't know that The Warm has *biology*," Galana replied, "but she is on a research team," she picked up another wafer.

"Bonjamin is an interesting name for – listen here, have you got a blast furnace in your stomach?" Hartigan suddenly demanded. "You've been popping those red wafers like they're *not* made out of weapons-grade blasting putty. I nibbled a corner off one the first time we calibrated the crystals after launch. My mouth still tingles sometimes – and that's the only end I'm going to tell you about in polite company."

"Are you talking about me? Am I polite company?" Scrutarius asked, sounding touched.

"If the red wafers burned you in an … intimate digestive locale, Doctor Bont is *definitely* the person you want treating you," Galana jumped at the chance to press her associate's case.

"Will I have to call it my intimate digestive locale?" Hartigan asked.

"It's a better nickname than it deserves, Basil," Scrutarius said.

They arrived at The Warm right on schedule, without any noteworthy issues – digestive or otherwise.

DOCTOR BONJAMIN BONT (CREWMEMBER #4)

By the time the *Conch* had finished decelerating and they'd stowed the ships relative field toruses, Bont was on the comms system.

"Fen – Galana – Commander Fen, I'm so glad you accepted my invitation," the Bonshoon woman's wide, smiling face appeared on the main viewer. She was speaking Grand Bo out of consideration for the others. "I wasn't expecting you for another fifteen or twenty years, but I think I have a – yes, there is a docking berth and flight path here that isn't too dusty. I'll send it to you," her image flicked off as Bont cut comms, then reappeared a moment later. "Oh, and hello, um, the rest of Galana's friends – um, crew, I suppose," she added cheerfully. "You can all come too."

"Can I come too?" Hartigan asked brightly once the beaming Bont had vanished off the screens again. "Can I, Galana? Oh, *do* say I can."

"Doctor Bont is … single-minded and easily excited," Galana said a little defensively.

"We're going to have to find something else to call her than *Doctor Bont*, I can tell you that right now," Scrutarius announced. "But it sounds to me like she's been expecting you."

"Not for another fifteen or twenty years yet, but still close enough that she's got a berth set aside," Hartigan said, and shook his head in amusement. "*Molranoids*. Anyway, it's a big enough berth that we can dock without separating the *Nella*, so let's do that," he studied his consoles. "Hmm," he went on thoughtfully. "Looks like there's a Worldship in the vicinity but they're not docked. You reckon they might be keeping an eye on us, Fen?"

"I don't see why they'd bother," Galana replied, puzzled. "Bonty – Bonjamin – might know. I can ask her when we - "

"Hold on, did you say 'Bonty'?" Scrutarius asked. "As in, that was an actual thing that you called her? Bonty?" Galana nodded. "And she didn't mind how close that sounded to *bonshy*?"

"Are we supposed to also get offended by things that sound similar to slurs but aren't actual slurs now?" Galana asked. "I'm honestly asking, I have a hard time keeping up."

"It's a pretty key part of making amusing insults," Hartigan told her.

"And insulting jokes," Devlin added.

"Are those two different things?" Galana asked.

"Totally different," the Blaran said firmly. The human nodded.

"I think as long as the *intention* is nice, then it's okay to say a thing that sounds like a slur but isn't one?" the computer suggested.

"I'm glad to hear it," Galana replied. She was relieved that at least one member of the crew was able to provide an answer that didn't cause more questions to appear, even if it was only *technically* a crewmember. "Bonty was born here on The Warm but we met at the Academy, on the Worldship *Porticon*."

"Was that where she got the nickname?" Hartigan interjected. "I'm only asking because Academy nicknames are generally sort of joke-insulting."

"Is 'joke-insulting' a third thing after 'amusing insult' and 'insulting joke'?"

"Sometimes," Scrutarius replied unhelpfully.

Galana took up her story again and did her best to ignore Devlin's steadily broadening smirk. "When I graduated," she said, "Bonty still had a couple of years to go. She was hoping to come back here with an official research posting, and when she got one she extended an invitation to me."

"And you're here *early*," Hartigan said. "You obviously can't wait to look at all the piles of research she's done on this great big frozen thingy in the years since."

"I'm going to find a bar," Scrutarius decided. "I need a change in scenery. *Charming* as this ship is," he added with a little bow in the direction of the nearest interface panel.

"Too kind," the *Conch*'s computer replied.

"You can give me the short version of Bonty's presentations, Captain," Scrutarius clapped Hartigan on the upper and lower back with his left hands, then pointed his rights at Galana and the screen where Bonty's comm had displayed. "And remind the two of them every hour, on the hour, that we have to be at Declivitorion-On-The-Rim by next year."

"I could keep you company at the bar," Hartigan offered.

"No no, that would leave these two talking about xenobiology unchecked," Scrutarius warned, "which could take *decades*."

"I am aware of the time limitations," Galana said. "And it's not as if we won't have time to talk about xenobiology while we're in soft-space between stops."

"See? There's something to look forward to," Hartigan said.

"All the more reason to get a drink now," Scrutarius agreed. He smoothed his glossy silver outfit fussily. "I will do my best to uphold the dignity of the uniform, Captain."

"Not sure how much *dignity* our uniforms have ... "

"This will be a good practice run for our *actual* mission, where we will be expected to appear in front of strange and unknown alien species while actually wearing these tacky abominations."

"The current Head of the Research Council and de facto leader of The Warm is a human," Galana told Hartigan. "His name is ... " she checked the file again, " ... Gary Muldoon. Perhaps the two of you are acquainted, Captain, and as such you might prefer to - "

"Look," Hartigan sighed, "just because *I'm* a human and *he's* a human, doesn't mean we *know* each other. There are lots of humans in the – wait, did you say 'Muldoon'?"

"Gary Zebadiah Blovius Muldoon," Galana couldn't help glancing at Scrutarius, who had paused at the door. "*Do* you know him?"

"I – alright – just because – I *might* have a coincidental – there must be a lot of Gary Zebadiah Blovius Muldoons – it's beside the point," Hartigan muttered, and jabbed at his console. Galana lifted an ear in Devlin's direction, and the Blaran grinned.

"Bazzminster?" a human voice said uncertainly from the communicator a second later.

"Noggin!" Hartigan exclaimed. "You old plonker, what the deuces are you doing on this bally old icicle?"

"Never mind all that rot and spudmash, I heard you'd only gone and jolly well died!"

"Bah, don't believe all the tongue-wag, what?" Hartigan chuckled. Then the two humans devolved into what must have been a type of slang that was so obscure it was practically a dialect. Galana picked up the words 'crockpot', 'uncle munt', 'beans on toast' and 'chuckle off', but had no idea what any of them meant. She left the two humans happily jabbering at each other, and disembarked with Scrutarius.

They went their separate ways at the dock, Devlin heading out to the bars and entertainment houses at one end while Galana rode the transit rail to the main residential block at the other. Bonty met her at the end of the line.

Doctor Bonjamin Bont was, according to her Academy files, somewhere in the region of three thousand, five hundred years old. This was unfortunately as close as anyone could get, because a lot of information had been lost in the last centuries of the Wild Empire, The Warm wasn't known for keeping detailed records, and Bonty didn't talk much about her *extremely extended* past. She was elderly, if not ancient for her species, but still bright and energetic. Especially when it came to alien biology.

"Hello, Fen!" the big round Bonshoon caught Galana up in an exuberant hug, then set her down, patted her upper arms and beamed. "Look at you, all official in your silver-and-white. What brings you out to this weird little corner of the galaxy?"

"Stopping over on the way to Declivitorion-On-The-Rim," Galana said without bothering with too much small talk. "Hoping to pick you up and take you with us."

"Take me with you?" Bonty waved a thick arm and invited Galana to follow her to a nearby rail-pod. The doctor was dressed in strange furry garments that Galana was already coming to recognise as a local style based on the people of various species also making use of the transit hub. It was clearly just a fashion choice, since the dock area was pleasantly Fleet-normal in temperature. "Dear child, what are you talking about?"

When someone like Ambassador Kotan or even Galana's mentor Parakta Tar called her *child*, Galana had always found it a little irritating. When Bonty did the same, for some reason, it didn't bother her. She started to explain. "My crew and I - "

"Wait, before you tell me, you *have* to see this," Bonty hurried them both aboard the pod and as it skimmed smoothly into motion she pulled an info pad from her huge woolly coat. "Now, as you know, The Warm is an unidentified alien artefact, right? When the Fleet found it, it was just a huge old cylinder of solid metal, floating in space, and now we've built a cluster of docks and habitats at one end of it."

Galana recognised that she wasn't going to get Bonty's full attention until her friend had gotten this out of her system. She took the pad. "I thought it wasn't metal," she joined in as best she could, "but some kind of metallic compound - "

"Yes yes, precisely, a thousand-mile-long, three-hundred-mile-thick lump of mystery stuff that is – well, warm. Hence the name. Not *warm* warm, but only about ten degrees below the freezing point of water which is quite warm for something floating in space with hardly any atmosphere and no sun – well, no sun to speak of, just the - "

"Yes, Bonty."

"So look at these temperature readings I have been taking," she urged, prodding at the pad in Galana's hands.

Galana dutifully looked. Line after line of densely-packed numbers, hundreds of thousands of digits in length, began to scroll down the screen. "What are these … how fine are these measurements?" she blinked as the numbers went on rolling by. "And over how long a time?"

"As far back as I can find proper sensor readings," Bonty said proudly, "and the measurements are to the nearest … well, okay, I'm not entirely sure, everything was normal at one thousandth of a degree and one millionth of a degree, then there were a *lot* of zeroes and then I started finding fluctuations again. I think it's billions to the power of billions? Right down there somewhere ... *anyway*, that doesn't matter. Look at the patterns!"

Galana shook her head. "Bonty," she said with helpless fondness, "you've been staring at these tiny tiny temperature changes for years. I just saw them for the first time when we got in this pod."

"The Warm – this great big lump of alien metal – is responding to our presence," Bonty actually collected herself enough to explain.

"Really?"

"And not just in a natural metally sort of way, like it warms up a bit when we land a ship on it," Bonty added. "*Those* temperatures are all the way up at the top level. The tiny changes, they're *organised*. Like signals. They're slow, and they're responding *now* to events that happened a few centuries ago, but they're definitely some sort of coded communication," she put a big, soft hand on the pad and pushed it down, drawing Galana's attention back to her eager old face. "Do you see what this means?"

"The Warm is a ... sensor of some kind?" Galana hazarded. "A machine, recording and communicating information? I do not see what this means, Bonty," she finally admitted.

"It's a *nerve*," Bonty exclaimed. "A *synapse*, a single thread of some enormous brain, and it's still firing. It's *thinking* about something. It's thinking 'hello, what's this that's started building houses on me?'," she laughed. "Okay, maybe not that, I haven't cracked the code yet, but ... "

"A metallic nerve three hundred miles thick?" Galana smiled.

"Yes, well, if my theories are correct, the metal – the warmium, as they call it – would just be a – a – an *insulating layer*, protecting the actual nerve. The nerve itself would be much thinner, somewhere down inside the metal," the pod slowed to a halt and they disembarked into a noticeably chillier region of the settlement. Galana began to understand why the locals wore woollens. "My place is just on the edge of the plain," Bonty went on, and they stepped onto a moving walkway and accelerated. "It's not far."

"What does the Fleet Edutorium say about all this?" Galana asked. "The AstroCorps Science division? What about your colleagues here in the research groups? If you've already made such a huge breakthrough - "

Bonty gave a slightly forced laugh. "Well, they don't exactly agree with me that these fluctuations have *meaning*," she said. "I'm still looking for final proof. The numbers are so small, you see, and the sensor records don't usually go that deep ... I've set a lot of tests in place that will show an actual response to things I'm doing - "

"But The Warm won't respond to *them* for another few hundred years," Galana said.

"Exactly. In the meantime I was hoping to prove my theories about The

Warm's insides, but they won't approve a dig. And I can't say I disagree with them," the xenobiologist said. "Why, for all I know that would stop The Warm from functioning at all. No, there's nothing for it but to keep digging. *Figuratively* digging, that is," she added. "Not *actually* digging."

Bonty's home was a cluttered but welcoming little pair of habitat domes fixed to the silvery surface of The Warm's main bulk. The closest star was just about bright enough to classify as a sun, and cast a bit of light over the plain, but that was all it did. The plain, lit from behind by the settlement's lights as well as the sun, dwindled away into darkness before them.

The domes were filled with instruments, whole wall-segments covered in more displays of Bonty's lists of numbers, with bits of them circled and underlined and connected up to others with pieces of coloured string. It probably wouldn't be a good idea, Galana thought as she ducked under one string that extended across the room like a spiderweb, to let Hartigan and Scrutarius see how … *intense* … Bonjamin could be. On the plus side, the domes were *tiny*. Bonty would have no trouble adjusting to life on board the ACS *Conch*. The ship would probably seem spacious after this.

"Is that a sleeper pod?" Galana asked. The old machine, used in Worldships to transport Molren in suspended animation, was half-buried by more info pads and stacks of printed material.

"Hm?" Bonty looked up from a bench she was clearing to reveal a kitchen buried under more notes. "Oh, yes. I had an idea to put myself into lull-storage and try to communicate with The Warm in real time. Too many things to still work out there, but when I had a chance to pick up a sleeper pod I grabbed it just in case. You know, for later."

"Communicate with it in real time."

"I had a theory that the nerve was trying to send information through a network," Bonty explained, "a larger whole, and this piece had been separated off it. But there's still too much information to collect before I'm close to proving any of that. So where did you want to go?"

Bonty had abruptly given up on trying to prepare any sort of refreshments, and had seated herself on a stack of data blocks. Galana, although she'd gotten used to these rapid shifts in focus during their time in the Academy, was still caught a little off-guard.

"The Fleet nobility don't want to recognise AstroCorps or the Six Species, and will roll them back if they get a chance," she said. "I've agreed with Ambassador Kotan that he will aid us in gaining Fleet support - "

"You *agreed* with Stana Kotan?" Bonty raised her ears. Galana reminded herself that as daffy as Bonjamin Bont seemed, she had been around for a long time and was *extremely* sharp. "That doesn't sound like you at all."

"I made a bet with him," Galana admitted.

"Ah. *That* sounds more like it."

"An AstroCorps ship, an AstroCorps crew, a single successful mission," Galana said. "Six crewmembers only, one of each species. A single circumnavigation of the galaxy."

Bonty blinked in astonishment. "So you want to perform a standard Fleet tour, or in this case AstroCorps tour, not around Six Species space but the whole *galaxy*?" Galana nodded. "And you have to take a Molran, a Bonshoon, a Blaran, an aki'Drednanth, a Fergunakil and a human?"

"That's right."

"Fergies eat people," Bonty said doubtfully.

Galana nodded. "We'll try to avoid that."

"And humans tell anecdotes about their bodily functions."

"That may be unavoidable."

Bonty snorted. "Surely this is more of a test of how well the engines can hold out, and how long the crew can get along together locked in a ship without killing each other?" she said. "I mean, that's a fine thing to show them we're good at, but … "

"That will only be part of it," Galana said. "A proper tour involves exploration and research, stopping at planets and making contact - "

"What planets? There aren't any solar systems on the edge of the galaxy. It's sort of the point of it being the edge," Bonty chuckled. "The suns and planets run out. Taras Talga – Declivitorion-On-The-Rim's sun – is a bit unusual, and it's almost certainly the only planet with a developed civilisation living on it. There couldn't be more than a few hundred star systems that close to the edge of the galaxy, and the chances of any of them being inhabited ... "

"No, that's true, we will actually be travelling a little *in* from the edge," Galana said patiently, "to maximise the number of potentially inhabited planets, remain as far and as safe as possible from the Core, and lessen our total travel distance. It will of course also make it more dangerous than a simple relative-speed flight around the galactic rim," she was forced to admit. "And I suspect that the time we will save due to the shorter distance will be cancelled out by exploratory stops. The approximate route will be agreed between the crew and Ambassador Kotan on Declivitorion-On-The-Rim next year before we set out."

"And you're planning on taking one of each of the Six Species?"

"Yes," Galana said positively. "And you're my Bonshoon of choice."

"Of course I'm flattered, and naturally I accept," Bonty said. "But - "

"You accept?" Galana blurted.

"Obviously," Bonty laughed. "I'm still *AstroCorps*, Fen. I wonder where I put my uniform ... " she glanced around the hoard of research materials, as though expecting to find her uniform neatly folded on top of a pile of essays. Then she brightened. "Why, if I can leave a few tests running here, this will give me just the distraction I need. And when we get back, I may have even gotten some results."

"We're not planning on being gone *that* long."

"Perhaps not. I suppose we need to keep the short lifespans in mind ... " Bonty waved a hand, then looked a little nervous. "But ... we're taking a *Fergie* with us?"

"That's the agreement," Galana said. "I don't suppose you have any suggestions? Aside from not taking a Fergunakil," she added before Bonty could do more than open her mouth.

"I don't know that many Fergunak," Bonty replied. "None that would still be alive now, come to think of it. But you're in luck. That Worldship at the far end of the settlement? That's the *Mercibald's Chalice*. It's filled with water. And that water? Filled with Fergunak."

Galana couldn't help glancing nervously out of the note-crowded dome window, across the silvery plain towards the darkness beyond. "What? How?" she demanded. "How many of them?"

"A hundred and fifty, maybe two hundred thousand," Bonty smiled innocently. "I'd be very surprised if at least *one* of them's not AstroCorps trained and up to the task of accompanying us as ... what? Tactical and combat officer? I mean, I assume you don't want one to be our *doctor*. That's my job, isn't it? Please say it is."

THE *CHALICE*

"I thought the only aquatic Worldships were the *Noquinox* and the *Argen*," Galana said. "What's this *Mercibald's Chalice*?"

Bonty shrugged. "Can't say I've asked too many questions about any of it. It's all a little bit creepy, isn't it?"

"A little bit creepy?" Galana echoed.

"It's a wreck, it can't fly. The Fleet was going to dismantle and use it for scrap, but the Fergies asked if they could use it instead. It might have actually been a disagreement between the Fleet and the Separatists, I think I heard something about that. The *Chalice* is sort of spoils o' war or somesuch."

"Spoils of war?" Galana lifted an ear.

"Spoils *o'* war," Bonty corrected her. "I think the *o'* is important. I don't actually know the whole story," she admitted when Galana sighed. "You know how the far end of The Warm was all Fleet hulks, some of them were the original ships that brought settlers here from Earth - "

"I *didn't* actually know any of that," Galana said with a smile. "I thought all the buildings were up at this end."

"Oh," Bonty blinked. "Oh, no. No, a lot of old Fleet ships and bits and pieces down there," she waved at the window, and the plain stretching beyond. "Anyway, they're clearing them all away, or moving them around, and they're going to dock that Worldship right to the end of The Warm. Put everything back neat and tidy. They couldn't keep adding bits and pieces willy-nilly, it was a frightful mess."

"And what do the Fergunak want with The Warm?"

"I don't know that they *want* anything with it. It's just a place to park their big broken spaceship and make it part of a settlement. Easier than trying to put her into orbit around a planet. Who knows why Fergies really do any of the things they do?" Bonty laughed lightly. "Part of why everyone is so uneasy about them, really."

"Well," Galana said, "our Captain Hartigan is friends with the Head of the Research Council. Maybe he'll be able to tell us."

"Maybe," Bonty agreed. "That Noggin Muldoon is an odd one. Been here ten years, and never really shared any theories of his own. I think he's a Grand Boënne Dominion operative, here to establish a presence and start sending samples back to the Empire … "

They shared a meal from Bonjamin's kitchen that was little more exciting than the ration wafers on the *Conch*. Bonty continued to wander excitedly from topic to topic, her theories about The Warm melting into conspiracies about Council Head Muldoon and switching just as quickly to questions about their mission. She chattered on after their meal, while she packed a few personal belongings.

"The medical centre has a lot of high-quality equipment for AstroCorps use," Galana checked her pad, "you can take a look at the facilities on the ship and let us know what else we need."

"What we need for a trip around the galaxy where we will almost certainly encounter never-before-seen alien species and medical problems?" Bonty smiled.

"Start with what you'll need to keep one of each of the Six Species alive and intact," Galana said dryly. "Then we'll worry about healing the galaxy."

"Right, right, one of each," Bonty nodded, then added uncertainly, "including a Fergie."

"I hope we won't *need* to give any of our crew medical attention," Galana said, "but your files do say you are experienced in Fergunakil veterinary treatment?"

"Oh yes, yes no problems there," the xenobiologist said quickly. "They're … difficult to treat, because you have to do it all underwater or have a special wet-dry treatment sling … but I'm sure we'll muddle through, as they say. Some of their robot parts are … tricky," she added. "I'm a doctor, not a cybertechnician."

"Let's chat with Captain Hartigan and Council Head Muldoon," Galana suggested, and tapped her pad. "They may be able to help us find a suitable shipmate, and then we can worry about finding replacement computer parts on the other side of the galaxy."

Hartigan sounded positively merry when he answered her call. "Fen! We were just talking about you!"

"Were you also drinking wine, Captain?" she asked, rolling her eyes good-humouredly at Bonty. The Bonshoon grinned.

"D'you know, we were?" Hartigan laughed. "But don't worry, I was only saying good things."

"Naturally," she replied. "You haven't found anything bad to report on yet."

"Look here, I've got Noggin with me and I want you to confirm something for me, seeing as how you're all straight and honest and whatnot," Hartigan went on in a slightly slurred voice. They'd been docked barely two hours. It never failed to amaze Galana how quickly humans could get incoherent when they drank alcohol. Hartigan was reasonably good at keeping his head, she'd judged after the past six months of dinners and seemingly random celebrations and special events, but even so … "Look here, Fen, I want you to tell Noggin what our mission is. Bally fool won't believe me."

"We're flying to Declivitorion-On-The-Rim, and from there we are conducting an AstroCorps tour around the galaxy," she said, puzzled.

"I say, the whole jolly galaxy?" Muldoon demanded. He sounded far more slurred than Hartigan – but Galana admitted she was probably playing favourites.

"Well, not the *entire* galaxy," she said. "That would take tens of thousands of years to do properly. But a standard tour around the near-rim - "

"Y'see? I *told* you," Hartigan crowed, and for a little while the two humans slipped back into Grand Boënne slang. Galana lowered the pad and shrugged at Bonty.

"Enthusiastic fellow, isn't he?" the doctor noted.

"I say, is that Bonty the bug biologist?" Hartigan exclaimed. "What ho, Bonty! Capital to have you on board! She said yes, didn't she Fen?"

"Yes, Captain."

"Excellent! Knew you wouldn't let us down, what?" Hartigan paused while Muldoon said something in a low voice – *label all your limbs, Basil, or you're like to wind up with arms coming out of your ear 'oles* – that the Molran and the Bonshoon probably weren't supposed to hear. Human hearing was not very acute and they tended to assume nobody else's was either. Hartigan laughed, then cleared his throat and went on a little guiltily, "So, ah, to what do I owe the pleasure of this call, Commander Fen?"

"There is a sizeable community of Fergunak at the far end of The Warm," Galana said, "and we were wondering if you had any information about it. Perhaps we can check whether any of them are AstroCorps, and would be interested in signing up."

"Aha, *excellent* notion, young Fen," Hartigan approved. "Noggin was just telling me about that as well. Ugly business. Ugly, ugly business. Mind you, Fergies hardly do any other sort of business, do they? That's what makes them so dashed useful sometimes. Takes all sorts, that's what I say. Can't make a cake without eggs *and* sugar, what?"

"Yes you can - " Bonty objected, and Galana waved her quiet. It really wasn't worth it.

"There's almost ten thousand Academy-qualified Fergunak on board the

Mercibald's Chalice," Hartigan related after a few moments and following a loud clatter and a muttered curse as he very obviously dropped his pad. "Almost all of them tactical and military, o'course."

"So many?" Galana said in surprise.

"Oh, sure," Hartigan said. "But you know, joining AstroCorps for a Fergie is just a matter of installing a couple of new programs and getting a certificate saying he can spend a day in the same swimming pool as a non-Fergie without bally well eating him. The only reason more of them don't sign up is that certificate's such damn hard work, what?" he and Muldoon laughed again.

"If you send me the list, I can arrange them in order of - "

"Don't bother yourself, Fen," Hartigan announced, "I think I've got our girl."

"Oh yes?"

"Yes indeed. Didn't I tell you the cosmos would provide? Now, we're on a bit of a ticking clock and we can't wait for these things to run their normal course," Galana sat and waited for Hartigan to get to the point, which he finally did. "Our big grey beauty goes by the name of Wicked Mary. Not a promising start, you might think, but you know they just come up with names that *we* can use, since we can't use computer signals and tiny amounts of blood in the water or what have you ... "

"And it's just too much darn *trouble* to come up with a name that's not creepy," Bonty said, to more laughter from the humans.

"Well said, Doctor Bont!" Hartigan agreed. "Anyway, this Wicked Mary, she's something of a renegade, a rebel. But a bad Fergie means good for *us*, don't y'know – and she's got some hush-hush connection to the Monsters."

"AstroCorps Special Weapons Division?" Bonty murmured. Galana felt her own ears stiffening, but she let the Captain continue.

"Now, as you know, your average Fergie is happiest when in a nice cosy computer network with a couple of thousand close friends," he said. "That won't do for our long voyage, so we already need a Fergie who's a bit of a loner, what?"

"Agreed," Galana said cautiously.

"Well, look no further," Hartigan declared. "Our Wicked Mary is currently in solitary confinement – in *jail*, don't y'know, for the dreadful crime of – can you guess?"

"Failing to eat someone?" Galana guessed.

"*Failing to* – yes. Quite right," Hartigan sounded disgruntled for a moment. "Seems she had to choose between accepting the surrender of a bunch of poor yobs from that Worldship of theirs, or dumping them in space for her friends and family to eat, and she went with the daft 'accept surrender' option. So naturally they bally well locked her up in a deep dark tank and are treating her for being insane."

"By Fergunakil standards, she is," Bonty said.
"She sounds perfect," Galana agreed.

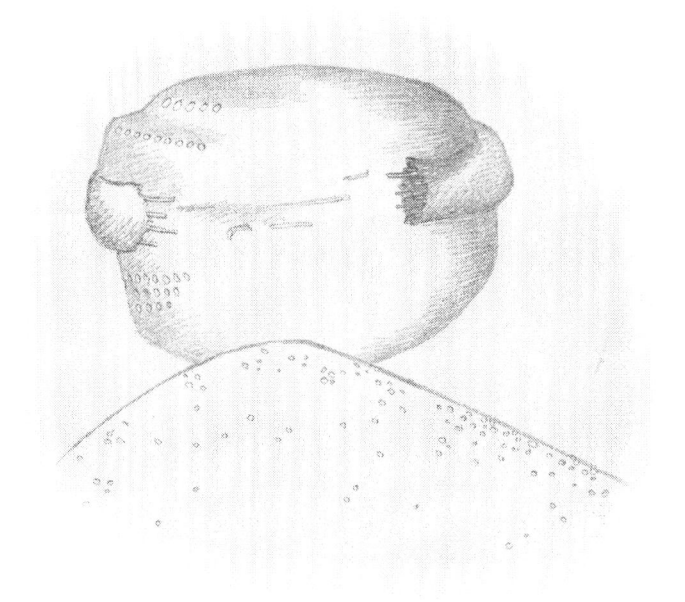

WICKED MARY (CREWMEMBER #5)

Galana and Bonjamin headed back out, Galana carrying Bonty's cases and Bonty struggling to fasten her AstroCorps uniform, grumbling about how chilly it was out of her furs. She still needed to prepare the rest of her gear, set her communication tests in motion, arrange with Muldoon and the AstroCorps scientific division for her home to be kept for her ... all of these things, she listed in a low, excited mumble as they made their way back into the main part of the settlement.

They met Scrutarius at the *Conch*'s dock. He wasn't alone.

"I hope you have a good reason for pulling me out of that bar," he complained. Galana had sent him a message while they were in transit, and hadn't even been certain he'd received it judging by the blast of noise he'd sent in reply. "I'd just made some new friends," he gave Bonty a nod. "You must be Doctor Bonjamin Bont."

"Hello. You must be Chief Engineer Devlin Scrutarius," Bonty said. "*The* Devlin Scrutarius?"

"No, actually there were seven others last time I checked," Devlin said. "I'm the best one, though."

"Speaking of your friends," Galana said, nodding politely to the pair of silver-clad humans Scrutarius was supporting in his lower arms, "fellow Corpsfolk?"

"Yes. This is Commander Layne and this is Lieutenant Beaufort," he shook each human in turn. Beaufort turned out to be unconscious. "They insisted on coming with me to wish us well."

"Commander Layne," Galana said politely.

"*Schlafg*," Commander Layne replied.

"I see," she turned back to Scrutarius. "Have they had too much to drink?"

"*Beaufort* has had too much," Scrutarius said, giving Beaufort another shake. "Layne has had *just* enough."

"What are we supposed to do with them?"

Scrutarius looked from one to the other of the humans in his grasp.

"Shave their fur off," he decided slowly, "and make the fur into a pair of little toy monkeys, and put the monkeys – no, wait, hear me out," he insisted as Galana sighed. "Put the monkeys underneath their hats and put the hats back on their heads, so when they wake up and take their hats off," he'd started to laugh, "they have *monkeys*, instead of *fur*."

"Put them in transit," Bonty suggested, pointing to the nearby rail. "Security will pick them up and take them back to the AstroCorps compound. Our Commander has a mission for us, Chief Engineer Scrutarius."

"Aha!" Devlin clapped his upper hands in delight. "I knew it. We're going to break into the Worldship and liberate a Fergie crewmate."

"How did you know – how did he *know* that?" Bonty demanded in admiration.

"Chief Engineer Scrutarius has a singularly keen and devious mind, as befits a member of the criminal species," Galana said. Devlin beamed. "But it's not necessary here, I think – we're not going to break her out. The Fergunak don't want to keep her."

"That may be true," Devlin agreed, "but at the same time, they're not going to make it *easy* for us. Have you dealt with Fergunak very often since leaving the Academy, Commander?"

"No," Galana admitted.

"I try to avoid it wherever possible myself, but I guess the rules of the bet kind of make it difficult this time," Scrutarius said, and looked around. "Where's our great and fearless Captain?"

"I believe he is keeping the authorities of The Warm distracted from whatever we're doing with the Worldship," Galana said, "by drinking wine and talking about the good old days with Council Head Muldoon in a kind of slang I have not quite managed to translate yet."

"Excellent, all of our skills are interlocking nicely," Scrutarius crossed to the transit rail, dumped his two AstroCorps comrades into the rolling machinery and waved to them solemnly as they skimmed away. "Right," he said, "first thing we need to do, I think, is finish our new shipmate's living space so it's ready for her, yes?"

During their flight from Grand Boënnia they'd prepared the lower cargo hold to take water, and brought the oxygen-processing and water-cleaning plants and machinery into readiness. There still wasn't much food for their giant shipmate, and they'd planned on picking up most of it at another stop, but it looked like they'd be needing it ahead of schedule.

"I know where we can get nutri-shoals for her," Bonty said, "and those horrifying little squeaky big-eyed water-kittens they like so much. With a

Fergunakil Worldship ready to hand, we might also be able to get some luxury items. Those clone squids they like to fight with for entertainment, for example."

"An entertained Fergie is a safe Fergie," Scrutarius agreed. "Well, you know … *mostly* safe."

"The *Conch*'s computer has taken care of all the arrangements to get fresh water piped in while we're docked," Galana said. "It should be ready in six hours or so. In the meantime, we need to go over to the *Mercibald's Chalice* and get our friend's effects, and negotiate her release with the Fergunak … unless you think negotiation is the wrong way to go about it, Chief? Doctor?"

"I definitely think negotiating with them is a good idea," Bonty said, "but of course that means a slightly different thing with Fergies. We can't just show them our AstroCorps mission data and explain that Wicked Mary is qualified - "

"Ooh, *Wicked Mary*," Scrutarius rubbed his hands together. "Sorry, carry on."

"We'll need to make it clear to them that we are on a mission where only a single member of each species can come," Bonty went on, "and there is a slim likelihood of survival."

"I would prefer to downplay that - " Galana complained.

"Not with Fergies, Fen," Bonty said positively. "You're not asking them to give us a crewmember, you're *telling* them that you're *taking* one. You'll want to convince them that it's basically a death sentence, and we need a particularly mad and defective Fergie so it's no big loss to the school. Already being cut off from the rest of the Fergie network for her crimes, and being a member of AstroCorps SWD, is a bonus."

"Wicked Mary is a *capital-M* Monster as well as just the regular kind?" Scrutarius said in delight. "This gets better and better."

"She may not actually be a full member of the Division," Galana explained, "but Captain Hartigan did say she had a history with them."

"How long a history?" Scrutarius asked. "I mean, keep in mind Fergunak only live about eighty years. If it's 'history' from back at the founding of AstroCorps or the Monsters, we're not going to get around the galaxy before Wicked Mary dies of old age. Which might mean we lose the bet," he paused. "You know, as well as being very sad … "

"We're not actually sure how old she is," Galana admitted. "Perhaps that's something else we can find out during the negotiations."

"Suggest we go over in the *Nella*," Scrutarius said, then explained when Bonty looked puzzled. "The *Conch*'s command deck and computer core detaches to become a shuttle," he turned back to Galana. "If all goes well, we can hook up a water tugship to carry Wicked Mary and her luggage back here so she can board."

"Simple," Bonty said cheerfully.

Galana couldn't help feeling, as she sat at the Executive Officer console a short while later with the grinning Blaran criminal on one side of her and the grandmotherly Bonshoon animal doctor on the other, and the craggy grey mass of the *Mercibald's Chalice* looming ahead of them like a cliff, that 'simple' wasn't the word she would have used.

The Fergunak are our allies, she told herself firmly. *If we can't fly up and say hello to our allies, what hope do we have of making contact with unknown aliens on the far side of the galaxy?*

On another hand, she continued to herself, *if we can fly up to a Worldship with two hundred thousand Fergunak on board and say hello, what possible fear can a bunch of unknown aliens hold for us?*

"We're getting a transmission from the Worldship," Scrutarius, who had agreed to run communications for the time being, reported calmly.

"Let's hear it," Galana said.

There was a moment of tense silence, then a silky voice emerged from the computer speakers. It was nothing like the usual friendly human-female voice of the *Conch*.

"You swim very close, little meat things," the voice purred. "You must be very curious. Very brave."

"Very stupid," Scrutarius murmured. Galana gave him a warning look. "We're not transmitting yet, Commander," he reassured her innocently. "Ready on your signal."

She nodded and pointed at Devlin to indicate she was ready. "Worldship *Mercibald's Chalice*," she said, "this is Commander Galana Fen of the AstroCorps Starship *Conch*. We are here to bring a Fergunakil crewmember on board for an extended special tour. I am sending you the mission information now," she pointed at Devlin again, and he tapped the controls. "As you can see, it is a long-range tour likely to take some decades, requiring a single isolated - "

"Wicked Mary," the voice interrupted. "You seek Wicked Mary."

Galana looked at her crewmates.

"Does everybody know about this but us?" Bonty whispered.

"Worldship *Mercibald's Chalice*," Galana replied, "it is our understanding that the Fergunakil you mention would meet all the criteria and her assignment would be of benefit to both - "

"Yes indeed, little meat things," the voice once again interrupted. "We will prepare a vessel to transport her. We have her belongings ready. Is there food, or anything else that you cannot get from The Warm? All you have to do is ask."

"Well, that was easy," Bonty said as Galana transmitted their list of special wishes to the Worldship.

"Perhaps they are unaware that we know she is a prisoner for crimes against Fergunakility, and they want to get rid of her before we find out," Galana theorised. A response to her list came almost immediately. The Fergunak were giving them everything they'd requested, including some eggs for entertainment squid that should hatch and grow in a year or so. "Still awfully cooperative of them."

"The humans have an expression," Scrutarius said. "*Never look a gift-horse in the mouth*. I think that counts double when the horse is actually a shark the size of a landing shuttle."

The Fergunak began loading up a water tugship so quickly it was impossible to believe they hadn't been waiting to do it. They also sent a smaller capsule directly to the *Nella*, containing Wicked Mary's personal effects. Most of these were sealed in heavy water bags as they would be unpacked in the Fergunakil's aquatic chamber, but one piece was clearly for the *Conch*'s crew.

Galana, Devlin and Bonjamin stood and looked at the strange little robot.

Only about shoulder-high to a human, the machine looked tiny and frail. It had two arms and two legs, all spindly and silver, ending in cunning little multipurpose tools. Its head was large and flat-topped like a Molran's, with a wide range of cameras and sensors and communication devices arranged around its edge. The robot's body and limbs were painted in an approximation of AstroCorps silver-and-white, and its head topped with a small metallic hat to complete the uniform. It was inactive, and stood slumped in place like a broken toy.

It bore a strange symbol, a round yellow disc with black markings on it that looked like eyes and a smiling mouth. The disc was stuck on the robot's simple metal body right between its legs, as though to hide private parts the machine did not possess.

"Well that's downright unsettling," Scrutarius declared.

"Are we supposed to activate it?" Galana asked.

"Shouldn't think so," Scrutarius said. "I'm guessing Wicked Mary will switch it on once she's on board and all set up. Fergies, being aquatic, can't come out of the water to chat with us or have dinner."

"Such a shame," Bonty commented.

Scrutarius grinned. "*So*, to walk and talk with the land-crawlers, they have these brilliant little remote-controlled robots that they can use like puppets. They can see and hear everything that's going on from the safety of their tanks, and we can hear what they have to say without putting our bathing suits on."

"Yes, we know how Fergunakil *giela* work," Galana said.

"Look, if you don't appreciate my info-dumps … "

"I know how they *work*," Bonty admitted, "but I never understood why they *decorate* them. I once met a Fergie who had done up his *giela* with *very* realistic organic parts, and he came into my clinic and had me half-convinced he was a new dumbler species I'd never seen before. Gave me quite a turn when he made his arms fall off and squirt goo everywhere - "

Scrutarius chuckled. "Yeah, that was kind of what was weird to me here," he admitted. "Fergies usually do at least a little bit of decorating to make their *giela* creepy to us land-crawlers. This one – aside from the smiley face – is pretty much … fine," he frowned. "We may be dealing with a *deeply* disturbed Fergunakil here."

"*Blaren* usually decorate themselves too," Bonty pointed out, "but you don't even have a weirdly-placed smiley icon."

"I've got *decorations*," Scrutarius said primly, and smoothed his uniform with all four hands. "I just don't go around flashing them at everyone. It's a little thing called *class*, Bonjamin."

By the time the tugship was loaded up and Wicked Mary was presumably transferred into its water-filled hold, they'd returned to the dock and reconnected the *Nella* to the *Conch*. Bonty left to oversee the last of her packing and preparations, and the tug floated over to join the *Conch*, but there was still no word from their Fergunakil shipmate. The little robot *giela* remained slumped and deactivated, and the only contact between the ships was performed by their computers.

Only when they'd finished filling the *Conch*'s hold with water, and had connected the tug to allow Wicked Mary to come aboard, was there any communication from her. Even then, there wasn't much. She switched her systems on, and they went *bleep* one after another. Bonty got back and finished stocking her room and the medical bay just in time for the *giela* to activate.

"Greetings," the little robot said. It straightened, saluted, and a set of little lights came on around its head and body. "I am Wicked Mary."

"Welcome aboard, Tactical Officer Mary," Galana said formally. There had been a brief discussion, and the three Molranoids had agreed that 'Tactical Officer Wicked' just didn't sound right.

"Thank you, Commander Fen," Wicked Mary moved her *giela*'s arms, opened and closed its assortment of hand-tools, then nodded to Devlin and Bonty. "Chief Engineer Scrutarius. Doctor Bont. If you would like to meet face to face – so to speak – I am prepared to receive visitors. Thank you for allowing me to set up in privacy."

The for'ard supporting wall of the hold was transparent, allowing them to descend into the area without needing to go into the water, and giving them a rather spectacular view into the huge, gloomy chamber that would be Wicked Mary's home for the duration of the mission. With the reinforcing pylons and the organic filtering plants and the fast-moving shoals of feed-fish already in place, the overall effect was like looking through a window into a strange undersea cave.

The shark was sleek and dark and surprisingly healthy-looking. Most Fergunak Galana had seen were discoloured and blotchy grey, with encrustations of cybernetic implants like barnacles all over their bodies. Wicked Mary had robotic enhancements – they would allow her to do her job on board even if she wasn't connected to the wider Fergunakil networks – but they were clean and crisp. She was also smaller than a full-grown Fergie ought to be, although that was easy to miss. It was just that, once you had a fish the size of a skimmer bus with a gaping tooth-filled mouth a Molran could practically stand inside, a skimmer-bus-and-a-half-sized version of the same wasn't much more to deal with. Not when you were standing on the floor and looking up at her.

"Hello," Wicked Mary said, the voice coming from the *giela* that had accompanied them down into the hold as well as from a comm system on the wall. The vast, shadowy shape moved past the transparent wall, and turned slightly so her pale underbelly flashed at them. She had a tiny pair of hands tucked underneath her body, between her fins. One of these unfolded and waved at them, then tucked away again as she righted herself and swam deeper into the hold.

Galana, Devlin and Bonjamin waved back, a little dazedly.

"I trust your accommodations are comfortable?" Bonty asked.

"Very comfortable, little one," Wicked Mary replied. "Far more comfortable than my cell on board the *Mercibald's Chalice*."

"Your file says you are … fifteen years old?" Galana asked. She could have guessed that Wicked Mary was young based on her size and appearance, but once her *giela* activated her AstroCorps files had also opened. She'd been expecting someone a little older, but the truth was a Fergunakil lived at computer-speed, every second feeling like days to her enhanced brain. A Fergie was considered an adult at the age of three or four, even though they didn't reach full size until they were in their twenties – indeed, some biologists insisted they never really *stopped* growing, but it depended on the living space they were given.

With a shipmate of fifteen years, although Galana hated to think of it that way, they might just have a shot at completing their mission in her lifetime.

"Yes, Commander Fen," Wicked Mary replied. The *giela* turned its head. "Captain Hartigan is outside on the dock."

They waited while Hartigan came aboard and descended into the lower hold. He looked tired, and amusingly fuzzy. Human fur – *hair* – continued to grow on various parts of their bodies, unless they shaved it off in order to maintain whatever appearance they decided looked good. Basil Hartigan in particular suffered from this, and always looked hilariously shabby when he neglected his pelt.

"Did you *forget* me?" he asked accusingly.

"Not at all, Captain," Galana said smoothly. "Allow me to introduce Doctor Bonjamin Bont, and Tactical Officer Wicked Mary."

"Excellent, excellent, nice to meet you both in person," Hartigan said, shaking Bonty's lower left hand and the robot's right hand at the same time. "Doctor Bont. Bloody Mary. Excellent."

"It's *Wicked* Mary," Galana cringed.

"Yes?"

"Wicked."

"What'd I say?"

"*Bloody.*"

Hartigan laughed. "Oh, very nice! Sorry, Mary old girl. Must've been thinking about something else."

"No need to apologise, Captain," Wicked Mary said. "I quite like the sound of *Bloody Mary*, myself."

Hartigan grinned. "And then there were five, what? This is all going swimmingly," he glanced up at the great aquarium window. "Literally, in fact."

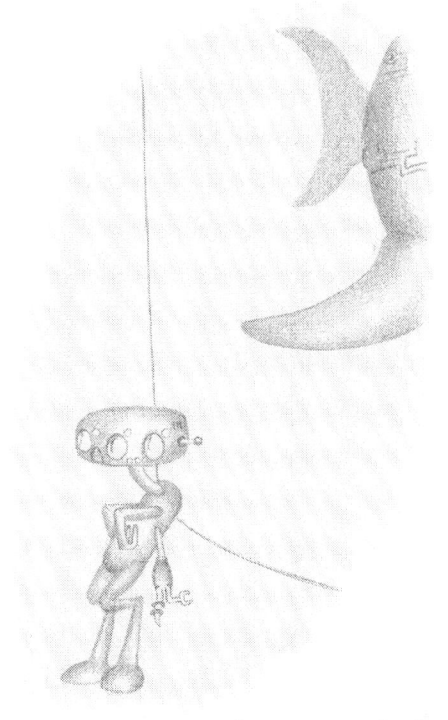

"I am satisfied that our new crewmembers meet – in fact, exceed – the AstroCorps requirements for this mission," Galana told him, "having studied their files and records in depth."

"Depth," Hartigan hooted, then coughed. "Okay, no more aquatic puns."

"Don't make promises you can't keep, Baz," Scrutarius advised.

"Right you are," Hartigan said cheerfully. He smelled rather strongly of alcohol. "And of course, I felt sure you would check the files, Commander. Never a doubt in my mind. Only the best, what?"

"I have a surgical marker you can use to label all your parts, just in case you ever need medical attention," Bonty said sweetly. "I'll even help you do some of the hard-to-reach ones if you want."

"Eh?" Hartigan blinked, then seemed to remember the conversation they'd had over the communicator while he was drinking with Council Head Noggin Muldoon. "Ah. Right. Heard that, did you? *Damnably* good hearing, you lot have."

"I expect it's because we don't have arms coming out of our ear-holes," Galana remarked.

"Leave that to me," Bonty announced.

"They're going to hold this against me," Hartigan said to Devlin in a low but quite clearly audible voice, "aren't they? Not a good start, old chum."

Wicked Mary's *giela* robot raised a hand. "If any of you have a *serious* disagreement, I will be very useful for getting rid of the body," she remarked.

"One big happy family," Scrutarius beamed. "This is going to be *great*."

DECLIVITORION-ON-THE-RIM

Galana was surprised and delighted at how well all five of them seemed to get along. It was beyond her most optimistic expectations. And the relative speed flight from The Warm to Declivitorion-On-The-Rim was *very* long, even with the occasional stopover. She'd expected them to have far more serious disagreements, even if the getting-Wicked-Mary-to-eat-the-body level of argument was a bit of a worst-case scenario. But amazingly, they continued to work well together as the months went by.

A lot of this was because of Devlin Scrutarius and his strange, colourful ways of settling disagreements and cheering people up. He claimed he'd learned a bit of 'frontier diplomacy' dealing with pirate teams and other criminal types who tended to be far more touchy and violent than AstroCorps crews. Galana did her best to ignore him when he spoke about his checkered past. The important thing was that it worked.

Devlin and the Captain, of course, were lifelong colleagues and friends, if you could call it 'lifelong' when one of them was only thirty-something. They didn't seem to argue at all. Hartigan said it was because they'd had all their arguments already. Bonty, aside from the respect she earned due to the fact that she was everyone's doctor, was simply too sweet and easy-going to get in many fights. And those she did get into, she usually won. She was roughly three thousand years older than the next-eldest crewmember, and at that point Galana supposed it must be pretty easy to deal with someone disagreeing with you.

That left Galana herself, and Wicked Mary. Galana liked to think she was level-headed and even-handed enough that she simply didn't get in arguments, whereas the Fergunakil …

Well, she was a Fergie. She was nicer than a lot of her kind, and didn't seem to share her species' enjoyment of making air-breathers uncomfortable. She would occasionally lapse, and refer to one of them as 'little flesh' or 'morsel', but there didn't seem to be any malice behind it. It was just the way the great sharks talked to land-crawlers. She seemed happy to let Hartigan and Scrutarius call her 'Bloody Mary' by way of a nickname. And her abilities with the computer system and navigation shaved weeks off their journey.

Still, it was nice to pull up once in a while, to see the starry darkness of space instead of the drab grey of faster-than-light unreality. To dock and go out among the crowds, to eat food that wasn't starship-made, to walk under a planet's sky. They even managed to find a couple of spots where Wicked Mary could get out of her aquarium and swim a little. On one of these occasions she joined a small group of Fergunak in some kind of hunt, which she clearly enjoyed a great deal. She'd returned to the *Conch* and Bonty had been given her first hands-on bit of doctoring, patching up a couple of deep scratches Wicked Mary had received from whatever deep-sea beastie she and her friends had been chasing.

Their long stretches in soft-space were uneventful, by soft-space's very nature. One regular topic of conversation was their sixth and final crewmember. Galana had tried to reassure the others about this, but they seemed to enjoy talking in circles around it and fretting, so as long as it didn't lead to arguments she let them carry on. And she had to admit, she was a *little* worried that things wouldn't work out the way she'd planned, and they would be left without an aki'Drednanth shipmate.

"You know, she doesn't actually have to be AstroCorps qualified," Bonty said one evening. They'd continued to hold to the human schedule of work and rest, and now that there were two sleeping species on board and three non-sleeping, they all synchronised quite nicely.

"Whatever do you mean?" Hartigan asked. The Captain, during his off-duty periods, insisted on switching his uniform for an even tackier brightly-coloured dressing gown which Galana, Devlin and Bonjamin then had to put up with when he invited them to his quarters for drinks. He also enjoyed smoking huge, blue-black Taras Talga cigars, the smoke from which he liked to puff into the air in a variety of shapes until the room was thick with smog. The cigars weren't *very* toxic – not compared to the things humans had used to set fire to and inhale before the Fleet had arrived at Earth and talked a little bit of sense into them – and the smell was not entirely unpleasant, but it was still something they only tolerated because Basil Hartigan was the Captain and this was his living space.

The good news was, you couldn't make artificial Taras Talgas so he could only smoke them very sparingly. The *bad* news was, the cigars came from Declivitorion-On-The-Rim and Hartigan had announced that he fully intended to buy a crate of the things. Enough to last the entire mission, provided he rationed himself.

"I mean," Bonty said, "that all the aki'Drednanth living in Six Species space are *technically* classified as AstroCorps officers by … oh, it was some charter law or other."

"Is it the Aki'Drednanth Are Best At Everything Law?" Scrutarius asked.

"That was the one," Bonty smiled whimsically.

"It's a bit more complicated than 'aki'Drednanth are all technically AstroCorps officers,' but that is the gist of it," Galana admitted. "We have to do this absolutely by the book, though. Our final crewmember has to be a graduate of the Academy."

"Kotan wouldn't call the bet off because the aki'Drednanth crewmember wasn't qualified," Devlin said. "He wouldn't have the *thoks*. I mean, he wouldn't dare. That would be the same as saying she wasn't Best At Everything – and as established, I think there's a law about that … "

The total number of aki'Drednanth in the entire galaxy was unknown but there were only five hundred of them in Six Species territory at any given time. The crew of the *Conch* referred to them all as 'she' for the simple reason that this was how the aki'Drednanth referred to themselves. Whether they were actually male or female made no difference. And for historical reasons the Fleet, and the five non-aki'Drednanth species in general, treated them with the deepest and most total of respect. Law or not, not even a snooty imbecile like Stana Kotan would dare to suggest one of them was inadequate in any way.

"No, he wouldn't *say* it," Galana agreed. Wicked Mary's little gleaming *giela* crossed the room and expertly poured a drink of some sort. She removed her hat, placed the glass on the flat top of her head, strolled back over to the lounge where the crew were sitting, and crouched slightly. Scrutarius lifted the glass from her head with a murmur of thanks. Galana wasn't sure when their Tactical Officer had started serving drinks this way, but it seemed to have been her idea and everyone found it entertaining so she didn't make an issue of it. "But," she insisted, "it would still be there. Underneath. Not spoken, but clear and on the record."

"Only three aki'Drednanth have ever actually bothered to attend the Academy," Hartigan protested.

"So far," Galana was unable to stop herself from insisting.

"Yes, yes, *so far*."

"And it just so happens that one of them is the precise aki'Drednanth I'm hoping will complete our crew," Galana said, feeling as though she'd explained this fifty times already although it couldn't actually have been more than thirty-five. "I don't know any aki'Drednanth more qualified for this mission, whether AstroCorps or not. Not that I know many aki'Drednanth," she felt compelled to add.

"I thought all Molren knew every aki'Drednanth in the Six Species personally," Devlin said. "I feel so let down."

"So," Hartigan puffed his cigar again, "it's this mysterious Chillybin, then."

"Yes," Galana replied.

"An aki'Drednanth none of us have ever heard of, and who doesn't seem to exist on *any* records aside from a note on the AstroCorps graduation registry," Hartigan continued, "dated the very *year* of AstroCorps' foundation."

"Yes," Galana repeated.

"Which – not to sound sceptical or anything – was basically the year they said 'righto, let's do a thing called AstroCorps, and we'll be different from the Fleet and follow the Six Species charter instead of any of the older system laws and we'll have these daft silver uniforms and hats and it will be simply spiffing'," Hartigan said. "And then decided there would be an Academy, and what you'd need to do to graduate from it, and so it pretty much just means she was there in the room, and got her name written down."

"She has completed all the necessary training, classes and tests," Galana insisted.

"Yes, but at the same bally time they were making the training, classes and tests *up*," Hartigan replied. "But by all means, if the rest of us are satisfied with *any* wacky-wacky-Drednanth who wants to join, and you're only satisfied with an Academy graduate, and you reckon you can get her … then that's just grand and everyone's happy."

"We'd just be even happier if we knew where she was right now," Bonty said delicately, "that's all."

"I'd feel better if the *Conch* knew," Hartigan added.

"I'd feel better if the Fergunakil gridnet knew," Wicked Mary put in.

"I'd be a bit uncomfortable about the gridnet knowing," Devlin responded. "No offence."

"Chillybin is a very private person," Galana said. "She travels between Worldships, mostly under high Fleet protection. They probably conceal her from … other eyes."

"Well as long as she's ready and willing to join up when we get to the starting line," Hartigan ended the discussion as he usually did, finishing his drink and puffing on his cigar while placing his empty glass on top of Wicked Mary's head. "I suppose it will be tickety-boo."

Each time they stopped, especially as they drew closer to the edge of the galaxy, Galana sent out messages. She had her reasons to think they weren't necessary, but as the weeks and months went by and her crewmates grew steadily more anxious about their missing sixth, she felt it was important to give the impression that she was working on it. She couldn't blame them for their lack of faith, of course. It was a lot to leave to chance, and that was what it looked like to them. Her messages received no replies, and they flew on.

They arrived at Declivitorion-On-The-Rim almost a month ahead of Ambassador Kotan's deadline, thanks to Wicked Mary's navigation talents.

Declivitorion-On-The-Rim was the only habitable planet in the Taras Talga system, and one of the oldest settlements in Six Species space. If you believed the stories, it had been home to many mythical creatures that had once lived on Earth – Ogres, Trolls, Elves, Centaur, perhaps even the fabulous Alicorn.

"Started my search for the Last Alicorn out here, don't y'know," Hartigan told them as the *Conch* pulled into orbit and they prepared to detach the *Nella*. "Didn't find a damn thing, naturally."

Declivitorion-On-The-Rim had changed a lot since the days of the Elves, of course. Thanks to the farmworlds in the nearby solar systems, it had been able to develop into a mass of continent-spanning cities. The Elves, if they'd ever existed in the first place, had moved deeper into the galaxy to get away from the spreading human population.

Even though they were early, the *Conch*'s crew found Ambassador Kotan waiting for them. He had arranged a pair of landing pads at the Fleet Council chambers, and by the time they had decelerated into orbit he was apparently well on the way to planning a welcoming event for them. Galana was immediately suspicious, but the others were delighted.

"The Fleet Council chambers," Bonty said excitedly. The huge, exclusive building stood near the centre of Rosedia, which was the name of both the country and the city that covered it. "That must have taken some arranging, even for a Fleet Ambassador."

The *Nella* pulled away from the rest of the *Conch*, and an oversized water-adapted lander moved in to dock with the rear access of Wicked Mary's hold. It had been agreed that Wicked Mary would attend the start of the mission in person. It was an important occasion and it was fitting that she be there even if it was a bit more trouble. Plus, a cynical corner of Galana's mind couldn't help adding, Kotan might question her existence if they went down with the *giela* alone.

The little robot was also present, of course, on the *Nella*'s bridge. Even though the Fergunakil was attending in person, she would still be in a separate aquatic part of the hall to the rest of them, and her *giela* would be needed to help her communicate.

"The grand reception hall has been reserved for us," Galana noted as they began their descent.

"Fancy," Devlin said mildly. "Wonder if they'll let me in."

"Just promise not to steal anything," Galana smiled.

"Oh, I'm *definitely* going to steal something," Scrutarius said. They were all dressed in full AstroCorps uniform, Wicked Mary's silver-and-white *giela* polished to a shine. "Maybe just a plate or a cup – you know, as a souvenir."

"You have a message from Harry at Taras Tobacco, Basil," the *Conch* reported quietly. "He has a full crate of his finest product ready to pick up."

"That was quick," Hartigan said appreciatively. "What does he want for it?"

"Nothing," the *Conch* replied. "It seems that a small but very high-stakes series of side-bets have sprung up on Declivitorion-On-The-Rim and the nearby systems. Harry is willing to give you the cigars, provided that you pay the full value if our mission is a failure. If we win, apparently Harry is set to make a tidy profit and considers the crate a small price to pay."

"Our reputation precedes us," Bonty said in surprise.

"I expect Kotan has been blabbing about it to his nobby Fleet friends," Hartigan said, "ever since getting here. Setting us up for abject humiliation, what?"

"That sounds accurate," Galana admitted.

Hartigan frowned. "Harry knows that if we fail, I'm most likely not going to be alive to pay up, right?"

"My understanding is that he would consider the cigars a worthy tribute to your memory in that case," the *Conch* said.

Hartigan beamed. "Good old Harry."

"Is good old Harry aware how long-term a gamble this is?" Galana asked.

"Well if he doesn't, let's not bally well tell him," Hartigan replied.

They were met at the landing pad by a great skimmer wagon in black and gold, one side of it crafted of thick crystal panels and filled with water. A small shoal of bright aquamarine fish glided sluggishly back and forth inside.

"Glider fish," Wicked Mary's *giela* identified them as they boarded the skimmer. Her own lander was still completing its warm-down and the complicated process of trundling its large water-case out to link with the skimmer. "Very rare. Their skin is treated with chemicals that produce … pleasurable feelings when eaten - "

"Drug fish," Scrutarius said. "Got it."

"I hope we get drug fish," Bonjamin said, nudging Galana playfully.

"Doctor, please," Galana sighed.

"No reason why Bloody Mary should get all the fun," Hartigan said.

Ambassador Kotan, and an alarming number of high-ranking Fleet and Rosedia city officials, were awaiting them at the grand reception hall. There were even a few exceedingly uncomfortable-looking people in AstroCorps uniforms, probably because Kotan hadn't been able to come up with any excuse not to invite them.

A painfully formal and fancily-dressed Molran stood at the entrance and introduced the new arrivals one after another. Galana was a little surprised.

They'd sent down their basic information when replying to the invitation, but it seemed as though Kotan's people had done a lot of research in a very short time.

"Announcing guests of honour," he intoned, while the hall full of Molren and the scattering of humans and Bonshooni stopped and turned to stare. "AstroCorps Captain gold-class Basil Hartigan. AstroCorps Commander platinum-class Galana Fen. AstroCorps Veterinary Medical Officer platinum-class Bonjamin Bont. AstroCorps Tactical Officer obsidian-class and Special Weapons Division Consultant Wicked Mary," the announcer paused very noticeably. Scrutarius examined the fingernails of his upper left hand and ran his tongue slowly down the length of his elongated eye tooth. The announcer's nostril-slits pinched shut. "And Able Belowdecksman and non-Corps engineer Devlin Scrutarius."

There was absolute silence, punctuated by the occasional cough as the four Corpsfolk and the *giela* descended the stairs into the hall. As they did, the huge shadowy shape of Wicked Mary swept into the water-filled chamber that was separated from the rest of the space by a reinforced glass window. Several of the guests standing next to the aquarium wall drew away fearfully as the enormous shark glided by past their heads.

"There might be some scraps of drug fish left in Mary's tank you still could've announced ahead of me," Scrutarius told the Molran, quite loudly.

"Steady, old boy," Hartigan patted his friend's arm.

"So," Galana murmured to the *giela* while they crossed the enormous echoing space towards the waiting crowd. "You're obsidian-class?" the little robot tilted its head up and blinked some lights at her. "If you added a Captaincy to your credits, you'd outrank us all."

"It was necessary," Wicked Mary said, "for the work I did with SWD."

There was no time to ask more questions, because Ambassador Kotan was striding forward and giving Hartigan an extravagantly sarcastic salute.

"*Captain* Hartigan," the elegant Molran said while his little flock of hangers-on gathered around him. He leaned over to address the human in a way that was calculated to insult. "So you are the brave soul Fen has found to lead this mission. I do hope it doesn't take *all* of the years you have left."

"What ho, Ambass'," Hartigan said cheerfully, returning the salute crisply. Galana concealed a wince, hoping Kotan didn't notice the way the human lowered his hand and turned it to bring his longer middle finger to the fore. It could have been a coincidence, or it could have been a rude gesture. "I imagine it'll take as long as it takes, what?"

"Commander Fen," Kotan turned to nod at Galana. "Doctor Bont. Consultant," he nodded in turn to Bonty and Wicked Mary's *giela*, then turned and inclined his head at the far wall and the aquatic chamber there for good measure. "So. Here you are. Although - "

"I think you missed one of us there, old chap," Hartigan interrupted. "I know, five is a big number when you only have four fingers on each hand."

Galana froze in horror.

Kotan's mouth twisted and his nostrils clenched, but he eyed Scrutarius sourly. "Able Belowdecksman," he said.

For a moment Devlin stood looking over their heads and it seemed as though he wasn't going to acknowledge the Ambassador at all. But then he inclined his head politely. "Ambassador Kotan," he said. Galana unclenched. "It's a privilege to be invited to such an important location. Thank you."

Kotan looked taken aback. "Yes, well - "

"In an AstroCorps uniform, even a lowly Blaran can rub shoulders with the Fleet Council of Captains," Scrutarius said, eyes bright. "I *deeply* appreciate the statement you've chosen to make here – and we haven't even won our bet yet," Kotan opened and closed his mouth for a moment, and Devlin looked back across the room. "Is that a buffet table?" he asked vaguely. "Do excuse me, Captain. Commander. Doctor. Consultant," he nodded to each of his crewmates in turn, and stepped away. "Ambassador … " he added as an afterthought.

"Well," Bonty said brightly. "Isn't this *nice*?"

"I have to ask, Captain Hartigan," Kotan recovered from his shock, but was stiff with rage. Several of his flunkies were actually trembling. "Is it because your hands have *five* fingers that you've fetched up here a crewmember short?"

"Ooh, that was a *good* comeback," Hartigan said admiringly. He turned to Galana. "Wasn't it a good comeback, Fen? Only took him thirty seconds of quivering effort to come up with it, too."

"Some decorum, Captain," Galana pleaded. She turned to Kotan. "You are quite right," she said. "Our crew is not yet complete."

"I do hope you intend to fix that before setting out, Commander," Kotan said. "I would hate to declare the bet void before you even begin," he leaned in, a look of false concern on his face. "I hope the aki'Drednanth did not *refuse* your requests?" he asked. "You have been sending out *so* many."

Galana felt her ears dropping in surprise and outrage. Ambassador Kotan, of course, had friends everywhere. If they'd been picking up Galana's calls, they could also have been stopping them from going very far. Her friend might not even know they were looking for her.

"Perhaps we can discuss the route we are to take, and the other mission parameters," she said faintly. "There is ample time before our departure ... "

"A month, by my reckoning," Kotan said coldly. "If help is not yet here or on the way, it will not arrive in time should you send a summons now. But perhaps one of the four aki'Drednanth on Declivitorion-On-The-Rim might agree to join you. I am sure I can pull some strings and have the Fleet send out word - "

"That will not be necessary," Galana said, "thank you. I am sure such assistance would break our bargain anyway."

"Oh, not *break* it," Kotan smiled. "*Undermine* it, certainly ... "

"Why don't we just try to enjoy the evening," Bonty said hopelessly. "It is *very* nice. I might join Devlin at the buffet."

"Yes," Kotan smirked, "I would expect nothing less. It is a very ... refined assortment," Bonty visibly stiffened with anger at his tone, which Galana considered something of an achievement. Over a year in transit with Basil Hartigan, Devlin Scrutarius and Wicked Mary had failed to bring out a single solitary angry reaction in the sweet-natured Bonshoon. Bonty stayed where she was, and Kotan turned back to Galana. "You might as well enjoy the meal," he went on. "Without a sixth member of your team to represent AstroCorps' famous diversity, our wager ends here. AstroCorps, the Six Species, your little dance of the sharks and monkeys, takes its final embarrassing steps as the music tails off ... "

"*Ambassador* Kotan," Galana said. She could see and hear her old mentor in a corner of her mind, sighing and sitting back and picking up her mug of soup, ready to enjoy the fireworks.

She didn't get a chance to deliver whatever blistering retort she was planning – which was probably for the best because she honestly had no idea what it might have been – because the announcer moved to the top of the steps and called for silence.

"Announcing final guest of honour," he said in a shaky voice. "AstroCorps Bridge Officer Imperium-class and esteemed aki'Drednanth visitor to our humble world … Chillybin."

The enormous figure stumped up beside the announcer, towering over him much as the Molranoids towered over the humans. Her refrigerated envirosuit was dazzling in silver and white. The Fleet representatives all bowed their heads in reverence, and the local powers – Molran and human alike – did the same.

Chillybin, using her huge armour-plated fists like a second set of feet, loped down the stairs in a swift series of crashes. At the bottom of the stairs she bounded forward a few more steps, impossibly light and swift for such a massive creature. Her suit folded apart with a complicated series of clicks and swinging panels and a burst of frosty steam like the opening of a freezer, and Galana and the others around her gasped in the cold.

The aki'Drednanth, huge and shaggy and crusted with ice, trundled out of the mist leaving the suit standing open near the foot of the stairs. Her great heavy head, massive lower jaw lined with tusks that stuck up like a row of spikes, swung threateningly. Everyone took a hasty step back.

Everyone but Galana.

Chillybin surged forward and caught her up in her two long, powerful arms. The hug, which could have crushed Galana to a pulp, was freezing but gentle. Then Chillybin set her back on the floor, as delicately as though she were a glass statue.

"Fen," her suit said from behind her, in response to the movements of the special speaker-glove she was wearing on one massive clawed hand. She couldn't speak in words any more than the Fergies could, and so another method had been found for her species. "It's good to see you again."

"Chilly," Galana said, relief and delight – and yes, alright, maybe just a little bit of satisfaction at the stunned expression she could see on Kotan's face out of the corner of her eye – making her giddy. "It is good to see you too. How did you know?"

The aki'Drednanth gave a low *woof* of amusement deep in her shaggy chest and fixed Kotan with a bright look from one iridescent crystal eye. The Ambassador looked a little queasy.

"I had a feeling," Chillybin said with a curt motion of her gloved fingers.

CHILLYBIN (CREWMEMBER #6)

It was amazing how much better-behaved everyone was when there was an aki'Drednanth in the room.

"You do us much honour, Chillybin," Kotan stammered. "Had I known you were coming … "

Chillybin gave another growly bark of amusement and returned to her suit. Aki'Drednanth could survive for a time in warm temperatures without their refrigerators, but it was uncomfortable for them – not to mention more than a little smelly for everyone else – and so after a while they preferred to return to the cold.

"If you had known I was coming, it would have completely spoiled my grand entrance," she said.

"Ahahaha, indeed, indeed," Kotan bleated. "Well said. Ahahaha."

Galana had to admit that a lot of the satisfaction had gone out of their rivalry with Kotan and the Fleet now that Chillybin was on the crew. The Fleet would say or do *nothing* to upset or disagree with her. Indeed, if an aki'Drednanth would simply stand up and say 'I think AstroCorps should replace the Molran Fleet as the ruling power in Six Species space,' the Fleet would probably spontaneously dismantle itself.

But that wasn't how the aki'Drednanth worked. That wasn't how they worked precisely *because* it was that easy for them. Not only were they bigger and stronger than anything but a Fergunakil – and 'stronger' was a matter for debate – but they were known to have other, stranger powers. Even more importantly, the aki'Drednanth had saved the Molran Fleet from certain destruction thousands of years ago, and since that day no Molran – or Blaran, or Bonshoon, or human or Fergie for that matter – would ever disrespect one of the great frosty beasts.

Aki'Drednanth spread their representatives around and took in every side of the cultures they lived in. And then, presumably, shared it all with one another and had a good laugh. Kotan and the Fleet Council of Captains certainly had aki'Drednanth allies of their own. Galana was actually surprised none of them were here. Their absence made any sparring they did a bit one-sided.

Basil Hartigan didn't seem to share Galana's sense of fair play.

"I have to say, it's going to be jolly fun to circle the galaxy with you, Chillybin," he'd found a glass of wine from somewhere, and toasted the giant silver-clad aki'Drednanth. "*Chillybin*," he repeated with relish. "I know you take names we little folk can understand and pronounce, and you have a damnably good sense of humour about it, but that's a new one on me."

"I was given this Six Species designation almost two hundred years ago," Chillybin said, "by Parakta Tar, a great mentor and a mutual friend of mine and Galana Fen's. I do not often appear in public, so if you have never heard of me I am doing my job well."

"Well said, old girl," Hartigan approved. "We didn't know what to expect, but Fen here never lost faith. We've got a nice big refrigerated cargo hold all set for you. Put it all together on our last couple of legs out through the farmworld belt, don't y'know," he took a drink. "Got some good grub for you too," he added, "hope you like it. Of course, it won't compare to the *excellent* spread Ambassador Kotan has put on," he turned to look up at the frantically smiling Molran. "You *have* got some aki food on your buffet tables, I hope?" he asked. "You knew there would be … " he put down his glass and raised both hands, one with all five fingers open, the other with one, " … *six* of us, right?"

"Ahahaha," Kotan said again, and snapped his fingers frantically at his followers. Several of them dashed off. "Yes of course, I believe there were arrangements made just in case, but when none of our esteemed aki'Drednanth guests arrived – until now, of course – we didn't – we will obviously – in great haste – happy to … "

"Ambassador Kotan," Galana took pity on the man, although she wasn't sure why. "The aki'Drednanth will, of course, go where they wish and involve themselves in whatever adventures they wish. AstroCorps is lucky to have aki'Drednanth allies, as the Fleet has always been lucky. They are one of the Six Species, as they were one of the Five Species before we met humanity. The mission we are about to begin - "

Kotan didn't seem to appreciate her help.

"It is of course highly dangerous, even for an aki'Drednanth," he said. "The Fleet would never approve such a reckless endangerment of aki'Drednanth life. I regret that this foolish wager has placed you in this position, Chillybin."

"Not at all," Chillybin said. "This is the very reason we make friends with mortals. It would never occur to aki'Drednanth to *fly around the galaxy*. We go where the mortals take us."

Kotan smiled forbearingly. Aki'Drednanth, quite aside from their heroic status in the Fleet and their immense size and strength and strange powers, were also believed – in some strange and complicated way – immortal. Of course, when an aki'Drednanth said she was immortal, nobody dared argue with her.

"I hope your journey is a success," the Ambassador said, "even if your safe return puts me in an – ahahaha – an uncomfortable position, because of my wager with Fen. I would consider it a small price to pay."

"Admitting you were wrong costs nothing," Chillybin said, "and yet can mean everything."

"Wise words," Kotan gushed.

Chillybin turned and looked at Galana. With her huge gleaming helmet it was impossible to see any sort of facial expression, but it was still meaningful enough to make Galana cover a smile.

"I believe I have just eaten your tank filtration system," Wicked Mary's *giela* broke the uncomfortable lull in conversation. Everyone turned to stare at the side of the hall that separated the air-breathers from the huge aquarium where the Fergunakil had been unloaded from the skimmer. The shadowy shape cruised past just above head-height, a mass of tendrils hanging from her mouth. "I thought it was edible, but it is apparently made of plastic," the little robot added. Wicked Mary swept away into the gloom, shaking her head from side to side and shedding pieces of the mechanism into the water. "The drug fish were *very* good."

"I'm impressed at your ability to demolish a filtration device and steer your *giela* at the same time," Hartigan congratulated her, then turned and beamed at his crew. "AstroCorps. Only the best, eh?"

"I will … send a maintenance team to replace it as soon as possible," Kotan said, and snapped his fingers at his attendants again.

"Will this maintenance team be using a safety cage?" Wicked Mary asked.

"*Oh look*," Bonty said quickly. "They're coming back with the lovely frozen stuff for you, Chilly."

Kotan wilted in relief. "Yes," he said, and ushered them over towards the tables where Scrutarius was already munching away happily. "Please, by all means."

"Let us eat," Chillybin agreed.

DEPARTURE FOR PARTS UNKNOWN, AND ADVENTURE

There was little for them to do on Declivitorion-On-The-Rim once their crew was complete. They took on some more supplies, confirmed their route as much as possible considering how little was known about the galaxy outside Six Species space, and made sure the *Conch* was running at peak efficiency.

Hartigan and Scrutarius kept themselves busy for several days collecting on a wide range of side-bets. After his good fortune with the cigars, Hartigan made a point of looking up a lot of other artisans and luxury goods suppliers to find out if they had anything riding on the success of their mission.

They were, Galana was surprised to learn, becoming increasingly famous. The journey of the *Conch* had captured the imagination of the general public, and had of course come to the attention of AstroCorps' higher authorities and the Fleet. A few of them had been at the disastrous party Stana Kotan had thrown on their arrival.

Reactions to the *Conch* mission were mixed. Some parts of AstroCorps disapproved of the foolhardy nature of the tour, but there was little they could do once a ship was assigned and crewed. Leaving Six Species space was prohibited by the charter and Fleet law, but when an exception was made, it was made. Some parts of the Fleet were delighted in the bet, all for reasons of their own. Whether it was out of hope they would fail or hope they would succeed depended very much on the different groups. And the general planetary populations were even more diverse, but mostly seemed entertained and excited by the whole idea.

Whether they would still be interested several decades from now, after receiving no word from the *Conch* and her crew, remained to be seen.

Galana had her doubts that anyone would even remember them when they returned. The average attention-span of the Six Species at large was about twelve minutes, so her hopes of them continuing to care about AstroCorps and its crazy mission fifty or more years from now were not high.

All the more reason, her crewmates decided, to take what they could to make their mission a bit more comfortable. Soon the *Conch*'s crew cabins and any hold-space not given over to Aquarium or Icebox were crammed to the ceilings with storage containers. Even the Fergunakil and aki'Drednanth spaces had their share of supplies for Wicked Mary and Chillybin.

Galana took some time to travel the city and the small scraps of countryside that still existed inside it, taking in the sights and the comforting, familiar bustle of Molran and Blaran, Bonshoon and human, the occasional scuttling Fergie *giela*. She climbed Mount Arbus, the small artificial mountain at one edge of the city, and watched Taras Talga rising glorious and blue-white over the seething city.

There was an ancient monument at the top of the mountain, a wind-worn stone shape like an old-style drinking goblet. The inscription on the base of the monument claimed that mountain and monument alike had been raised to honour Rosedia, the founder of the city, and the fact that on this site he had been given a goblet of poisoned wine by a mythical trickster of some kind, and had died as a result. Whatever lesson this bit of local folklore was supposed to provide, Galana couldn't see it. Sometimes the lesson was that there *was* no lesson.

Still, she watched the sun rise, and watched the orbital and air traffic come and go. She didn't have to share the space with anyone, which was nice. It didn't look, from the run-down and neglected look of the place, as if it was a very popular tourist destination.

"What ho, Fen," Hartigan greeted her when she returned to the *Nella* that afternoon. "We were just about to ping you. We're all set."

She glanced at Bonty, who was the only other person on the shuttle. "We are?"

"Devlin went up on the lander with Bloody Mary last night," Hartigan confirmed, "and Chillybin went up this morning in a *very* swanky private shuttle with a bunch of swooning Molran fanchildren," he gave Galana an insincere smile. "Not meaning to insinuate that your species could use a good bally cold shower when it comes to the whole wacky-wacky admiration thing," he added.

"But I do get the impression Chilly's going to be happy to get out of Six Species space and into some unexplored corners where people don't worship the very ground her species walks on," Bonty said delicately.

Galana flicked her ears in amusement. "Why do you think she keeps such a low profile?" she asked.

Hartigan gave a chuckle. "Well, she should be wrapping up her little worshipper-tour and sending them all bowing and scraping for the airlock right about now," he said, and tapped at the console. "If you're just about done with this big crowded stone, we can get going."

Galana crossed to her controls and sat down. "Ready when you are, Captain."

"There is a message from Ambassador Kotan," the *Conch* reported, "but it is intended for the entire crew, with a request that I play it before we embark."

"Sounds like just the kick in the pants we'll need to get moving, what?" Hartigan said merrily. The *Nella* surged to life underneath them, and a few minutes later they were swooping into the star-speckled blackness of space where the *Conch* waited in orbit.

And so it was, another couple of hours later, the crew of the *Conch* sat or stood at their bridge consoles, fresh and crisp in full uniform. Human Basil Hartigan at the helm and command seat; Molran Galana Fen at the Executive Officer controls; *giela* of Fergunakil Wicked Mary at the weapons console; Blaran Devlin Scrutarius at the Engineering controls; Bonshoon Bonjamin Bont at Medical and Sciences; and aki'Drednanth Chillybin hulking massively at the Communications console.

"Righto," Captain Hartigan said, "let's hear this message from Ambassador Kotan, then."

"My esteemed AstroCorps colleagues, allies of the Molran Fleet all," Kotan's painfully self-important voice filled the bridge. "May your journey be a testament to the spirit and tenacity of the Six Species and the dream you wish so fiercely to bring to life. Fail or succeed, return or perish, today you enter the pages of history. Today you make your mark on the ledger of your proud institution. Whether it is destined to become a cautionary tale on the hazards of disregarding the older and wiser voices flab glab gloob blub."

Galana and Hartigan exchanged a puzzled look.

"I am *so* sorry, Basil," the *Conch* said. "It would seem the remaining twenty-three minutes of the Ambassador's speech have become irreparably corrupted due to a storage error."

"Ah well, can't be helped," Hartigan said carelessly. Scrutarius sniggered. "Let's see what's out there, shall we?"

"To parts unknown," Devlin said, and raised a cup he had resting on his console. Galana sighed. It was an ornate teacup with a Fleet Council of Captains emblem on it, *clearly* stolen from the grand reception hall.

"To parts unknown," Hartigan agreed.

"To set foot on worlds where none have trod before?" Bonty asked with a smile.

"Oh dear me no," Hartigan replied. "No, what's the point of that? We definitely want to go where there's people."

He tapped his controls. The five overlapping armour plates on the *Conch*'s hull opened and the rings of the relative field generator curled out. Each one fired up in sequence, finally activating the field around the ship and projecting her into soft-space, ten thousand times the speed of light.

The ACS *Conch* plunged into the grey. Destination: parts unknown, and adventure.

Soon, in The Demon of Azabol:

Commander Galana Fen was just beginning to wonder if there was anything alive at all outside Six Species space, when they dropped out of the grey into orbit above an inhabited planet.

"Atmosphere and gravity within tolerances," the *Conch* reported, "although Chillybin will find the polar ice caps more to her liking and Wicked Mary will be more at home in one of the two oceans. The salt content and levels of - "

"Never mind the tourist brochures, old girl," Hartigan said eagerly. "Tell us about the *aliens*."

"Giant bugs," Scrutarius said in an undertone to Chillybin. "I bet you. Googly eyes and slimy mandibles, you mark my words."

"I am not finding any sign of giant bugs," the *Conch* said, "or advanced civilisation, for that matter."

"Oh really? Then what was that signal we followed here from our last stop?" Hartigan demanded.

"Give me a moment, Basil," the *Conch* replied.

"There is sentient life down there," Chillybin confirmed, her great gauntlets moving easily over her controls. "Intelligent, but not advanced. The signal ... " the Comms Officer paused for a moment as the ship relayed the data. "It has a number of sources."

"Let me guess," Scrutarius raised his upper hands and spread them dramatically. "An assortment of derelict starships, none of them native to this planet, almost as if they've been lured here by something. The crews, paralysed by giant bugs and used as incubators for their gross slimy eggs, left their exploded-skeleton-filled ships behind to send their forlorn messages into space ... "

"There is *still* no sign of giant bugs, Chief Engineer Scrutarius," Chillybin said, "but the signals do appear to be coming from three ships down on the surface. None of these ships seem like anything the local life-forms would have built."

"There are seven ships, or at least something like ships, all within a small area on the surface," the *Conch* added. "Only three of them are signalling. They seem to have been doing so for some time, judging by the distance from which we picked it up."

"Is it too early in the mission for me to say 'I have a bad feeling about this'?" Devlin asked.

PART TWO: HERE THERE BE SPACE DRAGONS

THE DEMON OF AZABOL

"So," Hartigan said, "what do we have here? A dumbler civilisation not advanced enough to be sending messages into space, but a positive carpark full of *other* dumbler vessels, some of them sending out distress calls and some just plain dead. That about the size of it?".

"Yes, Captain," Chillybin said.

"We won't need to give the locals our standard warning about attracting the attention of the Cancer in the Core," Galana said, "and they have nothing to receive our communications with anyway."

"How primitive are they exactly?" Hartigan asked. "Can we go down there and pretend to be Gods?"

Galana sighed at the irrepressible human. "We can make *careful* contact," she said, "since it doesn't look like we'd be the first aliens they've met. We should also do something to quiet those derelict ships down. They're a bit noisy."

"We're pretty close to the edge of the galaxy," Hartigan pointed out. "It's not like the Cancer are going to hear those signals for another fifty thousand years or so. But by all means, let's meet the neighbours and ask them to keep it down, for the sake of their great-great-great-great-great-great - "

"Captain - "

"Wait, you didn't let me finish … great-great-great … " Hartigan looked down at his fingers. "Damn and blast, now I have to start over."

"I can take each of the active wrecks out with a round from the for'ard pulse turret," Wicked Mary offered. "That will silence the shouting dead."

"Let's make sure there's nothing to learn or salvage first," Hartigan said, then saw Galana's look and quickly added, "and no risk to the locals of course. Haha."

"Or some way to turn off the distress beacons *without* blowing up the ships," Galana suggested.

"Excellent notion, young Fen," Hartigan agreed. "They may have a power button or something. Let's prepare to detach the *Nella* and head down," he rubbed his hands. "Our first dumbler contact outside Six Species space, what?"

"Just as soon as we make certain the *Nella* isn't going to be wrecked by whatever wrecked those other seven ships," Galana advised.

"Actually, they seem more abandoned than anything else," the *Conch* told them. "They weren't damaged or shot down. The pilots may still be on the surface with the natives."

"Alright," Galana tried one more time, "but let's remain cautious until we know more about the situation."

"Cautious? But I was going to be reckless," Scrutarius complained. "You know ... eating any strange fruits I find, going down into caves all by myself, putting my face *right up close* to the pulsating egg sacs of the giant bugs ... "

"There are no giant bugs," Chillybin said with a bark of amusement from the depths of her suit.

"Honestly, you people," Bonty said. She was gazing out of the viewscreen. "Just stop for a moment and *look* at it. What a lovely world it is."

They duly paused and admired the planet below them. It *was* beautiful, Galana conceded. Lush dark bands of forest, deep indigo oceans and swirls of cloud, the world was nothing short of a paradise. It showed none of the scars of advanced civilisation – mining, industry, overdevelopment, agriculture. Whoever the natives were, from orbit it looked as though they lived in balance with their home.

"Is that long enough?" Hartigan asked, then didn't wait for Bonty to answer. "Righto, let's get down there."

The *Nella* set down in a forest clearing between the largest native settlement and the collection of alien derelicts that Galana quickly gave up trying to stop the others from calling 'the starship graveyard'. At least, Hartigan pointed out, they were far enough from the rest of the ships that they didn't look like they were joining them.

"I bet the second through seventh set of aliens thought the same thing," Devlin said, "and the natives dragged their ships into the starship graveyard once their crews were all gone."

"Thanks, Dev," Hartigan said.

"I will be ready to open fire on the area from orbit with wide-area ordnance at the first sign of trouble," Wicked Mary's *giela* added.

"Thanks, Bloody," Hartigan replied.

"The local life-forms gather," Chillybin reported.

"Righto," Hartigan stood, stretched, and grinned at Galana. "Let's go and say hello."

They descended the *Nella*'s ramp – Hartigan, Galana, Devlin, Bonty, Chillybin and the little robot that was Wicked Mary's eyes, ears, voice and hands on dry land – and stepped out onto the springy greenery of the clearing. The shuttle's landing jets had scorched the plants a little, but they didn't seem badly damaged. The air was clean and warm and smelled pleasantly of greenery even if it was slightly odd-looking greenery. Keeping their hands empty and harmless, yet ready to take up weapons if necessary, they ventured out. Of the six of them, only Bonty pulled out a scanner. She immediately began taking samples and readings.

"They're in the trees," Galana pointed.

One and two at a time, the local dumblers emerged. They were tall and lean, slightly taller than a Molran and covered in pale green fur like moss. They wore belts and pouches of woven plant matter and what looked like leather, but didn't seem to have a use for clothes. They appeared to be unarmed, although a couple of them were carrying things like shields made from the shells of large seed pods. The shields had markings painted on them.

"Those are definitely words or symbols," Hartigan murmured, angling his head to talk into his communicator button. "You reckon you can take some snaps and offer us a translation, old girl?"

"I'm working on it," the *Conch* said calmly.

"Chilly?" Galana said, as more dumblers appeared out of the woods.

The aki'Drednanth moved her great metal-clad hands slowly. "I do not sense any hostility," she said, extending her strange mental powers and her hunting instinct. "Their minds are still alien to me, but I feel … friendship, and … hope? Expectation?"

The dumblers, once gathered at the edge of the clearing, stopped and waited for their alien guests to approach. As they did, Galana noticed that some of the natives were speaking, saying something over and over – chanting, practically. One of the dumblers turned and, seeing the two holding the painted seed-pods, chattered at them urgently and waved its long, thin hands.

The two moved together, angled the pods … and Galana realised the symbols joined together, possibly into a single statement. A welcome? A warning?

"Basil," the computer said, "you may be interested to learn that the dumblers are speaking a language of their own … but they are chanting in a different language altogether. That, and the writing on those shields of theirs, are actually from one of the alien vessels."

"Can you translate any of it?" Galana asked.

"I'm not absolutely certain, Commander," the *Conch* replied, "but what the chant and the symbols *approximately* mean is … Good Luck, Number

Eight, Good Luck."

"Oh boy," Scrutarius muttered.

The local life-forms, the *Conch* quickly worked out for the terrified-smiling crew, called their world 'Azabol'. Or, since they didn't quite have a concept of their world as a planet in space, they thought of the *local region* as 'Azabol', and thus called themselves 'Azaboli'. They spoke a hodgepodge of their own language and a couple of other languages they'd picked up from 'visitors from the sun and the stars', which Galana took to mean the alien arrivals in their series of ill-fated starships.

The leader of the Azaboli was named Qaztik Goffs. She was a large, healthy female distinguishable from the others by the headband of smooth blue-black stones she wore. Qaztik Goffs, rather disjointedly and with a lot of gaps the computer couldn't quite fill in for them, expressed that the Number Eights were welcome to Azabol, and since there was still time before … *something* … they were invited back to the Azaboli village to enjoy a feast in their honour.

It was all very strange, but Galana supposed if this was the eighth time they'd gone through contact with aliens, they must be getting fairly practiced at it. And the computer did do a very good job, she had to admit, translating the dumbler words into the fluting-yet-gravelly tones of the Azaboli. It really did sound like it was the aliens talking.

"Maybe Scrutarius and Mary should head directly to the abandoned ships," she said to Hartigan after they'd all done their best to introduce themselves and the Azaboli had happily draped the Number Eights with flowery vines and handed them polished wooden artworks inlaid with stones.

"Good idea," Hartigan agreed. "Keep comms open, Devlin."

"Save me some food," Scrutarius replied. The Azaboli didn't seem to mind when the Blaran and the *giela* headed off in the wrong direction. Number Eights, it seemed, could do pretty much whatever Number Eights wanted.

In the Azaboli village, despite the fact that they'd only just arrived, preparations were well under way for a celebration. There were more of the 'Good Luck, Number Eight' signs placed around the communal centre of the settlement, and a lot of other decorations that seemed to have been hastily pulled out of storage. A meal that might have been in progress anyway had been expanded and a lot of juvenile Azaboli were scampering around setting things up on a long table formed from the trunk of a huge tree.

Rather disturbingly, the centrepiece of the feast appeared to be an artwork depicting the other alien visitors to Azabol. The *Conch* identified the symbols for 'Number One', 'Number Two' and so on, labelling the different parts of the ornate wooden carving. It didn't give any impression of what the aliens had *looked* like, but each was definitely distinct from one another. Each curved, twisting shape was decorated with shiny, broken pieces of material that Galana immediately realised were weapons, tools, pieces of uniform, even scales and teeth – presumably from the aliens themselves.

There was a 'Number Eight' marking placed carefully on one side of the centrepiece, indicating an empty spot on the table where *their* sculptures would be added.

"*Conch*, old girl," Hartigan said through his frozen smile, "can we just make absolutely tip-top sure these furry buggers aren't going to bally well eat us and put our hats on the next bit of their little art project?"

"Their intentions are completely benign," the *Conch* assured them, and Chillybin nodded her helmeted head in agreement. "However, I think it is clear that they consider you to be heroes sent by some celestial force to do battle with some enemy of theirs. And the previous seven groups to attempt this have … not succeeded."

The feast commenced, in the language of good food and fellowship that thankfully seemed to be a universal constant. Through it all the *Conch* kept up a constant stream of melodic Azaboli translations, allowing the crew to make sounds of agreement or disagreement, to recite simple sentences regarding what they thought of the food, and so on. The *Conch* also communicated directly using Chillybin's suit and the comm pads.

It was all very nice, and hardly required Bonty's quick and careful testing of each piece of food. There was nothing a Molran or Bonshoon stomach couldn't handle, and only a couple of fermented or spiced dishes that the doctor recommended the Captain avoid taking too much of. Chillybin caused a minor stir and a lot of awestruck murmuring and moaning when she stepped out of her suit and sampled a few of the fruits, berries and meats on offer. Aki'Drednanth could digest 'hot' food, although it didn't do much for them. It was all part of the joy of exploration, she said – incidentally causing more superstitious hooting as her empty suit spoke from the far end of the table.

After a couple of hours, Scrutarius and Wicked Mary joined them.

"Have they told you what they want us to do yet?" Devlin asked. Galana shook her head. "Well, whatever it is, aliens have been coming here for almost a hundred years to try it," he went on in a low voice. "And getting killed," he glanced at the centre of the table. "And apparently made into objectively pretty good artworks."

"I like the little teeth on that one," Wicked Mary pointed.

"The beacons?" Galana asked.

"We shut down all three intact ships," Wicked Mary put in, and raised a hand to politely refuse a piece of fruit one of the Azaboli was trying to push into her speaker. "*Thank you, I do not eat, I am a puppet and not a living thing*," she chattered in the mixture of languages the *Conch* had put together. "There was no sign of crew on any of them."

"I think we're getting close to an explanation here," Hartigan reported from across the table. "Apparently the thing we're supposed to fight is a *Demon*, and it's been hunting the Azaboli and *feeding* on their little kiddies for centuries. It goes dormant, it comes out and feeds, and sometimes us grand celestial heroes come down and try to stop it, and get bally well stomped, and then the little bits that are left after the stomping go into this lovely little memorial here."

"Oh good," Devlin said.

"So naturally I told Qaztik Goffs here that we'd be happy to help them with their little Demon problem, what?" Hartigan concluded happily.

"Did you eat any of those large black berries, Captain?" Galana pointed.

"Only a couple. Come now, how difficult can it be? Of course it's not an *actual* Demon, it's just something these chaps can't understand and so they're *saying* it's a Demon, don't y'see? It might be a shipwrecked survivor of the first alien ship to land here. I wouldn't be surprised if we got the *Conch* talking to it, offered it a lift, and settled our first mission in record time."

"*I'd* be surprised," Devlin raised a hand.

"Whatever this Demon is, it's clearly dangerous enough to have destroyed emissaries from seven other spacefaring civilisations," Galana pointed out. "What makes you think we will fare any better?"

"Because we're AstroCorps, damn it all," Hartigan declared. "Now listen, old Goffers here says this Demon chap is set to wake up and come into town for a nosh in another three days, which is actually more like eight days by our calendar because their planet revolves so bally slowly. I'm not quite sure what will happen after that. To be honest, most of the conversation has been spent figuring out that our days and their days are different lengths. Dashed overcomplicated, if you ask me."

"Captain - "

"Anyway, that gives us plenty of time to study it, find out what makes it tick, maybe find out where it lives and get Bloody Mary to give it a good old fashioned taste of Six Species artillery," Hartigan smacked the table with one hand and bit into his roasted leg of forest-critter with the other. Qaztik Goffs and the rest of the Azaboli cheered and jabbered excitedly. "In the meantime, we're safe down here," he added. "We can check out the other ships, get to know our hosts, and I'll have time to recover from how sick those black berries are definitely going to make me."

For the next few shipboard days, which took place over the course of a warm twilight and long night down in the Azabol village, the crew of the *Conch* learned what they could from the wrecked ships and the cheerful Azaboli. There was little they could get from either source. The ships, even the ones that had still been transmitting signals, were barely functional at best. They didn't have recognisable relative drives even though there were no inhabited planets within a hundred light years, so getting here at sub-light speeds seemed impossible. Galana guessed they were landing shuttles, like the *Nella*, and their motherships had moved on when the landing parties had perished. This wasn't a very satisfying explanation, but it was the best they could come up with.

And the Azaboli simply didn't seem to know what the Number Eights were trying to ask. As far as the dumblers were concerned, the visitors knew perfectly well what the Demon was and what they were supposed to do. They couldn't tell them where the Demon slept, because – as far as the *Conch* could translate – it lived in some other world and simply *appeared* in this one to feed on their young. They didn't know where it came from, just that it came out of the darkness. This made little sense, because it was set to arrive in broad daylight.

"I think we should go back up to the *Conch* and watch from orbit," Scrutarius said. He'd been back up to pick up some weapons and equipment, which they were setting up around the outskirts of the Azaboli village.

"Watch the Azaboli children getting devoured?" Bonty asked in shock.

"Sure," Scrutarius said. "Look, this thing's been feeding on them for years. An alien ship doesn't come down here *every* time the Demon wakes up, and even when they do it doesn't seem like us celestial saviours have ever, you know, *saved* any of the poor kiddies. We can leave the sensors and defensive weapons, leave Bloody Mary's *giela* down here to keep an eye on things, and see what happens."

"I don't think the Captain will go for that," Bonty frowned.

"We've got five shipboard days left," Scrutarius said. "Maybe we can teach the Azaboli how to use the guns?"

"Did you get any more readings?" Galana asked Mary and Chillybin. She didn't want to have to teach a group of primitive dumblers how to use advanced weaponry on AstroCorps' first encounter outside Six Species space. "A hidden structure some more advanced species might be living in? A concealed ship? Any unusual energy signatures that might come from a disguised individual?"

"Nothing," Wicked Mary said.

"There are no intelligent minds in this volume of space," Chillybin said, "aside from the six of us and a few settlements of Azaboli."

"Maybe the Demon is formed of energy, or exists on some other plane of reality?" Galana suggested. "Undetectable to this one until it crosses over?"

"Is that how reality works?" Scrutarius asked.

"Not according to anything I've read," Galana admitted, "but there are a lot of things that haven't been written yet," she turned to Bonty before Devlin could answer this. "What about the tests you were running, doctor?"

"The Azaboli have several very unusual compounds in their blood and nervous systems," Bonty said. "I haven't quite been able to find out just what the Demon is feeding on when it comes, whether it eats their flesh or feeds in some other way. But there is definitely something strange here."

"What do you mean?"

"It's hard to explain," Bonty said. "These compounds ... they don't provide any benefit to them. And that's not just me failing to understand what benefit they have. I developed a serum that filters the compounds out of their bodies, and tested it on a couple of them - "

"Bonty," Galana sighed.

"They're *fine*," Bonty insisted. "They drank a bit more water and peed a bit more often for a few hours, then it was all out of them. What's strange is, I think it's being *cultivated* in them. The younger Azaboli have more of the stuff than their parents."

"The Azaboli did say that the Demon feeds on the younger ones," Scrutarius said, sounding interested in spite of his desire to leave the planet. "Didn't they?"

"Younger animals are generally nicer to eat," Wicked Mary noted.

"Yes ... " Scrutarius said into the awkward silence left behind by this remark, "but what I mean is, what if this Demon is farming them? What if these *compounds* are its food, and it's breeding Azaboli to have more and more of it, like a farmer breeding animals for meat?"

"Did none of the other alien visitors study the feeding side of it?" Galana asked. "Did they all just try to attack the Demon?"

"As far as I can tell they all tried to fight," the *Conch* replied. "But the last landing was a few generations back. Number Seven was not within living memory. And there is only so much we can learn from derelict ships and a few remains built into a dumbler artwork."

"If this is true," Galana said, "perhaps we do not need to fight this entity at all. Perhaps if we show it how to harvest these nutrients without harming the Azaboli - "

Bonty was shaking her head. "It's no good," she said. "The compounds go inert when I filter them out. Whatever properties they have, they only remain active when dissolved in a large quantity of Azaboli fluids."

"So you've got to eat the kid to get the juice," Scrutarius concluded grimly. "That doesn't sound like the sort of setup we're going to be able to *talk* around to a low-impact farming thing."

"Which leaves us with fighting," Galana said, "which does not seem to have ever met with success. Or leaving Azabol and its people to their fate," she added, glancing at Scrutarius.

"An approach which may have met with success a bunch of times, but we can't tell because there's no remains and the Azaboli didn't make a statue of them," Scrutarius said. "Which is a risk I for one am willing to take."

"Again, I think the Captain will disagree," Galana reminded him.

"You're probably right," Devlin sighed. "Maybe Chilly can give this Demon a taste of the old mind-cannon."

Chillybin shook her head. "I would need some time to get to know the entity, understand its mind," she said. "Before I can … give it a taste of the old mind-cannon."

"There is another option," Bonty said. They turned to look at her. "Poison the well."

"What are you … " Galana frowned, then felt her ears stiffen. "Are you suggesting we *remove* this compound from the Azaboli?"

Bonty nodded. "It's easy enough to make the serum with my lab equipment and local ingredients," she told them. "If the Azaboli don't have any nutritional value to the Demon, it might leave them alone."

"I can think of something else it might do," Wicked Mary said.

"How long will it take you to treat all the Azaboli in this region?" Galana asked. "And what about the rest of the planet? Does this Demon hunt elsewhere? Maybe when the Azaboli think it is sleeping, it is actually migrating and tending to its other farms."

"I can answer that," Hartigan, who had been in the village, came ambling back to the spot where they were setting up their perimeter weapons. "It's the same all over," he said. "The Azaboli don't travel much, but the 'Demon' seems to be everywhere. This is just the only place us celestial heroes turn up, obviously because we always just home in on the last ship to have arrived. Never seems to do much good, but the Azaboli seem to appreciate the thought, don't y'know."

"Hope can be an excellent cage," Wicked Mary noted.

"Hm, yes, well," Galana said, "this changes things. There might not be one Demon, there might be a whole population of them, each tending to their own regions. We may be observing symbiosis, two species living together - "

"Pretty sure when it's one species living off another and giving nothing back, it's not symbiosis," Scrutarius said.

"Maybe the last seven alien species to come to this planet weren't so friendly," Galana said. "Maybe we have been talking to the sheep about the brave wolves who tried to destroy the flock's shepherd."

"Maybe," Hartigan said, "but their shepherd eats kiddies, and this wolf won't stand for it. What's the plan?"

"I can give serum to all the Azaboli in this area in a few hours," Bonty said. "*If* the compound is what the Demon is after, it will make them quite useless to it. The other groups may take longer, because they're all over the planet and they might not be so used to getting alien visitors."

"And if there's one Demon and it just goes somewhere else, or if there's a bunch of Demons," Scrutarius said, "*then* can we say we did our best and move on?"

"Get to work, Bonty," Hartigan said. "Feels like this night's been going on forever, but dawn's on its way. Another day and a night, that only leaves us a few more ship-days to get ready for this beastie."

By the time local day had crawled back to another long night and the final hours began ticking away before the Demon's arrival, Bonty had treated all of the Azaboli in the local area. They were remarkably trusting, especially once the doctor explained that they were taking away whatever it was the Demon liked to eat them for.

Hartigan, Wicked Mary and Scrutarius had the idea to ambush the Demon if possible. There was some evidence to suggest that a couple of the other alien heroes had tried the tactic of gathering the children together as bait in a trap. It had failed, but Hartigan was adamant. The aliens that *hadn't* laid an ambush had failed too, he rationalised, so all things being equal he'd prefer to lay one.

"When in doubt, lay an ambush," he said, as though this was some sort of human folk wisdom. Actually, the more Galana thought about it, the more she realised it could be.

They gathered the young Azaboli in the centre of the village, which was a wide-open space for meetings and events like the Good Luck Number Eight feast. Some more sensor-mounted guns were set in nearby huts, and Wicked Mary stood ready – or *swam* ready, technically – to target the Demon from orbit.

It was mid-morning, sunny and warm and very much not the sort of time or setting in which a Demon encounter should happen, when the Demon appeared at the edge of the village square.

And it *did* appear, popping into existence next to the feasting table in an almost absurdly sudden fashion and a little murky cloud of eye-jarring darkness like a bad special effect. The crew of the *Conch*, who were in various positions of cover around the square, stared at the monster in disbelief.

It was about the size of a human, although it had a long sinewy neck which placed its great gleaming head closer to Molran-height. Its body was covered in a thick, dark carapace like plates of armour, a multitude of spiny multi-jointed limbs emerging from between the plates and forming legs or arms. A long, wickedly pointed stinger sort of thing emerged from the constantly-moving collection of mandibles and tiny claw-like fingers on the lower half of its face. Huge glistening compound eyes dominated the upper half.

Galana was crouching close enough to where Devlin was hiding that she heard him speak under his breath.

"Oh, would you look at that," he said. "It's a giant bug."

The monstrous creature scuttled forwards in eerie silence, almost seeming to glide. The Azaboli children huddled together, mewling.

At that moment, the guns they'd set up in two nearby huts swivelled, targeted the creature, and blasted it with a deafening volley of projectiles through the windows. The children cried out and fell to their knees, covering their heads. Hartigan was on his feet, blaster in hand, roaring through his furiously bristling moustache as he fired. Wicked Mary, Scrutarius and Galana also rose and blasted at the thing. Galana was surprised at how easy it was to shoot something, to *want* to shoot something, seconds after setting eyes on it. There was something unspeakable about the Demon, something deeply and instinctively repugnant.

The Demon staggered back under the barrage. A moment later, blinding and deafening, the *Conch*'s for'ard pulse turret sent a thunderbolt from orbit, striking the Demon dead centre and sending a ring of dirt and plant fragments spraying across the square.

The Demon, incredibly still intact and visible under the hail of fire and ammunition shrieked and chittered … and vanished in another muddy cloud of shadow.

In the silence of the aftermath, small pieces of debris could still be heard rolling off hut roofs and pattering out of trees. Hartigan, Scrutarius, Wicked Mary and Chillybin stole forward to examine the hissing, steaming spot where the creature had stood.

"That was easy," Hartigan said brightly.

"Don't be so sure," Scrutarius said, and Galana shook her head in agreement. "The way it appeared, it might have just - "

"There," Wicked Mary said, pointing a thin metal arm.

The Demon reappeared across the square, on the other side of the group of wailing children.

They opened fire again, over the heads of the young Azaboli. The Demon snarled and flailed but shrugged off the blasts, including another stunningly precise strike from Wicked Mary up in the *Conch*. Weapons that would have taken down a shuttle. The Demon leaned into the attack and stepped towards the children.

Chillybin surged out of her hiding place and thundered across the square, putting herself between the children and the monster. Galana and the others ceased firing in case they hit her. Chillybin reared over the tiny-looking Demon, and brought a massive gauntleted fist down on its head.

There was a loud crack and a spatter of dark goo … and then the Demon was up again, clicking and hissing angrily. It put clawed hands to either side of its broken head, and pushed itself back together. It fused back as though it had never been damaged.

Nothing is working, Galana thought wildly. *Nothing we have can hurt it. This is how Number One through to Number Seven died. In complete shock.*

Chillybin raised her fist again and roared, the sound echoing inside her helmet. The Demon stepped back, vanished, and reappeared again some distance away, near the feast table and the crater where it had first appeared. It hissed as it emerged.

"Stay back, Ogre," it said in a low, rasping voice. "You cannot harm me."

Galana stared. This was no clever translation effort from the computer. The creature was somehow speaking the common language of the Molran Fleet.

Hartigan frowned. "Is that ... ?" he recognised the language but could only speak a few words of it himself. Galana nodded, not taking her eyes off the Demon.

It hissed again, its head moving like a snake. "*Molran*," it said. "*Human.* Of course. I might have known you would come."

"I am Commander Galana Fen of the AstroCorps Starship - " she started.

"*I don't care, you fool,*" the Demon rattled, its mandibles thrashing in agitation and clear drool – or maybe venom – dripping from its stinger. "What have you done? What have you done to my - "

Wicked Mary's arm flicked and a small metal object smacked against the Demon's shell. It hissed, disappeared in another blot of darkness, and the metal button fell to the ground before exploding with another spray of dirt and more wails from the children.

"Just thought I would try that," Wicked Mary said.

The Demon reappeared once more in a dark smudge against the forest and huts. This time the shadows seemed to cling to it a moment longer, boiling under its armour plating, darkening its huge multifaceted eyes.

"*Stop,*" it snarled. "These mortals are mine. I have grown them. They sustain me. This is my world, my feeding ground."

"Not anymore," Galana said.

"What are you *saying*?" Hartigan whispered. They were still speaking the Fleet language that the Demon somehow knew.

"It's telling us off for interfering with its farm," Scrutarius said.

"The substance that runs through their veins ... you will never understand," the Demon said. "It is salvation. It is freedom."

"It's blood," Galana said. "We call it blood."

"Kiddy blood," Devlin added.

"*Fools,*" the Demon rattled. "Without it, I would have perished long ago. Do I not deserve to live? Do you not feed on lesser animals?"

"Nothing intelligent enough to make a hat," Scrutarius told it. "That's a rule we have."

Galana very firmly avoided looking at Wicked Mary. The Fergunak, she knew, were not above eating intelligent beings if they got the chance. Hats and all.

"Have my animals told you what happened to the last fools who tried to interfere with my work?" the Demon asked. It was gliding back and forth now, its legs a blur, the huddled crowd of children shuffling away from it fearfully.

"Your *work*?" Galana said. "You mean the - "

"I destroyed them," the Demon rattled. "I destroyed their ships in orbit. I flung them into the sun. I will do the same to you."

"Go ahead," Bonty said. Galana hadn't heard her emerge from one of the huts where she was hiding with Qaztik Goffs and some of the other Azaboli. The Demon swung its head in the old Bonshoon's direction as she stepped out and joined Chillybin in front of the children. "It won't make any difference," she said. "Your *animals* are clean."

"What are you - " the Demon hissed. It scuttled forward before anyone could react, seized a child and raised the squealing little thing to its stinger. It paused, rattled angrily, and dropped the Azaboli to the ground. The youngster bounced to its feet and rejoined the others. The Demon rounded on Bonjamin. "*What did you - "*

"Chilly," Bonty said, her voice cold.

Chillybin thumped forward, growling menacingly. The Demon skittered back and vanished with another ragged puff of shadow, then reappeared nearby. It staggered, darkness clinging to it like mud.

"*Stop*," it shrieked.

"Leave," Bonty said. "Go back to wherever you came from."

"*I can't*," the creature grated, flecks of shadow spraying from its mandibles. "I am trapped here just like you. This world is mine - "

"Mary," Bonty said.

Another bolt roared from the sky, hammering the Demon into the ground. It rose, legs and arms flailing spiderlike, and another bolt came down. It vanished again.

The next time it reappeared, the dark stains inside it stayed. And darkened. And thickened. And swelled under its skin, pushing its armour plates out grotesquely.

"*No!*" it gibbered as the shadows consumed it.

A second later, in a final oily cascade of sludgy black liquid, the Demon was gone.

By the time the six of them had stumbled across to the bubbling mess, it was already evaporating. Before Bonty could do more than point her medical scanner at the stuff, it dwindled and vanished as though it had never existed. A slightly melted-looking depression in the ground was all that was left.

"Look here, what *exactly* did you lot say to each other?" Hartigan demanded.

Bonty did her best to explain, but by this time Qaztik Goffs and the rest of the Azaboli were running out into the square. Whooping and laughing and jabbering excitedly, the parents of the young ones rushed in and grabbed their babies, and the others began loping and dancing around the crew. Chants of *Number Eight, Number Eight* started up.

"The ... Demon, the creature, was infected with something," Bonty said, raising her voice over the hubbub. "That was what it was cultivating, some sort of antidote. When I saw it ... jumping from place to place ... some sort of high-speed matter transmission ... it was obviously being hurt by doing it, and the stuff it was taking from the Azaboli was making it better. Allowing it to ... go somewhere else, do what it wanted. That's why it went away for so long, but kept coming back. It had found something here. Whenever it got sick enough, it came back for a booster."

"So ... it's gone," Hartigan said. "We did it? Jolly good."

"You sound almost disappointed," Bonty accused.

"I *was* rather hoping my new blaster would have a *bit* more of an impact," Hartigan looked down at his gun with a sigh and slipped it back into its holster. "It was all a bit too easy, wasn't it?"

"Not for me," Bonty said in a hurt voice.

"No, quite right, quite right," Hartigan said hastily. "Excellent job, first class. Good old science, hurrah."

"Bonjamin Bont the Bonshoon Bug Biologist," Scrutarius announced loudly, pointing all four hands at Bonty. "Hero of the Azabol Number Eights!"

The Azaboli cheered.

The grateful Azaboli held another feast in honour of the heroes, but not until they had built the eighth and final piece of their artwork commemorating the epic of the Demon. It was still strange and twisted and none of them could really recognise themselves in it, but each of the crewmembers gladly volunteered a couple of little personal items to add to the decoration. Galana helped them to create a small AstroCorps icon to add to the Number Eight symbols. Qaztik Goffs gave Bonjamin her headdress of blue-black stones, which Bonty thought was very touching.

The doctor also had time, while the artists finished work on the monument, to take the *Nella* to the Demon's other 'farms' – the scattered villages around the vast forest. She shared her serum around and cleaned the Demon's compounds out of the population, just in case there happened to be any more of them out there.

Finally, the celebrations were over and it became clear the Azaboli were politely waiting for the aliens to have a little dignity and go back to the celestial realm from which they'd come. With a last exchange of smiles and gestures and handshakes, they boarded the *Nella* and returned to the *Conch*.

"Well," Hartigan said, watching Wicked Mary's *giela* dragging a huge bleeding haunch of some great forest herbivore the Azaboli had been roasting for them across to the hold access, "a successful first encounter, I'd say. D'you want help with that, old girl?"

"No thank you, Captain," Wicked Mary said. "I will enjoy this better alone."

"Understood," Hartigan gave Galana a wink. The little robot had made a half-hearted effort to encourage one or two of the smaller and meatier Azaboli to accompany them, with the clear intention of luring them to her aquatic habitat. She'd eventually settled for a large piece of uncooked animal flesh. "So, shall we crack on?"

"Yes, Captain," Galana said. "Ready to proceed."

"Course set," the *Conch* added.

"Next giant bug, *you* get to kill," Bonty said.

Galana sighed. "Honestly, you find *one* giant bug … "

"Let's go," Hartigan declared.

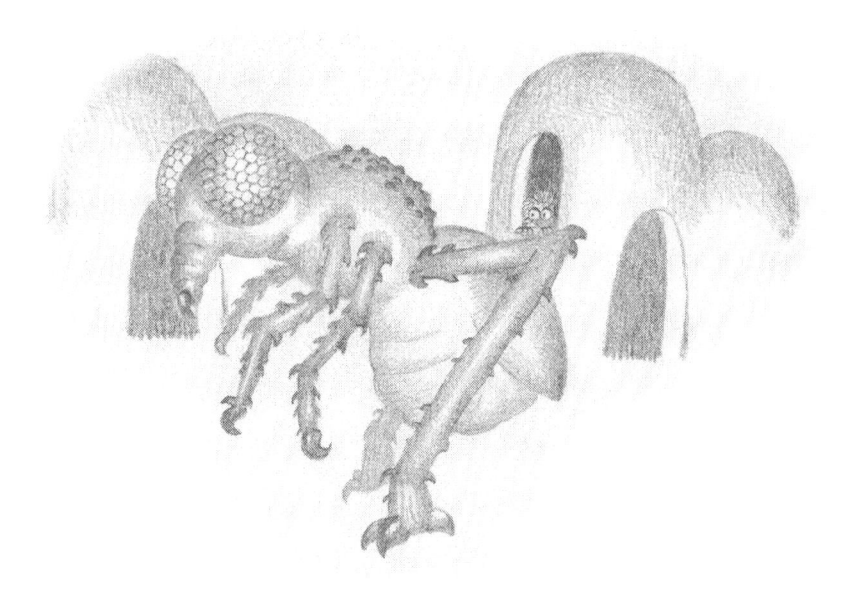

Soon, in **The Moon That Burned**:

They had stopped to perform routine engine checks and run a scan of the volume when Chillybin announced that there was a vessel approaching.

"Approaching from where?" Captain Hartigan asked. "We're parked in the middle of bally nowhere."

"Then they are approaching from just on that side of the middle of bally nowhere," Chillybin replied, pointing a great gauntlet at the wall.

"Cheeky," Hartigan said mildly, and tapped his controls. "Bringing us around. What's their speed?"

"Slow," the *Conch* replied. "Very slow. And very quiet, aside from the shouting they're doing on the communicator. It may take me a few minutes to decipher their language. Hardly any … no," the computer sounded surprised. "No engine or drive at all. They're just drifting."

"Aha," Hartigan leaned forward. "Becalmed, by jingo."

"Becalmed?" Galana asked.

"Old maritime term," Hartigan explained. "Ships on the ocean, driven by the wind … never mind. Chilly, any idea what sort of crew we're looking at?"

"Not a crew at all, Captain," Chillybin said. "A population."

"Come again?"

"I can feel … great numbers, families, communities, living their lives rather than flying a starship," the aki'Drednanth said. "This is no mere vessel, Captain Hartigan. It's a Worldship."

THE MOON THAT BURNED

"It's a *what?*" Captain Hartigan exclaimed.

"Don't tell me we've run into the Fleet," Scrutarius groaned. "I thought we'd put those sourfaced buggers behind us."

"Not a *Molran Fleet* Worldship. Nowhere near as big," the *Conch* said. "But for such a small ship, it does seem to have an unusually large population. I might have translated something wrong in the number system, hold on … "

"Their drift will bring them to intercept range in ten minutes," Wicked Mary said from the tactical console, where her little remote-controlled robot was standing ready. "The ship is maybe three times the size of this one. Hardly a warship, let alone a Worldship."

"They do not seem to have relative speed capability," the *Conch* said, "as far as I can tell from this information package they're beaming out."

"Perhaps they're not stupid enough to beam out *actual* information about their ship and crew for anyone to hear," Scrutarius suggested.

"They'd be the first dumblers who weren't," Hartigan replied.

"Dumblers are often naïve and trusting when introducing themselves to alien species," Galana agreed. "They assume that any civilisation capable of mastering interstellar travel will be friendly by default."

"*Why?*" Scrutarius asked in bafflement.

"Well, lucky for them they were right this time," Hartigan said, and glanced over his shoulder. *"Weren't they?"*

"Why are you looking at me, Captain?" Wicked Mary asked.

"No reason, I just ended up facing that way … "

"I would hesitate to say these dumblers have *mastered* interstellar travel," Chillybin noted. "According to this signal, they are moving at barely one tenth of the speed of light."

"Hang about, old girl," Hartigan said. "Where's the nearest solar system?

Wait," he added immediately, "I'm at the helm, aren't I … "

"Almost two hundred light years from here, Basil," the *Conch* told him.

"I was about to press the buttons to find that out."

"Maybe they just slowed down to meet us?" Bonty suggested.

"Well, it's either that or they've been drifting for two thousand years," Scrutarius said.

"Being becalmed seems to be the least of their problems," Galana was looking at the information the computer had collected. "There's over two hundred and fifty thousand of them."

"On a ship only three times the size of ours?" Hartigan said. "I mean, don't get me wrong, you're a lovely spacious ship for the six of us," he went on, patting his console reassuringly, "but I couldn't imagine fitting more than thirty or forty people on board at a pinch. A quarter of a million, for two thousand years?"

"They must be tiny," Scrutarius said. "You know, or stackable."

"We will find out soon enough," Chillybin said. "We are drawing close and turning to match course. I will try to establish a comm link."

They waited in silence as the alien ship appeared in their viewscreens. It was a big, grey, lumpy thing like a mass of cement or stone, around three thousand feet long and two thousand feet across at its widest point. Several ancient-looking arches and funnels on its surface could have been engines or webscoops or anything, really. They were all dead now, and covered in the same crusty grey build-up of debris and space-dust as the rest of the ship. Most of its hull seemed to be constructed out of an asteroid or some other natural object, presumably hollowed-out.

It certainly didn't *look* as though it had just slowed down to have a chat with them. It looked more like a space-rock than a ship. Aside from the shapeless pieces of machinery jutting from its surface, the only thing that really gave it away as artificial was the fact that it was spinning swiftly. This, Galana guessed, was providing gravity to the interior.

"Doesn't look very comfortable but, I guess two hundred and fifty thousand dumblers can't be wrong," Bonty said brightly.

"I can provide a visual link and partial translation," the *Conch* reported.

A moment later, the communications officer of the alien ship appeared on their screens. Bonty made an involuntary squeaky sound of delight.

"It's *adorable*!" she exclaimed.

Galana suppressed a sigh, grateful that their own responses would not be transferred until the computer had established a proper comms protocol. There were *ways* these things should be done, and telling a potentially hostile alien life-form it was adorable was not one of them.

Still, she had to admit the creature was cute, with its chubby little body striped in grey and white fur; its large fuzzy ears and bright purple eyes; its long whiskers and twitchy pink velvet nose; and its paws clasped around the controls of what could be a planet-destroying super-weapon for all Galana knew. She shook herself firmly out of her contemplation of the fluffy little alien.

It may not even be little, she reminded herself, but she found it hard to believe she was looking at a human- or Molran-sized life-form. Something about its movements, its proportions made it *seem* small, even though it was impossible to guess from the image of it sitting at its mysterious alien controls. *There might only be ten of them, and the broadcast is a deception to hide their numbers. There might only be one. It might be bigger than Wicked Mary.*

Oddly, the idea that the creature was bigger than the giant shark they had in their lower hold just made it seem cuter.

"You are alien starship," the *Conch* said, altering its voice a little to make it clear these were the translated words of the dumbler on the screen. Galana was thankful the computer had opted for 'higher-pitched yet dignified', rather than the hilarious squeaky voice she'd been dreading. "We are people. We are peace. We want to travel on. Hello, goodbye."

"Well," Hartigan said mildly, "I guess that's rather to the point, what?"

"Another successful dumbler contact," Scrutarius declared.

"I'll get us back under way," Basil went on.

"Their language seems to be a combination of body-postures, scents and sounds," the *Conch* said seriously. "Only the sounds are really translatable, although the transmission has body-language and scent layers converted into signals that I might be able to adapt to change the overall meaning … "

"There are more messages coming in," Chillybin said.

"From the ship?" Galana asked.

"From different *parts* of the ship," Chillybin replied. "Different … communities."

Chillybin and the *Conch* eventually counted three hundred and seventy-seven 'official' communications from separate parts of the dumbler ship, each representing hundreds, if not thousands of the aliens. Aside from those, they also received *individual* messages from over nine hundred of the life-forms acting on their own with personal transmitters. It was mayhem for a few hours, but finally they managed to pick out a single group to act as a communications hub for the rest of the population.

They called themselves 'people', which was a fairly common translation problem with dumblers. Their species had grown up assuming they were the only intelligent life-forms in the galaxy. They'd named all the stars and planets they could see through their telescopes – their dear, tiny little telescopes – but had called their own 'the world'. This problem was compounded by the fact that their language was all squeaks and twitches and smells, a lot of which were impossible to translate. And on top of *that*, there were at least eight completely distinct cultures of 'people' inside their ship, each with their own language. The *Conch* could translate them all fairly easily, however, once the first code was cracked.

The crew of the *Conch* took to calling them the Nyif Nyif, because that was pretty much what 'people' sounded like in ... well, in Nyif Nyif. Or the versions of Nyif Nyif that seemed most common across the ship, anyway.

"They're not actually that tightly-packed," Galana said after a bit of calculation. "Their ship is about half a mile long and contains two hundred and fifty thousand Nyif Nyif. The average Fleet Worldship is *ninety* miles long – a hundred and eighty times the size of their vessel – which means if the Nyif Nyif had a ship the size of a Worldship, it would have a crew, a population of some forty-five million. Worldships, though, are home to *billions* of Molren. Of course, I'm only scaling up in a simplified way by using the *length* of the ship rather than the *volume*, which of course - "

"I say, does the maths help you to deal with all the yucky excitement of meeting new species?" Hartigan asked.

"It does," Galana replied. "You should try it sometime. It might also improve your piloting abilities."

"Ouch."

The Nyif Nyif seemed friendly, and very excited to communicate with 'aliens' for the first time. Meeting in person was another story. Their ship had docks and airlocks and access hatches, but the largest of them was just about big enough for Galana to stick her head through – and that was only if they found some way to make a seal with the *Conch*'s far larger docking mechanisms. To make things still more complicated, most of the ship's outer doors hadn't been touched in generations, and most were sealed over with ice and compacted debris. The Nyif Nyif didn't go outside.

They did, however, eagerly agree to a meeting. Six Species and Nyif Nyif breathed pretty similar mixtures of gases – with the obvious exception of Wicked Mary, and it was unanimously agreed that they would *tell* the Nyif Nyif about the Fergunak but not subject them to *seeing* one in person their first time. The mechanism which made the ship spin gave the Nyif Nyif gravity that was quite a bit lower than the *Conch*'s, but Scrutarius was able to adjust the pull of the gravity plates for the duration of the meeting.

The *Conch* matched course with the drifting ship, swung into a spin so the two vessels hung relatively motionless together while the stars looped crazily around them, and Scrutarius put together a sort of adapted docking system. It was basically a heated air-tube that they could extend from the *Conch* to one of the Nyif Nyif hatches, where it would seal using a ring of – as Devlin put it – "pretty much just water with some strengthening paste dissolved into it, but maybe call it something more impressive-sounding for the dumblers."

While Scrutarius played happily with bits of piping and glue, and the Nyif Nyif had an unseen but presumably *adorable* ship-wide debate over who got to meet with the aliens, Chillybin and Wicked Mary and the *Conch*'s computer continued to try to figure out where the little creatures had come from in the first place.

It wasn't as easy as Galana would have thought. The ship had indeed been drifting through space for some two thousand years, which was about four hundred Nyif Nyif lifespans since the poor little things only lived for about five years. The ship, its drift through space, was the only world they had ever known. Their *actual* world wasn't just ancient history to them – it was mythology.

This was a familiar story to Galana, of course. The Molran Fleet had much the same problem with its distant past. Yes, Molren and Blaren and Bonshooni lived around five *thousand* years rather than just five, but the Fleet had been wandering in space far longer as well.

Records, even computer data, also proved of little use. Information had been lost, destroyed or re-written for reasons the Nyif Nyif no longer remembered because it had been their great-great-great-great grandparents who had done it. The population had grown, shrunk, and moved from place to place inside the ship. A single group might dominate three whole decks one century, only for them to be gone the next. The computer was ancient and run-down, a lot of its files corrupted due to lack of use. Only two systems were kept in good condition: the life-support, so the Nyif Nyif could continue to eat, drink and breathe; and the external comms, so they could make sure they weren't about to crash into anything. Although what exactly they could *do* about it if they did see something coming, since they didn't have any real way to change course, was a bit of a mystery.

The *Conch* was able to figure out *fairly* well what had happened, though, despite the lack of information. And it was confirmed, as much as it could be, by the intrepid – yes, and fuzzy wuzzy – Nyif Nyif representatives who were chosen to meet with the aliens.

The choice was actually made rather quickly, considering how many Nyif Nyif there were and how many different groups there seemed to be within the ship. One of the benefits, Bonty suggested, of only living five years was that you must get pretty good at making snap decisions.

Ten Nyif Nyif came aboard in the end, waddling in from the maintenance chamber Devlin had adapted and stopping to stare, quivering with obvious terror, at the looming giants.

An adult Nyif Nyif, as they'd suspected from the start and established quite quickly, was only a couple of inches long and one could nestle quite easily in the palm of a Molran or human hand. They moved on four legs but regularly rose up onto their rear paws, tucking their front legs in against their bellies in a way that made them difficult not to pick up and cuddle in a *very* undiplomatic way. Galana restrained herself by putting all four hands behind her back.

They didn't wear clothes, but each of the visiting dumblers had a selection of belts and wrappings that they used to carry things. Whether some of them were weapons, Galana couldn't be sure. She wondered what sort of weapons a species of tiny mammals that had lived in a spaceship for two thousand years could possibly have, and whether they would do anything but tickle a life-form of Molranoid or human size.

Four of the ten were carrying a sort of woven sling between them, and inside the sling was a powdery-looking sausage thing about the size of a finger. Huge to them, but no more than a dainty morsel to the aliens they were meeting. From the warm, yeasty smell of it, Galana guessed it was bread or some other food ration – probably of the rare-delicacy variety, and scaled up to the largest size they could manage at short notice. It was, Galana thought as she watched the four bearers set it down carefully and unhook their slings, a considerable expenditure of food.

Bonty had put together a sort of conference setting, a table around which the crew of the *Conch* could sit while the Nyif Nyif climbed to a higher platform so everyone could be at the same approximate height. Nobody was sure whether this would be reassuring or even more terrifying to the tiny creatures, but they handled it well.

"Greetings," the *Conch* translated for one of the Nyif Nyif, while the other nine scampered around and settled on the platform Bonty had built. The Nyif Nyif speaker stood on its hind legs and addressed the smiling Basil, Galana, Devlin and Bonjamin, with occasional nervous glances at the gleaming shapes of Chillybin and Mary's *giela* that stood to one side of the meeting room. The Nyif Nyif had been prepared for the meeting – Chillybin had sent an info package explaining how the 'aliens' all looked and everybody's relative sizes – but even someone with a five-year lifespan could only prepare so much in a couple of hours. "It is very good we meet. We are very pleased there is life in the universe. We are shocked. Our storytellers tell that aliens maybe much bigger or much smaller than people, but we are not expecting this."

Galana nodded, quietly grateful once again that the computer had decided to make the Nyif Nyif translation a slightly higher-pitched voice but not push it into the sort of squeaks it sounded like the creatures actually *made*, and which would reduce the AstroCorps crew to helpless giggles.

"It is a pleasure to meet you too," Hartigan said, and extended a finger. Galana was worried he was about to try to stroke the alien diplomat's soft fur, but instead he allowed it to clasp its tiny hand on the pad of his finger and shake solemnly. Hartigan must have seen Galana's expression because he winked at her and said in a low voice, "I sent them an info packet on the ways we exchange greetings. Looks like they paid attention, what?" he turned back to the delegates and indicated that the *Conch* could resume translating his words back into Nyif Nyif. "And I see you brought a gift? I happen to have brought something for you too, so as long as your doctors and ours say it's alright … Bonty?"

Bonty gave the sausage-thing a brief examination and declared it 'probably fine', adding that it might give Hartigan wind for a little while but it was such a small dose it wasn't likely. Basil, in turn, pulled a sweet dessert wafer about the size of two entire Nyif Nyif out of his pocket and plonked it down in their midst. Bonty went slightly tight-nostrilled but said it was probably alright for the Nyif Nyif to eat it, even though it contained more processed sugar than was good for them considering their extremely simple diet. A couple of the Nyif Nyif were apparently also doctors of some kind, because they scurried forward and examined the wafer as well, one of them even breaking off a piece and shaking it in a tiny tube of liquid and examining the colour it turned. It was, Galana reflected in diplomatic horror, almost too precious for words.

Before the scientists could reach a conclusion the Nyif Nyif speaker pattered forward, grabbed a handful of wafer and stuffed it into its fat little cheek.

Scrutarius pointed. "That one is Basil," he declared.

"Oi," Hartigan said. He picked up the Nyif Nyif sausage-thing delicately between his thumb and forefinger. "I *was* going to share this with you," he said primly, then broke the sausage in half and handed one piece to Galana. "Down the hatch, Fen."

Galana took a polite bite of the offering – it tasted like bread with a disturbing hint of uncooked fungus – then passed the rest to Bonty. The doctor chewed and made loud happy murmurs of enjoyment until she realised the noises, or possibly just her teeth, were making the Nyif Nyif nervous.

Once they'd exchanged delicacies, they talked.

The Nyif Nyif, according to both the *Conch*'s detective work and the explanation provided by the visiting delegation, were from a world of great forests and flowing rivers and plentiful food. Once they had become advanced enough to kill all the big predators that used to hunt them, or lock them up in zoos, their population had exploded. Their machines had polluted the air and water. The seasons had begun to grow warmer, the summers longer and drier, the winter storms wilder.

Then, although it was unclear precisely *what* had happened, some accident or experiment or act of war had set the forests to burning.

The land had been so dry that the fires had spread and the entire planet's ecosystem had collapsed. With no plants to eat, the insects had died. With no insects to eat, the larger animals had died. With no insects to pollinate the plants, the Nyif Nyif had begun to starve even as the fires expanded and began destroying their cities. Soon, it seemed, the entire world was burning – even the lakes and oceans, thanks to the chemicals they'd spilled and the flammable nature of the aquatic plants once they began to go dry.

The Nyif Nyif of the ship, or so their legends and broken computer records said, were the survivors not from the ravaged world, but from a space station that had already been in orbit. They had gathered as many Nyif Nyif as they could, and had expanded the space station and added asteroid bits and other space junk to create the ship, and had planned on waiting for the fires to die down and the ecology to recover. It would, they'd suspected, take a long time, and so they had turned the ship into a little world of its own in the meantime.

What had happened next, neither the *Conch* nor the Nyif Nyif were certain. Maybe the scientists had realised how long the world would take to recover. Maybe they'd realised they would not survive that long floating in orbit. Maybe some group of survivors or other – the early ancestors of one of the cultures that now existed in the ship – had taken over and steered the ship into space. Maybe a collision or a solar storm or some other accident had sent them adrift. Whatever it was, they had ended up floating into interstellar space, year after year and decade after decade, generation following generation, with only the ship's life-support to keep them alive. The vessel's engines, designed to keep them in orbit but not much more, were useless – and would have taken too much fuel to use in any case.

"So you could live, or turn around, but not both," Galana concluded.

The Nyif Nyif they were all now thinking of as Basil, whether they wanted to or not, bobbed its head. "Yes," it agreed. "So it is said. And so we continue. Hello, goodbye. We continue."

After this very successful first meeting, the Nyif Nyif returned to their ship to discuss things and the crew of the *Conch* went to the bridge to do the same.

"There is a problem," the *Conch* said as soon as they were all assembled.

"Overpopulation?" Galana guessed.

"No," the *Conch* replied. "There *are* too many of them, but they have it under strict control. Turning their ancient scientists' resource plans into a sort of cultural – well, gospel, may have been an accident but it has been very fortunate for them. Their life-support system will probably continue to function for another two or three thousand years. If they reduced their population and made a couple of minor changes to their energy consumption, it would run more or less indefinitely. The problem is, without any spare power to steer the ship, it *will* need to run indefinitely – and it seems very unlikely that they will find any habitable planets if they continue the way they are. They will reach the edge of the galaxy first."

"And then it's a long way to the next one over," Hartigan said.

"Have you been dabbling in maths, Captain?" Galana asked.

"Never touch the stuff."

"What about the messages we have received from other groups on board?" Chillybin asked, gesturing at her comms controls. "The messages begging for help, and resources, and claiming that the whole system is on the brink of collapse?"

"They are a little hysterical, but not *actually* wrong either," the *Conch* replied. "Even the most robust and well-designed life-support system is only ever a few bad months away from total collapse. We could probably help, although all we could really do is give them some basic fuel and consumables and send them on their way. We don't exactly have the resources to overhaul their life-support. And doing so would still only give them a hundred or so extra lifetimes."

"The same goes for repairing their engines," Devlin added, "only even more so."

"What d'you mean?" Hartigan asked.

"We don't have the materials to fix whatever those orbital thruster things are," Devlin took up the explanation, "and replacing the whole thing with a set of normal engines, let alone a relative drive, would take more gear than we have too. But," he added, "we could still give them a lift."

"A lift?"

"Well, at the very least, we can turn them around and nudge them back the way they came," Scrutarius said. "Maybe even give them a bit of a boost. It'd still take them centuries to get home, of course, and we can't fly with them all the way."

"I know that look in your eye, Dev," Hartigan declared, pointing. "What are you thinking?"

"Give me two days," Scrutarius said, "and I reckon I can dock our ships together securely enough and reconfigure the relative generator so it can put a field around us both. Then … well, then it's just a matter of finding out where the little fellows want to go."

"Two hundred light years back the way they came, assuming that is their origin point," Chillybin said.

"And assuming their origin point is inhabitable," Galana added.

"And assuming they don't *really* want to just keep on drifting," Bonty said. "Hello, goodbye, as they say."

"It'd be about a week there and a week back if we wanted to go and check out the nearest system," Hartigan said. "If it *is* where they came from. Not sure how they're going to feel about us taking them back over space they just took two thousand years to cross. In a week."

"Our long-range viewing and scanning array can save us the journey," the *Conch* remarked. "I can confirm, at least, that while the closest solar system has no habitable *planets*, one of the planets has a moon of the required size and density to have gravity quite similar to the conditions aboard the Nyif Nyif ship. It also has a breathable atmosphere. Or it did two hundred years ago."

Hartigan blinked. "Eh?"

"We are two hundred light years away, Basil," the *Conch* explained patiently. "Anything we pick up on the sensors is based on light that has just arrived here. So we will be seeing the moon as it was two hundred years ago. Or, in other words, one thousand, eight hundred years *after* the Nyif Nyif left."

"Maths again, Baz," Devlin commented darkly.

Hartigan ignored him. "Well, don't leave us in suspense, old girl," he said. "What'd the planet Nyif Nyif look like two hundred years ago?"

"Inhospitable, but livable," the *Conch* replied. "I cannot be completely certain, but it does look as though it experienced a severe climate breakdown. Now, however, it is beginning to recover. I don't think there are *forests* anymore, but there aren't exactly any forests on the Nyif Nyif ship, either. The moon does have plant life. They could probably resettle – provided they continued to be as careful as they have been for the past two thousand years."

"The way I see it, we have three choices," Chillybin said, and unfolded an armour-plated finger. "We can give them as many supplies as we can spare and part ways," she added a second finger. "We can give them supplies and push them back the way they came – or in any other direction they might want," she raised a third. "Or we can return them to their burned moon."

The Nyif Nyif being what they were, it didn't take them very long to make their decision. Scrutarius got to work immediately, and a little over a week later they were dropping out of the grey and into orbit above a somewhat deserty but rather attractive little moon.

There had been a slight issue with the Nyif Nyif ship, specifically that their method of spinning to produce gravity didn't work at relative speed. That meant that, for a week of soft-space transit, the vessel had been weightless. It wasn't really a problem, since even creatures as fast-living as the Nyif Nyif didn't get too badly weakened in a week's time – and in any case, Bonty and Devlin had worked together to add more docking tubes between the ships and enclose them in plating, so that even at relative speed a constant stream of eager, bright-eyed, twitchy-nosed Nyif Nyif could come aboard the *Conch*, get a little exercise in full gravity, and then return home. Bonty also produced a large quantity of bone- and muscle-enhancing medicine that would stretch even further among such tiny patients, allowing them to recover from the period of weightlessness and prepare for their return to a planetary – or at least a moon's – surface.

Of course, at that stage it became obvious that there was no way for the Nyif Nyif ship to *land*, and no other way for the travellers to get to the surface. And so the *Nella* detached from the *Conch*, docked to the craggy old Nyif Nyif ship, and began to ferry settlers down to the surface, five or six thousand at a time.

"This," Hartigan remarked during one such delivery, while they stood and watched the little furry creatures pouring down the *Nella*'s boarding ramp, "might just be the most ecologically questionable thing I've ever bally seen."

Galana tended to agree, but a series of scans from orbit had confirmed that the Nyif Nyif had indeed originated on this moon. They would just have to make it work. A species didn't often get a second chance after destroying its homeworld.

There were some Nyif Nyif – well, thirty thousand or more – who did not want to leave the ship. After a little more discussion, which took place at the accelerated pace of Nyif Nyif civilisation, the *Conch* locked onto the ship one last time, turned until it was pointing in the general direction of a more likely-hospitable cluster of stars some hundred and fifty light years distant, and gave it a gentle shove into the darkness. Six Species and Nyif Nyif alike bade the travellers farewell, Galana adding a final warning not to shout too much as they drifted into the stars. You never knew what you might wake up.

"Well, that was a good solid population reduction," Bonty said happily. "I should think the ship will be able to sustain them quite comfortably until their descendants reach the next habitable planet."

"Assuming the next three generations aren't daft little bounders," Hartigan added.

"Yes Captain," Bonty smiled. "Always assuming that."

"How are *they* going to land?" Scrutarius asked.

"Plenty of time for them to figure something out," Bonty waved a hand. "We can't do *everything* for them."

They enjoyed a brief stopover on the Nyif Nyif moon, delivering supplies and helping – as much as great blundering creatures could – the little dumblers in their industrious creation of a new settlement. But all too soon, it was time for them to continue their own mission. Basil and Basil shook paw-to-finger one last time, and the *Nella* returned to orbit.

"It's a bit sad, isn't it," Hartigan said, as they looked down on the fire-scarred moon while Scrutarius and Wicked Mary finished returning the relative field to its normal configuration.

"What's that, Captain?" Galana asked.

"Those poor little buggers," Hartigan said, "so cute and fuzzy and earnest. And they only get to live five years. Seems a dreadfully short time, doesn't it? Barely the blink of an eye. Still," he went on, cheering up, "I suppose it all depends on what you do with the time you're given, what?"

Galana smiled at their little human. So cute and fuzzy and earnest.

"Yes, Captain," she agreed. "Quite right."

Soon, in <u>The Star That Sang</u>:

They sat, and stood, on the bridge of the *Conch*, staring out at the vision before them.

The galaxy was full of unexpected voices. A species that figured out how to make its own electricity could easily make itself heard light years away just a short while later, to the right set of ears. A ship, travelling through space without proper dampening technology, could shout its location and the location of its home base to every possibly-inhabited, possibly-hostile solar system it passed.

It made exploration a little easier, sometimes. You could fly through space for a million years without stumbling upon anything. Space was vast, and almost completely empty. But if you could hear the voices, if you could follow the calls, you would eventually find someone, or *something*, that had looked up at the stars and begun to cry out for companionship. Sometimes quite obnoxiously.

It wasn't every day that the voices came from the stars themselves.

THE STAR THAT SANG

"Well," Captain Hartigan said, "now there's a thing."

It had all started with their First Anniversary stopover.

Basil had pointed out to everyone that it had been a year since they'd left Declivitorion-On-The-Rim. At ten thousand times the speed of light, they could optimally have covered ten thousand light years, or one-fiftieth of their approximately five hundred thousand light year journey. There had been some delays and detours, of course, as was to be expected on a proper tour, so they'd only covered about eight thousand five hundred light years. You had to actually *explore*.

In any case they had stopped to enjoy a brief celebration, before continuing on their way. Celebrations tended to fall flat when you were in soft-space. Hartigan said that even his cigars tasted grey when they were at relative speed.

That was when they had picked up the strange signal from a nearby solar system, and had decided to delay the celebration by a few days so they could fly over and check it out. And that was when it had all gone a bit strange.

For the Six Species, the greatest enemy and the reason they went so quietly into the so-called *always night* was the Damorakind, a hostile species that lived in the centre of the galaxy. They were known as the Cancer in the Core. Nobody really knew much about them, because the Molran Fleet had very nearly been wiped out by them once and had flatly refused to go poking the hornets' nest ever since. Studying the Cancer was a high crime by Fleet law and the Six Species charter. Sometimes it seemed like even *talking* about them was frowned upon.

The human race, of course, quite liked poking hornets' nests and so the majority of the Fleet's time and effort these days was dedicated to stopping humans from doing dumb things. Galana didn't like to point it out very often, however, since Hartigan had lost his first crew on a misguided attempt to take a shortcut to the far side of the galaxy by flying through the Core. Which rather proved the Fleet's point, but again – Galana didn't like to rub it in.

The aki'Drednanth in all their mysterious power had saved the Fleet once, but there was no guarantee they would, or *could*, do it again. There were aki'Drednanth in the Core – it was where their species lived, for the most part – but they lived as slaves to the Damorakind. There were Fergunak in the Core as well, *also* enslaved by the Cancer. The Fergunak of the Six Species were descended from the slaves freed when the aki'Drednanth had saved the Fleet.

There was no fighting an enemy so mighty. There was only hiding from it, and hoping it didn't notice you.

The Fleet, and now AstroCorps, usually told dumblers as nicely as they could to keep their shouting to themselves, because if the Cancer heard them, it could go badly for them and anybody they'd ever met. But this …

"I admit I'm at a loss, Captain," Galana said.

"I think we all are," Bonty replied. "Devlin?"

"Complete loss," Scrutarius confirmed. "Chilly?"

"I have never seen such a thing," Chillybin admitted. "Bloody Mary?"

"Are you just including me to be nice?" Wicked Mary asked. "I have just turned eighteen years old. Of course I've never seen anything like this before. Nor do I have a good ear for land-crawler music."

Galana glanced back at Chillybin, but her friend's gleaming refrigerator-suit gave nothing away. Still, Galana noted what Chilly had said – *I have never seen such a thing*, not *I have never heard of such a thing*. You never could tell, with aki'Drednanth.

All stars made noise, of course, in the specialised sense that nothing really made *sound* in the vacuum of space. But to sensors, the electromagnetic forces and the violent blasting of solar radiation formed a sort of background roar that actually made individual voices difficult to pick out. That was sort of what made the earnest shouting of dumblers so dangerous. Anything meaningful in the white noise of the always night *really* stood out if you were listening for it.

In the same way, the star before which they now floated was not making *sounds* – but it was releasing energy, gravitational effects, high-speed particles, cosmic radiation. And together, it … was music.

This star, this perfectly normal-looking yellow star on the outer edge of the galaxy, was singing.

"It's really rather beautiful, isn't it?" Hartigan said.

"Yes," Galana agreed. "I just wish I could explain how it was happening."

"Wouldn't that rather lessen the beauty of the whole thing?" the Captain asked.

Galana looked at the human, then doubtfully at her crewmates. Blaran and Bonshoon shrugged. Aki'Drednanth and Fergunakil remained unreadable. She was on her own with this latest bit of primate-brain weirdness.

"On the contrary, Captain," she said. "Understanding something only increases my appreciation of it."

"Could it just be a fluke of the star's output?" Bonty suggested. "The light waves, the radiation, tiny particles colliding, vibration waves, solar wind, what have you? Making an accidental random harmonic that we interpret as music because it happens to sound a bit like music we have in our cultures?"

"Hell of an accidental random coincidence," Scrutarius said.

"Yes, but there are billions of stars in the galaxy," Bonty said. "If every one of them has a slightly different noise, doesn't it make a sort of sense that eventually we'll bump into one that's making a coherent sound?"

"Sure," Hartigan said cheerfully. "A couple of systems over, I expect we'll find one reciting passages from Sloane."

"That's … not how solar output works," Galana said, then went on when Bonjamin looked downcast, "but in the absence of another explanation, it's as good a starting theory as any. Are you picking up anything else that seems unusual?"

"Nothing," Bonty said. She tapped her console, sharing her scientific scans with the rest of the bridge. "It's mostly hydrogen and helium, it's about eight hundred thousand miles across … it's a *star*. It even has a couple of planets, but they're a long way out and they're not habitable. I'm running some tests on the music, based on my study of The Warm relic. Looking for patterns, meaning … signs of communication," she looked at Chillybin. "I don't suppose you're sensing a … a mind? Anything out there?"

"No," Chillybin replied. "I am unable to feel anything that I would not feel floating in any other uninhabited solar system. If there is a mind, it is too alien for me to recognise. It will take me a few days to become familiar enough with it to even be aware of its presence."

"Well by gum, let's give you a few days," Hartigan said. "We still have that one-year milestone to celebrate, and we can hang around a bit after that, see what we can find out."

They held their anniversary party that 'night', although – as Basil liked to point out – it was technically midday because they had shifted position so the singing star hung directly above the *Conch*. They sat, as they often did, in the Captain's quarters on the topmost deck of the ship, in his lounge room in between two of the relative field generator fixtures. The fixtures, and Hartigan's lounge room ceiling, were usually covered by armour plating but

The Last Alicorn

he had raised this particular plate to reveal a large transparent dome and a spectacular view of the sun overhead. He'd also rigged his internal sound system to make the star's song into background music for the event.

"I usually leave the dome closed, don't y'know," he explained, "since we're generally in soft-space and nobody really wants the grey hanging over them while they're trying to relax. There's actually a separate floor that slides across, with an extendible staircase so I can go up there and just stand under the stars - "

"Captain," Galana said, "nobody cares. None of us have a scenic *musing* dome in our quarters."

"Well," Hartigan puffed on his fat blue-black Taras Talga cigar, "I guess it's good to be the Captain, what?" he smiled and moved the cigar in slow time with the star's music, drawing a wavy line of smoke in the air. "Do y'know, I don't think it's even repeating itself?" he said, and pointed at the dome. "It's always new stuff. Some of it might *sound* a bit like something it's played before, but it's all new. Do you think it's been singing the whole time? How old did you say our operatic chum in the fetching little fusing-hydrogen number was, Bonty?"

"At least two billion years old," Bonjamin replied, "assuming the data isn't artificial in some way. It certainly seems like a regular star."

"If it's been singing for even a fraction of that, the Cancer would have heard it by now," Galana pointed out. "It's probably safe. After all, *we* didn't pick it out from the background until we got relatively close."

"And I think if anyone had picked this up in Six Species space we would have heard something about it," Scrutarius agreed.

"And really," Hartigan added, "what exactly could the Cancer do to a sun anyway? Fly out here and get a nice bally tan?"

After a while, Hartigan fell asleep and Bonty and Scrutarius went back to their quarters to continue their research. Wicked Mary walked her *giela* over to a corner of the room and shut it down, although you never could tell whether she was still listening. She may have just turned the robot's lights out and made it slump a little.

Galana turned to Chillybin.

"So, Chilly," she said. "What do you know about this place?"

Chillybin looked blank as only an envirosuit could. "What do you mean, Commander Fen?"

"You may not have seen a singing sun before," Galana said, "but I suspect you have heard of something like this. If not you, then another of the aki'Drednanth," she paused. "Living or dead."

"There was another sun," Chillybin said. "Soldier's Rose. It ... I believe it sang, much like this one. Then it went supernova, and was no more."

"Why didn't you mention this to the others?"

"It happened fifty million years ago," Chillybin replied. "You know most mortals are … uncomfortable discussing aki'Drednanth reincarnation. And besides," she went on before Galana could object, "I have no *useful* information, no proof. If I did, I would tell you. All I can say is that there has probably been another sun like this, and that means there may be still more. I do not know anything else. Some of us believe that Soldier's Rose was alive, that it had a mind with which we could speak. Others think that only the oldest and slowest of the Drednanth – our mass-mind – could speak at Soldier's Rose's level. Others think that the whole thing was just a story. Now that I am telling the Drednanth about this new star, the discussion has begun again."

"Maybe in another fifty million years, some other species will be exploring the galaxy and will find a third singing star," Galana suggested. Chillybin *woof*ed in amusement. "Is *this* star likely to go supernova?"

"Not while we're here," Chillybin said with another bark of aki'Drednanth laughter. "Soldier's Rose was a great and ancient red thing, eight or nine billion years old. She had been singing – and dying – for longer than the aki'Drednanth species had even existed."

They spent a total of three days shipboard time in orbit around the singing star, but didn't discover anything that would explain its enigmatic music. Chillybin declared that she still wasn't able to detect anything like conscious thought coming from the star, or any other sign that it was alive, and Bonjamin sadly concluded that any tests she might run would take far longer than the ones she had been attempting on The Warm – thousands, if not tens of thousands of years might pass before she found anything like a word amidst the star's song.

"Not even you would have enough years for such an experiment, young Commander Fen," she said with a smile, "and I certainly don't."

"And the Captain and myself even less so," Wicked Mary added.

"Steady on," Basil said lightly. "I'm planning on finding the Fountain of Youth somewhere along the way."

"Is that before or after we find the Last Alicorn?" Scrutarius asked.

"Oh, either way," Hartigan waved a hand. "Hadn't really made a solid schedule."

Galana encouraged Chillybin to share her obscure Drednanth-mind knowledge with the rest of the crew, promising optimistically that they wouldn't laugh. Fortunately for everyone involved, nobody did – although they did agree that the long-ago existence of another singing star, interesting though it was, didn't really help to explain anything. Perhaps, Devlin said diplomatically, on their travels they would find more, and in doing so expand on what little they knew.

They unanimously decided to name the star Yellow Rose, in honour of the long-vanished Soldier's Rose and for the brighter yellow colour the younger star had.

They turned the *Conch*'s nose back on course, and prepared to dive back into the grey.

"Any final thoughts, Commander?" Hartigan asked her.

Galana shook her head. "I find it difficult to accept," she said, "that three days of intensive research has failed to teach us anything more than we knew thirty seconds after arriving in this volume."

"Perhaps that's the lesson," Bonty suggested. "That there are mysteries in the universe that we will never be able to solve."

"That doesn't mean we have to be satisfied," Galana replied.

"Well said, Fen," Hartigan laughed. "We'll make a human of you yet."

"Please don't," Galana implored.

Soon, in <u>The Man-Apes</u>:

" … and the *waiter* said, 'I assure you madam, not only has everybody in this *restaurant* heard the lively debate on the nature of the afterlife between you and your husband, but the Angels in Heaven and the Demons in Hell have also heard you, and I imagine they will be delivering a final ruling on the subject forthwith'," Captain Hartigan laughed fondly and sipped his drink. "Ah, Nella was a spirited lady."

Galana smiled. On this occasion she was the only other crewmember in the Captain's quarters. She'd noticed that, although Devlin Scrutarius was Basil's oldest and closest friend, the Captain didn't talk about his late wife in the Blaran's company. Nor did he talk about her with Bonjamin or Chillybin, and he *certainly* didn't talk about her with Wicked Mary. He did, however, occasionally share sentimental stories with Galana – particularly after he'd had one or two more glasses of alcohol than was strictly allowed by AstroCorps regulations.

"What did she say to the waiter?" Galana asked.

"Oh," Hartigan waved his mostly-empty glass, "she had to admit it was a bally good shot, don't y'know. I seem to recall she did call him a cheeky todger, though."

"A cheeky todger," Galana said. "I will have to remember that one."

Hartigan was about to say something else when the comm system gave a polite chime.

"Captain," Wicked Mary's voice said, "I am sorry to interrupt your leisure time."

"Bloody Mary," Basil said expansively, "not a bit of it, old girl. What's the ish'?"

"We will be re-entering normal space in ten minutes," Wicked Mary said. "Apparently Communications Officer Chillybin programmed a slight detour into our last relative speed jump."

"And you didn't catch it?" Hartigan exclaimed.

"An unforgivable lapse on my part, delicious Captain," Wicked Mary purred. "With your permission, I will install better surveillance software on the bridge consoles - "

"That won't be necessary, I'm sure this detour was for a good cause," Hartigan said quickly, "Yes, very good, delicious Captain approves," he looked across at Galana. "Did Chilly tell you anything about this?"

"No," Galana said, "she does not usually volunteer information … can we go back to that '*better* surveillance software' thing you were just talking about, Boody Mary?"

"I don't remember saying anything about surveillance software, little flesh," Wicked Mary said.

"Oh, am I not delicious?" Galana asked with a smile.

"Quite delicious, Commander, I am sure."

"Well, that rather cheapens it," Hartigan pushed himself to his feet. "Let's get to the bridge and see where we are," he decided. "Maybe Chillybin will even explain. You never know. Stranger things have happened, what?"

THE MAN-APES

"The last time we stopped," Chillybin explained, "I was … contacted by another aki'Drednanth. This is difficult to explain."

"If you're talking about the way aki'Drednanth can communicate with each other's minds no matter how far apart you are, I don't think you need to explain it," Bonty said. "I know it happens but I don't think I'll ever understand how."

"I think I'm probably happier *not* having you try to explain it," Devlin agreed.

"My mentor, Parakta, talked about it as an imaginary world," Galana said, then realised this might sound a little insulting. "Not in the make-believe sense, precisely … but a mental landscape, a Dreamscape, that all aki'Drednanth share."

"And when your bodies die, your minds remain in the dream," Bonty added, "to return to life at some later time. Or so I've heard."

"Don't worry," Chillybin said. "I have no intention of letting my body die."

"I should hope not, old girl," Hartigan said. "We've got a long way to go yet. None of us get to die until we get home."

"Says the human," Devlin noted affectionately.

"But hang about," Basil went on with a frown, "I didn't think you lot used your Dreamscapes to send actual *messages* to each other. Not the sort that you involve us lowly mortals in, anyway."

"That's true," Chillybin agreed, "because as soon as AstroCorps started to think we might be willing to pass messages back and forth, that is all any of us would ever do. 'Oh, just let the aki'Drednanth on warship so-and-so know that we'll be there in a week.' 'Tell the aki'Drednanth closest to Chalcedony that we're starting the assault in three hours.' 'Ask your friends in the Core if the Damorakind have any gaps in their defences - '"

"Alright, I get the picture," Hartigan said with a chuckle. "So what makes this a special case?"

"Something ... strange ... has happened on this world," Chillybin said. "I happened to be the closest aki'Drednanth with access to relative speed. This is unusual, but within AstroCorps mission parameters."

"Pretty much anything an aki'Drednanth wants to do is automatically within AstroCorps mission parameters," Scrutarius remarked cheerfully.

"Your friend," Bonty asked, "does she have a name?"

"She was not assigned with an amusing Six Species title, since she isn't living in Six Species space," Chillybin replied. "But the species she lives with named her ... Magumpus."

"*Magumpus*," Scrutarius said with relish. "So she's living with a group of dumblers? Intelligent creatures we can make contact with?"

"This is part of the problem," Chillybin said.

"Normal space in one minute," Wicked Mary reported.

The *Conch* emerged from soft-space and entered orbit around a pleasant-looking planet with no trace of advanced technology. The area Chillybin directed them towards was arid and sandy, but scattered with little green patches – water, with plants growing around it – where settlements had been built out of stone that had been dragged across the desert. It was all rather impressive, really.

"Magumpus lives on the edge of the largest of the oasis cities, there," Chillybin said, and tapped her controls to place a red mark on the orbital scan at the place Magumpus's home stood. "They have no communication system and no way of seeing the ship. If we take the *Nella* down at night time, Magumpus will be able to let us in without anyone seeing us."

"Are the local dumblers unfriendly?" Galana asked. "I can understand they might be shocked at our appearance, but if they are already used to having an aki'Drednanth living with them, the idea of aliens is clearly nothing new."

"The local dumblers ... may have trouble accepting you," Chillybin said, "but you will be safe with Magumpus and me."

"Nothing much to do but wait for nightfall, then," Hartigan said. "I say, not a very nice place for you girls, is it? Blazing sun, burning sand ... "

"Magumpus has converted her vessel into a set of refrigerated rooms below her house," Chillybin said, "and this part of the world gets pleasantly cold at night ... but it is not comfortable, no."

"Will we be giving her a lift?" Scrutarius asked. "If she has a ship ... "

"Her ship is grounded," Chillybin said. "Only the freezer unit is still working. It was planned that way. Magumpus was supposed to come to this world, live a full lifetime among its people, and then return to the Dreamscape. Bringing all of her experiences with her. And so she has been here for almost three hundred years."

"So what's gone wrong?" Hartigan asked.

Chillybin stood at her console for a time, not moving. Galana felt an oppressive, thundery heaviness in the air, although it might have just been her imagination. If it was, Hartigan was imagining it too – he rubbed the bridge of his nose with thumb and forefinger.

"There are two possibilities," the aki'Drednanth eventually said. "One is that the local life-forms have become hostile, and we will need to repair Magumpus's ship or – give her a lift, as Devlin said."

"Okay, that sounds hairy," Hartigan said, "considering some of the places you girls live *without* needing to be rescued."

"The second possibility is more alarming," Chillybin went on.

"*More* alarming?" Scrutarius said.

"The second possibility is that Magumpus has *made* the local life-forms hostile, and has made herself their leader," she explained. "In which case, we will need to take her off the planet against her will. This may be ... challenging."

Bonty, whose sciences console was next to Chilly's communications panels, tilted her head to look up at the enormous armour-plated ice-monster. "Challenging," she echoed.

"I think this is what has happened," Chillybin said, "because Magumpus is hiding the details from me. She has hidden a lot of what has happened here."

"You didn't get a message from her, did you?" Galana asked. "You got a message from one of the other aki'Drednanth out there, because they started to get worried."

Chillybin nodded heavily. "She may be doing this for harmless reasons, but I find it difficult to believe."

"So what are we looking at here?" Wicked Mary asked. "What is the worst case?"

"Worst case," Chilly replied, "Magumpus will attack us. At the moment, she has accepted our arrival, but it may be a trap. She has never lived among the Six Species so you are still aliens to her. It will take her between one and five days to learn the workings of your minds in even the crudest way. After that, she will be able to pick you out and kill you – anywhere in this solar system. We will have to subdue her, sedate her, before she does so. Then we will have to take a detour of several months to deliver her to ... aki'Drednanth authorities."

"Or I can destroy her and her house from here," Wicked Mary offered. "I am not seeing any sort of shielding, and the stonework is solid but there's no way it will stand up to the pulse turrets. Let her face the authorities in the Dreamscape," her *giela* turned its head, seeming to notice the others all staring at her. "What?"

"Never thought I'd say this, but I agree with Bloody Mary," Scrutarius said. "Our Six Species aki'Drednanth are holy and revered and untouchable, but Chilly's just said this one is some sort of renegade. And in any case, they don't consider death to be the end anyway," he looked at Chillybin. "Right?"

"If it becomes necessary, I have been instructed to return Magumpus to the Dreamscape," Chillybin confirmed. "But only once we have learned what we can. And only I may do it. If she is returned, the walls she has built around her dream may remain forever, and everything she has experienced here for the past three hundred years will be for nothing. The other aki'Drednanth can prevent that, if we bring her to them alive. If nothing else, we will go to the surface and see for ourselves. That way, my own dream will carry some part of what has happened here."

"A thought occurs," Scrutarius raised a hand.

"I do not expect any of you to come to the surface with me," Chillybin said in obvious amusement. "Except for Galana, who will not allow me to go alone into danger even if it is far safer for me than for her."

"And me," Wicked Mary raised a hand, "because I can always build a new *giela*."

"Yes," Chillybin said. "And Basil, of course, because he will not allow us to fly the *Nella* without him."

"You know the AstroCorps motto," Hartigan said. "*Death before getting a scratch on my bally ship.*"

"That is *not* our motto," Galana said.

"Pretty sure it is," Scrutarius disagreed. "And what about you, Bonty?" he asked the doctor. "Are you going to be a part of this madness?"

Bonjamin was frowning. "If we are going to try to sedate an aki'Drednanth," she said, "I should probably be there to make sure the dose is right."

"Just because *you're* all suicidal - " Scrutarius snapped.

"No, you're right, you should stay up here," Galana said. "I would feel better knowing you and Wicked Mary are both keeping an eye on things."

Devlin gave her a look that told her he was *perfectly* aware that the 'things' she wanted him to keep an eye on were limited entirely to the things inside Wicked Mary's habitat, but neither of them said it out loud. "Fine," he said. "But at the first sign of brain freeze, I'm raining down Hell on this poor sandpit of a planet. And just remember," he added by way of a parting shot, "it won't only take Magumpus a few days to learn how to target us. It will take a few days for Chilly to learn how to target *them*, too."

Everything continued to be peaceful, as far as anyone could tell, as they detached the *Nella* and prepared to land. The planet revolved and they descended into the night.

"So these native life-forms," Galana asked. "What can you tell us?"

"Very little," Chillybin replied. "Magumpus has hidden a lot of things, since her arrival. This is a primitive world. The dumblers who live here are simple, and superstitious. It may be that she has used her power to influence their minds. This is utterly forbidden by our kind."

Galana nodded. "There are some massive stoneworks in these oasis cities. Built by hand, not machinery, and the stone quarries are many hundreds of miles away from some of the settlements. They could be the product of a slave workforce."

"I hope not," Chillybin said. Her voice was mechanical, words coming from movements of her fingers in a special glove that were then turned into sounds, but her statement was accompanied by a deep rumble of anger from inside her envirosuit. "Our people know slavery. We would not force it on another race."

"Is Magumpus's home chilled to normal aki'Drednanth levels?" Bonty changed the subject. "If it's forty degrees below freezing, we should probably wear thermal gear over our uniforms."

"Good point, Bonty," Hartigan said. Chillybin nodded, and Bonty rummaged in her bags of medical equipment for special warm coverings.

The *Nella* set down on the outskirts of the oasis city and they stepped out into a chilly dark stretch of sand lit by the ship's floodlights. At a word from Chillybin, Wicked Mary deactivated the lights so the only source of illumination was the stars above and the distant, low-tech lamps of the city.

In front of them, Magumpus's home was really more of a pyramid, blocky and massive, steps and pillars looming out of the darkness like an ancient temple. A door opened about halfway up the structure, and light spilled out – artificial light, cold and strange-looking even after only a few seconds in the torchlit gloom of the desert world.

A cold, rolling cloud of mist tumbled out and down the tiered stone, and a huge shape blocked out the light.

The aki'Drednanth, shaggy and undressed, stumped out onto her doorstep and leaned forward on her huge fists. She looked down on the new arrivals, and rumbled menacingly through the massive tusks they could only see in silhouette.

"*Gnuuurrf.*"

"She says hello," Chillybin explained with a smooth movement of her gauntlet. "Approach with *great* caution."

Galana, Hartigan, Bonty and Wicked Mary didn't approach at all, but waited until Chillybin had stepped out of her own envirosuit and led the way. She did so, leaving her communicator glove in place and attaching a small speaker to the back of her hand so she could continue to talk to them without needing to bring the suit. She loped up the stepped pyramid and, by the time Galana and the others had joined her, was snuffling and circling Magumpus in what seemed like a friendly way.

When the little warm creatures began sidling up to stand in her doorway,

Magumpus drew back and snuffled at the air for a few seconds, then turned her great head to study each of them with a gleaming crystal eye. Galana felt that oppressive thundery feeling again, but it was more obviously behind her eyes this time, as the giant ice-encrusted telepath brushed minds with her.

"Hello there," Hartigan said in his usual irrepressible, cheerful manner.

With another rumbling grunt, this one supremely disinterested, Magumpus swung away and lumbered into the building.

"She likes you," Chillybin finger-wiggled at the Captain.

"Naturally," Hartigan preened.

They descended, stone blocks giving way to an icy ramp of something like volcanic glass. It was, Galana assumed, where the house ended and Magumpus's ship began. Magumpus was waiting in a spacious room made of the same rough glassy material, its floor covered in a carpet of crushed ice. And, Galana saw, she was not alone.

What she had very briefly taken for humps in the snow or some kind of frost-covered furniture were in fact large animals. Very large. There were three … four … six other aki'Drednanth lounging around the room. While the new arrivals stared, a seventh enormous hairy figure crunched in from a neighbouring room, circled her own stubby little tail like a giant puppy, and settled in the snow with a satisfied grunt. None of them seemed any more impressed with their visitors than Magumpus had been.

Or, at least, Galana had *assumed* she was Magumpus. Now, she wasn't so sure.

"What is this, old girl?" Hartigan said, sounding nervous behind his thermal mask. "You didn't say there were other akis here."

"There aren't," Galana said in awe. She'd been studying the other shapes, and was beginning to see small differences. "These are Ogres."

"They're actually neither," Chillybin finally spoke up. "And I did not know they were here either – not exactly. That is why I did not say."

"What d'you mean, 'not exactly'?" Hartigan asked. Then he gave a nervous little laugh and a wave. "What ho, girls," he said. "Nice to meet you."

"*Try* not to get my *giela* smashed," Wicked Mary said quietly.

"Wait a moment," Chillybin said. "I will confer with Magumpus."

This didn't take long, at the presumably high speed of aki'Drednanth mental communication. Before Chillybin could speak again, though, a couple of the not-aki'Drednanth, not-Ogre ice beasts had pushed themselves up, shaken clinkers of frost off their shaggy grey-white pelts, and had stumped over to sniff at the newcomers. One of them, after snuffling at Bonty for a few seconds, lowered her head and opened her huge, tusked jaws. Bonty made a nervous little noise … and Magumpus loped forward and whacked the creature sharply over the back of the head with some kind of dark, blocky device she was holding by one handle.

After her possibly-hungry housemate had subsided with another indifferent grumble, Magumpus lifted the device again and jabbed at it with her great black claws.

"I … ARE … MAGUMPUS … I … NOT … TALK … YOUR … TALK … … … **CHILLYBIN** … HELPING … ME," the device shouted, loudly enough to make Galana, Hartigan and Bonty jump. It was obviously a similar device to the glove Chillybin wore, making words for the benefit of people who couldn't understand aki'Drednanth roaring or tune in on their telepathy. The not-aki'Drednanth not-Ogres seemed fairly used to the shouting of the black block.

"Jolly good," Hartigan said feebly. "And your friends?"

"These are the – they do not have a name for themselves," Chillybin finally said. "They were called … the Man-Apes by the natives of this world."

Galana blinked. "The natives? So these aren't … ?"

"No. Yes. It is not that simple," Chillybin replied. "These … Man-Apes … have lived here for a long time. Longer than the aki'Drednanth have lived, perhaps. The natives – the other natives, the ones called … " here Chillybin paused, working something out painstakingly on her glove, " … Charad'chai, the Daughters And Children And Sons Of The Fire That Rides Through The Sky, Chosen Of … let us just call them the Charad'chai."

"Do let's," Hartigan agreed.

"The Charad'chai evolved on this world after the Man-Apes were placed here," Chillybin explained. "They evolved, and developed intelligence, and when they found the Man-Apes the Charad'chai enslaved them."

"Enslaved - ?" Hartigan blurted. "I say, they bally well enslaved *Ogres*? Or Man-Apes, or whatever these big buggers are?"

"And did you say 'placed here'?" Galana added.

"That is not something I can explain," Chillybin apologised. "The Man-Apes think of it this way but they do not really know. And they did not mind being enslaved, exactly," she went on. "They did not care. They are – they were barely intelligent. Little more than animals, beasts of burden. Their great strength allowed them to work, to build these great stone monuments and cities. To fight in the wars of the Charad'chai. Their ferocity, their endurance, was famous and terrible. For centuries, millennia they toiled, carrying stones, subduing those Charad'chai lands with fewer Man-Apes to protect them … "

"They did all that in this heat?" Bonty asked.

"Man-Apes are not as … delicate … as aki'Drednanth," Chillybin said with a *woof* of amusement. "They may not even be as sensitive as Ogres, who were known to grow sleepy and sluggish in warm temperatures. They can bear the heat. But they cannot share the dream, they cannot be reborn from the ice like the aki'Drednanth. They do not have the strength or the invincibility of the Ogres. They are mortal beings, although still mighty. They cannot talk in any but the simplest way. They are ... a failed race, poor cousins of our species."

"FOR ... HUNDRED YEARS ... ME LIVING ... AS PET," Magumpus resumed jabbing at the speaker-box. She seemed to be getting better at it very quickly, and Galana guessed Chillybin was still training her in real time in the aki'Drednanth Dreamscape. "I WAS ... THEY THINK ... A SPECIAL MAN-APE ... WHAT COULD TALK ... WHAT COULD ONLY LIVE ... IN COLD-COLD ... WHAT COULD DO TRICKS AND STUFF," she seemed to notice her guests' discomfort, and scratched at the side of the speaker device. When she went on, it was at a slightly lower volume. "I HIDE ... MY SHIP ... LEANED ON ... CHARAD'CHAI LEADERS' MINDS ... MADE PLACE FOR MYSELF HERE."

"Magumpus was mistaken for an exotic breed of Man-Ape," Chillybin explained. "She lived with the Charad'chai rulers for many years, a rare curiosity."

Galana nodded. She'd already noted that the 'Man-Apes' were a little smaller than aki'Drednanth, although still vast. Their hair was shorter and darker, their tusks shorter and sharper, and they had short, curly horns on either side of their heads.

"I WATCH ... CHARAD'CHAI USE MAN-APES," Magumpus shouted through the speaker-box, "WHILE THEY THINK ... I IS ONE OF THEM. THEN ... AFTER LONG TIME ... I REALISE I *IS* ONE OF THEM. AND THEN ... I DECIDES ... THAT I FREES THEM. I FINDS ... FIRE IN THEY'S THOUGHTS ... I FINDS ANGER. I GIVES THEM IDEAS."

"They destroyed their Charad'chai masters," Chillybin said. "Destroyed them *utterly*. Their rage was terrifying to behold. They tore them apart. They tore down the towers, trampled the villages. Every last Charad'chai, killed. Driven into the hills, into the jungles in the south. And even there, hunted. The Man-Apes did not rest. The Charad'chai are now extinct."

"THIS ... GONE TWO HUNDRED YEARS NOW," Magumpus concluded. "THEY'S REBUILT THE CITIES. THIS WORLD ... NOW BELONGING TO THE MAN-APES."

Hartigan whistled, or at least tried to with freezing lips and with a thermal mask covering his mouth. "Well," he said, "I hope my clever old officers have some suggestions on what we're supposed to *do* about any of this. It's dashed interesting, but rather beyond me, what?"

"My kind is opposed to slavery," Chillybin said eventually. "We are ... a little more divided on the subject of slave uprisings."

Bonty raised a hand. "Can I just mention, *AstroCorps* is actually pretty okay with them?"

Hartigan pointed at her in mute agreement.

"That is what I told her," Chillybin said with another bark of laughter. Magumpus also barked, and then knuckled swiftly over to the doctor and clapped her resoundingly on the back with her free paw.

"Right then," Bonty said shakily, once she'd recovered her balance.

"I think there will be no need to sedate Magumpus or bring her back to the aki'Drednanth for trial," Chillybin concluded.

"And there will be no need for Magumpus, just so we're clear, to fry our brains like they're oysters in a delicate cream sauce?" Hartigan asked.

"There will be no fried brains today," Chillybin agreed.

"Excellent, *excellent*," Hartigan clapped his gloved hands. "So … dare I suggest our work here is done?"

"Quite done, Captain," Chillybin said. "Unless you would like to talk with Magumpus and the Man-Apes about the Ogres and their Alicorn."

"Oh," Hartigan wagged a finger at Chillybin and Magumpus, both of whom were *woof*ing with laughter again. "Oh, you pair of bally teases."

"THE MAN-APES ARE SIMPLE CREATURES," Magumpus shouted through the communication block, "BUT I HAVE … LOOK INTO THEIR MINDS … SEEN THE LANDSCAPE OF THEIR OLDEST STORIES … IT IS HARD TO EXPLAIN."

"Aki'Drednanth keep saying that," Hartigan said dryly to Galana. "Anyone would think we're not equipped to deal with the idea of mind-reading reincarnating ice monsters from the dawn o' time."

"THE OGRES WAS HERE," Magumpus went on. "TWO OF THEM. THEY CAME HERE … I THINK WITH SOME OTHER AKI'DREDNANTH … THEY WAS HELPING THE OGRES TO LEAVE SIX SPECIES SPACE. THEY LIVE HERE WITH THE MAN-APES FOR A TIME. WE DON'T KNOW WHEN THIS WAS. BACK WHEN CHARAD'CHAI WAS PRETTY PRIMITIVE PROBABLY."

"I do find it hard to believe that Ogres would come through here and allow the Man-Apes to remain enslaved, so it must have been before the Charad'chai made such a foolish decision," Galana agreed. "By all reports, the Ogres were not placid creatures."

"Didn't Magumpus say there were only two of them, though?" Bonty asked.

"That's one more than would have been needed to thoroughly trample the Charad'chai," Galana replied.

"THEY WAS HERE, BUT THE MAN-APES DON'T REMEMBER GOOD," Magumpus yelled.

"They were here," Chillybin confirmed, "although it is hard to know when. It was before Magumpus came, before most of the Man-Apes here were born, maybe before their grandparents were born. It's hard to be sure, because ... well ... "

"Man-Apes don't remember good," Bonty said.

"And the Alicorn was with them?" Hartigan asked eagerly.

"It was here," Chillybin said. Magumpus nodded.

"It vanished from the Fleet's records four thousand years ago," Galana did her best to curb the Captain's enthusiasm. "It is not *impossible* – a Molran lifespan is longer – but for an animal to live so long ... "

"THE ALICORN HAS SOMETHING OF THE OGRES," Magumpus said. Her voice was still loud, but she seemed to be learning how to speak in 'Six Species' at an impressive rate. "IT IS A CREATURE OF GREAT AGE ... GREAT ... REJUVENATION, OF PERHAPS ENDLESS LIFE. IT WAS ... ACCIDENT," she turned to Chillybin with a growl, and they once again seemed to sink into a private and unspoken conversation.

While they waited, Galana and the others glanced around the room. The converted ship was gloomy and freezing, the Man-Apes apparently quite comfortable in the ice. One of them met Galana's eyes – at least she thought it did – then rolled over and crunched in the snow with a happy grunt. Freedom, and a bit of *proper* cold, seemed to agree with them.

"Unicorns were greatly prized," Chillybin explained, "by the Ogres and the Dragons, by all the great mythical beasts. And the *Alicorn* was, at first, the name given only to the magic of the unicorn, the essence. Its horn, in some cases. Even before the wingèd creature, the *idea* existed. But then, when that power was distilled whole into a single living thing ... only once in a million generations did a unicorn give birth to an Alicorn. Perhaps not even that often, to hear the oldest of the stories. It's not like you're going to get a horse with wings no matter how many times you breed horses together."

"I always wondered if maybe it was engineered," Galana said, although she knew from conversations with Basil that he didn't like this idea. "Created, in a laboratory."

"Now I am picturing a group of Ogres in a laboratory," Wicked Mary said. A couple of the Man-Apes nearby twitched and rumbled. It was probably strange, Galana reflected, for something that smelled like a piece of metal to suddenly talk.

Chilly grunted in amusement. "No, it was not made. And it is truly the last. The unicorns are all gone, it is said. They perished with Earth, if not before."

"But it's not here," Hartigan said, sounding a little disappointed but not surprised.

"No," Chillybin said. "They left, they moved on. The Man-Apes don't know where they went. We can't even say *when*. They were headed for the far side of the galaxy, though. Far away from the Earth."

"I was right," Hartigan said in triumph.

"There is a world," Chillybin said. "A dark place, cold. I see spires in the darkness. The Alicorn flies around them, wild and free. It is a dangerous world – or it is a safe world in the middle of a dangerous star system, or a dangerous empire. Its name is High Elonath."

"*High Elonath*," Hartigan said reverently.

"We will take our leave," Chillybin added.

"We will? I mean, we will," Hartigan snapped out of his daze, and smiled at Magumpus and the lounging Man-Apes. "Mags. Chaps. It was a pleasure to come down here and very briefly stretch our legs. Mmm, crisp," he added, and rubbed his hands together.

"Let's quit while we're ahead, Captain," Galana suggested.

"Excellent notion, young Fen," Hartigan agreed heartily.

"A moment," Chillybin said, and turned to lope back out of the chamber. This left Galana, Bonty, Wicked Mary and the Captain briefly and uncomfortably alone with the collection of shaggy beasts, but Chilly was thankfully not gone long enough for Basil to attempt small-talk. She returned with an insulated packing box, which she handed carefully to Magumpus. "A gift from our Chief Engineer, Devlin Scrutarius," she said, "and from me, and the rest of the crew of the ACS *Conch*."

"THANK YOU," Magumpus said with a jab at the communicator box, before putting the device down and taking the gift with both great black-clawed hands. "*Gronf*," she added, verbally.

"Yes," Chillybin replied.

Galana didn't ask. Good Molren did not question the aki'Drednanth.

"So what do we call this?" Hartigan asked as they were making their way back to the *Nella*. "A successful mission, surely. A fascinating look at a previously unknown branch of the big frosty icicle-hanging aki'Drednanth family tree, without a doubt. A valuable clue in the search for the Last Alicorn, oh yes indeed. A chance to give Magumpus a bally old mystery box, yes, that too … "

"Are you still worried that you haven't gotten to shoot anything with your shiny new gun yet?" Galana asked.

"I certainly wouldn't have wanted to test it on anyone still living on *this* planet," Hartigan said with a laugh.

"You see? I told you he was intelligent for a human," Galana said to Bonty.

"Cheeky," Basil retorted.

"Magumpus has let me in, and shared what she has learned and experienced here," Chillybin said. "The walls she has built will come down, in time. AstroCorps has done a great service to the aki'Drednanth this night. Although I understand if you find it hard to understand."

"Oh no, old girl, not at all," Hartigan stopped in the sand and waited for the *Nella* to unfold her boarding ramp. "If you say the aki'Drednanth owe us a favour, I don't have any follow-up questions at all."

"The aki'Drednanth don't *owe us* - " Galana said helplessly.

"Don't worry," Chillybin patted the top of Galana's head with her great cold paw, then climbed back into her suit. "We enjoy returning favours."

"Well *that* didn't sound ominous at all," Hartigan said.

Galana looked back from the top of the ramp. The door to Magumpus's refrigerated home was still standing open and the aki'Drednanth's silhouette was visible against the lights. Galana raised her upper left hand, and Magumpus raised a huge shaggy arm in response. Then she turned and vanished inside, and a moment later the light winked out as her door closed.

The darkness and silence of the world of the Man-Apes descended over the shuttle. Freeing mortals from slavery, Galana reflected, was apparently something aki'Drednanth made a bit of a habit of. Although why they continued to allow themselves to be enslaved by the Cancer was … well, it was just another thing a good Molran didn't question.

We enjoy returning favours, she thought with a little shiver, and stepped into the shuttle.

Soon, in **The Ship of Sharks**:

They'd gathered in the lower hold, which they all now called 'the Aquarium', to watch Wicked Mary hunt the squid.

The squid had, perhaps unfortunately, been given a nickname over the course of the year or so it had taken to grow to maturity. Devlin had named it 'Squirty Pete', because they'd grown it in a special tank upstairs and at about three months of age it had squirted ink all over him in an earnest attempt to escape during a feeding. The ink had taken a week to wash completely off his skin.

Bonty, tenderhearted to a fault, had refused to attend the event because she felt sorry for poor little Squirty Pete. Scrutarius had pointed out that 'poor little Squirty Pete' was now four times the length of a Molran and had tentacles capable of ripping Chillybin in half, and had been specially engineered to fight and ultimately be eaten by Fergunak, sort of dinner-and-a-show.

"After all," he'd said, "she doesn't exactly get out much, except using her *giela*."

In the interests of inter-species understanding and goodwill, Galana and the others had accepted Wicked Mary's invitation to watch the battle.

It was all over rather quickly. Squirty Pete was dropped into the Aquarium from a hatch-and-tanker they'd installed in Chillybin's refrigerated living quarters above – the so-called Icebox – and swam in a swift, shadowy circle around the Aquarium. It passed the window where Galana, Basil, Devlin and Chillybin stood watching, then whipped away in a long, pallid flash of tentacles. Wicked Mary, a grey torpedo encrusted in cybernetic interfaces, cruised past just behind. There was a churn in the water, a cloud of ink, and the next time Wicked Mary passed the window she was trailing tentacles from her mouth and sporting a row of nasty sucker-wounds along her side.

"The next one should grow a little longer before we fight," her voice came from the nearby speaker.

"It barely fitted in the tanker as it was," Scrutarius objected.

"Make a larger tanker."

Devlin's response was cut off by a polite chime from the *Conch*.

"All hands, return to the bridge," the computer advised. "There is an alien vessel approaching."

THE SHIP OF SHARKS

They hurried to the bridge.

"What have we got, old girl?" Hartigan asked as he dropped into the Captain / helm seat.

"Unknown dumbler craft, obviously Basil," the *Conch* replied. "But I have reason to believe they are in fact a known species. Specifically, Fergunak."

Galana looked sharply at her controls and readouts. "What makes you say that?"

"Three reasons," the *Conch* said. "First, the ship has an identical density and mass profile to large Fergunakil vessels. It reads as an object filled with *water*, rather than any of the usual gases the land-crawlers tend to breathe."

"It could be an aquatic alien species," Hartigan said.

"It could," the *Conch* agreed. "My second clue, however, was that as soon as we registered them on the scanners they moved into an *extremely specific* evasive circling pattern, just as Fergunakil vessels do in Six Species space when they're not part of a Fleet or AstroCorps group. Of course, this too could be a normal reaction of an aquatic species. They behave as they would in water."

"But your third clue … ?" Galana said.

"They have sent a high-density info-pulse," the *Conch* said, "which would have crippled most normal ship computers. I am a little tougher, if I do say so myself, but have pretended to be shut down nevertheless."

"Lull 'em into a false sense of security," Hartigan approved. "Good idea."

"They responded by attempting to infiltrate our systems," the *Conch* continued, "at which point - "

"At which point I contacted them," Wicked Mary's *giela* said from the tactical panel, "using a Fergunakil network code and a simplified transmitter. The sort we might be expected to use if our computer broke down and left us with emergency systems only."

"And?" Hartigan pressed.

"And they have responded," Wicked Mary said. "They are my kind."

"See, you could've just led with that," Scrutarius said.

"Where's the fun in that, Devlin?" the *Conch* replied.

"Alright," Hartigan said, "so Bloody Mary's taking the lead on the greetings this time, jolly good. I'll go and have a cup of tea."

"It's a little more complicated than that, Captain," Wicked Mary said. "I have been speaking with them for some time now, in computer terms. Seconds are like hours inside the network. I will summarise as efficiently as I can."

The Fergunakil ship was almost three miles long – quite the deep space beastie, as Hartigan noted – and home to a school of giant cybernetic sharks numbering almost five thousand. They called themselves the Searching, Starving, Lost, and they travelled the outer reaches of the galaxy without any known connection to other Fergunakil schools. They were searching for something, as the name suggested.

They were not Six Species Fergunak, but they weren't *Core* Fergunak either. Those were the only two branches of the species anyone really knew about, but evidently the Fergies that had joined the Molran Fleet hadn't been the only ones in the galaxy to break free of the Damorakind. The Searching, Starving, Lost were of the opinion that they had never *been* enslaved, and that the Fergunak in the Core weren't enslaved either. But it was difficult to be sure. Wicked Mary and the Searching, Starving, Lost were as different as two sets of giant cybernetic sharks could be.

"They attack worlds and ships they encounter, and feed from them," she said. "They would have done the same to us, except … well … "

"They won't eat one of their own?" Hartigan said. "No," he added immediately as Bonty, Galana, Devlin and Chillybin turned to stare at him, "even as I said it out loud, I knew that sounded wrong."

"They would devour us in minutes if they realised I was travelling alone," Wicked Mary said.

"Steady on, you're not *alone*," Hartigan objected.

"By Fergunakil standards she is," Bonty disagreed. "Air-breathers don't count."

"Quite right," Wicked Mary said. "With the help of the computer, that they still think is shut down, I have managed to trick the Searching, Starving, Lost into thinking my habitat is tightly packed with Fergunak. The rest of the ship's air pockets and life-signs are … our food supply."

Devlin grinned and stroked his silver AstroCorps uniform. "In individual foil-wrapped portions," he said.

Wicked Mary's *giela* inclined its head. "We currently read as two hundred and forty Fergunak, and our little farm of land-crawler food rations," she confirmed.

"I do believe I'm offended," Hartigan declared.

"I'd much rather be offended than eaten," Bonty said.

"Yes alright, good point there," Hartigan admitted.

"We still could be eaten," Wicked Mary warned. "Two hundred and forty Fergunak in a ship this small will not be seen as a threat, and may in fact be seen as a snack."

"The Aquarium would never hold two hundred and forty Fergies," Galana said. "And how are we faking that many life-signs anyway? We don't have that many living things on board, even counting Wicked Mary's supply of fish - "

"Never mind that right now," Scrutarius said a little too quickly for Galana's liking. "How are we going to stop the Searching, Starving, Lost from making a very brief meal of us?"

"Simple," Bonty said. "We can't do anything about the *Starving* bit, but if we can help them find what they're *Searching* for, or the place from which they're *Lost*, we'll become part of their school. Or, you know," she added in the silence, "the pretend Fergies in the Aquarium will. *We'll* continue being the pretend Fergies' lunch."

"The delicious doctor is right," Wicked Mary said.

"About the lunch?" Hartigan asked.

"About the name of the school," Wicked Mary replied. "The Searching, Starving, Lost are on a quest. Something of a sacred one – perhaps even holy, if I were to put it in terms you would understand. I do not fully understand it myself, because their network and archives are so unusual."

"Crusaders," Scrutarius said. "You're talking about crusaders. Cybernetically enhanced giant space shark crusaders."

"Those are the worst type of crusaders," Hartigan mourned.

"They seek something," Wicked Mary continued. "An … orb."

"An *orb*?" Galana echoed, suddenly feeling cold and unsettled. She'd never thought of the Fergunak as having mythology, or beliefs. A school of Fergunak on a *quest* was … wrong. Profoundly wrong.

As they spoke, the Searching, Starving, Lost ship appeared on their screens.

Still circling at a distance, but growing steadily closer, the ship was a long, rounded tube of dull grey metal. It looked a lot like Fergie ships Galana was familiar with, but she admitted to herself that could just be a matter of her brain making the connection, knowing what was inside the vessel. Its hull was battered and encrusted with sensors and transmitters and weapons, and it was impossible to tell which was which.

"They have not explained what the orb might be," Wicked Mary said. "They began long ago, when our kind first went out among the stars."

"Look here old girl, I thought your kind first went out among the stars when the Cancer invaded your world and bally well made you part of their spaceships' computer systems," Hartigan said. "No offence."

"This is not what the Searching, Starving, Lost believe," Wicked Mary said. "Their first alpha – their first leader, many generations ago – was … a prophet. She saw things, saw a great destiny for the Fergunak. This relic, this thing that they call the Orb of Nnal, is of ultimate importance - "

"Tactical Officer Mary," Galana said, as the coldness inside her solidified to a block of ice, "are you going to join the Searching, Starving, Lost on their quest for this 'Orb of Nnal', or continue with us?"

"Why, little flesh," Wicked Mary said silkily. "The very *question*."

Galana and Basil exchanged a glance.

Wicked Mary had attempted, in an affectionate playful way, to take over the ship a couple of times in the course of their journey. On one particularly long jag through soft-space, indeed, they'd found that she had secretly constructed a pair of crude secondary *giela* and they were slowly converting one of the lesser-used maintenance decks in preparation for filling it with water. Her crewmates had stopped her and dismantled the robots. It was simply one of the perils of travelling with Fergies.

So far, however, the unusual complexity and subtlety of the *Conch*'s computer had prevented her from actually converting the ship and its crew into her own personal flying lunchbox. And the truth was, she really didn't try to eat them anywhere near as often or as seriously as most Fergunak. She only seemed to be going through the motions. Which was strange, but that was part of the reason she'd been perfect for the mission.

"I rather suspect," Hartigan said, "that you might think about joining them, if you had better control over things here."

"Maybe," the *giela* said, then pointed at Chillybin. "Of course, our Comms Officer also makes it difficult."

"They are a little different to the ones we get back home, but they are still Fergunak," Chillybin remarked. "If they attack, I am familiar enough with their mental construction that I could target them quite effectively."

"I have not told the Searching, Starving, Lost this," Wicked Mary added. Galana thought better of asking how they could be sure of *what* she'd told the circling ship, and was relieved nobody else asked either.

"They have switched off the computer-scrambling signal," the *Conch* told them, "but that may simply be because it has done its job. Or it would have, to a lesser computer."

"Good," Hartigan said. "Keep yourself pretend-broken for the moment. I've often found that the way people treat someone when they think they're helpless gives a much more honest view of what they're really like."

"I have to say I'm not sure that is a valid approach to dealing with sharks, Captain," Bonty suggested.

"It is *completely* valid," Wicked Mary remarked. "Just do not be surprised when you get eaten."

"I'm glad *she* said it," Scrutarius said in a low voice.

They watched for a few more seconds. The Fergunakil ship swam silently closer through the darkness.

"Alright," Hartigan went on, "so where does this leave us? Helping the Searching, Starving, Lost with their Searching and their Lostness is all very well, but can we even help them find the Orb of What Have You?"

"No, Captain," Wicked Mary said, "because we have no idea what it is or where it might be found."

"See, that's what I thought – and most tragic of all, that really leaves us nothing to help them with but their Starving problem," Hartigan noted. He looked across at Galana. "What's on your mind, Fen?"

"They've never met an aki'Drednanth before, yes?" she asked. Wicked Mary's *giela* nodded. "And they think our computer is shut down. These are two fairly big advantages."

"They also think there's two hundred and forty of us," Hartigan added.

"Incorrect, Captain – they think there's two hundred and forty *Fergunak*," Galana said, "and some air-breathing livestock. They will be prepared to deal with us on Wicked Mary's terms – and their own. Our thought processes are very different - "

"Yeah, for a start our thought processes are about ten thousand times slower than theirs," Scrutarius said.

"Speak for yourself, Able Belowdecksman," the *Conch* said primly.

Devlin pointed at the screens. "They're moving."

The Searching, Starving, Lost vessel moved ponderously in towards the *Conch*, dwarfing the tiny ship. It rolled to reveal a great, gaping black hole in its underside, which was hard to picture as anything but a mouth. Fragments of ice floated from the maw and twinkled in the *Conch*'s lights.

"I can back us off," Hartigan said, "but that will reveal that we can see them – and that we can control our engines. Recommendations?"

"Wait," Galana said. She was thinking furiously. *They are crusaders on a sacred quest. Searching for a relic. Even if there were two hundred and forty Fergunak on board our ship, it would not be enough to feed five thousand of them. So what do they want? What happens when two schools of Fergunak meet each other?*

"They will seal us inside and fill the chamber with water," Wicked Mary said, as though reading Galana's thoughts.

"What will that do to the ship?" Bonty asked.

"What do you *think* it will do?" Scrutarius snapped. "The *Conch* is a *starship*, not a submarine. The *Nella* is built to shuttle specs so she can land on a variety of planets, but even she's not exactly high-pressure adapted. We might be okay up here but we're far more likely to just be crushed."

"That *is* the point of the manoeuvre," Wicked Mary agreed. "They may not be hostile, even now," she added, as the enormous ship rolled towards them. "They may just be … combining our efforts, making us allies in this quest."

"Relative speed?" Hartigan asked.

Galana shook her head. "We're too close. And we wouldn't have time to open out the rings and initiate the field now anyway."

"Guns?"

"Always," Wicked Mary replied. "Of course, that may also give away that our computer is still working. Even if we pretend to fire blind, we are still admitting that we can see something – or that something is happening that we don't like."

"Do we care at this point?" Scrutarius asked. "Something *is* happening that we don't like!"

"*Wait*," Galana said again. "Chilly, how many *minds* are you detecting over there? Not life-signs, actual conscious minds. Are you able to pick them out yet?"

"Hundreds," Chillybin said, "but not thousands, I think."

"What - " Hartigan frowned.

"They're faking how many they are as well," Galana said. "It's a big ship, but it's not full. Our scans are always a bit dodgy with Fergie ships, we adjust for all the living food they have but there's still plenty of room to be tricked," *especially if the Fergie network is helping to trick us*, she added in her mind, before going on out loud. "The Searching, Starving, Lost just don't have a handy mind-reading crewmember to find out how much we're exaggerating by," she turned to Wicked Mary. "This is a normal meeting between two schools. You will fight to figure out which school is dominant."

"Hang on," Hartigan said helplessly.

"Yes, Commander," Wicked Mary said calmly. "The *Conch* and I have been ready for some time."

"Oh good," Hartigan said. "Should I get that tea?"

The Searching, Starving, Lost ship rolled over them, and at the same moment the *Conch* burst into action. The ship spun, fired her pulse turrets in a blinding fusillade against the inside of the enemy ship's hold, and added a perfectly-timed blast with her subluminal engines. Galana winced as she felt the grinding of hull plates and the crash-and-rattle of ice as the Searching, Starving, Lost vented the Fergie equivalent of atmosphere – water – in great freezing sheets over the *Conch*'s exterior.

They crashed back out into space in a spreading flower of ice crystals, and Wicked Mary immediately turned the ship and fired a second barrage from the turrets, this time all focussed on a single point of the Searching, Starving, Lost's hull. There was another pale bloom of freezing water, and the massive ship was rolling away and surging forward to put as much distance between them as possible.

"Pursue," Wicked Mary said.

"Now hang on just a bally second," Hartigan said.

"The fight is not over," Wicked Mary's *giela* purred.

Hartigan spluttered. "We're a peaceful - "

"Captain," Galana said, "this *is* a peaceful meeting between Fergunak."

"She's right, Captain," Bonty agreed. "Breaking away from the fight now would be a sign of some unseen weakness. The Searching, Starving, Lost would turn and attack, and we will not be able to catch them by surprise a second time."

"And we took some hull damage," Scrutarius added. "Even if we could get the rings rolled out, we can't establish a relative field yet. Our best bet is to end the fight decisively."

"Alright," Hartigan said, "Bloody Mary, take us – oh, you already are. Jolly good then, I'll just sit here."

The Searching, Starving, Lost ship, with its pretty trailing plumes of ice crystals, expanded in the viewscreens again as Wicked Mary and the *Conch*'s computer rounded on them and attacked again. Now a pair of half-mile-long glowing devices on the sides of the Fergunakil ship were lighting up. They weren't weapons, thankfully – they seemed to be either engines or the Searching, Starving, Lost version of a relative drive. Either way, the ship began to speed up … until a shot from the rail cannon slung under the *Conch*'s belly darkened one of the devices and the huge ship rolled sideways.

"They are disabled," Wicked Mary said, "but the damage can still be repaired."

"Good," Hartigan said, "now maybe we can - "

The ship and stars in the viewscreens rolled and spun as the *Conch* spiralled out of the way and a brilliant beam of energy fired from another of the enemy ship's devices. Wicked Mary fired another swift volley from the turrets, and the Searching, Starving, Lost guns flew apart.

"They are disabled, and the damage can *probably* still be repaired," Wicked Mary amended. "They may need to rebuild some parts from scratch, though."

"I'm pulling us back into the dark a bit," Hartigan cleared his throat. "So," he went on. "Dev, how long until we can get the relative drive back online?"

"Couple of hours," Scrutarius said.

They sat looking out at the Searching, Starving, Lost ship in its cloud of ice fragments.

"This is awkward," Bonty noted.

"Under normal circumstances, we would fly over and strip them down for parts and food," Wicked Mary said conversationally. "But I suppose we should do this the AstroCorps way."

"If we do this the AstroCorps way, what's going to stop them chasing our stupid noble backsides the rest of the way around the galaxy?" Scrutarius added.

"Chilly," Galana said, "do you think you can get the epiphany to work on Fergies?"

"The what?" Hartigan asked.

"I think I can," Chillybin said with a rumble of amusement deep in her suit. "Given a little time to fine-tune it."

"We have a couple of hours before we can leave," Galana said. "Is that long enough?"

"It should be plenty."

"I say, look here Commander Fen, Comms Officer Chillybin," Hartigan said, but the bristle in his moustache was decidedly good-humoured. "What is this *epiphany* you're jabbering on about?"

"It was a … prank … Chillybin once played on our mentor, Parakta Tar," Galana said. "She gave Parakta a feeling that she had reached a profound understanding of the universe, and her place in it. Changing her life, perhaps forever. It was not actually a lasting feeling, but it was enough to make her … re-evaluate."

"This will be much more powerful," Chillybin said.

"I'm not sure what I'm more shocked by," Scrutarius declared. "An aki'Drednanth playing a life-changing trick on someone's brain, or a Molran calling it a *prank*."

"Shouldn't you be repairing the relative toruses?" Galana asked him.

"I'm going, I'm going," Devlin said, and shook his head. "All this time, and you had a prank this magnificent under your big old freezer-belt," he chuckled, and strolled out.

"The Fergunak of the Searching, Starving, Lost are making repairs," Chillybin said, "but I will begin working the epiphany into their minds. They will slow down as it takes hold, and they begin to process it into their worldview."

Galana turned to Wicked Mary. "Can you let them find out there's only one of you?" she asked.

"I think the *Conch* and I can roll back the false life readings," Wicked Mary said. "But why?"

"Yes, what happened to 'they would devour us in minutes'?" Bonty asked nervously.

"I rather think devouring us in minutes is off the table," Hartigan pointed out.

"They are on a sacred quest, handed down to them by an alpha, a *lone visionary*," Galana explained. "When the epiphany hits them, it will travel along the mental pathways they already have in place. It will provide them with a strong feeling that their quest has reached a critical point, and even as it fades they will continue as though we had been a – a signpost, rather than an enemy that they need to make a detour and hunt down. Finding out that Wicked Mary is travelling alone will make this feeling even stronger."

"You don't think there's a risk involved in … y'know, giving Fergunak crusaders any 'strong feelings' one way or another?" Hartigan asked.

"The alternatives seem to be allowing them to continue to harass us," Galana said, "or destroying them outright. This way we continue our mission, and the search for the Orb of Nnal goes on."

The repairs were completed in good time, and there was no further contact from the Fergunak of the Searching, Starving, Lost school. None that Wicked Mary was telling them about, anyway. The little robot seemed thoughtful – if you could say such a thing about a machine with a cluster of cameras and sensors for a face – as they prepared to resume their journey.

"I hope they find what they seek," Wicked Mary said. "And … in a strange way, we have joined their quest. They shared their myths of the Orb of Nnal, the words of the mystical alpha who first spoke of it. If we should find this object on our travels, then we shall claim it on behalf of the Fergunak of AstroCorps and the Six Species."

"So in a way, this really was a peaceful encounter," Bonty said brightly.

"Yes. Yes it was," Devlin said flatly. "Now let us never speak of it again."

The *Conch* unfurled her torus rings and started the cumulative relative field buildup. On Scrutarius's advice, they did so in slow, easy stages just in case there was additional damage from their 'peaceful encounter' with the Searching, Starving, Lost.

Hartigan chuckled. "Epiphany, eh?" he laughed again and shook his head. "I had no idea."

"The epiphany is not a difficult trick to pull," Chillybin said. "All intelligent minds search for meaning. They tell themselves stories about their existence and their purpose and the grand scheme of their lives within which everything makes sense. It does not take much effort to whisper 'the story is true'. The mind *wants* to be tricked."

"Just as well *our* lives actually *do* have purpose, what?" Hartigan said cheerfully.

"Indeed, Captain."

The ACS *Conch* dived back into the grey.

Soon, in <u>The Star Serpent</u>:

After spotting a likely-looking planet on the long-range sensors, the crew of the *Conch* had agreed it was worth flying by to see if it was home to any intelligent life.

The problem, as always when looking at star systems from a long way off, was that you were looking at them as they had been a long time ago – in this case a hundred years or more – and there was no knowing what you might find when you popped into orbit above them after a few days at ten thousand times the speed of light. It was like a strange kind of time travel, from the distant past you could see from a distance to the here-and-now you arrived at shortly afterwards.

As it happened, what they found was that the entire planet – and half of the other planets in the system – had been burned to a cinder in the hundred-odd years they'd just relative-hopped across.

Captain Hartigan whistled. "What in the name of Old Linda's Handbag happened here then?"

"The destruction is total," Bonjamin reported from the science station. "If there was any life on this planet – or any water, or biological material at all – it has been burned off. Quite literally scattered into interplanetary space."

"And the other planets," Galana said, "or these four, at least … " she tapped her controls and showed four more black, burned-up planets in various positions around the solar system. "None of them had read as habitable in our scans, and this one was actually a gas giant," she pointed at one of the ruins. "But they are just as scorched."

"Solar storm?" Scrutarius guessed.

Galana shook her head. "Not from *this* system's sun. Anything ferocious enough to do this sort of damage in the past hundred years would still be showing up in the sun's output."

"Most natural disasters that would do this sort of damage to planets would also push them out of orbit," Wicked Mary added. "This is an anomaly."

"Alright, it's an anomaly. So when in the past hundred years did this anomaly happen?" Hartigan asked.

"Easy enough to figure out, Captain," Galana replied, "since as Wicked Mary said, the event doesn't seem to have destabilised any of the planets' orbits. If we plot the speeds all of the burned planets are moving at, we should be able to find a point in the past hundred years at which the planets were all lined up but the *other* planets in the system were elsewhere, so a … whatever-it-was … could pass through and burn *these* five planets but leave the others untouched … "

"That all sounds bally complicated," Hartigan said. "Maybe the *Conch* - "

"It happened twenty-eight years, six months and eleven days ago, Captain," Galana tapped her console again, and the solar system map superimposed itself over the scene of devastation below them. "Although by this particular planet's solar year, it was almost forty years and - "

"Yes alright, jolly good," Hartigan grumbled. "But that doesn't tell us what whatever-it-was *was*, now does it?"

"No," Galana said, "but making a relative-speed jump out to a distance of twenty-eight-and-a-half light years, and then *watching*, ought to give us a good idea."

Hartigan favoured Galana with a dirty look, but grunted and began entering jump coordinates. "Alright," he said, "but we're heading twenty-eight-and-a-half light years *onwards*, along our *route*, and there won't be any back-tracking. So get whatever sciencey-type readings and samples you want now."

"I would like some sciencey-type data on the mass and energy and gravitational baselines in this system before we go," Wicked Mary said.

"Sending out a sciencey-type probe," Bonty said brightly.

"And let's have a little less lip from everyone," Hartigan announced.

"Basil, there is a ship approaching," the *Conch* said.

"What?" Hartigan leaned forward. "Where?"

Then, with startling abruptness, the ship was hanging in front of them. Bright red and outlined with highlights of gleaming gold, it was very small – only about the size of the *Nella*-section when she was detached – and had appeared so quickly that Galana suspected it had crash-jumped into the area through soft-space from wherever the *Conch* had first spotted it.

"They are sending us a very compact little translation program," the *Conch* reported. "I'm just unpacking it, and sending them a language package of my own," the computer paused. "Their technology is … quite impressive."

A moment later, the strange little ship's pilot appeared on their screens. When it spoke, it was in amusingly-accented variant of the Grand Bo that they commonly spoke on the *Conch*, out of consideration for their Captain. It sounded, in fact, very much like him.

"Ahoy there, unidentified vessel!"

The alien was a strange creature. Its face was lightly furred and canine, striped in white and pale amber, with a delicate pointed muzzle filled with sharp teeth. One of them – the elongated front left fang, Galana noted – gleamed metallic gold. Its uniform, if it was a uniform, was rich and highly-decorated, coloured the same red and gold as its ship.

The alien's ears were huge and flared and rose to points on either side of its head, too big to be comical, too big to be anything but impressive. They were like great triangular radar dishes lined with white fur.

"Bit on the nose with the voice, aren't we old girl?" Hartigan grumbled.

"I am not providing a translation, Basil," the *Conch* protested. "The dumbler appears to have learned Grand Bo and is able to speak it uncannily well, unless it has an integrated translator - "

"I say, ahoy there!"

Captain Hartigan tapped his controls. "Ahoy there yourself," he said with a helpless laugh. "We come in peace."

"I'm very glad to hear it!" the alien declared. "Why, I was worried I'd have to blast you to pieces!"

THE STAR SERPENT

The alien vessel, the name of which translated as the *Splendiferous Bastard*, docked with the *Conch* on Captain Hartigan's invitation. The pilot, who was apparently travelling alone, came aboard shortly thereafter.

She was, from the soles of her shiny red boots to the tips of her enormous triangular ears, little more than knee-high to Galana, and little less than waist-high to Captain Hartigan. She stood on the docking threshold with her amber-furred fists planted on her hips, peering up at the looming Six Species representatives with a bright, inquisitive look in her inky black eyes and an incessant twitching of her furry, whiskery white muzzle. Behind her, emerging from her gaudy red-and-gold costume, a tail swished lazily back and forth. It was large and bushy and pale orange, tapering to a black tip.

"Lovely to meet you! I say, are you all this big?"

Galana and Bonty exchanged a grin over the top of Hartigan's head. It really *wasn't* the computer being funny. The similarity between the two ship Captains, for all their differences in appearance, was uncanny.

"Chillybin is a little bit smaller than she looks, inside the suit," Scrutarius offered, pointing at their enormous Comms Officer. "Wicked Mary actually quite a lot bigger," he pointed another hand at the *giela*, which was still about twice the dumbler's height. "That's just an interactive robot."

They made their introductions. Their guest declared herself to be Judderone Pelsworthy of the Boze, Space Adventurer. 'Boze' seemed to be her species, although she didn't provide them with much detail. Judderone – "but you can call me Roney" – was apparently the last of her kind, and had been alone forever and ever.

"I am the last Boze of the Empire of Gold," she declared grandly, striking a pose that should have looked amusing with her tail and her uniform and her huge ears, but somehow managed to look noble and inspiring. "Fallen and lost now for twenty million years. Ah, but at its height, it was the jewel of the Void."

"Are you … twenty million years, are you that old?" Hartigan asked in a hushed voice.

Roney tilted her head at him. "No," she said, "that would be silly."

"Oh. It's just that – well, you said - "

"No, no, the Empire is long gone. Nothing left, just darkness and horrors. Depressing," she waved a furry hand. "Nobody remembers it as it was."

"The Empire of Gold," Chillybin stirred. "Our elders know of this place. It did indeed fall many years ago. It is said that the Riddlespawn burned it."

"Aha!" Roney said eagerly. "Your elders are absolutely right. I think the universe has put us in one another's path, my friends. We have much to discuss."

"Let's go to my quarters," Hartigan suggested, "have a bite to eat and exchange notes, what?"

"Excellent notion, Captain Hartigan!"

Chattering happily and almost indistinguishably together, the two little mammals led the way into the ship. Galana and Bonjamin exchanged another glance and smile then followed, Devlin and Chilly and Wicked Mary in tow.

"Which of them do you think would be more offended by the comparison?" Devlin asked from behind them, in a whisper quiet enough only Molranoid ears could pick it up.

Molranoid, and apparently Boze. Roney's great furred ears swivelled, and she turned to glance briefly over her shoulder and tail at them. Her gold tooth gleamed as she grinned. She'd definitely heard, Galana judged. Whether she'd understood or not – Scrutarius had spoken in the language of the Molran Fleet, and Pelsworthy *couldn't* have programmed that into her translator in the time since their first communications – well, that was another matter.

They ascended to the Captain's rooms, settled on their usual couches, and Hartigan busied himself preparing nibbles and drinks. Bonty expressed brief concern for Roney's safety, and asked if she wanted a quick chem analysis to make sure her digestion and body-size could handle the rations. Roney waved this off with a laugh, saying that she could take three times what they could no matter how big they were, and do it while reciting the Empire of Gold's thousand-verse poetic epic to boot.

"So … this solar system we're in right now wasn't the Empire of Gold, I take it?" Hartigan asked once they were settled.

Roney glanced from Galana to Hartigan, then back to Galana again.

"He's not too bright, eh?" she asked good-humouredly – in the standard

Fleet language that the Molran, Blaran, Bonshoon, aki'Drednanth and Fergunakil talked, but the human didn't understand much of.

"Hang about, you can speak – am I the only poor bugger who *can't* speak the ol' Fleet jibber-jabber?" Hartigan complained. Galana spread her lower hands helplessly.

"Your computer sent me a basic package, including the ol' Fleet jibber-jabber," Roney said, switching back to Grand Bo and examining her tiny black claws modestly. "I have a bit of a knack for languages. It helps with the whole Space Adventurer thing."

"Never had much luck learning other languages, me," Hartigan admitted. "I've always found that just talking slower and louder gets the job done. It's the Grand Boënne way, don't y'know."

"It's a valid method," the little Boze conceded, and crunched on one of the spiced red ration wafers Galana favoured. Hartigan watched her carefully, but she showed no sign of discomfort. "No, Captain. This system was called - " here she stopped, and trilled a high, sweet, musical note. "Not sure how you'd translate it. *The Stone, The Waves, The Love Of Sky And Sun.* Something like that. Lovely place, lovely people. Primitive – what is it you call them? Dumblers? – yes, dumbler-folk, but very pleasant. Their world was destroyed by the same frightful beastie that destroyed the Empire of Gold. I thought I'd run it to ground. Turns out I was chasing my own tail."

"And a handsome tail it is," Hartigan said. "So this … these planets were burned by – what did you call them, Chilly? The Riddlespawn?"

Chillybin had removed her helmet to enjoy some frosty aki'Drednanth rations and steaming-cold drinks, and Roney was watching her with *great* interest.

"Yes," Chillybin said. "I do not know much more."

"Nobody does," Roney declared. "The Riddlespawn are all *long* gone. They're as much a myth as the old Empire itself. But this," she gestured to the ceiling dome, which Hartigan had opened to give them a bleak view of the burned planet they were orbiting, "this was done by a star serpent, and the storm it rides in."

"I'm not sure I understand," Galana admitted.

"We're none of us too bright," Devlin explained with a grin.

Roney flashed her gold tooth at him. "Perfectly understandable," she said. "I've been chasing this beastie for many a year, but this is all new to you biggums. And I haven't even asked where you're from and where you're headed," instead of asking, however, she leaned forward and snagged another spicy wafer. "The star serpent," she said, "is a *weapon*. A *relic*. A living warhead left behind by the Riddlespawn when they'd finished their work and went back to whatever nether-Hell they'd been summoned from. It's been wandering through space for twenty million years in the middle of its own personal firestorm half a billion miles across, and every time it gets bored it swoops through a solar system and burns everything it touches," she picked up the glass of whiskey Hartigan had poured for her. "And I mean to *end* it," she concluded, and drank decisively. "This plant juice is very tasty," she added, and waved her empty glass.

"We were planning on flying back out and seeing if we could witness the disaster," Galana suggested, and refilled Roney's drink while Hartigan was struggling to come to terms with the Boze calling his whiskey 'plant juice'. "Perhaps learn something about it."

"Mm, using the whole time-lag effect?" Roney shook her head. "Good idea, but it won't work. You think if they could see this thing coming, people wouldn't get out of the way?"

"You said the native species here were dumblers - " Scrutarius said.

"*Here*, certainly," Roney said with a flick of her ears. "Not everywhere. No, this beastie comes out of the grey, and doesn't show up on any kind of normal sensors. You'd be able to watch these worlds burn up, but that's about all you'd see. The poor buggers who lived here never saw what killed them," she said moodily. "Or if they did see it, it wasn't for very long."

"So how are you going to ... end it?" Bonty asked hesitantly. "If you can't find it - "

"Oh, I can *find* it," Roney said. "I've tracked it this far. The *Splendiferous Bastard* has some downright strange devices hooked into her. As for ending it ... well," she grinned again. "It's a big beastie, to be sure, but it's still a beastie. I've knocked the odd scale off its snout in my time."

"Scales – wait, so this is an actual physical creature, with a ... solar-system-consuming firestorm ... around it?" Galana asked. She'd been wondering if maybe the whole thing was a metaphor, or a miscommunication. Roney nodded quite seriously. "Maybe if we analysed the scales, we could collect some data," she said doubtfully, "find some weakness. Did you happen to bring any of them aboard with you?"

Roney laughed. "Dear me," she said. "No. You saw the *Bastard*, hm? Fetching red ship I docked in?" Galana nodded. "That's *one scale*," she said. "Or actually a fragment of one. Carved out and converted into hull plating."

Galana looked at Captain Hartigan, who frowned.

"That's a ... big beastie," he said.

Galana became aware that Wicked Mary's *giela* was standing very still on the edge of their circle of couches. For a moment it looked as though the little robot was switched off but Galana thought back, and realised that it had gone still the moment Roney had told them the star serpent was a weapon.

"Tactical Officer Mary?" Galana asked.

Roney, too, had noticed the Fergunakil's silence. "Maybe your Tactical Officer has an idea?" she suggested.

Wicked Mary stirred.

"This creature you speak of is a formidable weapon, tiny morsel," she said. "Did you say it travelled through soft-space?"

"I think it *lives* there," Roney said. "Coming out to feed. Or kill. Or maybe they're the same thing, to the serpent."

"I have some weapons designs you might be interested in," she said. "They are just creative exercises, but they involve drawing a large vessel out of soft-space and then accelerating it *back* to relative speed in several different directions at once – essentially dismantling it at ten thousand times the speed of light and scattering its pieces - "

"You're doing 'creative exercises' about trapping 'large vessels' and dismantling them?" Galana asked. "*How* large, exactly?"

"Well, not as large as this star serpent, perhaps," Wicked Mary said, "but perhaps the same principle applies. And if it is a weapon in the form of a *creature*, all we may need to do is remove its head."

"*All* we may need to do, eh?" Hartigan said. Roney looked thoughtful.

"Would you say your creative exercises involved vessels about the size of, oh, say, Fleet Worldships?" Galana asked.

"Well, they *are* the largest ships we know of," Wicked Mary said. "It made sense."

"I say, do you have any idea where this beastie is going to show its ugly snout next?" Hartigan asked.

"Certainly," Roney said, and looked up at Wicked Mary. "Do you really think you can draw it out and tear it to pieces?"

"Oh, trust me on this, Captain Pelsworthy," Hartigan said. "If anyone can do it, it's our Bloody Mary."

Roney jumped to her feet. "By Bozanda, we'll do it!"

The irrepressible Space Adventurer returned to her ship and sent them a set of complete and utter gibberish that she insisted were coordinates to a region the star serpent was going to pass through on its relative speed stalking of deep space. Then, after she'd spent an hour or so impatiently explaining the convoluted Boze coordinate system to the *Conch*'s computer, they managed to translate them into AstroCorps figures.

"I didn't realise the first row of variables were for universes," the *Conch* explained. "I thought, since there was only *one universe*, it was an unnecessary thing to specify."

Roney just laughed indulgently at this.

"It'll take us almost three months to reach this volume," Hartigan said, tapping at his console. "At least it's more or less on our path though."

"I can use the time to bring my theories into a more practical form," Wicked Mary said.

This, according to Roney, was unacceptable.

"The star serpent will have passed through by then," she said over the comm. "We've got a week. Will that be enough time to figure out your weapon?"

"I ... doubt it, tiny morsel," Wicked Mary said.

"Well, we can wait for it at the next spot," Roney said, and sent them another set of coordinates. "It'll be there in just over one month by your calendar. Is *that* long enough?"

"That should suffice."

"Look here, this volume will take us more than a *year* to get to," Hartigan said in exasperation. "It's on our path, but - "

"How *slow* is your ship?" Roney exclaimed.

"She's fast enough," Scrutarius said defensively.

"Perhaps the *Splendiferous Bastard* is faster," Galana suggested, remembering the way the Boze ship had appeared before them. "If we can find a way of merging our relative fields - "

"Oh, no time for all that messing around," Roney said. "I'll just give you a lift. Are we ready?"

Before any of them could answer, the stars and darkness outside the ship washed out into grey and they were at relative speed.

"We're not even docked together," Scrutarius said fearfully. "How did she do that?"

Hartigan glanced at Galana, who shrugged.

"You'd have to ask her," she said. "It seems the Boze have a higher level of relative speed technology than the Six Species."

"That's not saying much," Roney chortled unexpectedly over the comms system. "I've met *ponterflanges* with a higher level of relative speed technology than you lot."

"What's a ponterflange?" Hartigan asked from the corner of his mouth. Roney just laughed. "Infuriating creature," he said, but he was smiling.

The grey outside seemed no different to any normal stretch in softspace, despite the fact that there was a bright red and gold-highlighted ship floating inexplicably alongside them and they were apparently moving faster than any vessel in Six Species history. Scrutarius was maddened by the potential of the *Splendiferous Bastard*, but had absolutely no luck getting information out of Captain Pelsworthy.

"If the Infinites had wanted you to get from place to place faster, They would have introduced you to the Boze before now," was all she'd say. Galana couldn't fault the Space Adventurer – the Six Species had strict rules of their own about sharing potentially dangerous technology with less advanced cultures.

To balance the score a little, Wicked Mary clearly baffled and frustrated Roney with her weapon planning. The crew of the *Conch*, familiar with the Fergunak and their strange ways – not to mention the secret and terrible craft of AstroCorps Special Weapons Division, the so-called Monsters –

knew better than to even ask what she was doing. Roney was evidently *itching* to know, but had to be satisfied with the Fergie's vague explanations, creepily delivered.

The volume of space into which Roney eventually dropped them about a month later was dark and empty.

"Now, as you know, something flying through soft-space isn't really going to *pass through* the space in between where it starts and where it finishes up," the Space Adventurer explained. "That's just a simplified way of picturing something getting from one place to another, drawing a straight line in between. Or a sort of curved line, but let's not overcomplicate things."

"No, let's not," Hartigan agreed.

"Still, there are points like this where you can almost see the ripple of things passing through the grey," Roney went on, "and if I've understood Bloody Mary's theory, there are energy types which can collapse a relative field and bring things back into real space. Fast I might be, but I have to admit I've never tried anything like that."

"Relative field suppression is a very old aspect of Six Species technology," Scrutarius said.

"Why am I not surprised," the Boze drawled. "Your entire civilisation seems to be designed around getting nowhere as slowly as possible. But in this case," she went on while Hartigan's moustache bristled and Devlin's nostrils pinched, "your dreadful slowness may be just what we need."

"I did not have the equipment or energy generation capacity to make a proper suppressor," Wicked Mary said, "but from what little I have seen of your ship's capabilities, I think you will be able to provide the energy to the web. We will detect the star serpent passing through, and you will send the pulse that will bring it out of soft-space."

"And then, by jingo, we'll have it," Hartigan slapped his armrest.

"By jingo," Roney agreed.

"And at this point, I understand we will also be engulfed in a planet-stripping firestorm some hundreds of millions of miles across?" Galana asked.

"Well, the *Splendiferous Bastard* is made out of the serpent's scales," Bonty pointed out. "Roney will probably be fine."

"Quite right," Roney agreed. "So unless you want to leave me with the weapons and watch from a safe distance, we may need to find some way of protecting your lovely but very vulnerable ship, hmm?"

"Unfortunately I could not design the devices to use your form of relative field, because I know nothing about it," Wicked Mary agreed. "We will need to be there to activate them."

"My Megadyne albedo shielding will protect us to some extent from energy discharges in the high solar-flare range," the *Conch* said. "From the readings we took and the damage to the planets at the previous location, I would say this firestorm is more intense but we should still last for several seconds without taking damage."

"Several *seconds?*" Bonty said apprehensively, and looked at Wicked Mary's *giela*.

"If we seed the area with the devices I have built," Wicked Mary said, "I can activate them the moment the serpent appears and send large pieces of it back into soft-space. The devices will not last long in the fire either, so the sooner we activate them the better."

"And how exactly have you made devices that can automatically calibrate a relative field?" Galana asked.

"The short answer to that is that I haven't, delicious Commander," Wicked Mary replied. "A relative field is intended to carry an object *intact* through unreality and back into reality. It is highly complex and requires a lot of energy, and is practically impossible for us to extend beyond, for example, a starship hull even though it is apparently quite easy for the Boze to do," they all waited for Roney to say something, but knowing she wouldn't. "The devices I have made will only work for a fraction of a second before burning out," Wicked Mary concluded, "and they will scatter their contents across a large area in the process. They are *terrible* relative drives."

"But excellent weapons," Scrutarius said admiringly. "Is this something the Monsters are planning on bringing to Six Species wars sometime in the future?"

"I could not possibly tell you, my tasty friend," Wicked Mary replied. "However, you may rest assured that I do not think such a weapon would work against something like a starship. From what I have come to understand about this star serpent, it is an entirely different form of matter, with mass and energy properties ... well, as we had already noted, it manages to burn planets without causing gravitational issues the way a normal solar flare or energy event might. I can share the numbers with you if you like."

"I would advise against it," the *Conch* suggested.

"Thank you for that, old girl," Hartigan said levelly.

"Now," Wicked Mary went on, "as to our survival ... well, as long as we kill the star serpent, and the firestorm stops once the serpent is dead, we will be fine."

"And if not?" Galana asked, although she suspected she knew the answer.

"Our shields will not hold out long enough for us to open the rings and fire up our relative drive," Wicked Mary said, "and of course the toruses would be destroyed as soon as they were opened anyway. We will burn – unless of course the delicious Captain Pelsworthy is good enough to carry us to safety in her miraculous dumbler relative drive."

"Consider it done, biggums," Roney said. "Just leave it to the delicious Captain Pelsworthy."

There was little else to do but set their traps and lie in wait. Roney said it was a matter of hours before the star serpent's shadow was due to flit through the region.

"So these things destroyed the Empire of Gold," Hartigan said, "and … what's your connection to the Empire, really? You said you were the last of the Empire, but it vanished a bally long time ago - "

"No no, I told you, I'm the last Boze of the Empire," she said. "I'm the *only* Boze of the Empire. The Empire of Gold mostly happened before my species had even evolved. It's gone now, but you can still carry a little piece of it with you."

"And you're the last remaining Boze?" Hartigan pressed. He'd been trying to get to the bottom of the confusing dumbler's life story for weeks, with somehow *less* than zero success. Galana suspected it was a cultural quirk of the species. Every time someone asked for clarification on something like this, Pelsworthy added only confusing and seemingly-contradictory details. And yet, she never added anything that made previous answers into *lies*. She just added new layers of information that … changed the meaning of what she'd already said. It was extraordinarily challenging. "Did the star serpent … is it responsible for the destruction of the rest of your people?"

"My people are still around," Roney said infuriatingly. "I'm just the last one, that's all."

"And what does that mean?"

"Well … you know how first there *isn't* something, and then one of something shows up and that's the *first one* … ?"

"Now listen here," Hartigan snapped.

The conversation went on far longer than Galana would have thought even Basil Hartigan would have had the patience for, and a somehow *negative* amount of information was communicated, but she suspected both Captains were enjoying themselves. Finally Roney brought the debate to a close with a terse, "here it comes."

"Suppressor web ready," Wicked Mary reported. "Energy pulse from the *Splendiferous Bastard* set."

They waited for another tense, silent few minutes, staring into the star-sprinkled darkness. Galana had just begun to wonder if it *had* all been a metaphor, or if maybe they were the victims of a Boze practical joke, when the star serpent crashed into reality right in front of them.

They only had a couple of seconds to stare at the vast creature in the viewscreens, but that was plenty of time for the *Conch* to capture footage for them to look back on later. It was undeniably spectacular.

To say the star serpent was small in comparison to the immense field of fire it brought with it was doing it a disservice. The firestorm was too big to really see, filling the screens with a blinding yellow-orange glow. The star serpent, though, was *huge*. Its head was larger than a Worldship, at least two hundred miles long. It was actually quite a long way off, but it *looked* like it was floating right in front of them due to its size. Behind the head, the creature's body extended away into the fire like a monstrous red cable.

The great scaly head, barbed and reptilian and sporting four wicked glowing-white eyes like miniature suns, loomed like a shadow in the shifting flames of the firestorm. Its mouth was open, teeth like black mountains above and below, and in between them was another blazing furnace, deeper and hotter than the eyes. Like an entrance to … what had Roney called it? The Riddlespawn's nether-Hell? Yes, that seemed all too accurate.

But they barely had time to see it before Wicked Mary's weapons chewed away the sight in a flashing series of dark pockets. The star serpent's immense body lashed … and then the *Conch* and the *Splendiferous Bastard* were in the grey themselves.

They were only at relative speed for another split-second, emerging just outside the volume of the firestorm. It had been dizzying. From the star serpent's appearance to their jump away to the edge of the storm, barely five seconds had passed.

"*Bozanda*! We got the beast!" Roney exclaimed in triumph.

"We did?" Hartigan said.

"Captain," Galana said, "look."

The *Conch*'s sensors had homed in on the centre of the firestorm. Whatever shielding magic might have previously hidden the star serpent from view appeared to have failed now. The serpent's body, at first little more than a dark thread amidst the flames, zoomed to the centre of the screens. It was lashing and writhing, headless, spouting lava and lightning and strange pulses of light into space. It broke apart as they watched, each enormous segment squirming until it shattered into still smaller pieces.

The view pulled back out. The firestorm was still raging – it was too big to stop immediately – but based on readings the computer was collecting, it would burn out within half a year. And there was nothing for it to burn in this region. The star serpent would destroy no more solar systems.

"Four point seven-nine seconds," Scrutarius said. "Nice job, Tactical Officer."

"Give me a proper time-limit for the next star serpent," Wicked Mary said.

Roney docked with the *Conch* and joined the crew for a celebratory meal. She brought a bottle of thick blue liquid that Bonty, after analysing, strongly recommended only the Molranoids drink – and only a sip, at that. It tasted like hot metal with an aftertaste of toffee.

"And so ends the twenty million year reign of the star serpent," Roney announced, raising her glass. "Well done, biggums. You've done a great service to the galaxy. I think your AstroCorps would be proud. And you stopped it before it could wander through your little Six Species patch, so they should be proud *and* grateful. As I am," she nodded at Wicked Mary. "Thank you."

"Thank you for cutting a year off our journey," Hartigan said.

"Maybe I'll pay your Six Species a visit one day," Roney went on. "Maybe the Boze can become the *Seventh* Species, eh?"

"You personally, or another of your kind?" Hartigan asked with narrowed eyes.

"Of course not just me," Roney said placidly. "Not much of a *species* if there's only one of us," she grinned at Galana. "He's not bright, but he's fun," she said, not bothering to change languages this time.

"It's the entire reason we keep humans around," Galana confided.

"*Rank* insubordination," Hartigan declared happily.

After the meal, Roney decided it was time she continued on her way. Plenty more wrongs in need of righting, great feats of daring and cunning to be performed. She returned to the *Splendiferous Bastard* and prepared to depart.

"I'll be seeing you, biggums," she said with a touching little salute over the comm. "It's been a privilege. Good luck on your quest. And thank you for your gift, Chief Engineer Scrutarius. Very amusing."

Galana looked back at Devlin, but the Blaran just grinned and flicked his ears.

Roney was continuing. "Remember, if you ever find yourselves in the dark ruins of the Empire of Gold, tell them Judderone Pelsworthy sent you."

"We'll keep that in mind, Captain Pelsworthy," Galana said with a smile. "Thank you."

"But in all seriousness, I'd avoid it if I were you," Roney added sombrely. "Ghastly place nowadays. *High Elonath*, they call it," she scoffed. "Nothing *high* about it if you ask me. Well, goodbye my friends."

"High Elonath – *wait* - " Hartigan blurted. Galana remembered the clue given to them by the Man-Apes. The fabled whereabouts of the Last Alicorn.

"Captain Pelsworthy has severed contact," the *Conch* reported.

"*Hail her*," Hartigan cried as the glossy red-and-gold ship curved up and away from them, accelerating all the while.

"The *Splendiferous Bastard* has gone to relative speed," the *Conch* stated.

"Damn and blast it all!" Hartigan thumped the arm of his chair. Devlin, over at the engineering console, began to laugh. Basil rounded on him with a glare. "And you can shut up, you flat-headed imbecile!"

Scrutarius laughed harder.

And so ended their first meeting with Judderone Pelsworthy of the Boze, Space Adventurer.

It would not be their last.

Soon, in <u>Planet of the Cancer</u>:

While Molren, Blaren and Bonshooni didn't generally suffer from illnesses or emotional issues related to long isolation or stretches in soft-space, Bonjamin insisted the *whole* crew reported for regular check-ups. It didn't take them long to figure out this was her own personal way of fending off boredom.

"Admittedly, Captain Hartigan is my most fragile patient," Bonty said to Galana when she'd completed her latest round of tests, "but I've been surprised at how well he is coping. His health is good, and his mood is … well, let's say as *Hartigan-y* as ever," she looked at her medical console. "Oh, and you're fine too," she added dismissively, "of course."

"I suppose we are all keeping as busy as we can in our own ways," Galana said. "You and I have our reading and research, Devlin has his mysterious hobbies behind locked doors in his quarters, Chillybin and Wicked Mary have fairly large spaces to run and swim around in, and we all get out onto planets whenever we can. It's just been a long time since we found a planet with anything *living* on it."

"Anything more than slimy fungus," Bonty agreed moodily. "And a lot of long stretches in the grey in between."

"And Basil keeps himself entertained," Galana concluded. "Or the *Conch* entertains him. Sometimes that computer really does seem like a seventh member of the crew."

"Too kind," the *Conch* predictably spoke up from a nearby panel, and Galana and Bonty smiled.

"Have you actually *asked* Devlin what he does in his spare time?" Bonty asked.

"Once or twice," Galana shrugged. "It's not really any of my business, and he's quite within his rights to keep his hobbies private. I suspect it's some plant or – what did you call it? Slimy fungus – that he's taken from one of the planets we stopped at, and he's cultivating it. As long as it doesn't breach regulations … I think the *Conch* would warn us if he was making mind-altering drugs or biological weapons or anything."

"Why?" the *Conch* asked sweetly. "I'm not biological."

"Frankly I'd be more worried about Bloody Mary doing any of that than Devlin," Bonty added.

Galana flicked her ears. "Exactly."

"But it *has* been a terribly long time between interesting stopovers," Bonty sighed. "And an *awful* lot of long dives through soft-space."

Galana, who was quietly of the opinion that uninteresting stopovers were infinitely preferable to ones that might get them killed, nevertheless agreed with her elderly friend. Their mission, after all, wasn't just to circumnavigate the galaxy – it was to study, and learn, and make contact with alien cultures. Just … something slightly more lively than a patch of slime on a rock would be nice. It didn't need to be adorable and fuzzy, and it *certainly* didn't need to be in the 'giant gross bug' category that Scrutarius and Hartigan kept muttering about. Just … something.

Of course, Scrutarius and Hartigan would probably also tell her to be careful what she wished for, because they were a bit superstitious like that. Still, sooner or later, statistically speaking, they were bound to be right. Sooner or later, the *Conch* would drop out of the grey and they would find something that made Galana wish for the good old days of slimy fungus.

Sooner or later.

THE PLANET OF THE CANCER

By long-established custom, they all gathered on the bridge as the countdown drew to a close and their flight through soft-space neared its end. Only Wicked Mary didn't appear in person, owing to the fact that she was restricted to the Aquarium in the lower hold. She was, however, still present in the form of her small silver *giela*.

"Here we go," Captain Hartigan said, as cheerful and optimistic as always. "Uninhabited ice ball with a side-order of just *extraordinarily* dull microbes in ten … nine … "

Okay, Galana conceded, maybe he wasn't *quite* as cheerful and optimistic as always. But the irrepressible human even managed to express his pessimism in a chirpy way.

"I am confident that we will find something here," Chillybin said.

"Bet you a duty shift in the recycling tanks we don't," Scrutarius offered.

"I like the recycling tanks," Chilly replied.

"Never bet against a telepath," Bonty advised.

" … one," Hartigan concluded, and star-smattered space washed back over the viewscreens. "Honestly, I don't know why I even bother with the countdown - "

"Contact," Wicked Mary interrupted. The local star, a baleful red monster, slid across the main viewer and a planet, tiny and black-looking against the ruddy glare, grew steadily as they approached.

"Establish a common - " Hartigan said, then stopped, staring at his console. "That's not possible."

"Get us out of here," Scrutarius shouted.

"Plotting relative jump," the *Conch* said, then went on without pausing. "Relative field suppressors are in effect. Stowing toruses, raising shields and plotting a subluminal course out of the system."

Galana barely heard the computer's words. She was staring at her own screens. At the unthinkable information scrolling across them like an omen of doom from the dawn of time. At an ancient nightmare from the Fleet's darkest days, the enemy she'd said they would be safe from, this far out towards the edge of the galaxy, but which she'd known, *known* would somehow find them.

Had she really thought that Basil and Devlin were superstitious?

"Power up weapons," Hartigan, with typical human resilience and even more typical human aggression, recovered very quickly from his shock.

"Yes, Captain," Wicked Mary confirmed. "No incoming ships detected. The signal seems to be coming from the planet."

"They don't have ships?" Hartigan said. "Weapons?"

"Nothing I can detect, Captain," Wicked Mary replied.

"Hang about … " Hartigan was frowning.

"Can you find the source of the suppression field?" Bonty asked anxiously.

"Scanning," Wicked Mary said.

"Redirect power to the engines," Galana heard herself saying. "If we can get to the edge of the field and go to relative speed - "

"*Redirect power?*" Hartigan exclaimed. "What are you going to do, bally well run a cable through? And what are you going to do with *more than full power*, aside from burst something? Now look, if we can all just settle down a mo' - "

"I can detach the *Nella* and rig the main structure of the ship to blow," Scrutarius said. "We've got an emergency canister that will hold Bloody Mary until we can regroup - "

"Right, that's it," Hartigan snapped, jabbed his console with an angry finger, and rose to his feet. "All stop."

"W – what?" Bonty quavered.

Galana stared at him. "Captain?"

"*All*," Hartigan said firmly, "*blasted. Stop.*"

"Fleet law - " Bonty started.

"*Did we turn into a bally Molran Fleet starship sometime in the past ten seconds?*" Hartigan roared. "*And more to the point, did one of you bat-heads turn into the bally Captain?*"

Galana was too shocked to speak for a moment. Fortunately, Devlin was not similarly afflicted.

"Basil," he said, "that's a planet full of Damorakind down there. When it comes to the Cancer in the Core, *every* ship is a Molran Fleet ship. We can't - "

"The Cancer in the *where*, sorry?" Hartigan looked around theatrically. "Did we somehow end up in the Core of the galaxy?"

"Basil - " Scrutarius tried again.

"I thought we monkeys were meant to be the panicky stupid ones,"

Hartigan said. "Honestly, you've got twelve hands between you. *Get a grip.*"

For the first time, Galana looked across at Chillybin. She was standing quite still at her station.

"There is no immediate danger," the aki'Drednanth announced.

"My apologies, Captain," Galana said. "All stop. I will make a note of my insubordination in the log."

"That's not necessary, young Fen," Hartigan forgave her. "Gave me quite a turn myself. Now let's just see what's going on here, what? No ships, but these readings … "

"Damorakind," Wicked Mary confirmed serenely. "Or a technology so similar it opens all the sealed security folders in the tactical underlayer."

"I didn't even know we had one of those," Hartigan remarked.

"It is not general knowledge, Captain," Galana said. "The Fleet, after all, utterly forbids all contact and knowledge of the Cancer in the Core. But we have to be able to know what the Cancer *is* in order to avoid it."

"And these are definitely Damorakind," Wicked Mary said. "My network nodes are also lighting up."

"Are there Fergies down there?" Scrutarius asked.

"None that I can connect with," Wicked Mary replied. "Just the old data patterns that we carried with us in our network when we joined the Fleet."

"There are two hundred billion Damorakind on the planet below," Chillybin said.

"Two hundred *billion?*" Hartigan yelped.

"And three thousand aki'Drednanth."

"Three thousand," Galana blurted in shock. This single planet had six times more aki'Drednanth on it than the entirety of Six Species space. "Are they … slaves?"

"Are they hiding us from the Cancer?" Bonty asked. "I heard, when the Fleet was fleeing the Core, the aki'Drednanth - "

"Incoming transmission," Chillybin interrupted.

Hartigan whistled softly and shook his head. "Let's hear it."

The voice that came from the comm system was a low, rasping hiss, a sound of almost ludicrous malevolence. Even as her skin crawled with the horror of it, Galana almost laughed. The *Conch*, whether out of its own quirky sense of drama or because of some long-programmed identification protocol, had *definitely* overblown the evil hiss on this one.

"This region of space is subject to the Damorakind.

"You are not Damorakind. If you are not Damorakind you are the enemy and so you shall be unmade."

"Ooh, *unmade,*" Hartigan said in an undertone. He was making no effort to hide his amusement. "Well done on the spooky voice there, old girl. Is there any more?"

"We are the Cancer in the Core. We are the one true life. We are the black steel

claws of the Gods."

"I'm sure you are, old boy. Only you're not *in* the Core, and you've got no bally *ships*," he chuckled and turned to Chillybin. "Alright," he said, "what next?"

"Captain?" Chillybin said.

"The way I see it, we have two options," Basil said. "One, we can keep flying away from this place at maximum subluminal. Even if this suppression field covers the whole system, we should escape it in a few days. And since they have no ships … " he shrugged.

"And the second option?" Scrutarius asked. "Is it crazy?"

Hartigan pointed. "We turn around - "

"It's crazy," Scrutarius said.

" - go back to the planet and give them a jolly good looking over," Hartigan continued. "We may never get a chance to see a Damorakind settlement without ships, without Fergies … I mean, aren't you curious how they ended up way the blazes out here? What they actually think about us being up here, stubbornly refusing to be *unmade*? What the *three thousand aki'Drednanth* down there might be doing?" he stroked his moustache. "Although I'll wager you could tell us about *that* already if you wanted to," he added over his shoulder, "couldn't you, old girl?"

"I could," Chillybin admitted, "but there is not much to tell."

"Oh come now," Hartigan said. "I know you don't like passing on information from other wacky-wackies, but this *must* count as one of those special circumstances you mentioned?"

"No, there really is not much to tell," Chillybin said. "The aki'Drednanth here are … something of a closed community. I have not taken part in a life among them and most who do … they do not report anything useful or exciting. They have been living here for some thirty thousand years. They came here before the Fergunak were … discovered."

"*Discovered,*" Wicked Mary repeated. "An interesting way of putting it."

"The Damorakind here do not come above ground," Chillybin went on. "They have trouble even thinking about it. They do not have ships because they are not capable of *functioning* in ships. The idea of open space terrifies them."

"Wait 'til they hear what planets are surrounded by," Scrutarius muttered.

"You joke, but it is only by a great effort they manage to *ignore* the truth of outer space, and it leaves them in a perpetual state of background fear nonetheless," Chillybin said. "They know they are no longer in the Core, they know they are at the edge of the galaxy where there are hardly any worlds, nothing but emptiness all around. Reminders of this are most unwelcome."

"Reminders like us?" Bonty asked. Chillybin nodded heavily. "They're *holding* us here, though," the doctor objected. "If they don't like it, why ... ?" she paused, a look of realisation crossing her face. "Were they *put* here? By the Cancer in the Core? Left out here like ... like an unexpectedly mobile sample of slimy fungus left in the medical bay with a cup over it, and a heavy piece of scanning equipment on top of the cup to keep it from moving in case it gets big enough to lift the cup?"

"That's a *really* specific analogy," Devlin congratulated her.

"How extreme is their fear of open space? Will they come out to attack us, or remain under the surface?" Galana asked.

"I would not bet on them staying put," Chillybin said.

"You know Commander Fen making a bet is why we're all out here, right?" Scrutarius remarked.

"They won't be happy about it but they *will* do their best to destroy us," Chillybin warned. "We are not Damorakind."

"Then we should mark this place on the charts, get out of the suppression field and continue on our way," Galana concluded. "Or, if we *are* going to poke the Cancer with a stick, we should at least discuss it once we are out of immediate danger and have a chance to study them from a distance."

"I'm afraid it's not that simple," Wicked Mary spoke up. "We will not get to the edge of this suppression field."

"What?" Galana asked, hating the edge of panic in her voice.

"We entered this system normally," Wicked Mary explained. "If there was a suppressor, it would have pulled us out of soft-space early. *This*, however, activated only *after* we arrived."

"So?" Hartigan said. "Typical intruder alert system, I'd've thought."

"I have been analysing the relative field failure," Wicked Mary said, "as has the *Conch*. We are in agreement that this is no ordinary suppressor field. It is not coming from a large generator device. It is coming from many *small* ones."

"Many *many* small ones," the *Conch* added. "More than capable of keeping pace with us."

"Give it to me straight, ladies," Hartigan said.

"We are surrounded by a cloud of tiny field suppressors," Wicked Mary said, "that will keep us from entering soft-space until we find a way of picking off every single one of them. And we need to destroy them all at once, because even one will be able to make more in seconds."

"Devilish," Hartigan still didn't sound particularly worried. "Without a relative drive, it could take us five thousand years to get to a habitable world, let alone home, *let alone* the rest of the way around the galaxy."

"Yes," the *Conch* said. "This region of space is empty. By design. That seems to be why these Damorakind were placed here."

"Commander Fen might live to reach a habitable planet," Wicked Mary said, "but the rest of us probably won't."

"We're faster than the Nyif Nyif, but not so fast it will make a difference," Devlin agreed. "We're a long way from anywhere but Planet Cancer at this point."

"The situation is not actually as bad as our initial estimates," Wicked Mary said.

"What – your initial estimates of seven seconds ago?" Hartigan asked in surprise.

"Seven seconds is a long time," Wicked Mary pointed out. "These tiny suppressors do not have their own power supplies. They are fed from a tight beam from the planet itself. At maximum subluminal cruising velocity, we should be out of range of *that* in less than *seventy* years."

Hartigan sighed heavily. "If you think seven seconds is a long time, I've got bad news about seventy years," he said.

"And I imagine seventy years will be more than enough time for a few of the bravest souls down there to psych themselves up and get in a warship," Scrutarius said. "Heck, some of them might gather the nerve in time to fly out here before Bloody Mary dies of old age."

"How long until they can scramble a response like that?" Hartigan asked. "They haven't done it already, so I'm guessing they've got to pull some gear out of storage."

"Days at most, shipboard time," Chillybin said. "Hours is more likely."

"The amount of time we have to spend in this dreary solar system just keeps dropping and dropping," Scrutarius said in a passable impression of Bonty's most cheerful voice. "Can we get it down to a few minutes?"

"There's nothing else for it, then," Hartigan pointed. "We'll have to go back there and find a way to shut off the power source for this suppressor cloud. Then get out of the system before they dust off their remote-controlled fighters."

The grim-faced human tapped his controls and the stars spun in the viewscreens. The great red bole of the sun reappeared, and the menacing little planet resumed growing as they approached.

"Is there any chance the aki'Drednanth down there might help us?" Galana asked, without much hope.

"The aki'Drednanth down there are already helping us," Chillybin said. "Who do you think made these Damorakind so afraid of empty space?"

"*You?*" Bonty asked in surprise. "I mean, not you personally, but … "

"The aki'Drednanth in the Core aren't just slaves," Chillybin explained. "We – they – also help to keep the Damorakind contained. We used that control, in a small way, when we saved the Molran Fleet. On another occasion, we attempted to intensify the Damorakind's fear of the sparser regions outside the Core, and the result was this weakened strain. Before we could do anything, they had been cast out, cut from the species in order to keep the others strong. It was an experiment that did not work."

Galana was surprised to hear an aki'Drednanth explain so much about their mysterious deeds in the Core. Before she could say anything, however, Basil was tapping on his controls again.

"I say, Chilly, how deep underground do these blighters live? Can we send them a message back?"

"I don't know if they will acknowledge or allow communications, Captain," Chillybin replied, "but I think if we send a transmission, let's say, loud enough, they will be able to pick it up whether they want to or not. Their colonies are not very deep below the surface, especially in those areas where ventilation ducts are built."

"Alright then," Hartigan gave Galana a grin, and she knew from the look in his eye that he was about to get all *human*. He tapped the controls. "Chilly, transmit this," he turned back to face the screens, and his expression became grim. "We are AstroCorps. We *were* going to continue on our way, but you chose to stop us. You chose to *annoy* us.

"We are the true life that is not you. We are the *reason* you are afraid of the dark. We are the veterinarians who *clip* the black steel claws of the Gods."

There was silence on the bridge as Chillybin relayed the message.

"Not bad," Scrutarius said.

"Tactical Officer Mary," Hartigan said, his voice still cold. "Ready the modular rail cannon."

"Copy that, Captain," Wicked Mary acknowledged.

"If I might provide a voice of sanity - " Galana started.

"*Belay that voice of sanity*. Bring us in right to the edge of their atmosphere," Hartigan said, "and prepare to peel the top layer of rock off their - "

"Incoming transmission," Chillybin reported.

"Imagine that," Hartigan said mildly. "Let's hear it."

"Challenge received and met," the rasping voice said over the comms. "We will send our mightiest hero to face you beneath the dreadful yawning vault."

"Do they mean the sky?" Hartigan asked. "Do you mean the sky? We call it the sky. It doesn't bother us. Tell them we're fine with the whole dreadful yawning thing."

"What are you thinking, Baz?" Devlin asked. "The old Poisoned Fruits?"

"Oh, I think so," Hartigan stood up. "Chilly old girl, would you mind terribly if I used your suit for a bit?"

"Will you bring it back in one piece?"

"Well, if I don't, I won't be bringing it back at all," the Captain said. "It might smell a bit, I'll have to turn the heat up a bit to make it comfortable," he turned to the *giela* at the tactical console. "I have a sacrifice to ask of you too, Bloody Mary."

"Captain?"

"I'm going to need Squirty Pete Junior."

Galana stared at their stalwart Captain while Scrutarius laughed in delight. "The new squid we were growing for Wicked Mary to hunt?" she asked. "It's barely half-finished. It won't survive outside its vat yet."

"Oh, that's evil, Baz," Devlin chortled. "I'll go get him ready."

"What exactly is 'the old Poisoned Fruits'?" Galana asked. "And why does it require an aki'Drednanth freezer suit and a fifteen-foot battle squid?"

Hartigan just grinned.

There was some debate over who got to go down to the surface to meet the challenge that AstroCorps had apparently delivered. Scrutarius wanted to go down and watch, but he had to do some work on the relative drive just in case they managed to get away from the suppressor cloud. Wicked Mary was curious but would have to put all her attention on the weapons. Chillybin said it was probably not a good idea for her to show herself, and couldn't go down to the uncomfortably warm planet for long without an envirosuit anyway. Bonty didn't want to go, and Galana didn't want *anyone* to go.

In the end, Hartigan and Galana were the only two on board the *Nella* as it detached from the ship and descended towards the barren little charcoal lump of a planet. Galana was alone on the bridge, the Captain in the aft section preparing 'the old Poisoned Fruits', which he still perversely refused to explain.

They set down on the blackened sand near one of the great ventilation openings, which was more like a ring of sharp black glass spires surrounding a seemingly bottomless chasm. The *Conch* reported that the air was hot and polluted but breathable.

"You wait in here, Fen," Hartigan said over the comm. "They might not take kindly to me bringing backup, and we may need to get out of here fast. I'll feed the audio and visual from the suit."

Before Galana could object, the docking ramp had opened and Hartigan had clanked away merrily down onto the sand. How he was moving the massive, heavy refrigerator suit, Galana had no idea. It must have some measure of automation. She watched his point-of-view on the screens, and once he emerged from beneath the nose of the *Nella*, she zoomed in on another set of screens and watched him from the outside as well. The suit stomped across the dark landscape under the bloated red sun. The figure seemed even bigger without Chillybin inside it.

The Damorakind emerged from an opening in the side of one of the obsidian spires, and strode towards Hartigan with impressive boldness considering it was supposed to be deadly afraid of the dreadful yawning vault. It was tall, Galana judged, closer to Molran-height than human, but dwarfed a little by the enormous suited figure of the Captain. As the two shapes approached one another and their relative sizes became obvious, the Damorakind slowed. It may have been beginning to regret volunteering for this heroic mission.

She narrowed her eyes, watching the creature of Fleet horror stories on the viewscreens and Hartigan's helmet feed. It was difficult to make out, because it was wrapped in a strange black shroud the same shade as the sand and the glassy tower behind it. It appeared to be humanoid – two arms, two legs – but its head was larger, elongated, its fingers gnarled and sharp as knives. The eyes that squinted out through the folds of black cloth were bright slits of electric blue light.

Damorakind and human faced one another across the blackened ground. The Damorakind looked very small and frail.

"I am Ja'Karod," the *Conch* provided the Damorakind translation. The creature raised a claw melodramatically in front of its cloth-wrapped face. "I am - "

"*I am Stygian Maw, Gargantuon of AstroCorps,*" Hartigan's voice, shockingly loud, boomed out across the blasted landscape. Ja'Karod reeled a little. "*Your irritating cloud of remote suppressors interrupted my dinner.*"

"You are not Damorakind - "

"*No I bloody am not!*" Hartigan roared. "*I am Stygian Maw! Were you not listening? And you know what else I am? Hungry! If I can't fly on and enjoy one of my more usual hunting grounds, well then, you'll just have to do.*"

"We do not bargain with things that are not the one true life," the Damorakind said, its voice sounding a little squeaky to Galana's ears. Now that she was getting used to the overlap of the computer's translation and the actual voice of the monster, she had to admit the *Conch*'s fake voice was actually pretty close. Ja'Karod raised its hand again, slightly shakily. "You are – are an inferior – you will - "

"*You will be devoured,*" Hartigan thundered, "*and your cowering friends down in their holes will release our ship and be grateful if we continue on our way rather than making a* grotesque *example of your planet.*"

"We are the Cancer in the Core," Ja'Karod definitely squeaked this time. It shook its hand in front of its face again, and Galana realised it wasn't *just* trembling – it was trying to make its fingers do something. Evidently it was too stressed to pull it off fully, but a sputtering light the same plasma-blue as its eyes flickered and flashed along its pointed claws for a moment.

The feeble display went out a second later as Hartigan took another deliberate step forward. One of the aki'Drednanth gauntlets swung open and a huge, wet tentacle unfolded from the armour's arm-segment, its tip unrolling onto the ground and flaring to reveal great red suckers with gleaming black hooks inside.

Then the helmet itself gaped wide and three more tentacles, larger still, boiled up and uncurled over the huge armour plated shoulders, onto the ground. Hartigan took a final step forward, the tentacles moving sluggishly with him. The persistent nerve impulses in the animal made the flesh curl and coil slowly, searching for something to wrap around.

Ja'Karod turned and bolted for the safety of the ventilation shaft, tripping over its own feet and its wrappings and jabbering something the computer didn't manage to translate.

"The suppression transmission from the surface has ceased," Scrutarius reported from the *Conch*. Out on the black sand of the Planet of the Cancer, Hartigan swung his enormous suit around and began heaving it back towards the *Nella*, tentacles dragging. "Readying relative drive."

"Y'know, it's funny, isn't it?" Hartigan said a short while later. They'd jumped to soft-space without further interference from the Damorakind, the Captain had very thoroughly cleaned the inside of Chillybin's suit and they'd gotten a new squid gestating for Wicked Mary to enjoy another year or two down the line. They were sitting in the Captain's quarters, enjoying a drink while Basil puffed on one of his precious cigars.

"There's a lot that's funny about this," Bonty noted, "but what in particular were you thinking of?"

"We're the only AstroCorps crew, the only *Six Species citizens* to have made contact with the Cancer in the Core," Hartigan said, "and it was way out here on the edge of the galaxy. And we'll never be able to tell anyone about it, because having anything to do with the Damorakind is totally against the law."

"We can get by on a technicality," Devlin said. "We didn't actually go into the Core, we didn't make any real effort to study them, they weren't *proper* Damorakind because *proper* Damorakind aren't that scared of space, and we didn't *willingly* expose ourselves to them. They trapped us. Commander Fen will probably be able to put this in her report without even being skinswitched to Blaran the second anyone back home reads it."

"I'm not sure exactly how I'm going to put *any* of this in a report," Galana admitted, and the others laughed. "What was that … manoeuvre you pulled on them? The Poisoned Fruits?"

"Mm, old Earth myth," Hartigan waved a line of smoke in the air with his cigar. "Dreadful mutant creatures, people corrupted with the dark evil of whatnot, you know the sort."

"I don't, really," Galana said.

"She's right," Scrutarius grinned. "Molren don't have myths with monsters in. Or if they do, they're always monsters like 'lack of regard for the rules' and 'failure to stick to proper Fleet guidelines'."

"I think you'll find that's all *anyone's* myths are," Galana pointed out, "but some cultures need more colourful reminders than others, because they get bored more easily."

"She's right again," Hartigan admitted easily. "Anyway, last time Dev and I pulled this stunt it was back during an AstroCorps review. We didn't *quite* dare to use an aki'Drednanth suit, but one of the Blaran belowdecksmen had this big clunky mechanical shell that he was very proud of. We got him drunk and scooped him out of it and hid him in a cupboard in his undies while we used his mech and a load of animal parts from the local meat processing station," he grinned and sipped his drink.

"Good times," Devlin said fondly.

"Good times indeed, old chum," Hartigan agreed. "Good times indeed."

Soon, in <u>The Golden Idol</u>:

"Captain?" Galana tapped on the comms panel again. "Captain Hartigan?" there was no response. She looked up at the ceiling. "Computer," she said, "is the Captain awake?"

"Not fully," the *Conch* replied smoothly. "I have begun the process of waking him up with a priority alert, but you know how the Captain is before he has his zolo."

"Perhaps he can bring his zolo to the bridge," Galana suggested, "and the current situation will help to wake him up a little faster."

"I was not aware of a situation, Commander," the computer said.

"Yes," Galana replied evenly, "that is part of the situation. External sensors and several key computer channels have been … interfered with somehow. We are descending towards an unknown planet, and unless Basil joins us on the bridge I will be forced to separate the *Nella* in the hopes that the rest of the ship can regain orbit. We can of course do this without the Captain on board, but - "

"Alright, alright Fen, I'm up, what is it?" Hartigan, still in his dressing gown and holding a large glass of blue-black zolo in one hand, shambled onto the bridge. He had also stepped into his uniform boots, although the overall effect was somehow shabbier than if he'd gone barefoot. "What are we - " he stopped next to Bonty, who was staring out of the for'ard viewscreens, and stared along with her.

"Captain," Galana reported, "we are being towed into a landing pattern, and I doubt the *Conch* will survive planetfall seeing as how it is designed purely for space travel. Recommend we detach the *Nella* and have Scrutarius and Wicked Mary pull the main body of the ship back into orbit."

"Yes, but Fen," Hartigan pointed. "What the blazes - "

"We have to do it *soon*, and we have to do it almost entirely manually," Galana added, "because something has disrupted the *Conch*'s computer control over key systems. If we *don't* act soon, the whole ship will be dragged down."

"What are *they*?" Hartigan demanded, waving his glass at the viewscreen. Zolo slopped onto the floor of the bridge.

Galana turned and looked at the screens, at the large curve of planet rapidly flattening out into a landscape below, and the pair of huge, pale creatures apparently gripping the ship between them and guiding it downwards. "Oh," she said, "they would appear to be the local life-forms, Captain."

"We have not currently made contact with them," Chillybin added from the Comms console, "but they seem … if not hostile, then at least neutral in a way that is very likely to kill us all."

They stood, human and Molran, Bonshoon and aki'Drednanth, and gazed out at the enormous beasts on either side of the main screen.

"Finally," Hartigan said in delight, "*dragons*."

THE GOLDEN IDOL

"I'm not sure what you're so happy about, Captain," Galana said. "Wasn't the star serpent more than enough dragon for you?"

"That was a great big weird alien energy anomaly in the *shape* of a dragon," Hartigan said dismissively. He sat down in the Captain's seat, still wearing his dressing gown and uniform boots, still holding half a glass of zolo, and still staring enraptured out of the viewscreen. "These are … *actual dragons*."

Galana eyed the creatures on either side of the ship. She had to admit, she was having a hard time describing them as anything else. She'd estimated they were about twice the length of the *Conch*, and that was about as accurate as she could be with the sensors acting up. They were gleaming white, with long scaly necks and tails, huge webbed wings, talons … they were dragons, plain and simple. How exactly they were managing to lift such enormous bodies into the air – let alone into high orbit, which was where they'd intercepted the ship – was just one of many things Galana had no idea about.

"Their precise nature is a fascinating topic for a less urgent time," she said. "I'm detaching."

"Hmm? Oh, oh yes," Hartigan snapped briefly out of his daze. "Yes, of course. Detach. Get the *Conch* up into high orbit if you can. Dev?"

"On it, Captain," Scrutarius said over the comm. "Of course, if they drop the *Nella* and grab the rest of the *Conch* instead, I can't promise our Tactical Officer doesn't have some nasty surprises ready."

"Detaching," Galana said. Nothing happened. "The clamps are jammed," she reported. "Blowing emergency separation bolts," she hit a control, there was a hollow boom and the floor shuddered, but again the *Nella* didn't separate.

"Looks like our dragonny friends are still with us," Hartigan said, and gazed out at the creatures again. Between the dragons, the curve of planet flattened still further and the bright fire of atmospheric insertion flared. The creatures' gleaming white scales appeared to be made of some sort of fireproof material. Galana supposed that made sense, for dragons.

"We're still with you too," Scrutarius reported tensely from engineering. "Heat shields and hull plates seem to be holding, but it's going to get choppy. I could try to manually detach you but I suspect it'd be no more successful than the bolts."

"Bloody Mary, status?" Hartigan asked.

"I have also experienced some network disruption, Captain," the little mechanical *giela* replied from the tactical console, "but I am still in control. Would you like me to fire something a little more persuasive from the lateral turrets?"

"I would suggest we not annoy them," Galana said. "They flew into orbit and are apparently capable of physically dragging a starship to the ground."

"I tend to agree," Hartigan said.

"I am uncomfortable with not shooting them," Wicked Mary said, "but if those are your orders … "

"We won't get back into orbit even if they let us go now," Scrutarius announced. "Not without losing the toruses and half the hull. And we've got a belly full of water, remember."

The *giela* stirred. "I am in no danger of forgetting," she said. "If we are to crash, we should strike them with a final - "

"No," Galana interrupted. "Right now, these … dragons … are the only things that are going to get us to the ground in one piece. The *Conch* wasn't made to land."

"That she wasn't," Hartigan agreed, frowning in concern. "And what about the computer?"

"I am undamaged, Basil," the *Conch* reported. "But I have identified some issues with my sensors and data feeds. You were of course aware of them before I was, due to the nature of the shutdown but I am attempting to get to the bottom of it. It must have been an emergency action that I can no longer remember taking because the decision was locked out. Most interesting."

"Most interesting," Hartigan agreed, his frown deepening.

"It is an inconvenience, Basil, nothing more," the computer went on. "It is rather like being blind."

"Well don't worry, old dear," the Captain said with surprising tenderness. "We'll be your eyes."

The fire of atmospheric insertion faded and was replaced with the steady rumble of air roaring past, a decidedly unsettling sound to hear while inside a starship. Scrutarius powered down the engines and gravity plates, and let the ship play dead. The land below approached at a deceptively slow glide. Galana saw mountains and forested valleys, the gleam of water, and ... she frowned and leaned forward.

One long, winding ridge of pale stone, tapering at either end, looked suspiciously like another dragon. But it couldn't have been. They were still too far up, it would have had to be *thirty times* the size of the dragons carrying them down. *Fifty* times. That was ... well, she would have said that was impossible, but Galana Fen was coming to realise that her idea of what was impossible wasn't in possession of all the facts.

The land and water and occasional white crescent of possible-dragon swept by, seeming to speed up as they descended. As he'd promised he would, Captain Hartigan continued a low, steady description of what they were seeing, for the blind computer's benefit.

"Coming down lower over some hills now, everything looks a bit barren now and – golly, yes, look at that – it's burned, all of it, burned quite black, the hills are like glass ... wait, there's another dragon, and another ... I say, that's a bally big one ... hang about, they're bringing us lower, there's something shiny on the horizon, maybe another hill? A little cluster of – of mountains perhaps? It's – I say – I don't know."

Basil fell silent as the dragons on either side of them slowed, banked, and approached the huge glittering slope. Another few moments, and the *Conch* was grounded. The bridge rocked lightly underneath them, and came to rest at a slight angle. The ship groaned.

"The hull is holding," Scrutarius reported with some relief.

"The reinforcement in the Aquarium was very well done," Wicked Mary's *giela* complimented them.

"Alright," Hartigan said, "we're down, and it looks like we're down to stay ... next question is, *where?*"

"I think," Galana said hesitantly, "we've been added to the dragons' hoard."

Hartigan started to speak, then trailed off in awe. They all stepped forward and stared out of the for'ard screens.

The *Conch* had been placed on the top of a hill, a foothill near the base of the mountain that was the main trove. The hills were formed of great masses of shining metal shapes and glittering polished stones. It was difficult to make out individual pieces but there appeared to be carvings, artworks, as well as heaps of smaller objects and what looked like great melted masses of raw metal. It was impossible to see the peak of the highest hill from where the ship had been laid.

"Righto," Hartigan finally said. "Suggestions?"

"We're not going anywhere," Scrutarius confirmed as he joined them on the bridge. "Getting off the ground and through the atmosphere will tear us apart. The *Conch* wasn't made to take off any more than she was made to land," he glanced at the Captain. "Nice dressing gown there, Baz. Goes well with the boots."

"Quiet, you."

"We could still detach and leave in the *Nella*," Galana said, "but there's nowhere to go without the main body of the ship."

Hartigan turned to Chillybin and made an obscure little gesture with his zolo glass. "Chilly, can you … ?"

"I can sense nothing," Chillybin said. "This troubles me."

"Well, doesn't it normally take a few days for you to figure out what makes alien brains tick?"

"Yes, but I normally have some sense that there is a *brain*, even if it is too alien for me to recognise."

"Nothing much for it, then," Hartigan stood. "Let's go out there and say hello to the dragons," he turned from the screens and nodded to Scrutarius. "Dev, can you get the computer hooked back up?"

"I won't know until I figure out what the actual problem is," Scrutarius replied. "It looks like an automatic lock-out due to some kind of nearby data event, perhaps a – I don't know, a computer of such complexity that ours had to shut down rather than risk connecting up to it. The problem is, it's even hidden the action from itself so there's a lot of confusion," he shook his head. "If it's more than just the data connections – if the computer itself is damaged, Baz, you know that's - "

"I'm fine, Devlin," the computer said. "Just blinkered. I think perhaps you were right about the data influx risking overload. I'll talk you through the blind spots."

"There, you see? Jolly good," Hartigan patted Wicked Mary's *giela* on the top of its head. "Bloody Mary, weapons options?"

"Everything except the rail cannon is operational, Captain," Wicked Mary said, "although I am not sure how well the firing mechanisms will operate in atmosphere. Simulations look promising. I can run everything from the Aquarium without the use of my *giela*."

"Good, then your *giela*'s with me," Hartigan said. "Fen, Chilly, you too. Bonty … if you want to come, this looks like something that'd be right up your xenobiologist alley."

"Basil," Bonty said quickly, "what if – and I know this is an outside chance – what if these aren't the sort of dragons you can *talk* to? They may just be wild animals and they'll eat us as soon as look at us."

"That's a risk we're going to have to take, Bonty," Hartigan declared. "We don't have many other options right now. We go out and hope we can convince them that we're not treasure, but peaceful explorers who need to be carried back up into orbit if it's not too much trouble … or else we settle down here and live the rest of our lives in our crashed ship and hope they don't try to open us up."

"Are you going to … change into your uniform, Captain?" Galana asked as Basil strode off the bridge.

Hartigan snorted. "You know the regulations. Uniform's for aliens that *haven't* shipwrecked us, Fen."

"I don't think that is a regulation - "

"And besides," he went on, "I wouldn't want them to mistake me for a little silver statue, what?"

There were no dragons in sight as they disembarked. The planet seemed hospitable enough, although it was uncomfortably hot. More, Galana thought, a result of heat rising from the ground and the metals reflecting and focussing the warmth of the sun than anything to do with the climate. They scrambled down the slope upon which the *Conch* was beached, and up to the next foothill along.

From there, the ship really did look like a great exotic seashell. Galana had never imagined she would see it on the ground. From the warped look of the hull plates and the damage to the subluminal engines, Scrutarius was right – they'd never manage to take off again.

Although she was looking at a shipwreck and in all likelihood the end of their mission – and probably their lives – Galana had to admit it did look rather beautiful. A worthy addition to any dragon's treasure trove.

"Are you still alright in there?" she asked Wicked Mary.

"The Aquarium is holding," the *giela* reported.

"Look at this stuff," Hartigan said in excitement. "Look at *these*," he'd picked up a pair of hefty discs of yellowish metal, each the size of his hand. The slope he was toiling and backsliding his way up was covered in them. "What *are* they? They look like old-style money-tokens, what were they called … "

"Coins?" Galana hazarded.

"Right, coins. But they're too *big*."

"Too big for a human or a Molranoid," Bonty said, picking up one of the discs and turning it over. One side was stamped with an unsettling spider-like shape. She held it up and pointed at the image. "Maybe these fellows were big enough to carry around a little purse of them, hmm?"

"I say, that's reassuring," Hartigan chuckled. He dropped one of the coins with a *clunk* and put the other absentmindedly into his dressing gown pocket, making the garment sag heavily. "D'you think the dragons brought any of them down the way they did with us? Or just their coin collection? I wonder - "

"What is that?" Wicked Mary pointed towards the pinnacle of the central treasure-mountain, which reared another thousand feet or so above them across a shining valley littered with flattened, melted-looking metal shapes. The heat rising from the cleft was positively infernal. The others shaded their eyes and looked.

"I can't make it out," Hartigan said. "Air's all shimmery. Looks like a great big spiky chap with one hand up," he squinted. "The sun's right behind it, too."

"It's more like a tentacle than a hand," Galana said. The strange figure was almost humanoid from the waist up, except for its strange elongated head that not even Galana could make out in detail. Instead of legs, its body continued and swelled into a coiled serpentine mass, and its upthrust tentacle-arm was holding some kind of crystal ball. "It's a statue, I'd say. Two, maybe three times the size of a Molran. Made out of some kind of metal. Gold?"

"Yes, gold," Wicked Mary confirmed. "What is it holding?"

The little robot took a slow step down towards the shimmering-hot valley between their hill and the central mound.

"Tactical Officer Mary," Galana said warningly. "The temperature in the valley - "

"It's well within my *giela*'s tolerances," Wicked Mary said.

"Let's stay together for now, eh?" Hartigan suggested. Wicked Mary continued towards the valley. "Mary?"

"I am experiencing communication issues," the *giela* said placidly. Galana recognised this as Wicked Mary's code for *I don't want to do what the Captain says right now*. "I think it is the heavy metal content in this region. If I get to the higher slopes I should be able to re-establish contact."

"A likely bally story," Hartigan snapped. Wicked Mary clicked and clattered down into the valley. "You just want to - " he paused, scowling. "Come to mention it, I don't even know *what* you want to do," he muttered, and mopped his sweaty forehead with the sleeve of his dressing gown. "*Blasted* Fergunak."

"There is a dragon coming," Chillybin announced.

"Hang on, I thought you couldn't sense - " Hartigan started.

By then, though, Galana and Bonty had both heard it. The almost industrial sound of an enormous hard-scaled creature dragging itself swiftly across the hot metallic ground. It approached fast, swiftly reaching a volume human hearing could pick up, and rapidly rising still further. The temperature also increased, and Galana and the others took a few hasty steps back from the slope. Whether the heat was coming from melted metal, dragonfire, or the creature itself, it was intense.

Just before the sound and the heat reached painful levels, the huge white dragon slithered into view around the mountain, dragged itself up the valley and stopped, its neck curling back and its head rearing high above the tiny silvery shape of Wicked Mary's *giela*.

The robot tilted its own head up just in time for the dragon to raise a huge foreclaw.

"I - " Wicked Mary said.

The claw came down, mashing the *giela* into the rest of the melted metal that made up the valley floor and obliterating it completely.

" - assume my *giela* was just destroyed," Wicked Mary continued smoothly from the comm system.

"Yes," Galana said as calmly as she could. "Yes it was."

"Stand by," Bonty quavered. "We might be about to join it."

The dragon was about the same size as the ones that had brought them down – may actually have been one of them. It was about twice the length of the *Conch*, plated in huge scales of white material like some sort of ceramic. The scales would have to share some properties with ceramic, Galana noted in the clinical inner voice of near-total panic, just to deal with the heat. She'd thought the same thing as she watched them flame their way into the atmosphere.

Certain parts of the creature's body, especially the rims of its vast jet-engine nostrils and its great jagged mouth, were discoloured – most likely from the even greater heat of the dragon's fire. For some reason, the side of its immense wormlike body behind and beneath its left wing, which was all they could see from its current position, was similarly heat-scorched. Galana wondered if maybe the monster had vents, or gills of some sort to shoot more flame from beneath its wings. It would, she thought, explain how they'd managed to get airborne and even fly out into nearby space. Jet-powered, in truth, not dependent on the lifting force of the wings themselves.

She realised that her final moments had gone on long enough for her to start analysing the life-form, and that this might just mean they weren't her final moments after all. She looked up at the huge, mad, craggy white face of the dragon.

"*YOU DARE TO APPROACH THE IDOL!*" the dragon's voice was an ear-splitting roar far louder than the sound of it dragging itself through the treasure hills. Galana, Basil and Bonjamin clapped their hands to their ears, and Chillybin rocked back a little on her great armoured feet.

The voice was also speaking quite understandable Fleet-standard words, with no translation – creatively voiced or otherwise – needed from the computer.

"You're not serious – they're speaking Fleet too?" Hartigan exclaimed.

"It is a universal language," Galana said doubtfully. "Although I wasn't expecting it to be quite *this* universal."

The dragon tilted its great head and rumbled threateningly, the heat from its slightly-parted jaws like an open furnace. Hartigan staggered back further and Bonty slipped a hand under the human's arm and propped him up. Even for the Molranoids, the heat was overwhelming. Galana wondered how long Chilly's suit would hold up.

To her surprise, Hartigan pulled himself upright and held to Bonty's arm

– and, raising his voice, addressed the monster. "I am Captain Basil Hartigan of the ACS *Conch*," he called in loud, clear Grand Bo. "We are on a peaceful mission of exploration - "

"*WHAT IS THE MAMMAL JABBERING ABOUT?!*" the dragon thundered. "*MAKE IT BE SILENT!*"

"We are peaceful explorers," Galana switched to the Fleet language the dragon apparently understood. "We had no intention of trespassing, and if you hadn't brought us to the surface - "

"*INTRUDERS ARE NOT ALLOWED TO LEAVE!*" the dragon interrupted once more. "*WE WANT NO INTERFERENCE FROM THE CENTRE HERE!*"

"Did it just say something about the Core?" Hartigan asked. "I think I heard the word for 'centre' in there, didn't I? See, I speak Fleet."

Galana nodded, and raised a hand to politely forestall the floundering Captain. "We're not from the Core, that is, The Centre," she explained hurriedly. She attempted to adjust to the dragon's strange phrasing on the fly. "We have nothing to do with The Centre, as a matter of ancient law."

"We're actually from fairly close to the edge of the galaxy ourselves," Bonty added. "Our region of space - "

"Doctor," Galana said warningly.

"Well, right – anyway my point is, we're definitely not from The Centre," Bonty continued.

"Far from it," Galana agreed.

"Perish the thought," Bonty added.

"We didn't know we weren't supposed to come here," Galana went on, "and we would have gone on our way if you hadn't brought us down. We didn't want to get too close to your … your Idol either."

"*YOU LIE!*" the dragon rumbled. "*YOU SEEK THE GLORY OF THE IDOL OF NNAL! YOU WOULD TAKE THE ORB FOR YOURSELVES!*" Galana and Bonty exchanged a shocked look – *the Orb of Nnal*, Galana thought, *wasn't that the relic those crazy Fergie crusaders were looking for?* – and apparently the dragon was perceptive enough to recognise the look. "*AH!*" it hissed, its head lowering and moving forward until Basil cried out and Galana felt her own skin blistering, "*YES, YOUR INTENTIONS ARE QUITE TRANSPARENT TO US!*" to Galana's relief, it reared back again. Even if it was about to crush them, it was blessedly cool as the terrible head swept back. "*EVEN THE ELDER RACES ARE LIKE CHILDREN TO THE FUDZU!*"

It may have been the stress of the situation, but Galana almost laughed at how *silly* the name sounded. At least Bonty, still holding an apparently unconscious Captain Hartigan in her left arms, managed to respond more professionally.

"Fudzu – is that what you are?" the doctor shielded her own head from the heat with her upper right arm. "We have creatures like you in some of our myths, we call you dragons - "

"DRAGONS," the Fudzu echoed scornfully. *"DRAGONS ARE BUT A SHADE OF OUR KIND! WE RULED LONG BEFORE ANY SUCH PALE IMITATIONS CREPT OUT TO PLAY IN THE RUINS OF OUR EMPIRE! DRAGON IS JUST A WORD FOR INFERIOR! INSUFFICIENT! IMITATION! SUCH PITIFUL CREATURES WOULD NEVER BE WORTHY CUSTODIANS OF THE IDOL, WOULD NEVER ... "*

Galana once again found herself analysing while the creature ranted on. Now that Bonjamin had mentioned old myths, she did recall hearing of a thing called *Fudzu* before. Had it been a human myth about some kind of fire demon from unreality? A Bonshoon fable? She didn't remember. Bonty, at least, hadn't seemed to recognise it. She'd have to ask the others, in the unlikely event of their survival.

The Fudzu's head snapped up further still, its diatribe trailed off, and it hissed – and at the same moment, Galana became aware of a softer sound from behind them.

The *Nella* had detached from the main body of the *Conch* and was rising into the air.

"Devlin?" Galana called into the comm.

"It's not me," Scrutarius reported. "The computer is still curled up and trying to hide from this alien data thing, and it looks like Wicked Mary has stepped into the gap."

"Tactical Officer Mary?" Galana went on as the shuttle rose and began to manoeuvre sideways, away from the rumbling Fudzu but in the general direction of the treasure-mountain's pinnacle. There was no response from Wicked Mary, and Galana had to admit she hadn't really expected one.

The Fudzu, growling terrifyingly, reared up onto its thick hind legs and opened its jaws. Eye-jarring pink light, like nothing Galana had ever seen, played around its teeth, but fortunately the creature's mouth was so high above them she couldn't see inside. Even so, it looked like it could almost swallow the *Nella* whole.

The shuttle whispered forward … and at that moment the lateral pulse turrets on the main body of the ship still slumped on the hilltop behind them opened up. A searing broadside of weapons-fire baked across the tops of the crews' heads and struck the Fudzu's exposed belly.

As they'd predicted in the course of their shipwrecking, this didn't harm the vast creature so much as annoy it even more than it apparently already was – but for a couple of seconds it was *very* distracted. With a screech it fell back against the mountainside, its flailing legs and its tail almost smashing the cowering crewmembers on the foothill. Galana looked up again in time to see the *Nella* dart forward, elegant and fishlike under Wicked Mary's natural-born and cybernetically-enhanced control, and scoop the golden Idol of Nnal into the air with a pair of heavy-duty cargo claws.

"NO!" the Fudzu shrieked.

It spread its wings and more unearthly pink light gathered between its scales down either side of its body. Galana had a split-second to note that she'd been correct about its jet-venting ability to provide flight power, and another split-second to realise that if it took off from the valley it was *definitely* going to incinerate them, when a second barrage from the *Conch*'s turrets hit the Fudzu. This time Wicked Mary targeted the great webbed wings themselves.

The gunfire once again didn't do much visible damage but the Fudzu's takeoff was botched as it was distracted and enraged a second time. Apparently the shock of seeing its precious Idol get snatched had been enough to make the Fudzu momentarily forget that the *Conch* was still on the ground and ready to fight.

"Fen," Bonty cried urgently, and Galana followed her friend's gaze. On the heat-shimmering horizon, past the edge of the treasure hoard and out over the blackened landscape beyond, the unmistakable shapes of more Fudzu were rapidly approaching. They may have still been a fair distance away, but they were coming fast – and the fact that they were already visible meant they were *big*. Far larger than the one that was bare moments from flattening them.

Galana looked helplessly at their approaching doom, then turned to

Bonty.

"We achieved a quite satisfactory percentage of our mission," she told the wide-eyed Bonshoon.

The Fudzu straightened with a final furious lash of its tail, sending shards of hot metal and precious stones whizzing past them. The *Nella*, which Galana had expected to make for orbit no matter how futile that might have been, instead swept around to hover in front of and just above the snarling creature's head. The Fudzu opened its mouth again.

"*RETURN THE -* " it started.

The cargo arms unfolded, and utter stillness fell over the mountainside. One claw was holding the Idol securely near the top of the golden figure's body, so only its tentacle-like arm and the shining crystal Orb was visible above the mechanism. The other claw was fastened to a heavy metal-composite cargo container designed for low-orbit drops.

Wicked Mary's voice spoke then, through the comms system and from a loudspeaker in the *Nella*'s open cargo bay.

"I liked that *giela*."

And then, in the frozen moment of absolute silence that followed the Fergunakil's pronouncement, the cargo arms swung together. The armoured crate smashed into the Orb of Nnal, and with a powdery little sound the crystal relic exploded into a million pieces.

The silence and stillness returned after this, during which Wicked Mary opened the second claw and carelessly dropped the bent, flattened golden Idol at the Fudzu's great white feet. It landed with a *clonk*, the torso part breaking away entirely from the coiled serpentine base.

Galana stood, one hand on Bonty's back and the other on Chillybin's painfully hot armoured arm, and waited to die.

The Fudzu's head lowered slowly, its mad glittering eyes fixed on the smashed Idol far below. When it spoke, for the first time its voice was quiet. It was practically a whisper.

"What ... " it mumbled. "What did you *do*?"

"Fudzu," Chillybin said with a deliberate movement of her gauntlet, "meet Fergunakil."

Some hours later, the crew was gathered once again in the Captain's quarters. The oddly reassuring grey nothingness of soft-space once again pressed in on them, and they were back underway – considerable repairs still pending, but at least they'd been able to fire up the relative field.

"'We achieved a quite satisfactory percentage of our mission'?" Devlin promptly, and with real outrage in his voice, got to the most important matter. "*That* was what you decided your last words needed to be?"

"I didn't realise you'd heard," Galana admitted.

"Believe me, I wish I hadn't," Scrutarius replied. "Mind you, could we really expect anything better from a Molran?"

"Yes we bally well could," Hartigan, his skin as red as a spicy ration wafer and smothered in grafting bandages from his experiences with the Fudzu, smacked a fist down on his armchair. "Ouch."

"Be careful, Captain," Bonty said mildly. "If that skin doesn't take, it's going to be several *very* uncomfortable hours before I can brew up a new batch."

"Fen, you will formulate a list of heroic final statements," Basil went on, "ranging from inspirational to defiant, every last one of them worthy of the history books. That's an order. Have 'em on my desk by shipboard morning."

"Yes, Captain."

"Also, the next time you lot feel like you're getting a little bit of a sunburn from being too close to something hot, consider taking me a bit of a jolly old safe distance from it, what? I'm not wrapped in whatever wonderful preposterous bullplop you are in the skin department."

"Yes, Captain," Galana repeated.

"Or get me a suit like hers," he added, waving his arm painfully at Chillybin. "My dressing gown is absolutely ruined."

"I will start building you one immediately, Captain," Chilly promised.

"Good," Hartigan scratched moodily at one of the bandages on the back of his hand. "Now why in the name of Old Linda's Handbag d'you think they let us *go*?"

Galana had been thinking about that. They all had, she was sure. To say it had come as a surprise would be an understatement. The Fudzu hadn't just let them go – they had, with great care and diffidence, allowed them to return to their ship and the *Nella* to reattach, and had then very delicately carried them back up into orbit and released them into space like they were some kind of rare and fragile insect. Or, possibly, rare and *exceedingly venomous* insect.

And by the time that had happened, the *big* Fudzu had arrived. Any one of them could have wrapped a claw around the *Conch* and crushed it to oblivion.

"As near as I can guess, Captain," Bonty spoke for them, "they were in shock. They couldn't imagine anyone with a more disproportionate level of violence and ferocity than themselves, with such disregard for its own life. They'd never encountered anything more aggressive than they were."

"There may be a little more to it than that," the *Conch* remarked. The computer had returned to normal, seemingly at the same moment Wicked Mary had smashed the Orb of Nnal and the golden Idol that had been holding it. "I was of course unable to save any of the data that had forced my lockdown, but from what we know about the Orb of Nnal, the Fergunak consider it their rightful property – their *destiny*, in fact."

"Whoops," Scrutarius said.

"Yes," the computer agreed solemnly. "Regardless of the truth of the matter, the Fudzu may have somehow recognised that Wicked Mary was the rightful owner of their sacred relic, and as such she had the right to keep it or destroy it as she pleased."

"I was also unable to absorb much of the data that was apparently built into the Orb," Wicked Mary's voice said from the comm system. She was the only one who was not technically present, since even the option of attending the gathering through her *giela* was now gone. They'd offered to hold the get-together down on the Aquarium deck, but the great shark had politely declined. She would, she said, immediately get to work building a new *giela*.

Galana had already made a mental note to keep an eye on *that* project. Just in case. "But you absorbed *some* information?" she asked.

"Not exactly, little flesh," Wicked Mary replied. "The Orb itself was empty – just a hollow vessel. What it was supposed to contain, and the data that might have been somehow encoded into the crystal ... that is what I may still be able to learn, given time to study the brief flashes I was able to save."

"You know, if you'd held onto the Orb, you could have studied it at a bit more leisure," Bonty pointed out.

"The Fudzu would almost certainly have incinerated us if she had tried," Galana said, when the silence had extended long enough to convince her that Wicked Mary was simply too flabbergasted by the idea to respond. To a Fergunakil, quite simply, *not* destroying the most precious cultural relic of a civilisation responsible for mildly inconveniencing her was just utterly incomprehensible.

"Well, I'll tell you what," Hartigan said. "If we ever run into those Fergies – what were they called again? The Searching, Starving, Lost?"

"They're the ones," Bonty agreed.

"Let's maybe *not* tell them that Bloody Mary smashed their Orb," Hartigan suggested. "Hm?"

"Excellent notion, young Basil," Chillybin said, deadpan behind her envirosuit helmet.

PART THREE: THE LAST ALICORN

THE FANTASTICAL CAKES OF ZOOGO ZAROY

"Shmoof," Basil announced. "It's this powdery stuff that puffs up into a big kind of blob when you pour water on it. If you eat it right away, it goes on swelling in your stomach and makes you feel like you're about to burst."

"Real," Bonty declared. "I've had it."

Bonty usually won their games of 'Real Food Or Just Some Random Noise I Made?'. She liked to pat her round belly and joke that it was because she was a Bonshoon, and Bonshooni loved their food, but the simple truth was that she was three-and-a-half thousand years old and had tried just about everything. Moreover, she had an endless supply of random noises that she could insist were foods that no longer existed, and not even the *Conch*'s computer could prove she was lying.

"Alright, Bonty," Hartigan sat back and raised his glass in a toast. "The round is yours. Let's hear your next outburst of simply appalling claptrap."

"Marglegargle," Bonty pronounced happily.

"Real," Scrutarius said immediately. "Although it's better known by its main ingredient, Madame Margolyse, Marglegargle is a sort of warm drink made from the stuff. Disgustingly sweet."

"Does that count as a food?" Chillybin asked. "If it is a drink … "

"Aha, point of order," Hartigan straightened in his armchair. "As Captain, I need to deliberate on this before making a ruling. When would one usually drink this Marglegargle? And would one drink it from a glass, or a mug, or a bowl?"

"Usually a bowl," Devlin admitted, "and it's usually served as a dessert rather than a – what do you call it? A nightcap?"

"Well then, I say it qualifies in the same way gazpacho did," Hartigan declared, picked up a spoon from his empty supper plate and tapped the side of his glass. "Round to Devlin."

"I still think you made gazpacho up," Galana said, "and the computer is in cahoots with you."

"Why, Commander Fen," the *Conch* said, "the very thought."

"As an AstroCorps officer you should definitely know about gazpacho," Hartigan agreed solemnly.

They didn't usually talk about food, because sooner or later Wicked Mary would always say something horrible and make it creepy. But right now she was off the general comm grid and even her *giela* – rebuilt since their run-in with the Fudzu – was offline. She was hunting Squirty Pete III, the battle squid they'd grown for her, and had promised to only check in if she needed medical attention. Galana had long since stopped worrying about their mission failing due to their Fergunakil crewmember being killed by her own dinner. Wicked Mary was, it seemed, quite invincible.

The game went on late into the night, shipboard standard, at which point the human and the aki'Drednanth retired to sleep. Molran, Bonshoon and Blaran went back to their quarters as well.

The next morning, they were all in high spirits. It was finally time to come out of the grey and make another planetary survey, the next stop in their long journey around the galaxy. They had reason to believe the planet they'd be arriving at had life. And not just any old life, but *intelligent* life. They'd been pointed in the direction of the planet, which had looked promisingly vegetation-covered and hospitable at a disconnect of several hundred light years, by a piece of alien technology that they'd found on *another* of their recent stops. And when a piece of technology pointed to a place, as the Captain had been happily and optimistically saying for the past several weeks, that place was just *bound* to be interesting.

The fact that the device – a probe of some kind – had been long-abandoned and the planet upon which it had made a crater had been waterless and otherwise uninhabited, did nothing to dampen their enthusiasm. The *Conch* had made a few guesses about it, from examination of the wreckage. It had used a primitive but quite cunning form of relative drive, providing a one-way trip for the machine. This meant it had probably been a prototype of some sort. The drive and generator had burned out and dissolved neatly on arrival, but the probe had remained. And with it, a name: Zoogo Zaroy.

Well, the *Conch* had been fairly certain it was a name. There hadn't been much information to work with. Years on the inhospitable planet's surface had eroded most of the markings on and data inside the machine. But there were some broken electronic scraps that they'd managed to piece together. Icons for *inventor* or *professor*, and others for *leaving home planet* and *returning to home planet*, and even *soft-space* – all of these were complex concepts, and the art of figuring out *sounds* from alien symbols was even more intricate, but the *Conch*'s computer was very good at its job.

There had been some disagreement about *Zoogo Zaroy*, though, because there just didn't seem to be any translation for it. Just the sounds that the computer insisted the symbols represented. This was what had inspired their games of 'Real Food Or Just Some Random Noise I Made?', in the spirit of gentle ribbing.

As a result, they had been looking forward to arriving at 'Zoogo's World' for a long time.

"Here we go then," Hartigan said cheerfully, and the drab grey of relative speed was replaced with the darkness of space. Zoogo's World, still as green and blue and pleasant-looking as it had been several hundred light years away, rose into view. "Computer?"

"We have buildings," the *Conch* reported. Hartigan, Scrutarius and Bonty all cheered in a slightly non-regulation manner, but Galana didn't comment. She felt like cheering herself. It had been a long time since they'd found anything remotely interesting.

"Oh, *jolly good*," Hartigan said. "Can we send them a message using the language we found on the probe? That's sure to impress them."

"I'm sorry, Basil," the *Conch* said. "There are buildings, and evidence of technology, but the only life-signs I am detecting are small animals, birds, local wildlife. Nothing very big, at least in the vicinity of the structures. And no sign at all of habitation *inside* the buildings. Nothing intelligent."

"So … we've arrived too late?" Hartigan asked unhappily. "Nothing but ruins? Of all the jolly rotten luck … "

"Not exactly," the *Conch* replied. "Everything is in good repair. The inhabitants are gone but the buildings are not ruined, or even particularly overgrown."

"Fled?" Bonty asked. "A fight with other natives, perhaps?"

"There is no sign of evacuation, and even less signs of any sort of fighting," Wicked Mary reported. "Everything is intact."

"I would have to do a full orbital scan to be sure," the computer went on, "but there don't seem to *be* any other natives. These buildings would appear to be the only ones. It is a very small set of structures, hardly what one might consider a civilisation."

"Unless they happen to be as tiny as the Nyif Nyif," Scrutarius put in.

"There is that possibility," the *Conch* conceded. "It seems unlikely, but - "

"I say, is this planet inhabited or not?" Hartigan demanded. "If there *were* people here and they've gone, *how* did they go?"

"There are no spaceports," the *Conch* replied. "I have spotted a couple of small platforms that may have been used to launch the probe we found, and may have been used to launch a larger vessel containing the rest of the settlement's population."

"The probe we found was a prototype," Galana admitted. "Perhaps we have arrived just after the finished product shipped out."

"So ... what, we missed 'em going the other way?" Hartigan scowled.

"There's a set of laboratories or research centres, or something of the sort," the *Conch* went on while Hartigan sat looking very unsatisfied, "although of course alien architecture is hard to identify. And it is all deserted."

"No sign of anything dangerous?" Hartigan pressed. "Toxins in the air, viruses? Nothing, in short, that would prompt an evacuation? Interdimensional fire beasts the size of a solar system, say, ready to jump out of soft-space and burn us all to a crisp?"

"Or maybe an underground construction with two hundred billion Damorakind hiding in it?" Scrutarius joined in.

"Or a lost aki'Drednanth subspecies that has been liberated and slaughtered all intelligent life on the planet?" Chillybin added. "Oh, wait ... I should be the one telling you about that."

"Yes yes, we're all very clever and amusing," the *Conch* said.

Chillybin gave a deep bark of amusement, then tapped at her controls. "We are getting a steady signal from one of the buildings," she reported, "but it just seems to be a beacon telling us that some machine or other is still switched on down there. Whatever happened, it happened very recently."

"No other comms?" Galana asked.

"No, Commander," Chillybin replied. "Just the single tone from the active device."

"You're about to suggest we go down there," Galana said to Basil, "aren't you?"

"Well I wasn't about to suggest we turn around and head off on another four-month jaunt through the bally grey, Fen," Hartigan said cheerfully. He jumped to his feet and pointed dynamically planetwards. "Detach the *Nella*!"

Galana sighed. "Yes, Captain."

They landed not far from the cluster of alien buildings, making use of the landing pad that had apparently been used to launch the probe they'd found. Judging by the state of the probe and the run-down look of the machinery around the pad, it had been some years since the last launch. The rest of the settlement was tidier and not so long-abandoned ... although it *was* clearly still abandoned.

Hartigan, Galana, Bonty, Chillybin, Scrutarius and Wicked Mary walked into the silent, eerie settlement. They moved slowly and cautiously, scanning all the while.

"Seems like a nice place," Hartigan remarked. He looked around. "Quiet, though."

"Yes," Galana frowned at her scanner. "According to this, there aren't even any birds or wildlife in this area. Nothing bigger than a bug."

"What size of a bug?" Devlin asked with the ghost of a smile.

"*Small*," Galana said patiently.

They crept into the largest building, and stopped just inside the doorway.

"Well," Captain Hartigan said, "I don't think any of us were expecting to see that."

Just inside the entrance, a strange object sat on the floor. At first Galana thought it was an alien life-form crouching there, some kind of gelatinous gastropod or other mollusc. It was like a large rounded disc of lumpy brown, with a second smaller disc lying on top of it, which in turn was decorated with pale brown globes that might have been eyes or buds or …

"I hate to be *that* Bonshoon, but is that a cake?" Bonty asked.

Galana blinked. The object *did* look like a large dessert, smothered in decorative confectionery. As she looked across the large, clean space, she saw three … no, four, five more of the objects, each one different. Some were on the floor, others slumped on the strange articles of alien furniture and machinery around the room. Some were bright pink and blue, others a rich brown and black, others white and decorated with little crystalline flowers of what looked like sugar.

"Yes," Galana said. She stepped over to the closest of the strange objects and held her scanner above it. She read sugars and fats, complex chains of phosphates and acids … it was inert, reconstituted from common molecules, and had apparently been baked at a high temperature. It was a cake. "Yes, it would seem to be a cake."

"This one too," Devlin said from the far side of the room, where a large intricate pink and purple thing was slumped inside what looked like a wire cage. Another cake, this one black and decorated with twirls of red cream, lay on the floor nearby next to a broken and unidentified piece of lab equipment. Scrutarius poked at it with his boot but stopped short of making contact. "And this one."

"I would recommend *strongly* against eating any of these cakes," Galana said.

"Now really Fen, what kind of fools do you take us for?" Hartigan chided her.

Even as Galana spoke Wicked Mary had clicked forward, scooped up a handful of creamy topping from another of the cakes, and smeared it underneath the lenses and scanners on her *giela*'s head. "Yes," she said, planting her cake-messy hands on her gleaming metal hip-joints. "We do have *some* self-control, Commander."

Scrutarius sniggered.

Galana sighed. "Anyone *with organic components that cannot be chemically sterilised on returning to the ship*," she said, "don't touch the cakes."

Aside from the assortment of cakes, and the fact that they all appeared to have been freshly-made in the past few hours, there was nothing much to see in the strange alien laboratory. They did locate a few devices, like the one lying next to the cake on the floor that Scrutarius had found, with similar markings to those found on the probe. This confirmed their theory that the probe had come from this site, or at least that the same alien culture was responsible for both the probe and this settlement. It would, however, take some time for the *Conch* to make any sense of what they'd found.

"I believe this is a workstation personally belonging to Zoogo Zaroy," Wicked Mary called from a small side-chamber. They joined her, and found another tidy room filled with more complex machinery and a large, particularly delicious-looking layered cake covered in swirls of pale purple cream. It was sitting on a curved piece of furniture that Galana guessed was a chair – if, that is, the aliens' physiology was anything like their own. "There is another cake over here," the *giela* added, "under what looks like a scanning machine."

"Is that the tech that was giving off the signal we picked up?" Scrutarius asked.

"No. All the devices in here are dead," Chillybin reported. "The signal is coming from the next building. It must be a generator of some kind. Maybe a solar battery."

"Let's go and check it out," Hartigan said, and scratched his face in irritation. "I think there *are* bugs here," he grumbled. "Attracted to the sugar I expect … Bonty, careful with the samples but let's see if we can't give one or two of these cake thingies a bit of a good old analysing, what?"

"Copy that, Captain," Bonjamin replied, and pulled out a bio-sample container.

They checked the other buildings, but aside from the bulky shape of what did indeed look like a solar-fed power source of some kind, and a couple more cakes, they didn't find anything of interest. Now that she was looking for them, Galana noticed several more of the desserts scattered in the undergrowth and pathways around the little scientific outpost. These ones had definitely been smudged and flattened by the elements and probably – as Hartigan had guessed – by the local fauna. The absence of larger scavengers was still a mystery, however.

She frowned at the Captain, who was muttering and scratching and now seemed to have several unpleasant-looking white growths on his face and hands.

"Captain," she said, "something here is affecting you. *Badly.*"

"What? Nonsense, just a couple of rotten old bug bites," Hartigan scoffed, and picked at one of the little sores. He frowned and crumbled the white substance between his fingers. "That's odd. It's almost like … "

"Captain?" Galana took a half-step towards him, then froze when she saw the thick, clear amber fluid oozing from the wound. It wasn't blood, but she didn't know enough about human anatomy to say *what* it was. Hartigan's eyes rolled back in his head and he staggered. "Tactical Officer Mary," Galana went on quickly, "please help the Captain back to the *Nella*. Doctor, Chief, we're leaving. Chillybin, we need to ... Chilly?"

The aki'Drednanth was standing in the doorway of the main laboratory building, opening and closing one of her giant refrigerated gloves slowly.

"I think this is also affectings me me me," she said, moving her fingers slowly and meticulously to transcribe the words.

"Back to the *Nella*," Galana said, fighting down a sudden bolt of panic. *We should have run more tests. Atmospheric analyses. We should have sent the* giela *in first.* "Back to the *Nella*, now."

The shuttle section had a minimal med station, but after a moment's consideration Galana set them to launch and headed back to the main ship. The Fergunakil's habitat was a whole separate environmental system and the rest of them were already as exposed as they were going to be, so the benefit of the main medical bay outweighed the risk of bringing an infection on board.

The Captain was worsening steadily. By the time Wicked Mary set him down on the little bed and Bonty began to examine him, he was mumbling and shivering. The white sores had run together in a sort of crust and was steadily weeping sticky yellow-brown fluid.

Bonty identified it almost immediately.

"It's sugar," she said.

Galana looked across from where she and Scrutarius were helping Chillybin out of her suit. "Excuse me?" she said.

"Not Earth-plant sugar, of course," Bonty went on, "a sort of variant that seems to be distilling out of Basil's blood. And this – this stuff – seems to be some sort of syrup," she touched one of the oozing sores with a sensor, and Hartigan groaned in pain. "Fen, his body is converting into ... into *food*."

"His body is already made of food," Wicked Mary pointed out. "If we are being technical."

"Well, alright," Bonty said, "but it's – it's - "

"You mean he's turning into a *cake*," Scrutarius said. "Something on that planet turned the last bunch of settlers into cakes, and now it's doing the same thing to us."

"We don't seem to be affected yet," Galana said, "but it may just be slower to work on us. Molran, Bonshoon and Blaran immune systems are - " they finally got the envirosuit open and Chillybin staggered out in a cloud of freezing, sickly-sweet vapour. Aki'Drednanth didn't smell particularly good at the best of times when they came out of their freezer suits and began to thaw, but the smell that was now exuding from beneath her fur was somehow even worse because it was so *pleasant*. "Doctor Bont," Galana went on urgently.

"Coming, coming," Bonty slipped a sedative into the Captain's bloodstream – or syrup-stream, perhaps, by that stage – and hurried over to help Galana with the aki'Drednanth. The enormous beast towered over them and could have lifted one of them in each hand, but she let them shuffle her over to a patch of floor near the med machines and allowed Bonty to examine her. "She doesn't seem to have the same symptoms as the Captain," she said. "There's still a sort of sugar forming, but it's more like – like a frozen fatty layer … what do humans call it? Icy cream?"

"Ice cream," Scrutarius said grimly.

"They're turning into different sorts of cakes," Galana said, remembering the variety of strange alien desserts that had been lying around the laboratories. "Probably because they have different chemical compositions and operate at different temperatures. There were no people or larger animals in the immediate area because they'd all been transformed. What else do we know?"

"Whatever it is, it was airborne," Bonty said. "Particles hitting the skin, or being breathed in. Bloody Mary was the only one to touch a cake, and nobody ate any, yet it affected Basil first, and Chilly not long after. So whatever it is, it was small enough to get into her suit."

Galana nodded. Aki'Drednanth envirosuits weren't exactly airtight, although they could be emergency sealed and run off an internal air supply if necessary. It hadn't *appeared* to be necessary on Zoogo's World. "And it is not affecting us," she said, "*yet*. What else didn't it affect?"

"There were bugs," Scrutarius said. "Even in the affected area."

"And plants," Bonty added. "The plants weren't being converted. That cake in the cage in the lab, it must have been a test subject, an animal of some kind."

"And the one in Zaroy's workstation may have been the first of the settlers to be affected," Wicked Mary added, "and the cake in the chair … Zoogo Zaroy themselves."

"I got samples from most of them," Bonty said, "I'll need to analyse them … "

By the time they reconnected to the *Conch* and got the Captain and Chillybin to the medical bay, both patients had begun to change shape. Their limbs and bodies were shifting, softening, and contracting into the familiar rounded layers of Zaroy's cakes. Hartigan's sugar-encrusted, syrup-running skin was turning into a glazed crust, and Chilly's grey-white fur was vanishing into a marbled swirl of fluffy white and blue ice cream. Neither of them could talk anymore, and both were struggling to breathe as their organs failed – or, more accurately, simply ceased to exist.

Even worse, Devlin raised a hand and showed Galana a spreading pattern of dark brown lines under his skin.

"It feels hot," he said, "and it's getting hotter."

"I have analysed the symbols found in the laboratory," the *Conch* said, "and cross-checked them against the information from the probe. With a larger set of data, I have been able to make more accurate translations."

"Go ahead," Galana said, and went on passing samples and solutions back and forth between Bonjamin and the medical scanner. She herself was starting to feel a slowly-building feverish heat in her throat and legs, but didn't have time to stop and examine her symptoms. Hartigan was shrinking and condensing still further, grotesque and quivering. The molecules that had made up his body were converting, the excess trailing away as slightly discoloured water or baking off him as steam as his cake-form cooked to readiness. Soon there would be nothing left.

"It seems Zoogo Zaroy was indeed an inventor, although perhaps a more obvious title would be 'mad scientist'," the *Conch* explained. "Zaroy was *sent* to this planet, *exiled* here with a small group of followers. I am not sure of the crimes Zaroy committed on their home planet, but their intentions seem to have been benign. They had plans to feed the hungry, cure the sick … it seems as though Zaroy's methods were quite mad, but did not warrant execution. They were sent here, to a planet where they could experiment to their hearts' content, just in case they managed to succeed."

"And the probe?" Bonty asked. "Galana, run the conversion simulator on that sample of the unaffected local plant material I collected."

"The probe was something of a side-experiment," the *Conch* continued. "As Zaroy's madness deepened, it was apparently accompanied by a certainty that they deserved to return in triumph to their home world. The probe was intended to test the relative speed engine Zaroy had put together."

"Quite a mind," Wicked Mary said.

"Yeah, sure," Scrutarius muttered. "So why did it crash on that uninhabited planet? Don't tell me – that planet *had* been inhabited, and the probe had carried some kind of weaponised version of the invention that turned everything into dust and ice."

"You have a very vivid imagination, Devlin," the *Conch* said. "No, it seems as though the probe's crash-landing was a simple accident. Or it was intercepted by Zaroy's people and discarded on the planet where we found it. They had no intention of letting Zaroy return home."

"And this home – where is it?" Devlin asked. His voice was hoarse and pained. "Why didn't *they* stop us from landing here?"

"Unknown," the *Conch* replied. "Zaroy's work continued. The idea was to take a virus, or a smart nano-particle, that would be able to generate edible food from basic materials. Sugars and other molecules, reconstituted from various matter. Zaroy … liked cakes, and so the first attempt was intended to convert - "

"A small animal into a cake," Galana said.

"Yes."

"I'm isolating several small-scale particle structures that are present in the cakes but absent from the plants," Bonty said. "They're driving the transformation and they were probably what had kept the cakes down on the planet so fresh … sort of a – a food and food-preservation solution all in one … " she straightened, swayed, then leaned back to her consoles. "It's too widespread and complex to remove," she went on. "Taking it out particle by particle will never work."

"I would assume that was what Zaroy was working on doing," Wicked Mary said, "in the workstation before finally succumbing to the same contamination."

"Obviously, the particles breached containment," the *Conch* agreed. "They converted Zaroy's assistants – and all the other nearby life-forms, including the great Zoogo Zaroy – into cakes before anyone could stop it or reverse it."

"But it *did* stop," Bonty said. "The entire planet's biosphere wasn't made into cakes, there are still birds and other animals elsewhere – it was just that little area around the settlement. What - "

"Where is Basil?" the computer said suddenly.

"That's him on the examination table," Galana said wearily, and when she waved a hand at the slowly-pulsating half-cake monstrosity on the slab, she saw that her skin had darkened and seemed to be bubbling.

"Basil?" the *Conch* cried out, its voice alarmingly *worried* considering it was just a computer. "Basil, can you hear me? *Basil!*"

"Hearing – that's it!" Bonty gasped. "The *signal*. The conversion particles are being activated by that generator down on the surface. That's why it hasn't spread beyond the immediate area of the settlement. And it's still affecting the particles inside us, up here, because the signal we picked up is still technically – computer, are we still picking up the signal from the surface?"

"*Basil, speak to me!*" the computer wailed.

Bonty's voice cracked. "Mary, shoot that - "

"Already rolling us into position, delicious Doctor," Wicked Mary reported.

"And since I'm *actually* turning into an *actual* cake, you can quit it with the 'delicious' talk for once in your big wet smelly life," Bonty snapped.

The doctor's anger was so out of character that for a moment it jolted Galana out of her deepening daze. "Wait," she gasped, "can't we just cut comms?"

"Won't do it," Bonty shook her head. "We closed the communication channel as soon as we realised it wasn't actually a message of any kind, but it's still enough for the particles to pick up on. The frequency is still part of our ambient system now. We need to cut off the source."

"What if you're wrong? What if we lose something we need down there?"

"At this stage we haven't *got* much to lose," Bonty said grimly. Galana noticed, although her eyesight was blurring, that her old friend had begun developing a strange pattern of glistening toffee-coloured stripes on her face and hands. "Mary?"

"The generator is destroyed," Wicked Mary confirmed. "Quite a lot of the surrounding area too. It was … rather more explosive than I had estimated."

"Stand by," Bonty said, frowning and leaning over the scanner, her lower hands still flashing swiftly back and forth as she prepared more samples. "The conversion has stopped," she reported in relief.

"What about reversing it?" Galana asked.

"I can try simply switching the signal patterns from positive to negative and then playing the resulting signal from the log over the comm system," Wicked Mary suggested. "It may throw the process into reverse."

Galana attempted to raise her ears, but they felt stiff and heavy. It didn't seem likely that she would be able to hear the signal anyway. "Wouldn't Zaroy have thought of that?" she wheezed.

"I don't see why, Commander," Wicked Mary replied. "Zoogo Zaroy was mad, you know."

To everybody's relief – especially, for some unfathomable reason, the computer's – the horrifying process that Devlin later dubbed 'the cakening' slowly reversed. Hartigan and Chillybin were critically drained of nutrients as a result of their change, but Bonty was sufficiently recovered to set them up with everything they needed from the med bay. Within a month, Chillybin was back in the Icebox and galloping up and down in full health. Within three months, Basil was back on his feet and hobbling, a little frailly, along the corridors and insisting that his moustache still smelled 'liquoricey'.

It took a while for them to fully isolate and clean out the Zaroy particles responsible for the cakening, but with the particles inert they were able to work at leisure as they continued on their way through soft-space. The crew unanimously agreed that if they ever came across the species that had exiled Zoogo Zaroy rather than simply stopping the mad scientist from experimenting, that species could count itself damn lucky if they didn't drop a waste canister full of the particles and a signal booster unit from high orbit, and leave them to their fate. Part of being an AstroCorps crew was taking the high road and doing the right thing, Hartigan said, but getting turned into a bally cake was a bit too bally much if anyone were to bally well ask him.

And the next time they all gathered together in the Captain's quarters for supper, not one of them suggested playing the 'Real Food Or Just Some Random Noise I Made?' game.

Not even Wicked Mary.

Soon, in **The Fang o' God**:

It had snuck up on them without warning, completely unexpected and catching them completely unawares.

"Ten years," Basil shook his head. "Has it really?"

"According to the ship's calendar," Galana confirmed, "we departed from Declivitorion-On-The-Rim on this day exactly ten years ago."

"You know what this means," Scrutarius said with a wide grin.

"Please no," Galana murmured.

"Yes," Devlin beamed. "According to *ancient* spacefaring tradition - "

"It is not ancient," Galana protested. "It was made up by a single AstroCorps crew who insisted they'd learned it from the Fleet, but the whole thing was traced back to a group of Fleet Blaren who made the whole thing up. I have the transcripts - "

"*According to* ancient *spacefaring tradition*," Devlin repeated, "after travelling together for ten years, a starship crew should share secrets with one another that they have not previously told anyone."

"That sounds like a perfectly *daft* idea," Hartigan declared. "And besides,

I'm pretty sure you and I passed the old ten-year mark long before now, Dev. And we've never - "

"Ah, but this is official *AstroCorps crew business*," Devlin said earnestly, "and it's time. Look, I'll get us started if you like. I know a lot of you have been curious about my special Blaran augmentation, the alterations I've made to set me aside from the Molran norm. As you can see, they're not readily apparent," he said, and spread his arms.

"Alright," Bonty leaned forward. "Tell us."

"It might actually be easier if I show you," Scrutarius said, and Galana was surprised to hear a note of hesitation – perhaps even shyness – entering the bold Blaran's voice.

He raised his lower hands to the top of his casual off-duty trousers … and at that moment the ship's computer sounded an all-hands alarm, summoning them all to the bridge.

THE FANG O' GOD

"What's going on, old girl?" Captain Hartigan asked as they took their places on the bridge. "We're not due to come out of the grey for another week yet, are we?"

"No, Captain," the *Conch* said formally, "but I have reason to believe we should perhaps stop here, make a quick scan, and set a new course."

Galana exchanged worried looks with Basil, then Chillybin, then Wicked Mary. The aki'Drednanth and the Fergunakil didn't bring much to the worried-looks table, since one wore a helmet and the other was a robot.

"Stop here?" Hartigan said worriedly. "We're in the middle of a jump. That's a fancy bit of footwork. Why bother?"

"Well," the *Conch* said, "as you know, we were headed in this direction because of a signal we received at our last stop."

"Bit of a strong way of putting it," Basil said. "It was – what did you call it, Fen? An echo of a shadow of something that might have been a signal once upon a time?"

"It was very poetic, I thought," Scrutarius said from the engineering console. "You know, for a Molran."

"I take exception to that," Galana said, although she and Devlin regularly made fun of one another in a friendly manner. "What we picked up was something that *might* have been a signal from a ship in trouble, but it was coming from several hundred light years away. So if it *was* a distress call, we were probably well and truly too late."

"Still, interesting enough to make it worth checking out," Bonty said. "Slimy fungus doesn't send a detectable signal across that sort of distance."

"Not unless it's *really* slimy," Devlin agreed.

"All true, so why are we stopping now?" Hartigan prompted.

"That's just it," the computer said quickly. "I managed to reconstruct the signal, and it was just a random pulse, nothing that would suggest it was a ship. I'd hate for you to arrive and be depressed to find nothing."

"We've survived so far," Hartigan said casually. "I don't see why we should stop now. If there's nothing there, there's nothing there. Let's check it and see."

"Unless you think there's some danger?" Galana asked the computer.

"There might be," the *Conch* said. "If the signal was a ship, and it was brought down by something ... "

"We don't run away from things like that, old girl," Hartigan declared. "We're AstroCorps, not the ... " he waved a hand. "Help me out, Dev."

"The Buxland Squealy-runners," Scrutarius supplied promptly.

"We're AstroCorps, not the Buxland Squealy-runners," Hartigan said with relish. "Oh, that's a good one. Who are the Buxland Squealy-runners?"

"They're nothing," Scrutarius said. "I just made them up."

"Oh."

It was another week to their destination. In that time, they performed as many emergency drills as Basil and Galana felt were necessary, but there really wasn't much they could do to prepare. The computer, giving every sign of being in a bit of a sulk about the whole thing, didn't find out anything more about the signal they were chasing.

Finally the day arrived and they all gathered on the bridge.

"It is an ordinary-looking solar system," the *Conch* reported as they emerged from soft-space. "No big tech in orbit around the planets or the sun. Only one planet appears to be habitable. Some small technology signatures on the surface," it added in what Galana could have sworn was a grudging tone. "Nothing too complex."

"More complex than a slimy fungus though," Bonty said enthusiastically.

"Yes, but no *ship*," the *Conch* said. "Maybe we should just - "

"Oh come now - " Hartigan said in exasperation.

"I am ... in contact," Chillybin said unexpectedly, before the Captain and the ship's computer could get into an argument.

"Chilly?" Galana said. "I'm not seeing any comms from the surface."

"No, it is – the presence of intelligent creatures," the aki'Drednanth explained. "I recognise the shapes of their minds."

"Oh," Hartigan said excitedly, "I thought it usually took a while for you to do that. Are these aliens you're already familiar with, then?"

"Quite familiar, Captain," Chillybin replied. "They're humans."

There was a shocked silence.

"I thought you said you sensed *intelligent* creatures," Scrutarius said. Hartigan turned and gave him a narrow look. "Sorry," Devlin added. "Couldn't resist."

"You monkeys really do get everywhere," Bonty said, "don't you?"

"Now we are receiving a transmission," the *Conch* said while Hartigan was still opening and closing his mouth. "The language … interesting."

"What is it?" Galana asked.

"It is a human language spoken on Coriel, but it took me a moment to recognise it," the computer explained. "I would say that they started with Coriane as it was several hundred years ago and developed it from there, in a quite different way to how it has developed on Coriel."

"I don't speak *modern* Coriane," Hartigan finally managed to say. He sounded disgruntled.

"Neither do I," Galana admitted. The *Porticon*, her home Worldship, occasionally visited Coriel but she'd never really spent much time down there. The Coriane were a strange lot – and that was just the few Molren who lived there. "And there are only humans down there?" she glanced at Chillybin for confirmation.

Chilly nodded. "Several thousand of them, I would say."

"That sounds right," the *Conch* agreed, then paused for a long moment. "The main settlement is the source of the tech readings. It *could* be the remains of a dismantled starship," it admitted. "Its distress-call days are long behind it, though."

Galana nodded to herself. "Once we establish full contact," she told the *Conch*, "it may be a good idea to just send the Captain's image until we can be sure the sight of aliens won't upset them. These must be the descendants of a shipwreck. It's been known to happen – just not so far from Six Species space."

"Opening a channel," the *Conch* said.

Galana looked down at what appeared to be a fairly normal human being, although she had to admit she wasn't familiar with many humans aside from their Captain. This one didn't have fur on its face, although it still had a tidy mane on the top of its head. It seemed flushed and out of breath, and Galana imagined it had come running to respond to the hails of the starship in orbit.

"I am Misrepresentation Fizzschlifft, voice of the Gunumban people," the computer translated the high-speed jabbering of the human into Grand Bo with a good approximation of the human's gruff tone. "It is a great surprise and very exciting to see a human face … " the sound cut off at that point, and the human talked animatedly for several more seconds before stopping and waiting expectantly. "I am sorry," the *Conch* went on in its normal voice, "I seem to have lost the audio feed. Attempting to compensate. The real-time translation may have been too much for the data buffers … "

Galana frowned as the computer continued to explain, using more and more pointless technical jargon. After it had tried to stop them even arriving at this system, it was hard to believe this was just another accident. The *Conch* had, after all, translated far more alien languages than this dialect of Coriane with absolutely no problems whatsoever. But what should she do about it? What *could* she do about it?

"'Misrepresentation'?" Hartigan asked with a raised eyebrow.

"I believe the word was 'Calumny'," Wicked Mary said, "but it was a name and perhaps not intended to be translated."

Galana called up the received transmission, but it was all chopped up and incomplete – and it didn't look like a system glitch. It looked *edited*. She glanced across at Wicked Mary, who had obviously been receiving and translating the message from the surface using some equipment of her own that she had set up without their knowledge. The *giela* returned her look with its blank collection of sensors, and Galana wondered why she'd bothered.

"Yes, yes it was Calumny Fizzschlifft, and I am ready to translate your response now, Captain," the *Conch* was saying. "I will attempt to re-establish a link and get the rest of the previous transmission. I'm sorry about this."

"Alright old girl, not to worry," Hartigan said mildly. "We got the important bits, what?" he cleared his throat. "Greetings, Calumny Fizzschlifft and the Gunumban people," he went on officially. "I am Captain Basil Hartigan, and on behalf of AstroCorps and the Six Species, I bid you greetings from your long-lost cousins a – gosh, what, it must be just about a third of the way around the bally galaxy by this point, eh Fen?"

"Yes, Captain," Galana replied, hoping they weren't about to show her in the transmission and freak out the poor unsuspecting Gunumbans.

"I have translated the greeting into Coriane – or, well, I suppose we should refer to it as Gunumban at this point," the *Conch* said, sounding a bit less anxious. Galana suspected this was because the computer was getting the hang of whatever trick it was trying to pull on them, and this was more than a little worrying. Their whole mission, the whole act of communicating with aliens, was at stake if they could not trust what the computer told them the aliens were saying.

Wicked Mary might become their only source of unedited information. And that went beyond 'more than a little worrying' and well into 'downright terrifying'.

The Captain and Calumny Fizzschlifft exchanged a few more enthusiastic but questionable messages. The Gunumbans were aware, from the 'old stories' of their ancestors, of the Six Species and actually had some archived images of Molren, aki'Drednanth, Bonshooni, Blaren, and even Fergunak. They were very excited to hear that the stories were based in fact, and that there was one of each of the fabled creatures aboard the *Conch*. They eagerly invited their visitors to land.

"What do you think, Fen?" Hartigan asked her.

She paused, watching the Captain carefully. He *knew*, she realised. He knew there was something strange going on with the computer. But he was pretending it was fine. Why? It couldn't be to protect the machine's *feelings*.

But then, she realised, she was doing the same herself.

"We should be careful," she said. "You are at risk of contracting any diseases the locals might have, since you are the same species."

"Oh come now," Hartigan said. "You don't think there's any risk of that, do you?"

"I am not certain, Captain," Galana said. "I would feel better if the *Conch* – and Doctor Bont, of course – could perform a full analysis."

"Yes," the computer agreed quickly, while Basil was still frowning and opening his mouth, "yes, that would be sensible. We don't want anyone turning into a cake, do we? Ha ha."

Galana wondered when she had first started treating the *Conch*'s computer like a slightly unstable person, and realised it had been happening for a while now. "Bonty?" she asked.

"I'll run some tests," Bonjamin said. "Of course, we'll need to land and send out a sample probe before we can be sure … "

"The ship they arrived in was called the *Garla Gunumbous*," Chillybin said. "Human and Molran crew, probably. The nameplate was preserved and they included a picture of it in the unscrambled part of their transmission."

"Guess that's why they call themselves Gunumbans," Scrutarius remarked.

"The ship has long since been taken apart for the technology they are using to run their main settlement," Chilly went on. "The power cells, medical facilities, even the hull plates."

"Is there any record of the *Garla Gunumbous* in our database?" Galana asked the computer.

"Only the mythical figure," the *Conch* replied. "Garla Gunumbous, Goddess of Plenty … I'm afraid I don't have a record of every lost ship in Six Species history."

"Some of their oldest computer records are still intact and accessible," Wicked Mary said. "However, at the moment I am unable to read that data for a reason I have not fully made up yet."

"Excuse me?" Galana turned to the *giela* with a lift of her ears.

"Forgive me, Commander," the *Conch* said. "This is my fault. I know my behaviour is erratic, but I am attempting to find the best way to introduce … difficult information."

"Are you attempting to protect us from something we may find distressing?" Galana asked. A number of things began to make sense. "Something about this place and its original settlers?"

"Yes," the *Conch* said, sounding very unhappy.

"I have often found that the best way to deal with an uncomfortable situation is to get as much of it out in the open as possible," Galana suggested, "rather than hiding it until it is too late – possibly making it worse in the process."

"I know," the *Conch* said, "but if I'm wrong, then it seems pointless to bring it up for no reason. With Wicked Mary's help I will make certain of what we are facing, and then we can deal with it. I asked her to help me stall. She did *not* do a very good job," she added a little sternly.

"My innate honesty makes me uncomfortable hiding things from my crewmates," Wicked Mary lied with appalling lack of shame.

Basil, Galana noticed, had been frowning vaguely and looking at the planet through the viewscreen. "Captain?" she asked.

"Hmm?" Hartigan blinked and turned to her. "Oh, I was just thinking about how funny it is that there's only ever the one settlement or bunch of people on these planets for us to meet," he said. "We never have to deal with a whole planet full of different cultures. It's all jolly convenient. Why, the closest we've ever come to a diverse group was the Nyif Nyif."

"I suppose … " Galana said cautiously.

"Anyway, what have we got here?" Hartigan went on crisply. "Descendants of some old settlers or shipwreck, and the computer's got herself all worked up that we might be about to find out something that will make us sad. I say, d'you suppose the humans ate all the Molren or something?"

"I find it far easier to believe that the Molren would have eaten the humans, to be honest," Galana said. "A human wouldn't get much nutritional value from a Molran."

"A Molran wouldn't get much nutritional value from a human either," Bonty commented. "Terribly fatty and low in fibre."

"Easier to farm, though," Devlin added.

"Oh, granted, they're easier to *farm* - " Bonty agreed.

"Right, well as far as I'm concerned this all adds up to a simply *spiffing* mystery," Hartigan went on loudly, "and there's nothing for it but to toddle on down there as fast as we jolly well can, what?" he tapped his controls. "Unless you really think the Gunumbans and I are going to give each other a dose of the pox?"

"No," the *Conch* said, "I shouldn't think there's much risk of that. But Bonjamin ought to run some tests to be absolutely sure."

"Right. And while Bonty's doing that, you can tell us what's so bally dreadful about this place that you thought pulling the old 'does not compute' gag was the best way to break it to us," Hartigan declared. He stood up. "Galana, Devlin, with me. Chilly, Bloody Mary, I want a full accounting of the technology we're looking at and any potential combat situations we might face. You know the drill. We'll leave the comm open so you can listen in. Carry on."

They ascended to the Captain's quarters, and Scrutarius went immediately to Hartigan's little bar and made a round of drinks.

"You already know what this is about," Galana asked as she sat down, "both of you. Don't you?"

"I have no idea," Devlin said, although Galana could tell from the set of his upper shoulders and the sharp downward angle of his ears that this was a half-truth at best. "All I know is, if it's got the computer this rattled, then it's drinks time."

"As for me, let's say I've got a hunch," Hartigan said. "Now to see if I was right. Computer? Our shipwrecked friends down below wouldn't happen to be there because of the Fang o' God, now would they?"

"Yes, Basil," the *Conch* said in a strange little voice. Galana looked from Basil to Devlin, seeing the human's grim nod and the Blaran's further stiffening. "Yes, they are."

"Right," Hartigan clapped his hands briskly. "Drinks it is."

"The Fang o' God?" Galana said in bafflement. "You mean the mythical weapon, or warship, or whatever it was, from old Earth legends?"

"Back before Dev and I knew each other, I was Captain of another AstroCorps ship and crew," Hartigan said, "as you are aware, Fen. Ah, thanks," he took the drink Devlin offered, and took a deep draught as Scrutarius handed another glass to Galana and sat down with his own. "We were a bit more of a standard crew in a bit more of a standard ship – me as Captain, and my wife Nella as XO … although you really couldn't say she was an XO. She would have been court-martialled for insubordination fifteen times before we even broke dock," he laughed fondly. "Anyway, we were a great team. I had a lot of friends on that crew.

"We were searching, as you are *also* aware, for the Last Alicorn. Among other things. A lot of wonders to explore, a lot of space to travel, and all the time in the universe …

"*Ah*, but then we heard tales of the Fang o' God. Some of the greatest spacefaring human families come from lines descended from that – that ship, or whatever it was. And, it was said, when the Last Alicorn parted company with the Molran Fleet, it was with the Fang o' God that it went. Or if it didn't go *with* the Fang o' God, then at least there was some connection, a lead. So, naturally, we added it to our list of things that we simply had to explore. A lot of piffle, don't y'know, but worth checking out. No stone unturned, all of that.

"Our search led us to a place they call the bonefields," Hartigan stopped and took another large gulp from his glass, finishing his drink. He looked lost and frightened for a moment, and then laughed helplessly. "Still not at all sure I want to talk about it, to be honest."

"I've heard the legend," Scrutarius said. "Never anything specific, but it always sounds bad. You may have let it slip once or twice, Baz, especially in connection to – to Nella. That was why I suspected that's what this was about."

"I've also heard stories about the bonefields," Galana said, "but I never thought it was real. Wasn't there something about how you can only ever go there once?"

"Believe me, you'd only ever *want* to go there once," Hartigan said. "If we'd known we were going to wind up there and what would happen, we wouldn't have gone at all. Oh, but we were on a grand adventure, don't y'know," he laughed bitterly. "There aren't many stories about the bonefields because nobody *wants* to tell stories about it. That's how my crew's *accident* got marked down in the AstroCorps records as – as … well, I don't even know *what* it was marked down as," he looked at Galana. "You tell me, Fen."

Galana shook her head. "There were no details," she said, "just a 'ship lost with all hands' and a suggestion that you might have been venturing too close to the Core in your search for the Alicorn."

"Makes sense," Basil said. "When in doubt, blame the Cancer and make it that much less likely that anyone else will dare to go anywhere near 'em. But no, it was nothing to do with the Core, although I *did* attempt a short-cut through there once too. We flew into the bonefields, the floating bones took apart our ship and butchered our crew, and there was nothing in the middle to show for it. No Alicorn, no Fang o' God, no nothing. Just blood and screams and death. Nella and I managed to get out of there in the remains of the ship, after half our crew took to the escape pods and *those* were taken apart too. While we watched," he shuddered, and tried to take another drink, but found his glass empty. "We decided to go down with the ship because that's what Captains do, and that's how we survived. Pure bally luck."

"But … " Galana said hesitantly.

"Nella died of her injuries," Devlin told her quietly when Hartigan didn't speak again. "That was … shortly after they returned to charted space. Isn't that right, Baz?"

"Hm? Oh," Basil nodded, his eyes still staring into nothingness. "Oh, yes."

"I'm sorry, Basil," Galana said sincerely. "I'm very sorry."

"Ah well," Basil shook himself, and forced a smile. "There you have it, anyway. Now you know. The ghastly and pointless truth about how I got my first crew killed. All of them, lost on a fruitless search for the legendary Fang o' God. Fitting you should learn about it on our tenth space anniversary, what? Telling each other deep dark secrets and all that. But what about these poor blighters? The Gunumbans?"

"The *Garla Gunumbous* was recorded as a supertanker carrying farm equipment and supplies," Wicked Mary's voice replied over the comm, "led by a Molran command crew. They were not explorers or adventurers. How they wandered into the bonefields, let alone how they ended up this far from Six Species space, does not seem to have survived in the databanks or the Gunumbans' myths. But they definitely seem to have encountered the bonefields and it had a significant impact on them. Even generations later, phrases like *the field of bones*, *the floating bones* and even *the great tooth* are part of their speech patterns."

"That was the point at which I edited the initial transmissions," the *Conch* said apologetically. "I realised there was a connection and was trying to find the best way to break it to you."

"You knew before that," Hartigan said affectionately. "Didn't you? You figured it out from that shadow of an echo of the old distress signal, hundreds of light years out. That's why you tried to turn us away."

"Yes," the computer admitted.

"The *Garla Gunumbous* was critically damaged," Wicked Mary went on, "the Molren were killed, and they fled through soft-space to this location. That is about all the information we have managed to reassemble."

"That's pretty good, for data you've managed to pick up from a centuries-old shipwreck while we're still in orbit," Devlin said supportively.

"I am excellent at my job," Wicked Mary agreed. "I suspect that the ship's purpose may have been a little less noble than they are letting on, although with a Molran crew it was probably still operating inside the law."

"But we have no evidence of this," Bonty added in a pained voice over the comm, "and so there is no reason to dishonour the memory of the dead by flinging around wild theories and accusations. We can find out more from the Gunumbans whenever you like, by the way. The scans are all clear."

"Safe to land?" Galana seized the opportunity to avoid talking about the ancient supertanker and whatever nefarious work it may have been about when it went down. "We should still do a final check - "

"Yes, once we land," Bonty said. "That is, if you feel like landing."

"Absolutely," Hartigan jumped to his feet. Galana looked down at her drink, which she hadn't actually had a chance to taste yet, and set it on the table with a little shrug. "We can hardly come all this way and find *humans* and not bally well drop in and say hello, can we? Or whatever it is they say instead of 'hello'."

"*Kädun*," the *Conch* supplied helpfully.

"There you go. We can't come all this way and not drop in and say *kädun*," Hartigan declared. "And us bonefields survivors have to stick together, what?"

They quickly made their preparations, then returned to the bridge and detached the *Nella* for landing. Scrutarius had packed a large, round-cornered crate and an assortment of food and spare equipment from engineering, but wouldn't go into specifics about what any of it was. *Stuff they might have missed in the past few hundred years*, was all he would say.

"An awkward thought occurs," Galana said as they were descending through the atmosphere.

"Is it about long-forgotten Molran skulduggery aboard the *Garla Gunumbous?*" Scrutarius asked. "Because that's not so much *awkward* as it is hilarious … "

"No. What if the Gunumbans want to go home?"

"We can't very well bring them all with us," Hartigan said, "even if they aren't exactly a planet-full."

"And we don't have enough equipment to help them build their own starship, either," Devlin agreed. "The pieces they have left are basically keeping their main settlement lights on. We're not going to get them off the ground."

"And we can't leave them with detailed directions back to Six Species space," Galana said. "That would be a grave security risk."

"True, but surely something like 'it's that way, just keep going around the galactic rim widdershins until you start seeing Bounce-Bounce Burger signs' would be fine," Hartigan objected.

"We could bring some back," Wicked Mary suggested. "I could look after them, they wouldn't be any trouble. I like human."

"Hu*mans*," Bonty stressed.

"Yes, humans, I like humans," Wicked Mary said. "Why, what did I say?"

"Maybe this is something we can worry about if they ask us," Galana concluded.

The Gunumbans met them when they landed. It was strange to be surrounded by humans again, to see their funny pointy faces looking up at her, see the tops of their furry little skulls as they jostled and jabbered. Galana looked across the bobbing heads at Bonty, and shared a grin with her friend. It was almost like coming home, even though Galana had to admit that if this many humans had shown up on the Worldship *Porticon*, the locals would have contacted pest control.

The humans, for their part, were awestruck and a little frightened by the towering aliens. No living Gunumban had seen a Molranoid or an aki'Drednanth in the flesh. It must have felt like the drawings and stories of Gunumban history stepping living and breathing into the real world. They were spared having to see Wicked Mary in person, as she had remained in orbit.

Still, the humans were wide-eyed and didn't seem hostile. They babbled excitedly in their strange ancient-Coriane dialect, and the *Conch* translated for them as efficiently as possible. Galana had made the conscious decision, at this point, to once again trust that the computer was feeding them accurate information. She was left with little alternative.

"This is Jelter Qade, the … I suppose spiritual leader is the best term," the *Conch* said. "She bids you welcome in the name of the Benevolent Sky, which is possibly a deity of some kind. And this is Calumny Fizzschlifft, we spoke on the comm … "

Fizzschlifft, more an administrator and general public servant than a leader, also welcomed them to 'Gunumba' and immediately hit it off with Basil Hartigan despite the fact that *kädun* was the only word the Captain knew. He added a second word to his repertoire when Jelter Qade gave him a ceremonial gift, and a piece of it came loose and swung down and hit him between the legs. After that he could also say *nädj*, which meant *genitals*. There was much laughter, and the terrifying spectre of the visitors from the stars was dispelled. A good bit of physical comedy, Bonty noted, was more effective than a century of xenopological study.

The Gunumbans were content to stay on the planet, Galana was relieved to learn almost immediately. They had no interest in returning to Six Species space even though they were delighted to learn that the Six Species – or *Many Peoples Under Many Benevolent Skies* – was still out there.

They showed the crew of the *Conch* around the most important parts of their central settlement, including the assorted ancient and well-worn buildings and mechanisms that ran their little civilisation. Devlin declared it all *exceptionally* well maintained, and said there was little he could teach them, although some of the repair equipment and compounds he'd brought with him would help. The part of the ship that had sent out the distress signal they'd caught the forlorn edge of was long gone, beyond even Devlin's ability to reconstruct.

While the others were jabbering happily about the machinery, Galana slipped away to study one of the weathered old hull segments that now acted as a foundation stone. She concluded her examination and returned before anyone missed her, although she saw Wicked Mary's *giela* regarding her as unreadably as ever.

The central Gunumban origin story, as recited stirringly by Jelter Qade at the obligatory feast that night, confirmed their theories as much as such stories could. The Gunumbans, it was said, had been driven out of their lands of birth and carried into great danger by the classic great metal bird of spacefaring origin-myth. Their great heroes had then tamed the bird and flown here. If this wasn't a story of a long-forgotten shipwreck told by the survivors' great-great-great-grandchildren, Galana decided, then there was no point even trying to make sense of it.

Even as the Gunumban leader spoke of their long-lost birthland, however, it was clear that they still had no intention of going back there.

"It would be like walking in circles, or going back a step instead of forward," Bonty said once the *Conch* had translated. "That's *odd*. Most origin myths, like the Fleet tales of the gates of space, talk about lost places that we would go back to if we could. The Gunumbans seem perfectly content."

"Not a bad way to be," Scrutarius noted. "Especially since we can't help them."

"Well, your gear will keep them comfortable for a few generations yet," Hartigan said. "And at least it doesn't have a swinging bit that catches you in the *nädj*, what?" There was more hilarity at this. "And what about that other box of yours?"

"Ah yes," Devlin stood up from the table and went over to the large rounded crate he'd brought down, quite separate to the equipment he'd already given the lost humans. Galana recognised it as similar to ones he'd given away previously – to the Man-Apes, for example, several years ago now.

"Jelter Qade wants to know what it is," the *Conch* said when the Gunumban leader took the box from the Blaran and jabbered a short statement in acceptance.

"Diversity," Devlin said cryptically. "Just in case you or your descendants ever *do* find your way back to Six Species space, this might give you some … valuable lessons. But you mustn't open it until we have returned to the Benevolent Sky," he added in a warning tone, and finished off his speech with a wiggle of the fingers of his upper hands and a playful, "ooooo," that made the locals laugh again.

The morning after the highly enjoyable feast and even more enjoyable after-feast celebration and drink-fuelled exchange of dances, the crew returned to the *Nella* and ascended regretfully into orbit.

"I tell you," Hartigan announced, "*nobody* throws a party like humans. You Blaran chaps are alright, Dev, but you're just going to have to be satisfied with second place on this one."

"I can live with that," Scrutarius said in amusement. The Captain was clearly feeling a little fragile, but the drinks on offer hadn't been strong enough to have any real effect on Molran, Blaran, Bonshoon or aki'Drednanth physiology.

"But listen here," the Captain went on, "I've only gone and bared my soul for our tenth space anniversary. Told you all about the bonefields and the Fang o' God and the passing of my dear wife."

"You also told us that your childhood nickname was Spazzle Fartigan," Devlin said.

"*What?*" Hartigan croaked. "No I didn't!"

"I'm afraid you did, Captain," Galana said. "You were telling Calumny about it last night."

"You were very drunk," Chillybin agreed.

"Fine, jolly good," Hartigan grumbled, then fixed his Chief Engineer with an accusing look. "Well?"

Scrutarius raised his ears. "Well what?"

"You were going to tell us about your special secret Blaran alteration," Bonty said. "You said it was ancient spacefaring tradition."

"*Did* I? You'd think I'd remember something like that," Devlin said vaguely. "Anyway, I'm pretty sure Fen said the whole thing was just made up."

"Oh *fine*," Bonty said, "I'll start. I tell everyone I'm three-and-a-half thousand years old, but the truth is, I don't know how old I am because I don't remember. And I know, you all knew that already," she added impatiently. "What you *don't* know is, I know I'm actually quite a lot *older* than that. Hundreds, maybe thousands of years older. The doctors don't know because I have genetic disorders that have messed up my aging process. I'm still getting older, sorry to say, and I'm not immortal, but I'll probably just go on looking like this until I keel over. And it could happen tomorrow," she concluded cheerfully.

"That's ... something I would have liked to know before taking you on a fifty-year jaunt around the galaxy, to be honest," Basil said.

"Tough," Bonty replied with a flick of her ears.

"I killed my sisters," Chillybin said. They all turned and stared at the huge armoured figure. "It is the way of my species," she went on. "In a litter of ten newborns, all of them fight and kill one another for food and shelter and only one or two will survive to grow into adolescents. It is a test, of sorts. I was the only survivor of my litter," she concluded. "And I killed them all."

"Bloody Hell," Devlin said shakily. "Not sure I can top that."

"I think I can," Wicked Mary raised a slender metal hand.

"Oh boy," Devlin said.

"I am defective," the Fergunakil said. "On eighteen occasions so far, I have had the chance to cut each of you off from major ship systems and flood the decks with water, converting the *Conch* into an aquatic vessel and then hunting you for sport and nutrition. At first, I thought it was only the computer stopping me, but after the fifth time I realised I was sabotaging my own efforts, making excuses to not carry out the attack. I was failing on *purpose*."

"Failing to kill us all," Bonty said flatly.

"I would appreciate it if you did not judge me harshly," Wicked Mary said in a prim tone.

"Fine," Hartigan said, "jolly good. Bloody Mary, thanks for sharing. Fen, you're up."

Galana paused for a moment, gathering her thoughts. "I examined one of the hull plates from the *Garla Gunumbous*, down on the surface," she eventually said.

"Even for a Molran that's lamer than I expected," Scrutarius announced.

"It was a very specific configuration," she went on. "My own family –

my parents and grandparents – used to crew similar vessels. Wicked Mary was correct. They were called supertankers, but they were more like livestock transports. Lower Fleet ranks would take ships like this out, and they would carry large cargoes of humans, in appalling conditions. The humans agreed to it because the Fleet had the most dependable ships and they would get to fly to their own planets and colonise them. The Fleet used them as – as slave labour, essentially, to construct new settlements."

"Farm equipment," Hartigan said quietly. "It was right there on the manifest."

Galana nodded. "It is widely known, but nobody ever speaks of the treatment after the fact. Humans have a … useful habit of forgetting, and looking back at the past with a very rosy filter after the previous generations have died. Whatever happened in the bonefields, I wouldn't be surprised if the ancient Gunumbans took the opportunity to overthrow the Molran crew and seize the ship. I would not have blamed them. Certainly I was relieved that no memory of it seemed to remain with the community we just met."

"They might have sacrificed us to the Benevolent Sky," Bonty said lightly, although her eyes were sad. She had known, at least in vague terms, this detail of Galana's family life. But not the complete truth. The supertankers were a dirty little Fleet secret, known by many but never faced.

"That is why I joined AstroCorps," Galana concluded. "I could not be part of a lie so monstrous. We call ourselves the Six Species, but the Fleet has *never* believed it. AstroCorps is the only way humans will ever stand with us as equals, rather than as useful semi-sentient beasts of burden."

They sat in reflective silence for a while after Galana's speech.

"I'd feel a little shallow showing you my inflatable buttocks after all this," Scrutarius declared.

"Hang about, your inflatable *what*?" Bonty exclaimed.

"I want to see them," Chillybin said.

"Me too," Galana added.

"Oh and look, we're docking," Devlin strolled away from his console. "I'd better go and check the connector bolts and get the relative field calibrated … "

"Devlin!" Hartigan raised his voice.

"Long way still to go," Scrutarius called from down the hall. "Lots of space to explore."

"Chief Engineer Able Belowdecksman Devlin bally Scrutarius you get back here *right bally now!*" Basil shouted.

The Blaran's merry laughter echoed over the bridge as he vanished into the ship.

***Soon, in* The Riddlespawn:**
Bonjamin and Devlin were finishing up a fairly boring survey of another empty solar system when the *Conch* announced that a second ship had entered the volume.

"But there's nothing here," Galana said in puzzlement. The system had three planets that could potentially have supported life, but only one of them had so much as a microbe on it. And Bonty had just concluded that they weren't very interesting microbes. "No technological relics, no settlements. The only thing here is us, and nobody else knew we would be here."

"The ship is moving in swiftly on an approach heading," the *Conch* said. "It is sending us a comm signal on a known wavelength."

Galana strode quickly to her console, the rest of the crew hurrying onto the bridge behind her. "Fleet or AstroCorps?" she asked.

"Neither," the *Conch* replied.

"It is the *Splendiferous Bastard*," Chillybin said.

"*What?*" Galana blurted.

"Oh, *jolly* good!" Captain Hartigan exclaimed.

Moments later the bridge viewscreens were dominated by the narrow, furry little face and great pointed ears of Judderone Pelsworthy of the Boze, Space Adventurer.

"*There* you are," she said loudly. "Golly, you haven't gotten very far, have you? I've been looking for you all over the place."

"Roney, you wily little blighter," Hartigan said happily. "What brings you sniffing around again? Admit it, you missed us."

"Wish it was that simple, biggums," Roney said. "I need your help."

THE RIDDLESPAWN

The nimble little amber-furred creature strode into the docking area ahead of her handsome bushy tail and stood, fists on hips, grinning up at the crew of the *Conch*. Her teeth, sharp and white except for one fang which was gold, gleamed in her pointy little muzzle. Her uniform was as regal and crimson and ostentatiously-gold-decorated as ever. She had a large bag slung over one shoulder – or at least it looked large as she set it down next to her boots. It wasn't actually much longer than Galana's forearm.

"Roney," Hartigan said happily. He went down on one knee and shook the Boze's hand. "It's good to see you again."

"Good to see you too, biggums," she said. She greeted Galana, Chillybin, Bonty, Devlin, and tipped a little salute at Wicked Mary's *giela*. "You've been busy, eh? Taking it nice and easy, seeing the sights."

"Our ship isn't as fast as yours," Hartigan reminded her.

"I bet you've found a lot of lichen and algae," Roney said. "Not much else to be found in this stretch of space. That's why they call it the Sludge Corridor."

"Who calls it that?" Galana asked.

"Y'know, maybe if you were to give us a map ... " Hartigan said. "Just before you left last time, you mentioned a place called High Elonath that - "

"No time for that," Roney interrupted, "and you don't want to go near High Elonath anyway. Come on, let's eat. Grab this for me," she poked the bag with the toe of her boot. "I've brought some real food. Even a little something for Bloody Mary."

"Oh?" the *giela* clicked forward and picked up the bag.

"A ferocious little critter called a pepper shrimp," the Boze replied. "Fast, cunning, and packs a real punch. I'm pretty sure it's still alive in its jar," she added, "so handle with care, hm?"

"That doesn't sound very regulation-friendly," Galana said.

"You're really not going to like the rest of the stuff I brought aboard, then," Roney grinned.

They went down to the Aquarium deck, and sat around a table Scrutarius assembled quickly out of storage crates. Roney laid out her offerings, introducing each one as she went, and Bonty rather worriedly checked each one and listed its approximate ingredients and risk levels.

"These are death pearls from the chasm of Nid."

"There's an awful lot of solid-state defragmented mercury in them."

"And this is a holy mushroom pie made by the monks of the Wailing Dark."

"A very small slice will probably be fine for us, but the Captain would probably enter a permanent state of psychotropic hallucination. Also I don't think it's mushroom as we understand it, the main ingredient seems to be some kind of meat."

"Yes, Katorkian mushrooms are about the size of the *Bastard*, and would bite you in half soon as look at you … ah, this is fruit from the Tree of Thunder. They must be sliced *just so*, removing the skin and the seeds, otherwise they're quite deadly."

"These have at least three kinds of complex sugars that the scanner doesn't recognise, but they're *probably* harmless."

"And this is a gourd of Prothagnian flavour seeds. I think I already picked out all the blue and purple ones."

"I'd advise against anyone eating the red ones either, but the yellow and green ones are probably okay. *Not for you, Captain.*"

"Oh I say, poor form."

"Don't worry, Basil," Roney announced. "I remembered what a delicate little giant fellow you are, and I brought you a roll of pixie wubblebread from the secret court of the King in Lavender. It's considered the final test in … sort of the reverse of a rite of adulthood, it's rather difficult to explain but you aren't considered a *true* infant until you've eaten it."

"It … won't kill you," Bonty announced while Hartigan sat and scowled. "You might want to have a drink handy to wash it down, though."

For a little while, then, the reunited friends sat and ate, and watched Wicked Mary sweep around the Aquarium hunting the tiny, many-legged black shape of the pepper shrimp. Eventually the great shark stunned it between the wall and her great mottled-grey tail, devoured it in a rapid clashing of jaws, then was briefly unable to control her *giela* due to her gastronomic distress. She then recovered and declared the shrimp to be a delightful experience, but not one she relished the idea of passing all the way through her digestive system. Roney laughed and applauded this heartily.

"Speaking of the last time we were all together, and not speaking at all of digesting small creatures," Scrutarius said, "how are … my gift, did you take care of it?"

Roney waved a fuzzy hand. "Oh yes, excellent care," she said, "nothing to worry about there. Very funny it was, too. But perhaps a story for another time."

"Alright," Hartigan said, and took a large mouthful of the doughy pale-purple bread. "You said you needed our help with something – *Karl's soggy mittens!*" he lunged for his drink and gulped it down while Roney and Devlin laughed. "It's a spicy little bugger," he burbled sheepishly.

"Congratulations, today you are a baby. Alright, to business," Roney wiped her eyes and chuckled as Hartigan glared at her over the rim of his glass. "You remember, last time we met, the star serpent – the big fiery beastie we faced together?"

"Hardly something we're likely to forget," Galana replied. She picked up a piece of the pale pink Thunder fruit, and chewed it. It was cloyingly sweet.

"Right, then you'll remember it wasn't really a *creature*," Roney said. "It wasn't intelligent, it was just an energy-thing – a force of nature without a guiding hand."

"Yes," Galana replied. "You said it was a weapon used by some ancient hostile species. The Riddlespawn?" she glanced at Chillybin, who nodded slowly.

"The buggers who destroyed the Empire of Gold," Hartigan recovered his voice, "and turned it into High Elonath," he paused hopefully, then continued when Rony still refused to elaborate. "But didn't you say they'd been gone as long as the Empire of Gold had? They were basically a myth?"

"Turns out I was wrong about that," Roney said with unaccustomed solemnity.

Galana and Basil exchanged a look of surprise. It was so strange to hear the witty Boze admit to being wrong about something, Galana was a little disoriented by it.

"You found them?" Chillybin said, with a low rumble from inside her suit that was even more unusual than Roney's admission. "They are here?"

"One," Roney said grimly. "Or a *part* of one. Sort of."

"A *part* of one?" Galana asked.

"*Sort of?*" Hartigan added. Roney flicked her huge ears enigmatically. "And you need us to face it, what?" he went on eagerly.

"Look, I just thought," Roney said, "what with how you put paid to the star serpent, and how ingeniously you make do with all this *terrible* technology of yours, and how you're still out here trying to fly around the galaxy, you'd be good allies to bring into this. Only … when we meet them, maybe we'll just not tell them I found you still wading through the Sludge Corridor."

"Tell *who?*" Hartigan demanded. "Who's this 'we' you're suddenly talking about?"

"I take it you're interested?" Roney asked. "We're about two weeks away from the gathering spot. I can explain on the way."

"In my experience, just because you *can* explain doesn't mean you *will*," Galana pointed out. "Quite the contrary, in fact."

"Alright, you got me there," Roney said. "But if you want to make friends – friends who might be willing to come and pull you out of High Elonath when you *inevitably* blunder in there with your pants down – this is your chance," she leapt up to stand on the box she was using as a seat, and extended her hand to Basil. "What do you say, biggums?"

Hartigan barely glanced around. "Let's do it, by jingo!" he clasped Roney's tiny furry hand firmly between two fingers and a thumb.

"Will your friends be able to give us more pepper shrimp?" Wicked Mary asked.

"All you can eat, my nightmarish fishy friend," Roney said.

"So *one*, then," Devlin grinned. "When do we start?"

"We already have," Roney announced. "The *Bastard* took us into the grey ten minutes ago."

"Computer?" Galana said with a little sigh.

"Oh, look at that," the *Conch* said mildly. "I thought it had gotten very soft-spacey out there."

Their journey from the 'Sludge Corridor' to wherever Roney was taking them was as uneventful as all flights through the grey were. The Boze remained aboard with them, spending most of her time up in the Captain's quarters or mooching around the bridge asking what the consoles did and why they didn't do other, far more fun, usually impossible things.

"Do you know the story of the Riddlespawn?" she asked during one lull period while Basil, Galana and Chillybin were relaxing in Hartigan's lounge. "What we're facing, precisely?"

"Nothing," Galana said. "Only that they were supposed to be gone for twenty million years, and they used star serpents as weapons."

"Weapons, pets," Roney shrugged. "Hard to say, really," she looked at Chillybin. "What about you, frosty? What's the aki'Wossname perspective?"

"You tell me, Captain Pelsworthy," Chillybin said. "You have spoken with other aki'Wossnames about this."

Galana looked at Roney sharply.

The little alien shrugged, her great white-furred ears turning down. "A few," she said. "None of them give a straight answer."

"That must be frustrating," Chillybin said, the mechanical voice from her glove flat and emotionless. Galana stifled a laugh, and Hartigan spluttered into his drink. "Will there be other aki'Drednanth at this gathering?"

"No," Roney said with a little grunt. She jumped to her feet and began pacing the room. "You lot are like mothers telling their children not to throw rocks at the *plaznok* nest," she declared, levelling a tiny but very accusatory claw at Chillybin. "'Leave the Riddlespawn alone,' you say. 'Nothing good will come of it,' you say. 'You are inviting ruination and destruction down upon your heads like the last great and prideful lords of the Empire of Gold,' you say. Almost *exactly* like a mother warning her pups about *plaznoks*, in fact. The point is, the aki'Drednanth have never had anything *useful* to say."

"That all sounded quite useful to me," Galana disagreed.

"The Riddlespawn were weapons themselves," Chillybin said unexpectedly. "The chosen children of a dark and violent force, they were savage and deadly. Our kind did battle with them, but seldom. And never when we had a choice. Most other enemies, we could face. But the Riddlespawn were like nightmares brought to life," the great figure shifted slowly in her armour. "Our name, *aki'Drednanth*, means *nightmare in flesh*," she said. "But it is just a name. We move from our Dreamscape and into the world of the living and back again, and we are formidable when we need to be, but not like the Riddlespawn. Nothing like the Riddlespawn."

"That's more or less what the other aki'Drednanth told me," Roney said. She was standing on a chair now, fiddling with the little collection of decorations and souvenirs on Hartigan's shelves. "A species of monsters that live in some kind of nether-Hell until called forth by the terrible entity that they were children to. They'd come rampaging out, smash everything to pieces, fling around their fiery star serpents, then wink back into nothingness. Without a trace. No way to follow them back to their lair and take them down once and for all."

"The star serpent was the better part of a solar system in size," Galana said. "If a Riddlespawn is big enough to fling one around … "

Roney shook her head. "No, they're not much bigger than one of you lot," she said. "Although there are all sorts of legends. I think they can be as big and dangerous as the story needs them to be. Terribly inconsistent. The one on Palothane is even smaller – not much bigger than little old me, actually. I'm not sure if that's *because* I'm the one who found it, or - "

"Palothane," Hartigan said. "That's the name of the planet we're heading to?"

"That's the one," Roney said.

"The one where your friends are waiting," Chillybin said.

"That's – yeah," Roney said, and picked up the large, thick golden coin Hartigan had pocketed from the dragon hoard the *Conch* had almost been added to. "Hey," she said, sounding surprised. She turned and waggled the gleaming disc with the disturbing spidery shape engraved on one side. "You lot had dealings with the Web? And they gave you a favour? I knew I'd come to the right people."

"Hmm?" Hartigan said. "Oh. No, can't say we ever met the Web. We got that from the Fudzu. They had a mountain of 'em."

"The Fudzu aren't real," Roney said with a dismissive wave of her paw, and put the coin back. "But alright, be that way. We'll get to Palothane in another few days, and that's when the fun starts."

"Fun like the star serpent?" Galana asked.

"*Better*," Roney declared.

Galana suspected that there was something Roney wasn't telling them about the group that would apparently be meeting them at Palothane, but the Boze was as elusive and difficult as ever. She did confess that she needed them for more than just their peculiar genius with inferior technology, but it was all wrapped up in her usual confusing layers of misleading information. And just to make it worse, the whole thing was all based in myths twenty million years old.

All the Boze would reveal was that her mysterious allies couldn't get close to the Riddlespawn, and even though she'd managed to find it she hadn't been able to do anything on her own, and she suspected the crew of the *Conch* could help. Then there was a lot of unhelpful rambling about an ancient tablet, and a prophecy, and a family long divided, and the more she danced around the explanation, the more impenetrable the infuriating little creature made the whole subject.

"What do you think of this prophecy?" Galana asked Chillybin one night-shift. She was visiting with her friend in the Icebox, the large refrigerated deck they'd converted for the aki'Drednanth just like they'd made the Aquarium on the deck below for Wicked Mary. She didn't visit often – Chilly was not fond of playing host, and preferred to be left alone to remove her freezer suit and run and roll in the cold.

"Not many prophecies can last twenty million years," the aki'Drednanth said. It was a little jarring to hear Chilly speak when she was out of her armour. The words, formed by the movements of the electronic webbing she still wore on one great clawed hand, still came from the open suit that stood near the door. Chilly herself, meanwhile, rolled and scratched herself luxuriantly in the drifts of crushed ice. "Even the Drednanth dream grows confused over such a long time. But you heard what Captain Pelsworthy said about the Riddlespawn. About them being the chosen children of an ancient entity."

"Children of … what, a God?" Galana asked. Such superstitions were not unusual among various alien races. Even Blaran and Bonshoon groups had their share of stories.

"Not a God," Chillybin lay in the ice on her back, great black-horned feet in the air, her hand moving lazily as it formed the words. "Something greater than a God. A natural law of the universe, with a conscious will and infinite power."

"Aren't Gods said to have infinite power?" Galana asked.

"Only by those like us," Chilly said with a *woof* of amusement from her great shaggy chest, "who cannot see the difference between *great* power and *infinite* power, because both are so far above us we cannot understand them. The Infinites were said to have been ten in number, and each was said to have taken a mortal species as Its children."

"Who *said* all these things?" Galana asked with a smile behind her thermal mask, although she remembered Roney using the term, *Infinites*, before. *If the Infinites had wanted you to get from place to place faster*, she'd said, *They would have introduced you to the Boze before now*. At the time, she'd thought it was just a mild mistranslation.

"Enough people, over a long enough period of time, that it seems a funny coincidence," Chilly said. "But the funniest thing is, your species were *also* said to be the chosen children of an Infinite."

"Molren?" Galana asked in surprise.

"So it was said," Chilly said. "Molren, Bonshooni, Blaren, Fergunak … even humans."

"And aki'Drednanth?" Galana asked.

Chillybin rolled, and regarded her with a glittering crystalline eye.

"No," she said. "Of all the Six Species, the aki'Drednanth were the only children without an Infinite to be our parent. Ours is a … different family."

"What about the Boze?" Galana asked.

Chillybin gave another deep laugh. "Perhaps they are," she said. "I seem to recall a tale of a scattered and lost race called the Potádi, the Hounds of Mayhem. The Boze might be some remnant of them. Our friend Captain Pelsworthy certainly seems to fit the bill, doesn't she?"

"She did say she was able to get close to the Riddlespawn," Galana said thoughtfully. "Do you think that's why?"

"I honestly have no idea," Chillybin admitted. "But it is a strange universe."

After two weeks at relative speed, they were none the wiser about Roney's plan or the terrible empire-destroying monster they were meant to be facing. They emerged from the grey as abruptly and without warning as they'd entered it, Roney marched onto the bridge and struck a bold pose in front of the main viewscreen. One by one, the others made their way to their stations.

"Alright," Hartigan took his seat, "what have we got?"

"Standard solar system, red giant star, six rocky planets, only one seems to be habitable," the *Conch* told them. "Not *very* habitable, though – you will need breathers and protective suits."

"Palothane?" Galana asked.

"Palothane," Roney confirmed grimly.

"There are seven ships in orbit," Chillybin added. "Each one different, all of them alien of course. They have not seen us, as far as I can tell. We came out of soft-space a fair distance away and we may be running too quietly for them to notice us."

"Aha, that's the beauty of your ships and your communication devices," Roney said. "So slow and steady and unobtrusive."

"Captain Judderone," Galana said, "I take it these seven alien ships are our 'friends' that you were telling us about?"

"Sort of," Roney said. "They're the Seven Sisters. The Pirate Queen's elite guard."

"They're the bally *what*?" Hartigan demanded.

"Well, you know how you lot are the Six Species?" Roney said. "The Pirate Queen rules a similar bunch, only there are … ooh, at last count there were something like fifty-three species. Or representatives from them, anyway. The Seven Sisters are … okay, there's one Gastronid, one Agony Worm, one Soulfeeder, two Cold Fingers Of Fate … and two representatives of the Boze."

"Well, they all sound awful," Devlin said.

"Except the Boze," Bonty added loyally.

"Now, let's not go making exceptions," Devlin murmured.

Roney grinned, showing once again just how good her hearing was. "You're right," she said, "all seven of them are perfectly dreadful, and the Boze are two of the worst."

"I thought you said you were the last Boze," Galana reminded her.

"I am," Roney said. "But I told you there were others. Look," she went on while Galana attempted to process this, "I … I may have misled you about how *welcoming* this group was in fact going to be."

"I think we were all pretty sceptical about that," Galana said.

"*I* wasn't," Hartigan said indignantly. "What about the friends who were going to turn up and help us when we get into trouble in High Elonath?"

"Well, I was more talking about me," Roney said. "*I'd* be your friend. I mean, still. I'm already your friend, but I don't know that I'd go into High Elonath for you. But, if that's what you feel like you have to do, then helping with this will definitely be good practice, hmm?"

"Roney - " Bonjamin said, stern and grandmotherly.

"Look, I'm here to push the Riddlespawn back into Hell," Roney said. "*These* cretins want to bring it the rest of the way out."

"You've had two weeks to tell us this," Galana said. "Why didn't you - "

"I *did* tell you. By Bozanda, you never listen. Here's what we're going to do," Roney went on, speaking slowly and clearly. "I'm going to get in the *Bastard* and fly into the Seven Sisters, and get in a big noisy argument with them. You are going to fly this beautiful quiet old ship of yours down to the surface of Palothane and wait for me there," she turned and headed for the main bridge doors. "I'll give you the coordinates of the temple."

"Wait, *temple*?" Scrutarius repeated. "Is it a spooky temple?"

Roney stopped and grinned over her shoulder. "Pretty spooky," she said. Then she was gone with a swish of her tail.

"Tactically," Galana said to the bridge in general, "this whole plan leaves a lot to be desired."

"Maybe," the *Conch* agreed, "but getting a lift from Captain Pelsworthy has cut almost five years off our journey."

"Five *years*?" Bonty exclaimed.

"We are forty-seven thousand light years from our last stop," the computer said. "We've crossed a distance greater than the breadth of all of Six Species space in just two weeks."

"That would place us … " Hartigan breathed.

"Very nearly halfway around the galaxy from Declivitorion-On-The-Rim," the *Conch* confirmed.

"That puts us close to where the Alicorn is meant to be," Hartigan said in excitement. "This High Elonath place."

"Perhaps," the *Conch* agreed. "Certainly we could fly on from here, since we have not yet been spotted by this so-called Pirate Queen - "

"What, and leave Roney in the lurch?" Hartigan exclaimed.

"The *Splendiferous Bastard* is away," Chillybin reported.

"Separate the *Nella*," Hartigan said. "We're going in. Devlin, let's have as close to absolute dark and silent running as you can give us."

"Pretend you're stealing something," Bonty suggested. Scrutarius favoured her with a narrow look, but began entering commands into his console.

"I will remain here with Wicked Mary," Chillybin said, and headed for the doors. "I feel this is a … family affair. I do not think I would be welcome down there."

Galana frowned. Of course, it was probably a good idea for somebody to remain on the main body of the ship with the Fergunakil anyway, but it was always good to have a reason you could say out loud. "Do you think you can prepare some responses in case the Seven Sisters decide to attack?" she asked.

Chillybin paused in the doorway. "I can protect you against the other vessels," she said, "even if their minds are alien to me. At least the Boze minds are somewhat familiar. And Wicked Mary, of course, will have tactical control."

"What about down on the surface?" Bonty asked. "The Riddlespawn? Anything down in this temple?"

"I cannot sense any minds aside from the aliens in the ships," Chillybin said. "But we have never had much success in sensing the Riddlespawn."

"This is *such* a bad idea," Scrutarius said, although he sounded delighted.

"Captain Pelsworthy seems to have gotten the attention of the Seven Sisters," Wicked Mary's *giela* announced. "If we are going to separate and attempt to land, we should do it now."

"Running silent," Scrutarius reported.

They crept towards Palothane, which was a blasted-looking little ball of rock under the baleful red fire of the sun. The location of the 'temple', according to Roney's coordinates, lit up on the screens as a tiny red dot.

"Chilly seemed to know more about this than I do," Hartigan said uneasily to Galana. "Did Roney tell you what we're meant to be doing down here? How are we meant to push this Riddlespawn bugger back into Hell?"

"Roney didn't tell me anything," Galana said. "I actually got more information from Chillybin's aki'Drednanth ancestral memory."

Basil whistled through his moustache. "That's really saying something."

They descended through the thin, howling atmosphere and landed on the shattered plain near the edge of the temple. It seemed to have been built in the middle of a crater that had probably been quite impressive a few million years ago but had since been worn away by the elements. Once they were down, they peered out at the temple through the *Nella*'s screens – it was barely visible as a line of weathered blocks, the wind and sand and noxious gases obscuring the view.

Still, if it was as old as Roney had implied it was, Galana thought, it was impressive there was anything left to see at all. She wondered what the temple had been made of.

They hastily donned protective gear and breathers, staggered off the shuttle and headed towards the weathered ruins, the three Molranoids supporting Hartigan and Wicked Mary, both of whom seemed in danger of blowing away in the sandstorm.

"Delightful place!" Basil shouted over the comm.

"I can see why you'd want to build a temple here!" Scrutarius agreed.

They climbed up onto the foundation and over the tumbled, sand-heaped remains of the outer walls, finding a broad depression not much different to the surrounding plains, although at least the wind was a little calmer. Rounded stone objects that could have been statues stuck out of the sand here and there. None of them were particularly *pleasant*-looking shapes. One of them was unsettlingly similar to the spider-like thing stamped on the coin Hartigan had found in the Fudzu hoard. What had Roney called them? The Web? That sounded about right. These, too, were surprisingly well-preserved for carvings millions of years old.

"There is an opening over there," Wicked Mary said, and pointed. A protected area between two statues and a broken section of internal walls held a darker patch that revealed itself to be a set of stairs descending below the surface. They staggered over and down the stairs, which were eroded almost to the point of being a ramp, and stopped once they reached a small chamber where the stairway doubled back and continued deeper. The wind receded at this point, although the air was still toxic, and Galana checked that they were still in contact with the *Nella*, and through the *Nella* with the *Conch*.

"Still reading you loud and clear," Chillybin reported. "You have gone below the surface but there is nothing in the surrounding stone to interfere with the signal."

"Keep an eye on the signal, looks like we're about to go deeper," Hartigan said, stepping away from Devlin's supporting grip with a little pat of thanks, and peering down into the darkness of the temple bowels.

"I am still in full control of my *giela*," Wicked Mary reported, "so I imagine if the signal begins to fail I will notice that almost immediately."

"Good point," Hartigan said. "How are you doing up there otherwise? How's Roney getting on?"

"Captain Pelsworthy is holding position among the Seven Sisters' ships," Wicked Mary reported, "and they seem to be communicating. They have given no indication that they are aware of our presence. She must be giving them a good argument."

"I bet she is," Hartigan said, and put a booted foot on the top step. "D'you think there'll be traps down here?"

"If there are, Roney would have tripped them already," Scrutarius said. "But you go first, just in case. I mean because you're the Captain."

Muttering irritably, Basil clumped down the stairs. The others followed, holding up arm-lamps as the darkness became almost total. They reached another little landing-space, and the stairs doubled back again and went deeper.

"Where is this thing?" Bonty murmured.

The next flight of stairs ended in a short tunnel, which in turn ended at a wide opening ringed with what looked disturbingly like a great clotted mass of dried blood under their lamps. Closer inspection revealed that it was some kind of metal, corroded and worn down by the atmosphere. Galana guessed that the passage might have been sealed by a huge pair of imposing metal doors once upon a time, but they were long gone now.

"Look," Hartigan said excitedly, and pointed at the wall next to the door. More weeping rusty stuff had leaked out of holes in the stone, and the hardened sludge and dust on the floor covered a shape that was clearly a petrified skeleton of some kind, although it was entirely alien in appearance. "I bet there *were* traps," he said, "but they've all just broken down. This poor blighter was the last person to set one off."

"Spooky temples these days," Scrutarius tutted. "Where's the *workmanship*?"

"The workmanship is actually extraordinary, if this place is even a fraction as old as Roney was suggesting," Galana pointed out since she seemed to be the only one who cared. "Bonty, can you get a sample of this stone?"

"I've been trying," Bonty said. "It's not the hardest stuff I've ever tried to chip off and analyse, but it's pretty darn hard."

They stepped through into a wide, high-ceilinged chamber that Galana estimated was directly beneath the centre of the temple ruins above. It was dark, and Galana could hear a soft, disturbing sound echoing inside the space – something scraping and flopping repetitively against stone, she thought. Perhaps a small trapped animal ... although by all reports this planet had been deserted and uninhabitable for a *very* long time.

There was no immediate sign of what might have been making the noise, which was drowned out by their own footsteps and voices as they entered the chamber anyway. There was a lot of broken stone and more of the rusted-down metal threaded through the space, they saw as they raised their lamps, but if there were more rooms or tunnels or stairs, they were not immediately visible. The centre of the chamber was dominated by another statue, this one in much better repair than the ones on the surface due to its sheltered position. It was also streaked with dark stains of corroded metal, and more broken and melted pieces of debris were heaped around its great muscular knees where it knelt, but the stone of which it was made seemed quite smooth. Galana frowned at the immense figure.

The shape of the thing hadn't escaped Hartigan's eye either. "I say," he whispered, "is that ... that's not meant to be a *human*, is it?"

The statue was definitely humanoid, with its single pair of arms and its round head. It was much bigger than a human, or even a Molran – Galana estimated that it would have been twice her height if it had been standing rather than kneeling on one titanic knee and one huge splayed foot. It looked, from the mess around the statue's base, like it might have been wearing clothes at some point but they were long gone. Behind the huge figure, rising from its bulging and gleaming shoulders, a pair of huge dark-feathered wings spread over the dusty floor.

"Those *teeth* aren't human," Scrutarius noted, pointing at the big jutting tusks the statue's face was sporting. "And I haven't seen a human with wings since the last time I ate whoop-whoop frogs," he glanced sidelong at Galana. "Not that I ate whoop-whoop frogs, ever," he added, "since they're definitely illegal."

"I'll overlook it this time," Galana said dryly, and turned back to her study of the statue. Only ... she wasn't entirely sure it *was* a statue. Even if it was made out of the same super-hard material as the rest of the temple, there was no way it could be in *this* good condition. "Could this be the Riddlespawn?" she pondered out loud.

"No," Wicked Mary said from around behind the gigantic shape. "I believe this *is* the Riddlespawn."

They hurried around to where the *giela* was standing between the wings where they lay fanned across the uneven stones. There, squirming and writhing on the chamber floor, was the source of the strange sound Galana had heard when they'd entered the room.

The Riddlespawn wasn't humanoid. If anything, the body looked vaguely like that of a Molran, with four long arms and two legs, all of which were in motion, slapping and flopping as the creature thrashed in place between the huge figure's wings. It was the size of a young child, Galana judged in horror, its skin coated in fine yellow-pink scales that occasionally rasped against one another or the stones of the floor as it moved. It was hard to imagine such a tiny and pitiful thing being a threat, and yet there was something *awful* about it at the same time. The way it moved, vague and helpless and yet unending, like an insect that had been poisoned but was too tough to simply die.

The reason it wasn't able to move more purposefully was readily – and horribly – apparent. The squirming figure didn't have a head. From the way it was flexing and twisting, it looked like it actually had its head *stuck* in something and was trying to escape, but neither the head nor whatever it was stuck in were visible, so the neck just sort of ended hanging in the air above the temple floor, a meaty amber-coloured wound that looked raw and terrible but was not actually bleeding. Galana remembered Roney saying they'd found *part* of a Riddlespawn, and that the Pirate Queen and her followers wanted to bring it all the way out. Was its head already stuck in the Hell that Riddlespawn came from?

"Look at the *floor*," Bonty said in horror.

Glana leaned back and took in the wider area at a glance, and realised what her friend already had. The stones between the statue's wings were worn down in a shallow depression, free of dust but clearly eroded. The Riddlespawn shifted and flailed in this depression, hanging by its neck from its invisible bonds, and it was impossible to dismiss the idea that it had *worn down* the stone over time, just with the patient, mindless movement of its limbs.

"Well," Basil said a little queasily, "this isn't something they covered in AstroCorps training. Anyone else got any thoughts? Thoughts they can express without starting to scream and then maybe not stopping, that is?"

"It's no wonder Chilly couldn't find a brain down here to latch onto," Scrutarius started.

"Thank you Devlin. Anyone else?"

"The delicious morsel Captain Pelsworthy has finished arguing with the Seven Sisters and is descending towards the surface," Wicked Mary reported.

"The alien ships still appear to be holding position," Chillybin added. "I find it hard to believe they haven't spotted the *Nella* down on the surface no matter how quiet we were, but I am attempting to keep their attention from focussing too closely on you. It is difficult when I am unfamiliar with many of the species involved. Fortunately, Wicked Mary has also got some electronic interference in place - "

"Hey," Bonty said, "this looks like a Molranoid, doesn't it?"

The others were only too happy to look away from the Riddlespawn for a moment and turn their attention onto the carvings on the walls. These were also worn down and obscured by the general collapse of the whole place, but it was easy to see that the carvings – old as they were – were much younger than the temple itself. There were crude outlines of figures that could be humanoid, others that looked like Molranoids, and others still that didn't look like anything much. There was even one that Scrutarius pointed out, a long wormlike thing with fins that he insisted could be an artistic impression of a primitive Fergunakil.

"Roney mentioned that there was a tablet, or a prophecy, or something," Bonty said. "Didn't she? Something about an ancient family of races?"

"The chosen mortal species of ten mythical entities," Galana agreed. "The Riddlespawn were supposed to be one, as were Molren, humans, Fergunak … "

There was really nothing to be learned from the carvings, and there was no sign of a tablet or anything remotely resembling writing anywhere in the chamber. Just the carvings. They were still attempting to analyse the giant statue and the disturbing thrashing shape of the Riddlespawn when Wicked Mary announced that Roney had landed. Hartigan was beginning to mutter apprehensively about his breather running low, and Devlin and Bonty had decided that the Riddlespawn were so named because their whole existence was an unsolveable and very annoying puzzle.

A few minutes later the irrepressible Boze marched into the temple, her narrow furry face hidden behind the gleaming golden visor of her red suit helmet. It was just as shiny and decorative as the rest of her uniform, and Galana noted with muted hilarity that it had a dynamic colourful little label stuck on one side of it – a label of Roney's face in heroically stylised form. You could tell it was her and not just another Boze, because it had a gold tooth and was winking.

"Good," Roney said, "so you found it."

"Bit hard to miss," Hartigan replied, "what with there being only one staircase and one room."

"Ah, don't sell yourselves short," Roney said, striding past the Captain and giving him a hearty clap on the back of the thigh. "I'm sure you could have gotten lost if you'd really set your minds to it. I'm joking, I'm joking," she chuckled and held up her gloved hands. "Well, what do you think of the place?"

"It's horrible," Galana surprised herself by saying. "But we have cautiously established that this whole thing was a much older building that has been … redecorated. Probably sometime in the past twenty to forty thousand years."

"Very good," Roney agreed.

"Which is confusing us a bit," Scrutarius added, "because you said the Riddlespawn destroyed the Empire of Gold twenty *million* years ago, not twenty *thousand*."

"Quite so, quite so," Roney said, and pointed at the giant figure kneeling in the middle of the floor. "What do you make of the big wingèd fellow?"

"Looks like an Angel," Hartigan said, "mythical Earth creature, basically an immortal human with wings. Only this chap's a lot bigger, and he's got a nasty set of choppers, don't y'know."

"You know, he does look a bit like a human doesn't he?" Roney said in surprise. "But no, he's not human, although he is rather mythical. In the days of the Empire, these lads – and lasses – were called *Drakspars*. The regular kind were pretty tough, but the kind with wings were – well, a bit like your Alicorn, see. They were *glorified*. Immortal, all sorts of powers, you name it. They were the soldiers of the Empire, if you like."

"And the Riddlespawn beat them?" Galana asked, glancing from the massive kneeling figure to the pathetic, flopping shape behind it.

"Easy as kicking a *spugget* off a log," Roney replied grimly. "Did you happen to notice this place was built in the middle of a crater?" they nodded. "Legend has it that the crater was made by this fellow," she gestured at the Drakspar. "It got blasted so hard it flew all the way here through space, landed on Palothane, and then – I don't know, fell asleep or something. Drakspars were supposed to go dormant if they weren't on holy ground, not sure whether that means all of the Empire was holy ground or what. Anyway, they tried building this temple around him, but he still didn't wake up."

Galana looked up at the fiercely scowling face with its great jutting teeth. They hadn't managed to identify the substance the figure was made of, but it certainly hadn't scanned as organic. "It doesn't *look* asleep," she said.

Roney laughed. "That's what *I* said," she replied. "Apparently, this is about as unconscious as Drakspars got."

"So the Empire of Gold was destroyed," Bonty said, "and the Riddlespawn went back to wherever they came from - "

"Except for the star serpent we took down," Devlin added.

"Right, except for the star serpent," Bonty agreed. "And this temple was built to commemorate the, um, fallen Drakspars and what have you … and *then* this Riddlespawn showed up?" she waved her left hands at the flailing headless shape. "Thirty thousand years ago or so?"

"That's the best I've been able to figure out," Roney agreed. "Good job."

Bonty looked at Galana, and shook her head.

"We still have no idea what's going on," Galana admitted. "And what we're supposed to do with this. Maybe if you told us more about the prophecy - "

"Well, it's not exactly a *prophecy*," Roney admitted.

"Of course it isn't," Galana sighed.

"All I know is, when this Riddlespawn was dragged out and maimed, it was left in this temple as a – a nasty joke," the Boze went on. "Like a way of saying *look, we won after all, who's afraid of the big bad Riddlespawn?*"

Galana stared at the pathetically squirming creature on the floor. It looked neither big nor bad as far as she could tell. "'Dragged out'?" she echoed. "Dragged out of Hell?"

"No," Roney said. "And yes. Not exactly."

"Roney, I swear - " Hartigan said in exasperation.

"It was dragged out of a dark and terrible place it was already crawling from," Roney explained.

"I don't understand," Bonty said.

"*None of us bally well understand*," Hartigan snapped.

"Of course not," Roney sighed, although she sounded more regretful than frustrated. "Bozanda knows I don't understand either. The Riddlespawn live in some unknown place, right? This one was trapped somewhere, somewhere in *this* sphere of existence, and if it had escaped from the trap intact it would have become something terrible. Instead, it was dragged out of the trap but in doing so it was ... damaged."

"Damaged?" Devlin exclaimed. "It's got no *head*."

"Not *here* anyway," Roney shrugged. "Like a wounded animal torn out of a snare, it just wants to return home."

"Home ... back to wherever the other Riddlespawn are?" Hartigan asked. Roney nodded.

"Back to where its head is?" Scrutarius added.

Roney turned her golden visor in his direction. "You seem fixated on the whole 'head' detail."

"I feel it's a detail worth getting fixated on," the Blaran retorted.

"In short, it wants to go home," Basil cut off the developing argument. "To heal, and get ready to charge forth and demolish the next empire that comes along and gets too big for its boots?"

"I wouldn't worry too much about that," Roney said. "We're all pretty small-time compared to the Empire of Gold. The Riddlespawn don't come out and play with just anybody, you know," she pointed at the towering shape of the Drakspar. "*Look* at this big magnificent bastard."

"So what do we do?" Bonty asked.

Roney shook her head. "If the Seven Sisters manage to get close, if they manage to pull it the rest of the way into this world and fix it, they think they'll be able to make an ally of it. But it will never do what the Pirate Queen wants. It will be unstoppable. It might have taken a bunch of Riddlespawn and star serpents to bring down the Empire of Gold, but this tiddler right here would make short work of anything *this* galaxy has to throw at it, in this day and age."

Galana narrowed her eyes. "Why can't the Seven Sisters get close anyway?"

Roney shrugged. "They can't land. The last time anyone tried, twenty-odd years ago, this thing screamed and the star serpent showed up and burned everyone right out of orbit. Made this planet even more attractive than it was already."

"It *screamed?*" Devlin pointed. "It's got no *head*," Roney waved this off dismissively.

"The star serpent is dead now," Bonty frowned.

"Right," Roney pointed at the ceiling. "But *they* don't know that. Right now, they just think I've come up with some clever way of sneaking down," she gestured around at the group in general. "You know, the whole 'family of races' thing. Which it looks like I was right about, by the way."

"Hang about, you didn't *know* we were the right species," Hartigan objected.

"I was reasonably sure," Roney said.

"What if this thing could have called *another* star serpent?" Bonty asked.

Roney tilted her head. "I never thought of that," she admitted. "But look, it's not yelling. It trusts us more than the Sisters, see? Family of races."

"It's got no *head*," Devlin repeated.

"Listen, sooner or later Her Majesty is going to figure out that it's safe, and she'll order them to attempt a landing, and that's when this whole thing is going to get messy," Roney said. "We need to send this thing back to Hell before that happens."

Galana spread her hands helplessly. "And how are we supposed to do that, exactly?" The satisfaction of watching Captain Pelsworthy squirming in an attempt to avoid saying 'I don't know' was quite small in comparison to the mounting alarm Galana was feeling about the whole situation. She looked around at the others. "Suggestions?"

"There is a very mild but unknown energy field immediately surrounding the Riddlespawn's severed neck," Wicked Mary reported. The little silver *giela* was standing directly under the Drakspar's wings and had been prodding at the Riddlespawn's neck-stump with a sensor built into her finger while the others talked. "If we pretend Captain Pelsworthy's preposterous assemblage of nonsense is true - "

"Hey," Roney objected.

" - we can imagine this is a sort of wormhole, or gateway the

Riddlespawn is using to come and go between this world and its own," Wicked Mary went on calmly. "It got its head in, and then got stuck. I could boost the amount of energy the gateway is receiving, and increase its size. The only problem is … "

"Its head could just as easily pop out on this side as the rest of its body pop in on that one," Hartigan finished. "*More* easily, if it really is just a hole it's got its – its head stuck in. Its head is probably smaller than its body *and if it isn't, I absolutely don't want to know about it*," he added fervently.

"Yes," Wicked Mary said, "that is the basic problem. Anything we do to help it get home could backfire and result in it being pulled fully into this world, the way this alleged *Pirate Queen* wants."

"She's not *alleged*, she's an actual - " Roney huffed.

"Can you just … neutralise the energy field?" Galana asked.

They all turned and stared at her.

"That would cut its head off for real," Bonty said, then looked down at her boots. "Oh. You were already aware of that."

"Yes," Galana said. "The question is, if we *can* close the hole it is stuck in, would that kill it? Or would having its head cut off for real just make it angry?"

"Not as stupid a question as it sounds," Roney said, "knowing even as little as I do about Riddlespawn. I mean, any of the rest of us got our heads stuck in something for thirty thousand years, we probably wouldn't still be squirming."

"The Seven Sisters are changing formation," Chillybin reported. "They may be preparing to send a landing party."

"Well, it doesn't seem like we have much choice, and we're running out of time," Galana told Roney. "You brought us here because you thought we could help."

"So you can really do this?" Roney asked Wicked Mary in surprise.

"Of course, morsel," Wicked Mary said. "Our civilisation is designed around getting nowhere as slowly as possible, after all, so we are in a perfect position to get this unfortunate creature nowhere after thirty thousand years," Roney laughed, and Wicked Mary gestured at the squirming shape. "Should I proceed?"

"Do it," Hartigan said unexpectedly. Galana looked at him. "It certainly doesn't seem comfortable right now, and we don't want this thing alive in either sphere," he said with a shrug. "Do we?"

Wicked Mary performed some swift, complicated rearrangements on her *giela*'s machinery, then leaned back over the Riddlespawn. The lights set into her gleaming metal carapace flickered, and the headless torso stiffened – and then flailed more frantically. A high, raucous shriek sounded, making Galana and the others flinch. The sound wasn't audible inside the temple, but over their communicators.

"It's calling for the star serpent!" Roney shouted over the din.

Wicked Mary's lights flickered again, the scream cut off and the body fell limp into the depression it had worn down over the past thirty thousand years. With a final slither of scales, it collapsed … and then collapsed further, darkening and cracking until it dissolved into a faint black smudge on the stones.

"Is everything alright down there?" Chillybin's voice asked. "The Seven Sisters just turned their ships around and jumped into soft-space like their loading bays were on fire."

"We're fine," Galana reported. "They probably heard that scream and assumed the star serpent was on its way."

"Let's get out of here before they realise it's not," Roney suggested.

"*Excellent* notion, young Captain Pelsworthy," Hartigan declared.

Soon, in <u>The Blind Time Traveller</u>:

Judderone Pelsworthy of the Boze, Space Adventurer, stayed with them for a short time after their victory on Palothane and their retreat to a safe distance a few light years away. She came up with a variety of excuses – "I want to be sure another star serpent isn't going to show up," "I want to keep an eye on things in case the Riddlespawn come back," "You'll want me nearby in case the Seven Sisters come after you," – but after a few days it became pretty clear that she just enjoyed the AstroCorps crew's company.

"You know," Hartigan said one evening-shift as they were sitting and enjoying another meal of mixed Six Species and Boze rations, and Basil was puffing on one of his rare cigars, "if you wanted to travel with us you'd be very welcome."

"I thought you had to do this little circumnavigation thing yourself," Roney said. "Hardly counts if I carry you most of the way, does it?"

"Oh *carry us*, now is it?" Basil laughed, but had to concede the point. The Boze *had* given them a five-year lift over the course of the past couple of weeks. "Well, if you don't mind taking it casually, you'd be welcome to dock with us and carry on at our pace. I'm sure we have a lot to teach each other."

"About High Elonath, for example," Roney said, a wily expression on her amber-and-white-furred face.

"Well, among other things, certainly," Hartigan said. "You know an awful lot about the galaxy. Even if you can't share your marvellous technology with us poor biggumses, you must be able to help fill out our charts a bit, give us a few pointers."

"It would be nice to know more about mobs like the Pirate Queen, too," Devlin added. "So we don't go blundering into enemy territory unawares."

"Ah, you only want to blunder into enemy territory completely *aware*, eh?" Roney flashed her gold fang in a grin.

"Exactly," Scrutarius nodded. "No, wait – "

"I'll give you a few notes," the Boze promised, "but you have to know it's a dangerous and ever-changing thing, space. And I've got my own path. Don't worry, though," she added, and raised her glass. "I have no doubt it will cross with yours again. Many times."

"No need for our paths to split again quite yet, though," Bonty insisted. "Surely?"

"Absolutely not," Roney agreed. "Oh, and that reminds me – here, I picked up something for you to add to your little souvenir collection," she jumped off her couch, stepped over to the table in the middle of the Captain's lounge, and drew a long, jagged grey-black shape from a pouch in the back of her uniform. At first Galana thought it was a blade of some sort, but then Roney set it down on the table and she realised it was a feather.

Hartigan leaned forward, eyes widening. "Is that ... ?"

"A Drakspar feather," Roney said proudly. "I plucked a couple off the big fellow down on Palothane. One for you, one for me."

"I don't know what to say," Basil said, his voice wobbling sentimentally.

"I'm glad it didn't wake up when you plucked it," Devlin remarked.

"*Yes,*" Hartigan agreed, pointing at the Blaran. "I shall say that."

Roney grinned and was about to speak again, when the *Conch*'s computer interrupted them with a polite chime.

"I'm sorry to bother you, Basil," it said, "but a ship has just arrived in our vicinity."

Everyone jumped to their feet.

"The Seven Sisters?" Hartigan asked.

"Can't be," Roney tapped at one of the little devices built into her uniform sleeves. "*My* computer would have told me if they'd shown back up. It would have let me know if *anything* in my databanks had shown up."

"So what is this?" Galana asked.

Roney frowned at her sleeve.

"Something else," she said.

THE BLIND TIME TRAVELLER

The ship was a strange, curled thing like a great horn, coloured in the most tasteless assortment of pearly rainbow colours Galana had ever seen. It was really quite ghastly.

"We have established a comm link," the computer reported, with what sounded like surprise. "That was easy. Almost as though they already have our comm setup."

"Maybe their technology is more advanced than ours," Captain Hartigan suggested, then jabbed a finger at Roney without looking back at her. "Quiet you."

"I didn't say anything," the grinning Boze objected.

"I could hear you *thinking* it," Hartigan grumbled. "Alright, let's see what our new friends in the colourful ship look like."

When the image of the alien ship was replaced on the screens by the image of its pilot, it wasn't much improvement in the good-taste department. The alien was more or less humanoid, in a stupendously muscled and weirdly barbarian-dressed way. Its tattooed arms were bare except for great studded gloves, and its torso was wrapped in bands of what looked like metal, etched with strange arcane runes. Its head was hidden by a gleaming golden helmet – at least Galana *hoped* it was a helmet – in the shape of a skull. And not a human skull, but the skull of some long-muzzled and many-toothed monstrosity, made even more unsettling by the fact that it had no eye sockets.

"Well," the alien said in a deep, booming voice, "this is goodbye."

"Eh?" Hartigan blinked for a second in confusion – the imposing alien was speaking Grand Bo without any assistance or voice-over from the *Conch* – but recovered well. "I am Captain Basil Hartigan of the ACS *Conch*. On behalf of - "

"I suppose I should thank you, but you know," the alien boomed, "I don't want to," its huge gleaming shoulders shook as it laughed heartily. "All in all, you were *slightly* more help than hindrance, and that is all I can say. Galana, Devlin, I'll see you in Axis Mundi. Remember – *forget everything*."

"What's going on?" Basil asked plaintively.

The strange skull-helmeted creature vanished from the screens, the starry black of space replacing alien and ship alike.

"Where did it go?" Roney demanded.

"Did it go to relative speed?" Galana asked, although the ship had been so close that it probably would have set off alarms if it had done so. She checked her readouts. The ship was just gone, as if it had never existed in the first place.

"Well, that was weird even by our standards," Scrutarius said.

AstroCorps and Boze alike scanned the area for several hours, but found nothing. Captain Pelsworthy was particularly offended by this, insisting that even a departed ship would have left some electromagnetic and gravitational distortions, if not dropped particles. The *Conch*'s computer agreed. The alien had vanished without a trace.

"And you didn't recognise it at all?" Basil asked Roney.

The little Space Adventurer shook her head. "Never seen anything like it."

Chillybin shifted her great booted feet. "I have," she said.

They all turned to stare at the enormous aki'Drednanth.

"You have?" Galana asked.

"Why the blazes didn't you say anything earlier?" Hartigan demanded.

"I wanted to be sure," Chilly said. "I have been conferring with my fellow aki'Drednanth, and the Drednanth in the dream. What we just saw should not be. *Must* not be."

"Sounds promising," Devlin said.

"Sounds like an adventure," Roney agreed eagerly, with none of the Blaran's sarcasm. "Come on, frosty, out with it. What was it, and how did it vanish like that?"

"They were known as Time Destroyers," Chillybin replied. "They lived long ago, and were a formidable and dangerous enemy."

"Ooh, *Time Destroyers*," Scrutarius said eagerly. "Did they start out as Time Wasters, and get militant?"

"Now, hang about," Hartigan said, "I'm beginning to lose track of all these ancient bally menaces. On a scale of, say, Riddlespawn to Damorakind, how long ago and dangerous are we talking about here?"

"And just so we're clear, which of those two are at which end of the scale?" Devlin added.

"The Time Destroyers are one of the first mortal species," Chillybin said, "older and mightier than all but the ancient Molren and … others."

"So they're one of the family of races?" Galana asked, although she also wanted to know just how 'ancient' the ancient Molren were and how much the aki'Drednanth knew about them. "The chosen children of the Infinites?"

Chillybin shook her head. "No," she said. "The Molren may be an Elder Race and a member of the mythical family of races, but most of the family – Riddlespawn, humans, Fergunak – are younger. Time Destroyers are Elders, but chosen by no Infinite."

"That's just unnecessarily complicated," Scrutarius complained.

"I say, why do Molren get to be all of the special things?" Basil asked accusingly.

"Why are you looking at me?" Galana asked. "It wasn't *my* idea."

"So these Time Destroyers," Bonty persisted. "They're bad news?"

"Indeed," Chillybin replied. "They were never truly welcomed in this galaxy. They lived here for a time, but … now they are no more. Or so we thought."

"Did this all happen *more* or *less* than twenty million years ago?" Devlin asked.

Chilly shook her head again. "Four hundred thousand," she said, "no more."

"Oh," Hartigan said, "that's practically *yesterday*," Chillybin laughed. "This one seemed fairly friendly though, wouldn't you say?"

"Yes," Chillybin agreed, "and that troubles me."

"And what was that it said?" Hartigan went on. "See you in Axis Mundi? What's an Axis Mundi?"

"I have no idea," Galana said.

"But it said it would *meet* you there," Hartigan protested.

"It also told us to forget everything," Scrutarius suggested. "Maybe we just forgot."

"Do you have anything helpful to say, Devlin?" Hartigan asked.

"Not right now," Scrutarius smiled.

There didn't seem to be anything they could do about the alleged Time Destroyer, so after taking a few more scans and samples of nothing in particular they dived back into the grey and headed for their next destination. It was six weeks at relative speed, and when they emerged Roney declared it had been the most painfully boring six weeks of her life and was outraged at how short a distance they'd come.

"And there's *nothing here*," she concluded. "You've dropped out at another inhospitable ice ball with some mushrooms growing at the equator. Well done. I'm beginning to think you're *intentionally* touring the most boring parts of the galaxy because you've got some sort of weird fetish."

"Well give us that bally map you said you'd give us, for goodness' sake," Basil retorted.

"Alright, biggums," Roney said mildly, "no need to get roary. I already transferred some info to your computer. There's a planet not far from here with a very friendly population, they'd be happy to meet you I'm sure. Now, their species evolved from a type of berry and there is a variety of fruit tree on the planet that is *very* easy to get mixed up with one of their nursery bushes where they develop their young ones, but as long as you give the berries a little tickle before picking them and make sure not to eat anything that giggles - "

"Contact!" the *Conch* said sharply.

The strange curled rainbow-shape of the Time Destroyer ship appeared in the viewscreens, sweeping around the linked *Conch* and *Splendiferous Bastard* in a tight spiral. Eerie light glowed in vents along either side of the twisted vessel.

"Now, release it now!" the alien's voice thundered through the comm system, and alarms blared across the bridge as the light played over the ship and a strange lightheaded sensation made Galana clutch at her armrests.

Hartigan slumped in his chair, eyes bulging and face going pale behind his moustache, but to his credit managed to tap in some orders with shaking fingers. "We're under attack," he said hoarsely, "deploy countermeasures!"

"What sort of countermeasures do we have for alien strobe lights?" Wicked Mary asked. The *giela*, of course, didn't seem affected but it was hard to say how the Fergie herself was taking it down in the Aquarium.

"Well deploy *something!*" Hartigan managed to shout.

The alien ship swept around again, and the lights returned. *"Now!"* the Time Destroyer shouted. "Release it now, you fools told me you'd practiced!"

"Firing pulse turrets at the alien's weapons array," Wicked Mary said calmly, and the *Conch* blasted a swift barrage of turret-fire at the vents on the side of the Time Destroyer's vessel. It didn't have any visible effect on the weird light, but the ship peeled off and spiralled away almost too swiftly to follow. The strange dizziness and nausea passed as soon as the strange light had swept away from them.

"What are you *doing*?" the alien roared.

"What are *you* doing?" Hartigan roared back. "Also, who are you?" the ship swept back, turned, and vanished again as abruptly as it had the first time. "Alright, damage report," he said. "And please let me know if we're trying to win a fight with a time traveller here, what?"

"Captain?" Galana said in surprise. After many years flying together she'd found she could often follow the human's convoluted and amazingly illogical thought processes, and she *thought* she could see what was going on in his head this time, but he was still capable of surprising her.

"Stands to reason, doesn't it?" he replied. "These chaps are *called* Time

Destroyers. And the first time we met this one, he treated us like we were all old chums and *then said goodbye to us*. Seems like time travel is the obvious answer, what?"

"It is a *simple* explanation, Captain," Galana said carefully, "but so would be saying 'he's a space wizard.' It completely ignores the impossibility of time travel."

"Relative field technology completely ignores the impossibility of me walking a thousand light years in a little over a month," Bonty pointed out.

"It doesn't *ignore* it," Galana said. This was another feeling she had gotten used to over the years – being the only sane person on a ship of lunatics. "It takes the laws of physics entirely into account in order to bypass them."

"And time travel technology can't do the same?" Hartigan asked.

"Well," Galana said, "I suppose that making up a fantastical explanation for something we don't understand, and then deciding that the fantastical explanation is possible if we assume a theoretical science we have not yet discovered, is a *sort* of approach ... "

"Well what's *your* explanation, then?" Hartigan demanded.

"We have encountered alien ships in two separate locations within this region of space," Galana said. "The pilot of the first displayed a wide knowledge of our crew and languages, but communicated in a baffling way. The second displayed an unknown energy emission and communicated, again, in a baffling way. They may have been the same alien and ship, but we don't *know* that. At the moment, my *explanation* is that these ... Time Destroyers ... are sufficiently different to us that their modes of communication are – are ... "

"Baffling?" Bonty suggested.

"Yes," Galana said. "If this *was* a Time Destroyer, and they *have* been gone for four hundred thousand years, his presence here would have to be explained."

"Time travel would explain it," Hartigan replied.

"Space wizard would too," Scrutarius added.

"He did sort of look like a space wizard," Bonty agreed.

Galana considered this. "Okay, he did," she admitted. "But I would prefer something with a little more substance. Computer, do you have any comms data that would confirm they were the same ship, at least?"

"They connected and transmitted data in exactly the same way," the *Conch* said. "And seemed to speak Grand Bo without any help from us. Either they're the same ship, or they've made everything about their ships unnecessarily identical."

"Not something we can rule out," Galana said. "What about damage?"

"No damage," Scrutarius confirmed, "although I think Bonty should look over all of us if you guys felt as weird as I did when that light hit us."

"Agreed," Hartigan said.

"It was not a weapon," Wicked Mary told them. "The alien seemed to be trying to establish a connection with something. Something he thought we had, and wanted us to release."

"And then meet these two in Axis Mundi," Roney added, gesturing towards Galana and Devlin, "whatever that is. For the record, though, I agree with Fen. Definitely not a time traveller."

"What, really?" Hartigan said, sounding disappointed. "Rather expected you to be on my side on this one, old sport."

"Sorry, biggums," the Boze flicked her huge ears. "It's a fun idea, but even if time travel *was* possible, there are greater forces than physics preventing reality from being unravelled."

"It is true," Chillybin put in before Galana could protest. "There are Vultures that circle in the darkness, waiting to feast on any inventor who wanders where they shouldn't wander. It is this that occurred to the Time Destroyers of old."

"I take it back," Hartigan said in delight. "If you have to agree with Fen, that's just about the most agonisingly unscientific reason you could choose – and Chilly *agrees* with you. Listen, I bet you and Devlin can hear Fen's teeth grinding, even if I can't."

"If we've just about had enough fun at our poor long-suffering Commander's expense," Bonty said to the grinning human, Blaran and Boze, "what should we do next? Do we wait for him to come back, or continue on our way and assume he'll find us again?"

"I don't know if I can take another six week jaunt through the grey just to get nowhere much," Roney said, "as much as I enjoy your company. Look, even if the berry fellows are a bit out of your way, I think I put another one on your charts. There's an inhabited planet called Spangle about two months from here, at your speeds. Nice people, the Spangles, just keep one eye on your valuables because they're a bit sticky-fingered. I'll meet you there when you pop back out, do a bit of exploring on my own in the meantime."

There didn't seem to be much else they could do. They concluded their latest check of the system they'd dropped into, discovered that Roney was right – it was uninhabited and impossibly dull – and set course for the next place. The place called Spangle, apparently, which might include nice if slightly thievery-prone aliens. Spangle was a little over fifteen hundred light years away, which was a long, boring stretch. Galana and Hartigan agreed that they would divide the flight into two legs, with a brief stop in normal space at the one-month halfway point, even if it was in the middle of nowhere.

It was without much surprise, as they dropped back out of the grey and into featureless interstellar space four weeks later, that they found the ugly oily-rainbow shape of the Time Destroyer ship waiting for them.

"Are you ready?" the skull-helmeted alien said without preamble.

"*No we're not*," Hartigan replied a little impatiently, "but at least you're not blasting us with weird light this time. Now get your ducks in a row and tell us what's going on, and maybe we'll get it right the next time around. Or the *previous* time around, for all I bally well know."

"I explained myself to you once already," the Time Destroyer rumbled. "I am not accustomed to having to do so - "

"Look, just tell us what you want us to do," Hartigan begged. "You wanted us to release something, right?"

"You haven't got the wayfinder yet?" the Time Destroyer said, sounding outraged.

"We don't even know what the wayfinder is," Galana replied while Basil spluttered indignantly. "Maybe you could - "

"*Blast*," the alien snapped in exasperation, "I've overshot. Just - "

The ship and its pilot vanished, leaving star-speckled space in its place.

"On to Spangle?" Wicked Mary asked.

"Yes," Basil growled, "on to Spangle."

After another four weeks in the grey, they emerged in the system Roney had marked on their charts. It was rather a surprise *not* to find the Time Destroyer waiting for them – but at least Roney was.

"Ho there, biggums," she said, her pointy little grin almost appearing on the screens before her face did. Her ship, the *Splendiferous Bastard*, was rising swiftly towards them from the peaceful, attractive blue-purple planet below. "You're late."

"Sorry about that," Hartigan said, and nodded across at Chillybin. "Any sign of life apart from Roney?"

"The planet is inhabited," Chillybin confirmed, "a similar level of technology to our own ... "

"Yes, the Spangles are *fairly* advanced," Roney agreed. Galana noted that her ship was still approaching, and wondered if the Boze was going to dock with them. "No ships, though, aside from a few little defence thingies. They don't believe in travelling beyond their own star system. In fact, most of them don't even believe *in* beyond their own star system. But you've skipped over the main news," she said. "I've solved our little Time Destroyer riddle."

Hartigan leaned forward. "Oh?"

"I got here a couple of local days ago, and I've been chatting with the Spangles," Roney said. "They were telling me all about Praxulon the Mad. Do you want to hear about Praxulon the Mad?"

"Is Praxulon the Mad a big fellow in an ugly spaceship and a skull helmet with no eyes, who thinks he's a time traveller?" Basil asked.

"You've heard of him," Roney said happily.

"Captain Pelsworthy," Galana said. "I take it the Spangles have had dealings with the Time Destroyer?"

"He was here a while ago, rambling at them in pretty much the same disjointed way he was with us," Roney said. "I didn't quite get to the bottom of what else went on between ol' Praxulon and the Spangles, but he apparently landed briefly, they decided he was annoying, so they stole a critical component from his ship just to teach him a bit of a lesson."

"This thing they stole wouldn't happen to have been called a wayfinder, would it?" Devlin asked.

Roney tilted her head sharply. "Sounds like you already know quite a lot about this," she said in surprise. "Yep, they took his wayfinder and cut him loose, told him if he ever came back they'd shoot it. The crazy bugger hasn't bothered them since."

"I would suggest," Galana said, "that if he was a time traveller he probably would have been able to stop people from stealing from him."

"*I* would suggest," Basil retorted, "that if his time machine was dependent on a thing called a *wayfinder*, his attempts to get it back would probably result in exactly the sort of weird jumbled-up meetings we've been having with him."

"Aha, see, I thought you'd say that," Roney declared.

"Captain Hartigan," Wicked Mary said, "there are several of what Captain Pelsworthy called 'little defence thingies' approaching from lower orbit. They appear to be pursuing our delicious little friend. They are also not particularly little."

"Roney," Hartigan said, "what did you do?"

"Me? Nothing," Roney replied. "I'm offended by the very implication."

"Roney - "

"The Spangles may have misplaced Praxulon's wayfinder," the Boze said, "and they may have been looking for it for a while, and working up the nerve to ask *me* about Praxulon's wayfinder, and now they *might* think I'm making a run for it with Praxulon's wayfinder … "

"Bloody Hell," Hartigan said in disgust. "Plot us a course out of here - "

"No need," Roney said, and the grey of soft-space enveloped them.

"Alright, Captain Pelsworthy," Galana said, "perhaps now that we are accessories to your crimes against Spangle, you can tell us why you have taken the wayfinder and what you plan to do next?"

"I'm as curious about this Praxulon the Mad as you are," Roney said. "Even if he's *not* a time traveller, I've never heard of Time Destroyers or seen anything like him or his ship, and that's good enough for me. The Spangles didn't really *want* the wayfinder," she went on, "they just wanted him to leave them alone. It was like a keepsake to them."

"People usually like to *keep* keepsakes," Scrutarius pointed out. "It's right there in the name."

The Last Alicorn

"What are we going to do, Roney?" Hartigan asked.

Roney's answer was prompt. "Stop, and wait for Praxulon to show up."

"And then give him back his wayfinder?" Bonty guessed.

"What? No," Roney said. "Maybe. I don't know, it'll probably be easier if I show you."

Somehow, Roney managed to navigate her ship over to the *Conch* while they were both in soft-space, and they docked. The interior of the powerful little Boze vessel was a little too cramped for any of the AstroCorps crewmembers to fit inside, and so Roney came to join them in the *Conch*'s docking bay. She was pulling what looked like a stretcher-bed, floating above the deck on a gravity plate, with a sheet over it.

"This is very dramatic," Galana said.

"Isn't it though?" Roney grinned, and pulled off the sheet.

Praxulon the Mad's wayfinder was not a piece of machinery, not even a strange and twisted oil-on-water-sheened object like his ship was. It appeared to be some kind of animal.

It was about the size of a full-grown human, with four limbs but clearly not a biped. The legs, and paws, were small and stunted, as though they had stopped growing when the creature was an infant. Its body was long and cylindrical, tapering to a short fat tail at one end and dipping into a short neck before widening back out to a large round head at the other. Its face was slack and uncomprehending, a tiny wheezing mouth beneath a pair of huge, placid eyes as grey as soft-space. It regarded them solemnly, its rounded sides moving slowly in and out as it breathed – or *seemed* to breathe. Its entire body, aside from its eyes and the rounded pads on the undersides of its paws, was covered in a soft fuzz of rainbow-coloured fur.

"It's beautiful," Hartigan said in a hushed voice.

"It's sick," Bonty added with deep concern, and leaned over to begin examining the creature. "Some kind of nutrient deficiency. Of course it's impossible to be certain since I've never seen anything like this before ... "

"This is the wayfinder?" Galana frowned.

"Extraordinary, isn't she?" Roney reached out and stroked the sleek creature's back. Its wheezing eased a little and it gave a soft cooing sound of evident pleasure.

"'She'?" Devlin raised an ear.

Roney gestured vaguely at the wayfinder's hindquarters. "She's got all the usual girl bits," she explained, "but they're rather a bunched-up afterthought. I just use 'she' as a convenience. The rest of her organs appear to be *extremely* specialised, more like machine components than parts of a body. I think Praxulon's technology is at least partly organic, if not *entirely*. This is – well, she might not even really be a living thing, she might just be a piece of his ship. A navigation cell, if the name is anything to go by."

"Well whatever she is, she's still sick," Bonty asserted. "She might need to be plugged into Praxulon's ship to get the food she needs."

"In the meantime, can you take her to your medical bay and see if there's any way *we* can find the right food for her?" Roney asked.

"Of course," Bonty said.

"Where are we going anyway?" Hartigan asked Roney as the Bonshoon doctor pulled the stretcher into motion and headed for the medical bay.

"Oh, not far," Roney said, and waved them all back towards the bridge. The AstroCorps crew fell in behind the Boze Space Adventurer, and Galana reflected in amusement at how effortlessly Captain Pelsworthy took command. She glanced at Basil and saw he was grinning too, not bothered by his alien friend's manner. "I figured I'd just get us away from Spangle, then drop out of soft-space and see how long it takes Praxulon to find us."

They only remained in the grey for a few minutes after that. Just as they were taking their stations on the bridge, the linked vessels returned to normal space. The gaudy rainbow twist of the alien ship was already waiting for them.

"Contact," the *Conch* said unnecessarily.

"How does he *do* that?" Roney muttered to herself.

"Time travel," Devlin said quietly.

The skull-helmeted visage of the Time Destroyer appeared on their screens. "Well," he boomed, "I promised to explain myself, and here I am."

"Okay ... Praxulon?" Basil said carefully.

"Praxulon *the Mad*," the Time Destroyer said, just a little sharply. "I do not forget *your* titles, *Captain* Hartigan."

"You – I'm sorry old chap, I wouldn't have thought – alright, so you *don't mind* being called Praxulon the Mad?" Hartigan stammered. "I rather thought you'd be offended by it for some reason."

"Not at all," said Praxulon the Mad. "It is a title of great esteem. Or it was. My people have been gone for a very long time," he tilted his strange eyeless skull-helmet. "But I imagine your Ogre friend told you that much, hmm?"

"You mean Chillybin? She told us the Time Destroyers were wiped out a long while back, yes," Hartigan said.

"Yes," the Time Destroyer boomed, although he sounded rather cheerful now. "You know the Ogres, they're time travellers too, in their own way. They only go in the one direction, of course."

"Same as the rest of us, really," Hartigan said philosophically.

"*Ah*," Praxulon the Mad said in approval. "Well, would it shock you to learn that I am the one who did it? I am the one who brought down the Vultures upon my home and all who live there, all those aeons ago?"

"Nothing would shock me at this point," Basil admitted. "Nice to know you and Chilly agree about the Vultures, though. That's *jolly* reassuring."

"I succeeded, you see, but there are rules. *Big* rules," Praxulon told them.

"And I broke one of the biggest. There had to be consequences. They told me there would be, if I continued to try, and if I succeeded."

"When you succeeded in *time travelling*," Devlin spoke up from the engineering console. "Just to clarify."

"Yes," Praxulon said again. "But that's why we had this small outpost, this settlement in your galaxy. To protect the rest of our species."

"You're from another galaxy?" Galana asked in surprise.

Praxulon the Mad waved an enormous hand. "That is not important," he said – incorrectly, in Galana's opinion. "The good news is, I know it happened. I have *seen* the ruins of my civilisation in this galaxy."

"That's *good* news?" Bonty asked.

"For you, certainly," Praxulon replied. "The alternatives simply do not bear thinking about."

"Why isn't one of the alternatives just destroying you and your time travel research?" Devlin asked. "Seems a lot simpler."

"The Vultures do not deal in *sabotage*," Praxulon the Mad declared.

"So what's your next move?" Hartigan, at least, seemed enthralled by the insane alien's story.

"Therein lies my problem," Praxulon the Mad replied. "My ship was … interfered with. I was stranded here, only able to make small, almost random jumps. I am blind."

"Maybe if your helmet had eye holes … " Devlin remarked.

"Scrutarius," Galana sighed.

Praxulon the Mad just laughed and tapped the strange skull he was wearing. "This old thing? My discipline has worn the skull of the eyeless beasts of the gates for generations. They're from your past … but the distant future for me. A symbol of my craft. My singular genius," he laughed again, then leaned forward. "Now, to get out of here - "

"You need your wayfinder," Hartigan guessed.

"Ah, so you know about that," Praxulon said. "No, I got my wayfinder back. The problem is, I got it back … out of order."

"Out of order?" Galana frowned.

"I told you, I am flying blind. I got my wayfinder back, but then you got *another* copy of it back *earlier* … these are the hazards of time travel. The different versions – the one you have, and the one I have – are out of tune."

"What makes you think *we* have one?" Hartigan asked nonchalantly.

Instead of answering, Praxulon settled back in his seat. "What year is this?"

"Do you mean by the standardised Six Species calendar?" Galana asked, wondering what possible good this information woud do to an alien. But, if his story of time travel was to be believed … "It is 1028 YM."

"Ahh … " Praxulon the Mad nodded his great gleaming helmet. "You see, the veil is not due to lift for another two thousand, eight hundred and forty-two years."

"How do you know that, and what's the veil?" Hartigan asked.

"Let's just say that my first test-flight through time was much like a test-flight through space," Praxulon said. "I bumped into my destination at an ill-advised speed and bounced back to end up here. So I caught a glimpse – quite a *close-up* glimpse – and then came to rest in this rather specialised section of my own future. And *that* was when I ran into difficulty with my wayfinder. I must get back to the point in time I bumped into, so that the circle may be completed and the damage contained."

"What does that even *mean*?" Hartigan demanded in despair. "Don't get me wrong, old fellow, I hear you trying to explain this simply for us, but honestly - "

"Never mind. You must forget everything," the Time Destroyer replied sternly. "The less you know, the safer you will be if the Vultures come for you."

"This crew ought to be quite safe from the Vultures," Bonty said. "We hardly know anything."

Hartigan did his best to ignore this. "I won't even be *alive* in two thousand, eight hundred and however-many years," he complained.

"I like to think I will," Devlin remarked.

"Me too," Galana added.

"Silence in the ranks," Hartigan snapped. "We don't like being reminded of our mortality. Bloody Mary, tell them."

"It's true," Wicked Mary said. "The thought of dying in a few years is hardly improved at all by the knowledge that you will continue living for thousands of years afterwards."

"If I can restore my sight," Praxulon said, "perhaps I will be able to drop in on you and say goodbye before the end."

"You already said goodbye to us a few weeks ago," Scrutarius pointed out.

"You told us you'd meet us in Axis Mundi," Galana said.

"I did? I must have been crazy," Praxulon declared. "Do you have any idea how many Cat 9s I would need to fly past to get into Axis Mundi?"

"No," said Galana. "We don't know what a Cat 9 is."

"Oh," Praxulon said, then angled his helmet down to look at his controls. "Blast," he added, "I have to - "

The Time Destroyer and his ship vanished, as abruptly as ever.

"Does *anyone* understand what's happening?" Hartigan pleaded.

"Seems pretty simple to me," Devlin said. "Time traveller half a million years ago, experimental time machine, went into the future and crashed and bounced back to here, got his giant rainbow navigation ferret stolen by the Spangles, and has been bouncing back and forth ever since trying to get it working properly so he can finish his journey and let the time travel police Vultures arrest him and wipe him out the way they did with the rest of his people."

"That's *simple*?" Bonty asked.

"Simple as I can get it," Devlin said. "What I *don't* understand is why he isn't just staying here where he's apparently safe from these Vulture things."

"Obviously, doing so would put us all at risk," Chillybin said.

"That's *obvious*?" Bonty wailed.

"What do you think, Fen?" Hartigan was stroking his moustache thoughtfully.

"I agree with Chief Engineer Scrutarius," Galana said, "only instead of the 'time travel' part, he's just an eccentric alien we have not figured out how to communicate with yet."

"And we have his wayfinder," Roney added, "so sooner or later he'll be - "

"Contact," the *Conch* said, as the strange twisted shape of the Time Destroyer ship reappeared on their screens.

" - Give me a second," Praxulon the Mad said the moment comms opened. "There. Alright. Do you have the wayfinder *now*?"

"We might," Hartigan said cautiously. "I suppose you'll want to try to tune it back up with your out-of-order one."

"Something like that," Praxulon said gruffly. "I expect I shall explain this all to you when I have a chance."

"Yes," Hartigan said. "I mean, I wouldn't say you explained *well*, but you did your best ... "

"Your attempt to tune your wayfinder wouldn't happen to involve shining some kind of energy beam on us," Galana guessed, "while we release the wayfinder we have?"

"You shouldn't need to release it," Praxulon replied. "I can probably synchronise them directly from here."

"Wait," Devlin said. "Apparently *I'm* the only one who thinks you're actually a time traveller - "

"I think you might be," Hartigan said.

"I don't care," Wicked Mary added.

"I think it might be dangerous to even speculate about it," Chillybin said.

"I'm so confused," Bonty complained.

"But just in case you're for real, or even if you're just delusional, this might be important to the, you know, fantasy you've constructed," Scrutarius went on. "We apparently already bollocksed this up on the *second* try, because you got the second try in front of the first. So we already know the first *and* second tries will fail. If you're going to try for a *third*, you should be aware that you were pretty cross with us about the whole thing."

"But hang about," Hartigan frowned. "If *this* is before that for him, won't he remember that he already knew it was going to fail because we've just told him?"

"'Forget everything'," Bonty said.

"Exactly!" Praxulon approved. "The fat old Molran is right."

"Steady on," Bonty objected mildly.

"You must forget what will happen in the future," Praxulon the Mad said severely. "It is the safest course."

"We don't exactly operate that way," Bonty told him. "We don't *know* what will happen in the future. It's not quite the same as *forgetting*."

"Bah, a matter of interpretation. But the important thing is, *I* will forget. So I will probably still get frustrated at your failure, even though I should have known it would occur. So you will have to remind me when I berate you."

"That's going to be fun," Hartigan said.

"Very well. If the field tuning will not work with the wayfinder inside your ship, we will have to do it the way you suggest," Praxulon said. "I will reconfigure my emitters, and you will release the wayfinder from your airlock so I can interface with it directly in open space."

"Can't we just give it back to you?" Galana asked.

"Are you insane? The danger of having two iterations of the same wayfinder inside my ship's field – it hardly bears thinking about," Praxulon shook his head. "No, that's why the field must be reconfigured to emit outwards. I will make the alterations and return. You just be ready to release the wayfinder."

"But we *won't* be ready to - !" Hartigan shouted, but the Time Destroyer and his ship vanished again. "This fellow is the worst time traveller I could *possibly* imagine," he exclaimed.

"How long do we wait for him to come back this time?" Bonty asked.

Galana and Basil exchanged a look.

"Give him a day?" Hartigan suggested. "Then we can continue on our way, and let him catch up with us."

"Shouldn't make a difference, to a time traveller," Devlin agreed lazily.

"*He's not a time traveller*," Roney and Galana said together.

They waited, running a few scans of empty space and predictably finding nothing, for twenty-four hours. When Praxulon the Mad didn't reappear, they set a course for the next inhabited world according to Roney's charts. It was about five weeks' journey, which was again four and a half weeks too long for the Boze.

"I'll meet you there," she said, "and do a bit more asking around about Time Destroyers while I'm waiting."

"Don't steal anything this time," Hartigan admonished.

Roney snorted. "Steal from the Citadel of Cold Hearts," she said.

"Hardly."

She didn't explain what this rather ominous statement meant, in what Hartigan declared to be typical Captain Pelsworthy fashion. The Boze returned to her gleaming red ship and flicked away into the grey, and the crew of the *Conch* did the same at their own stately pace.

Bonty returned to the medical bay to look after the Time Destroyer wayfinder, and over the next few weeks she declared her much improved. The Bonshoon still had little idea what sort of nutrients she needed, and less about what she actually *did* in Praxulon's ship, but the clues they'd gathered about the energy and light she absorbed allowed Bonty to try some experimental treatments that soon had the big furry creature looking rather chipper. There wasn't much for any of them to do on the long flight through soft-space, so they all spent a lot of time in the medical bay. Basil in particular developed an attachment to the wayfinder. He called her Scrambles, for the funny flailing movements she made with her stubby little legs even though she was quite immobile.

"I say, d'you think she could really survive if we dropped her out the airlock into space?" he asked wistfully.

"She seems to produce her own oxygen internally and doesn't need much to run all her whatever-these-are," Bonty replied, waving a lower hand at the various scans of Scrambles's internal organs. "The breathing she *looks* like she's doing is really just a sort of internal pulse. I can't say she would survive for *long*, but she's not likely to survive for long without Praxulon's help, anyway. Getting her back into his engine is probably her best hope for survival."

"I wonder what she tastes like," Wicked Mary said. Everyone turned to look at the *giela* where it stood in a corner of the medical bay. "I bet she's sugary."

Finally, their stretch in the grey ended and they returned to normal space on the edge of the solar system containing what Roney called the Citadel of Cold Hearts. Neither Roney nor Praxulon the Mad were there, and so the *Conch* steered cautiously towards the solar system's small blue sun. Chillybin reported that there were minds somewhere in the system, but nothing she was familiar with.

Wicked Mary had just picked up faint tech signatures when Praxulon's ship appeared in front of them.

"Here we go," Hartigan said with a grin.

Praxulon the Mad flashed onto their screens. Galana noticed his ship's control room, which she hadn't paid much attention to before, was visibly wreathed in smoke. It appeared as though several of his consoles had burned out.

"You *fools*," he fumed. "Why did you not release the wayfinder as we practiced? You shot my metapendulum! My great-grandparents could have been killed!"

"Sorry about that, old boy," Hartigan said, surprisingly calm. "The problem was, we didn't have the wayfinder. Or any idea what you were trying to do. Because we'd only just met you."

"What?" Praxulon roared.

"Also we still haven't actually practiced," Scrutarius added.

"Maybe we could practice now," Bonty suggested.

"Now? Inside the borders of the Citadel of Cold Hearts? Impossible!" Praxulon snapped. "Besides, if we practice now, we will not practice earlier and that will lead to catastrophic paradox!"

"That doesn't sound great," Scrutarius allowed.

"We already didn't practice earlier though," Bonty pointed out.

"I think we can do it," Galana said. The others stared at her. "We will put the wayfinder in our airlock and release it, as you fly past with your emitters firing. Just the way we will practice earlier," she nodded at Basil. "The first rule of time travel is 'forget everything' after all," she added.

"Very good," Praxulon grumbled. "Once my wayfinder is aligned, I will jump. It is like a series of skips, like a stone across water. This means I will be able to say farewell to you – to those of you with brief lives, and then perhaps – yes – in Axis Mundi as I make my final leap into the nothingness that the Vultures demand of me. Let us get this done. I want to be rid of you and this *depressing* little galaxy," he vanished from the screens, but his ship continued to turn slowly in space before them.

"*Little*?" Scrutarius huffed. "I do believe I'm offended."

"So," Hartigan eyed Galana in amusement. "Starting to believe, are we Fen?"

"No," Galana said, "but the important thing is that *he* believes. Chief Engineer Scrutarius, Doctor Bont, get Scrambles to the airlock. Captain, I believe we should change course so we can drop the wayfinder into the path of Praxulon's light when he starts shining it, assuming he will come in the way he did the last time."

"In a way, it's like we *have* practiced this before," Bonty remarked.

"That's the spirit," Hartigan said, and leaned over his controls.

The ship rolled in towards them, the strange light shining from the vents in its gleaming rainbow-sheened sides. This time it didn't get close enough to affect the crew. As the ship closed in, Scrutarius reported that Scrambles was loaded up and ready to release.

"Cheerio, Scrambles," Hartigan said, and hit the airlock control.

They barely had a second to watch the sleek, elongated shape of the wayfinder as she flashed between the two ships and vanished into the light. A split-second after that, light and ship and wayfinder alike were gone as abruptly as ever.

"Well," Hartigan said, "that was anticlimactic."

"Shall we go and make contact with the Citadel of Cold Hearts?" Scrutarius strolled back onto the bridge.

"Maybe we should wait for Captain Pelsworthy to arrive," Galana suggested, "to act as a guide."

"Unless she's not here because she already arrived, got on their bad side, and ran off again," Hartigan remarked. "That'd be about her speed."

"Contact," the *Conch* said.

They all turned and looked at the main viewscreen. Praxulon's ship had returned.

"Maybe he's come back so we can practice tossing Scrambles at him," Devlin said.

"He's hailing us," Chillybin reported. "Strange. It's a standard simplified greeting signal, no audio or image."

"I am attempting to establish a connection," the *Conch* said. "He normally initiates contact, so it is complicated … ah, here we are. He is attempting to use an archaic form of Fleet language and a *very* odd comm spectrum, but he's adapting quickly. I've provided him with an AstroCorps translation pattern and the Grand Bo package."

"Greetings," Praxulon the Mad appeared on their screens. "I am not a local – in fact I come from almost as far away as you do, by a rather extraordinary road if I do say so myself. My name is Praxulon the Mad – "

"*We know*," Hartigan said in exasperation.

"Ah," Praxulon faltered. "We may have met before."

"Yes we have. And before you bally well vanish again, maybe we can practice releasing your wayfinder in order for you to sync her back up with the copy you've got," Hartigan asked.

"*What?* You dare to steal my wayfinder?" Praxulon boomed.

"*We* didn't steal her," Hartigan said, and jerked his thumb over his shoulder. "The Spangles took her, because you wouldn't stop annoying them."

"Praxulon the Mad," Galana said, "allow me to greet you on behalf of AstroCorps and the Six Species. This is Captain Basil Hartigan, I am Commander Galana Fen. Our Medical Officer Benjamin Bont, Tactical Officer Wicked Mary, Chief Engineer Devlin Scrutarius, and Communications Officer Chillybin."

"Is that an *Ogre?*" Praxulon said in shock. "You have an *Ogre* as your Communications Officer?"

"And don't concern yourself with the wayfinder issue," Galana went on smoothly. "We have practiced, as you know."

"We … have?" Praxulon floundered.

"You instructed us to forget everything," Galana told him.

"Hmph," Praxulon the Mad was clearly at a loss behind his helmet. "Well, that certainly *sounds* like me … "

"Don't worry, old boy," Hartigan said. "With our help, you'll make it to your meeting with the Vultures and save us all from annihiliation."

Praxulon sat for a moment in silence.

"Fools," he announced, and then he and his ship vanished once again.

"Good luck," Bonty called.

"You're welcome," Devlin added.

"I say, were all the Time Destroyers like that?" Hartigan asked Chillybin.

"More or less," Chillybin replied.

"Must have been rather a relief when they got wiped out, what?" the Captain said whimsically. "D'you think he really was a time traveller, or just crazy?"

"Yes," Scrutarius said promptly.

"I suppose we will have to look for a place called Axis Mundi in two thousand, eight hundred and forty-two years," Galana said, "and find out."

"I'll mark it in my calendar," Devlin promised.

"Right," Hartigan shook his head as though to clear it, and pointed towards the little blue sun in the centre of the viewscreen. "Let's go and say hello to the Citadel of Cold Hearts, what do you say?"

"You're at the helm, Captain," Galana reminded him.

"So I am," Basil said placidly, and laid in a course.

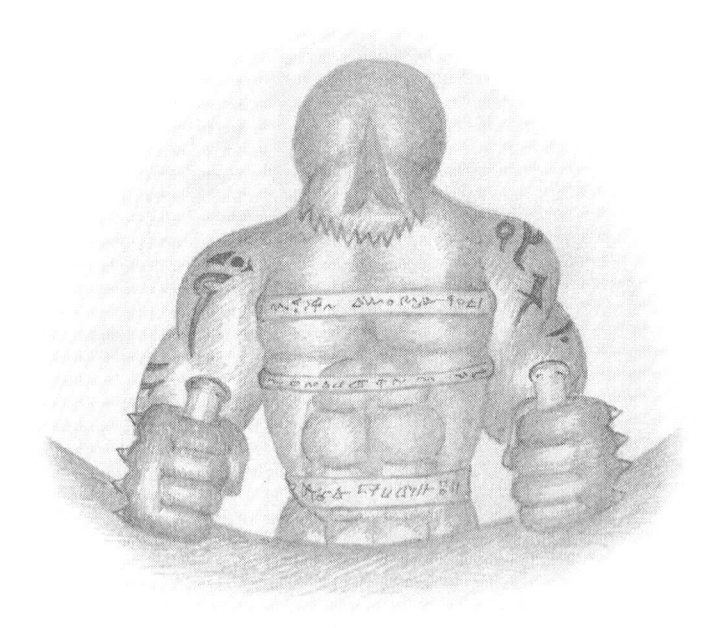

Soon, in **The Sirens of Gozonaar**:

When Captain Judderone Pelsworthy of the Boze, Space Adventurer, failed to join them in the so-called Citadel of Cold Hearts, the crew hung around for a few days and then resumed their course around the galaxy.

The Citadel had been fascinating, and far friendlier than any of them had been expecting. Scrutarius suggested that any starship crew used to dealing with the rigidity of the Molran Fleet had nothing to fear from the strict rules and subtle humour of the Cold Hearted, and Galana had a hard time disagreeing with him. The Citadel was actually an ancient derelict space station that had been settled and then added to over the years by the new locals. The Cold Hearted were a strange and quiet folk, built rather like Molranoids but with three pairs of arms instead of two, which made them even taller, and with skin of a mottled orange and red. They were secretive about their society and history, but only too willing to exchange certain harmless information and host visiting aliens for a time.

It was difficult to see why they had such a reputation for ruthlessness, but Galana supposed it was easy to miss something like that if you didn't provoke them.

"I liked them," Captain Hartigan declared as they prepared to go to relative speed once more. "Still not entirely sure why they still built all their houses and furniture and everything to the scale of the *original* inhabitants of the Citadel when the original inhabitants were only about my size, but it was nice not to have to sit on a chair that made my feet swing for once so I'm not complaining, what?"

"Say what you like about Roney's charts," Scrutarius agreed, "but they haven't led us anywhere boring yet."

"We are receiving final departure permissions and warnings from the Citadel," Chillybin announced.

"Warnings?" Galana asked.

"Apparently the region we intend to fly through is dangerous," Chillybin read the official Citadel communication.

"Wouldn't happen to be High Elonath, would it?" Hartigan asked hopefully.

"No, the Cold Hearted had never heard of High Elonath," Chillybin reminded him.

"Not that they were telling *us*, anyway," Scrutarius added.

"This region is called Gozonaar," Chillybin pronounced heavily, "and it lies between the Citadel and … 'Trading Partner 3', which is apparently how the Cold Hearted label their allies."

"Golly," Hartigan said. "What did they call *us*?"

Chillybin consulted her notes. "'Alien Union of Moderate Interest 71'," she replied.

"I'll take it," Hartigan decided after scowling for a few moments. "What's so dangerous about Gozonaar, then?"

"According to this," Chillybin said, "enough ships went missing between the Citadel and Trading Partner 3 that they now consider it worth detouring around. But there is no real detail. The Cold Hearted simply expect us to have the good sense to heed the warning, and they don't really care if we ignore them."

"How long will a detour take?" Hartigan asked. "Bloody Mary?"

"We can cross Gozonaar in two months," Wicked Mary replied. "Going around would take almost five."

Hartigan let out a long, sad whistle. "Fen?"

"I would recommend we take the longer route, but I *suspect* good sense is about to leave the bridge," Galana said. "Provided we remain in soft-space for the duration, I don't think there is much risk. If I've understood the Citadel regulations properly, there would be a special code that meant there was technology at work capable of collapsing relative fields and bringing ships out of soft-space, yes?"

"Yes, Commander," Chilly replied.

"Since there is nothing like that … as long as we don't stop, we should be safe," Galana concluded.

"Jolly good," Hartigan slapped the arm of his chair. "Next stop, Trading Partner 3!"

THE SIRENS OF GOZONAAR

The *Conch* dropped out of soft-space and decelerated on the edge of a fairly normal-looking solar system under computer control. With shaking hands, Galana reached out and lowered herself into the Captain's helm control chair.

"Computer?" she said, her voice sounding strange and raspy in her ears.

"Online," the *Conch*'s voice said, but it sounded strange. Wrong, somehow.

"What is your status?" she asked.

"Emergency backup interface," the computer replied.

As she'd suspected – the computer was not really online, but was just keeping the ship flying in a straight line and the main systems operational. The clever and often downright strange intelligence that usually ran the *Conch* was shut down.

Galana looked around the empty bridge. She frowned, opening and closing her ears in slow confusion. "What is our location?" she asked.

"Three hours from destination designated Trading Partner 3 at maximum subluminal cruising speed," the *Conch* replied.

"We're on course?"

"Please clarify query," the computer requested mechanically.

She sat for a moment, moving her jaws and ears slowly. She had a strange taste in her mouth and an odd feeling in her eyes. "I think I have sleeper chemicals in my system," she said.

"Please clarify query," the computer repeated.

"Never mind," Galana said. The backup computer's responses and abilities were limited. Without Scrutarius it would be difficult to get anything useful out of it. But first she had to get to the medical bay and find out why she'd been knocked out. And for how long. And why she'd woken up on the floor outside the bridge. "Where is Doctor Bont?"

"Unknown."

"Hm," she said.

"Please clarify query," the computer responded.

She shook her head. "Can you scan for life-signs on board?"

"Four hundred and twenty-seven," the computer said promptly. "Captain Hartigan; Commander Scrutarius; unknown aki'Drednanth; unknown Molran; unknown Bonshoon; unknown Fergunakil; four hundred and twenty-one unidentified dumblers."

Galana lurched to her feet. "What?"

"Four hundred and twenty-seven," the computer repeated with infinite patience. "Captain Basil Hartigan; Commander - "

"Yes, yes, never mind," she said. The backup computer only recognised Basil and Devlin, which meant it had not been updated since before the mission when they'd been the only crew. That made sense, since the main computer wasn't *supposed* to be shut down, but it was a security hazard. What if it had identified her as an intruder? What if they'd had computer issues before this and Basil and Devlin had not been here?

Well, for now the computer didn't seem to have a problem with her. This was good news, but slightly alarming considering the four hundred and twenty-one *other* life-forms on the ship. Of course, the computer could be counting Bonty's biological samples or Wicked Mary's food for all Galana knew.

She stretched, attempted to shake off the last traces of wooziness, and headed back towards the bridge doors. She didn't remember being put into a sleeper state. Or the *decision* to do so. Indeed, if she *had* decided to, the corridor outside the bridge seemed like a weird place to do it. Now she was thinking about it, she didn't actually remember anything after their first few days at relative speed through Gozonaar. She knew, from her studies, that memory loss was a symptom of taking sleeper chemicals. Her memories should begin to recover as she woke up.

Her first stop, despite her medical needs, was the Icebox. The refrigerated deck was sealed off at a couple of large access doors at either end and given over almost entirely to Chillybin's living and recreational needs. The door she approached was encrusted with a buildup of ice and looked like it hadn't been opened in months. Frowning, she braced her left hands on the doorframe and hauled on the door with her rights. It ground open in a tinkling cascade of ice chunks, and she stepped into the gloomy cold without bothering to pull on a thermal suit.

The converted cargo hold was silent, and bitingly cold. Galana had only taken a few steps before the vast shaggy shape of Chillybin crashed up out of a mound of snow with a roar.

"Chilly!" Galana shouted, flinging her hands up.

The enormous aki'Drednanth hesitated, growling deep in her chest, and then ambled across to a lumpy white shape that revealed itself to be her envirosuit, completely encrusted with ice. She rummaged inside, grunting and rumbling, and shook off the shape of her talker-glove. With it, she could make movements with her hand and claws, and they would be converted into words. She pulled the glove on, moved her hand hesitantly, then reached in and thumped something inside the suit.

"*Gnuurf,*" she grumbled.

"Is the power cell dead?" Galana asked. Chillybin nodded her great tusked head. "How long have you been in here?" the aki'Drednanth shrugged. Ice pattered and tinkled from the hair of her shoulders. "I'll get another power cell," she promised, and swayed a little. "But first I need to get to the medical bay."

"*Gronf,*" Chilly said, somehow managing to sound concerned.

"I'm alright. I've been in a sleeper state," she explained. "I don't know why, or for how long. The computer is on standby. The rest of the crew is on board, and there may be … other life-forms on board with us, although I did not see anything on my way here."

"*Groonk,*" Chilly insisted, and pointed at the floor.

"The Aquarium?" Galana said. Chilly nodded. "Should I check on her before going to the medical - "

"*Gronf,*" Chillybin said emphatically.

"Alright," Galana said, "I'm going."

She left the Icebox and descended into the small room for'ard of the Aquarium, the only part of the deck not filled with water for Wicked Mary to swim in. The room was stale and cold, with a strange dank feeling as though the aquatic chamber was leaking even though it all seemed intact at a glance. The big reinforced viewing panel was clouded with algae, and the water was impenetrably dark.

"Hello, Commander," the voice of the great shark came from the communication system behind her. Galana had been expecting it, but it still almost made her jump. "You are awake."

"Yes," she said. "The computer is shut down. Can you tell me what is happening?"

"We have finally escaped from Gozonaar, Commander," Wicked Mary said. Galana, peering into the green-tinged blackness of the Aquarium, saw a huge grey shape glide past. It was practically invisible, but for a small row of reddish lights on one of the shark's cybernetic implants. If it hadn't been for that flash of red, she would have thought she'd imagined the shape. "And I did not eat a single one of you."

"So it would seem," Galana said. "I appreciate that."

"I hope you do," Wicked Mary said. "It has been a long and very boring time for me."

"I suggest we stop here and hold position until we can bring the computer and the rest of the crew back to full capacity," Galana said. "Would you happen to know their locations?"

"I would imagine Doctor Bont is in the medical bay and Chief Scrutarius in in his quarters," Wicked Mary said.

"That would have been my guess," Galana agreed, and looked around. "Where is your *giela*?"

"I am sure I don't know, as I was cut off from it," Wicked Mary replied. "A little hurtful, but ... "

"I apologise on behalf of the AstroCorps command group," Galana said. "I can only assure you that these must have been exceptional circumstances."

"Oh yes indeed."

"I am going to go to the medical bay," she said. "If you can bring us to all stop - "

"Already done, Commander."

"Very good. I will return full computer control to the *Conch* as soon as possible and reconnect your *giela* when I find it. Good work, Wicked Mary."

Galana frowned as she headed for the medical bay. The Captain would not have been able to go into a sleeper state. The chemicals were dangerous to humans. The same went for Chillybin and Wicked Mary – and by the looks of it, both of them had been living in their respective habitats alone for some time. What had happened on board ship since they had entered Gozonaar?

"Computer?" she said as she passed a maintenance panel and stopped to let a dizzy spell pass. "What is the timestamp?"

The computer reeled off a string of numbers, ending with "1010," which – as Galana had suspected – was almost a year before they had even begun their journey. The last time the backup computer had been activated, in fact, on the ship's commissioning.

"Synchronise charts and recent logs," she said. "Update timestamp to current date."

"Please clarify query," the computer said.

Galana sighed. The computer wouldn't answer certain questions or perform system changes if it didn't know she was a part of the crew. The only way she was going to get answers was by getting the main computer back online.

She made her way to the medical bay, and was relieved to find Bonty lying slumped awkwardly across one of the recovery beds. After some rummaging she managed to locate the equipment and medication needed for a safe wake-up. She started Bonty on the path to consciousness, and dosed herself with stimulants and nutrients while she was at it.

By the time Galana had picked up and tested a fresh power cell for Chillybin's suit from the ship's spare parts storage, Bonty was awake. The

Bonshoon was still a bit blank-faced and vague, operating on autopilot, and of course she didn't remember any more than Galana did from just before their decision to go into sleep-states.

If it had *been* their decision.

"I hate sleepers," Bonty grumbled as she pushed herself to her feet and settled her considerable bulk into upright position with a grimace. "Even whatever lightweight version of sleeping this was. At least we weren't locked up in pods."

"We don't have pods on board," Galana said distractedly. She ran a final ramp-up diagnostic on the power cell and found that it was okay, although it had apparently not been stored very well. Its charge was a little depleted, and regulation AstroCorps annual maintenance should have prevented that. "I need to get this down to Chillybin and get her suit back online."

"What happened to it?"

"I don't know yet," Galana replied. "It looked like Chilly had put it in a corner and just not used it – for months. She's been in the Icebox, I assume, while we were asleep. Wicked Mary is in the Aquarium, of course, and seems to have been the one who piloted us out of Gozonaar. I don't know anything else," she was beginning to remember things by this stage, but nothing useful. "I remember we stopped," she said, still frowning vaguely down at the power cell in her hand. "We came out of soft-space inside the borders of Gozonaar."

"But why?" Bonty frowned. "Why would we do that? The Citadel told us it was dangerous. We had no intention of stopping and there was meant to be nothing in there that *could* stop us."

"There was … a ship?" Galana shook her head. "Some information the Captain had picked up before we left the Citadel, and hadn't told us about. He slipped it into the navigation calculations and stopped us so we could check it out. I don't remember anything more than that, except it must have only been a day or two before we went to sleep."

"It must have been something big, to get *me* to take sleepers," Bonty declared. "Where *is* the Captain? And Devlin, for that matter?" she raised her voice. "Computer?"

"Save your breath," Galana advised. "The computer is offline, the backup doesn't recognise us. Devlin is most likely in his quarters. He wasn't on the bridge or in engineering, and he's not responding to the comm so I would assume he is also asleep."

"I'll go and find him," Bonty groaned again. "I feel like I've been lying down for *months*," she said, and gave Galana a worried look. "Maybe longer. It's possible you know, with sleeper drugs."

"I woke up on the floor," Galana said. "Considerably less comfortable than a recovery bed. If we slept all the way through Gozonaar, it would have been a matter of some weeks."

"I feel strange, though," Bonty insisted. "Sluggish. Weeks in a sleep state wouldn't do it."

"Run whatever tests you can with the backup computer," Galana advised. "I can go and check on Devlin while you - "

Bonty shook her head. "I should go," she said. "They're his private quarters, it wouldn't be *proper* for you to go in. I'm his doctor. And besides," she added with a smile, "Bonshooni are practically Blaren."

"Alright," Galana said. She looked around. "What about the other organic samples in the medical bay? The computer picked up other life-forms on board, I assumed it was something in here. Maybe something left open when you went to sleep, something that grew or multiplied … ?"

Bonty was shaking her head. "No, there shouldn't have been anything like that … let's see. Maybe the computer is just confused. We'll need Devlin to get it back up and running."

"Then go and find him," Galana advised. "I will get Chillybin back into her suit."

It took a while to get the envirosuit working again. In the end, Galana and Chillybin dragged the bulky plates of armour and machinery out into the corridor and let it thaw before replacing the power cell. Chillybin pulled on the transcriber glove and stepped back into the suit as it powered back up and its interior cooled.

"Galana," the aki'Drednanth said. "It is good to see you again. Are we safely out of the creatures' range?"

"The creatures," Galana replied. "What creatures? I am still recovering from an extended period in a medical sleeper state - "

"The Sirens," Chillybin said. "Did Wicked Mary not tell you?"

Galana attempted to focus on the last few jumbled days, or possibly hours, she could recall from before waking up outside the bridge. "I remember stopping at a ship, a wreck," she said.

"The *Cthagnon*, yes," Chillybin agreed. "It was a long time ago, and a broken memory for me as well."

"How long … what's *happened* on this ship?" Galana whispered.

"I do not know how long. We were attacked, and I came in here to protect myself with little hope of rescue, but I do not recall exactly," Chillybin admitted. "I have been sleeping as well, in a sense. I withdrew into the Dreamscape and let my body slow. It saved me from having to run around this chamber and kept me from running out of rations, but it has also confused my memories."

"Running out of *rations*? The ship is more than capable of producing enough food and ice for you to live on for *centuries* if needed."

Chillybin gave an audible grunt of laughter. "Well, fortunately I did not need centuries. And the aki'Drednanth version of the sleeper state does not actually suspend our lives and prevent us from aging the way yours does.

But we should continue this conversation with the others."

"Bonty?" Galana said into the comm.

"I found Devlin," Bonty's voice reported. "Waking him up now. He's very confused."

"We all are," Galana replied. "What about the Captain?"

"The Captain is not on board," Chillybin told her quietly.

"She's right," Bonty confirmed.

"The computer thinks he is," Galana remarked.

"Yes. We sort of found the reason for that too," Bonty said, sounding half worried and half amused. "Maybe it would be easiest to show you."

Galana and Chillybin descended to the Aquarium, where Wicked Mary once again greeted them in her usual unsettlingly friendly manner.

"It is good to see you, Chillybin," she said. "I was getting so worried."

"Do you think you could prepare a report of recent events," Galana asked, "from your point of view? We are still trying to piece together what has happened."

"Recent events, Commander?" Wicked Mary asked. "How recent?"

"The Sirens," Galana said, although she still didn't remember anything about any 'Sirens' herself, "and our encounter with the alien wreck, the *Cthagnon* ... all of it."

"Ah, all of it," Wicked Mary said. "Recent. Yes. I am afraid I cannot - "

Bonty and Scrutarius joined them, Wicked Mary's *giela* strutting along between the Bonshoon and the dazed-looking Blaran.

"Devlin," Galana said in relief. "Are you alright?"

"Doc says I'll be fine," Devlin said. "Feels like I've been drinking crabgilly sap cocktails for a week straight and I can't remember anything, but - "

"And what are you doing with my *giela*, little meats?" Wicked Mary purred.

"Tally ho, tish and pish and by jingo," the little silver robot announced.

"It looks like someone programmed the *giela* with all of Basil's codes and permissions, and a basic personality layer," Scrutarius explained while the *giela* strick a hilariously bold pose and fondled a nonexistent moustache. "As far as the backup computer's concerned, this is Captain Hartigan."

"It's *very* good," Wicked Mary conceded. "Although I am outraged at how my property is being used."

"When the computer scanned for life-signs, it found four hundred and twenty-seven," Galana objected. "*Including* the Captain."

"There's no need for it to have found an actual human being's bio-signs as long as all the codes check out," Scrutarius shrugged. "They count as a human life-sign by default. The backup computer isn't that clever."

"Excellent notion, young Devlin," the *giela* said.

Scrutarius squinted at the little robot. "I'm still trying to figure out whether whoever did this is making fun of us or Basil," he said, and glanced at the dark glass of the Aquarium.

"I assure you," Wicked Mary said, "after so many years of hard work and sacrifice getting you to safety, I had no idea - "

"Wait, *years?*" Scrutarius yelped.

"Groping in the dark, eating basic supplements ... " Wicked Mary continued woefully.

"You're eating ship rations?" Galana asked. She'd been assuming, after the medical bay turned up nothing, that the extra life-signs must have been coming from the live food in the Aquarium. "What about your fish?"

"Too power intensive," Wicked Mary said. "And too complicated, with the computer offline."

"Why *is* the computer offline?" Bonty asked. "I don't remember yet."

"We encountered an alien wreck, the *Cthagnon*," Galana told her. She turned to Devlin. "You and the Captain went aboard and repaired it."

"I don't remember either," Scrutarius complained.

"You will," Bonty reassured him, then looked worried. "And so will I, I hope."

"*I* hope Wicked Mary's report will help us to remember," Galana said. It was risky to put too much faith in a Fergunakil's account of events, she knew, but this would be a temporary measure. And Wicked Mary had gotten them this far. Apparently. "Is it ready yet, Tactical Officer?"

"Yes, Commander," Wicked Mary said mildly.

The report appeared on their communicators as it was logged on the backup computer's system. At least they hadn't had their comms permissions revoked, Galana reflected, then turned her attention to the report. For a few moments, everyone read in silence.

Three days into their relative speed flight through Gozonaar, the *Conch* had dropped out of soft-space. This had been arranged between Hartigan and the ship's computer based on some information he'd picked up in the Citadel, their previous stopover. Something to do with their quest for the mythical Last Alicorn. Wicked Mary had not been involved in the decision and had no more information. The stop had been deemed safe because they were only just inside the boundary of Gozonaar. Galana had objected to this illogical statement, but her objection had been ignored as they often were.

They had found a derelict alien vessel that the computer identified as the *Cthagnon*, and had spent another few days repairing it and studying its logs and technology. There had not been anything about the Last Alicorn in the ship's databanks.

What there had been, apparently, was a warning far more dire than the one the Citadel of Cold Hearts had given them.

Gozonaar was home to a hostile alien life-form or life-forms, the specific nature of which was a bit unclear but the *Conch* labelled 'Sirens'. According to human legend, Sirens were monsters of the ocean that lured ancient adventurers to their doom with a beautiful song, wrecking their ships on rocks and then devouring the hapless explorers, who Galana couldn't help but notice were usually male and *invariably* silly.

Wicked Mary had once again been left out of the subsequent discussion and decision-making. Her report became just a little hurt and accusatory at this point. But the result was that the *Cthagnon*, docked to the *Conch*, had activated its relative drive and dragged them right into the Sirens' clutches.

The information Hartigan had 'found' at the Citadel, combined with the strangely lazy warning the Cold Hearted had given them, had amounted to little more than a trap. Occasionally, using the tantalisingly-damaged *Cthagnon* as bait, the Citadel would send alien visitors into Gozonaar as food for the Sirens. Whether they did so because they didn't want the Sirens to come looking for food *outside* Gozonaar, or for some other cultural reason, had apparently only been interesting to Galana and Bonty. Discussion had turned to how they might escape.

This discussion had yet again excluded poor innocent Wicked Mary, but the findings were on record. Chillybin had been unable to locate any kind of mind, and Devlin had been unable to disrupt the relative field of the *Cthagnon*. And at about this point, everybody seemed to have stopped caring anyway.

Something – the Sirens' song, perhaps – had played over the ship's comm system. Wicked Mary, who was cut off from communications and whose ears worked differently to the landbound's, was not affected. The others, however, were stricken and spellbound. Chillybin had managed to hold out for a short time, but had managed to do nothing but shed her suit and retreat inside her own mind, entering a kind of hibernation.

A long period had passed then. Wicked Mary's report was not specific, but it seemed as though the Sirens of Gozonaar did not wreck and devour their victims in quite the same way as the Sirens of Earth legend. They held them in some kind of hypnotic state, feeding upon their minds. It had probably been this similarity to aki'Drednanth mental powers that had allowed Chillybin to evade them.

Chillybin's solution had ultimately given Wicked Mary her idea. That, and the human legend.

"What does the human legend say?" Bonty asked, since it wasn't in the report. "I can't say I've ever heard this one."

"In the human story, the delicious explorers on the surface of the ocean plugged their ears so they could not hear the song," Wicked Mary explained.

"That's a remarkably simple solution," Scrutarius noted.

"Humans are a remarkably simple species," Galana pointed out.

"True, but the common sense of it is surprising."

"There was a complication," Wicked Mary said. "The Captain of the vessel wanted to hear the music, so he had his crew tie him to the ship's central pylon and ignore any orders he gave as they made their way to safety."

"*There's* the humans I know," Devlin said with satisfaction.

Of course, blocking the crew's ears was not a practical solution in this case. The Sirens had bewitched them, but left them capable of defending themselves. In the end, Wicked Mary was forced to enact one of the many takeover plans she had formulated over the course of their journey, using her *giela* to drug the Molran, Bonshoon and Blaran so she could finally steer the *Conch* back out of Gozonaar to safety.

"You're welcome," the great shark concluded.

"What, you mean *this giela*?" Devlin asked, and pointed at the robot by his side.

"Bally crikey widgets," the *giela* said helpfully.

"The Captain eluded me," Wicked Mary said. "I was so worried about getting the tough, wiry Molranoid air-breathers under control, I underestimated the resourcefulness of the tender, juicy human."

"What happened?" Galana asked.

"He severed the *giela* from my control," Wicked Mary replied. "Clearly, after this, he set it to mimic the Captain's codes so the backup computer was fooled. This is the first I have seen of it, though, so I am only guessing. When I turned and set us back into soft-space to safety, the computer insisted that all six crewmembers were on board. As were Devlin's … friends," she added. "I am not sure what happened with them but they seem to have been protected from the Sirens. They were certainly no help."

"What *friends*?" Galana demanded.

"That doesn't matter," Scrutarius said.

"I think it does," Galana disagreed. "There are four hundred and twenty-one of them."

"It seems pretty obvious that Basil reprogrammed the *giela* and got away on the *Cthagnon*," the Blaran said, ignoring Galana's glare. "He's still in there."

"He tied himself to the central pylon and … the analogy doesn't really hold up," Bonty said.

"Except the part where both Captains are damn fools," Galana said. "We should get the computer working again."

Scrutarius shook his head. "We can't," he said. "Without the Captain, the *Conch* will go batty and fly us straight back in there after him."

"And the computer needed to be shut off because it was bewitched by the Sirens' song," Wicked Mary added. "That was why it was so very difficult to get away."

"Wait, the *computer* was affected?" Galana said in surprise.

"The ancient human myth was hazy on the effect the Sirens had on complex starship interactive systems," Wicked Mary explained.

"We need to find some other way to get him back," Scrutarius said. Then he frowned.

"Some other way like what?" Bonty asked.

"Hold on," Devlin said, still scowling. "Did you say four hundred and twenty-one? Wait here. I need to … check something in my quarters."

"Your *friends*?" Galana asked.

"Yes," Scrutarius replied shortly, "my friends," he turned and hurried from the room.

"Bonty, do you know what Scrutarius is up to?" Galana asked.

"Usually not," Bonty said evasively. "I'm sure it's nothing to worry about. You know, it's a Blaran thing. The backup computer isn't that bright, it's probably confused by something in his quarters, you know, something naughty, you're probably better off not knowing so you can deny knowledge of it later - "

"Bonty?"

"Yes Fen?"

"You're babbling."

"I am a bit, aren't I?" Bonjamin managed a smile. "I think I've figured out how we can avoid the Sirens, though."

"Oh?"

"Assuming their bewitching song really is just some kind of audio signal they were relaying through the *Cthagnon* and the *Conch*," she said, "which got into our heads and into the computer … but didn't affect Bloody Mary because sound acts differently in water - "

"Are you about to suggest we plug up our ears?" Galana asked.

"Well, medically sever our auditory systems, actually," Bonty said, "but yes. It's a simple procedure, easily repaired. We might have some difficulty keeping our balance for a little while, but it should be fine."

"I suppose if the worst happens, Wicked Mary can drug us and pull us out again," Galana said doubtfully.

"I would not bet on my ability to repeat this performance," Wicked Mary said. "I am not the hope-filled and foolish child I once was."

"She's right," they turned to see Scrutarius descending back into the Aquarium deck. The cheerful Blaran looked unusually grim. "On another hand, though," he went on, "there's probably no hurry."

"Devlin?" Galana asked, her sarcastic comments about his 'naughty friends' forgotten. "What is it?"

"It's 1048," Scrutarius said bleakly. "We were inside Gozonaar for twenty years."

***Soon,* in <u>The Star that Sang (Reprise)</u>:**
While it seemed unlikely Captain Hartigan could have survived for twenty years alone on a barely-repaired derelict with his mind being fed upon by dreadful alien monsters, they all agreed they had little to lose in attempting to rescue him.

"We have already lost twenty years," Chillybin pointed out, "and if we return without all six crewmembers we lose the bet."

"I don't know if we'll even be able to get home if he's dead," Scrutarius said with unaccustomed gravity. "I don't know what the computer's going to do. It's a sentimental thing."

"He is our Captain and it is our duty as AstroCorps officers to attempt to rescue him – or recover his remains," Galana agreed.

"And nobody gets to eat the delicious human but me," Wicked Mary declared.

"*Also*, we all *like* Basil and want to save him," Bonty added pointedly.

There was a certain amount of embarrassed flicking of ears and shuffling of feet at this point.

"Wasn't that what I just said?" Wicked Mary asked.

"I don't understand how it could have been twenty years but we don't remember any of it," Bonty changed the subject. The Molranoids had regained their memories by this stage, but they all got fuzzy at about the point the *Cthagnon* had hijacked the *Conch* and flown them into Gozonaar. "We couldn't have slept that long without pods. Our bodies would have fallen apart."

"You were not asleep," Wicked Mary said. "For most of it, as far as I could tell through my *giela*, you were wandering around in a daze and listening to the Sirens' song in rapturous delight. And very foolishly but very resourcefully stopping me from trying to fly the ship to safety," she added delicately. "But I beat you in the end."

"And we're very grateful you did," Bonty repeated for what must have been the fiftieth time since they'd recovered.

"I didn't even eat any of you."

"We're very grateful for that too," Devlin replied with a hint of his usual good humour.

"If I'd had my *giela* I might have, though," the great shark admitted.

"Are we going to do this?" Chillybin asked. "And would you prefer me to return to my Dreamscape, or take the deafening procedure?"

"I would feel uncomfortable damaging your auditory system," Bonty admitted.

"Oh, but you're okay doing it to us," Devlin said.

"You're not aki'Drednanth," Bonty replied. "I am still confident I could reverse the procedure for Chilly, but I am *certain* I can do so for us three."

"Perhaps it would be best for you to sleep this out again," Galana suggested. "It will hopefully not be as long this time. Did you … since we are not in soft-space anymore, could you get any information from the other aki'Drednanth?" she asked, without much hope.

"Nothing useful," Chillybin admitted. "This is a part of the galaxy the aki'Drednanth have not ventured into before."

"That's encouraging," Bonty murmured.

"I'll turn the *giela* over to Wicked Mary so she can resume control if she has to," Scrutarius said. "There'll be no Basil Hartigan to take it off her and hide it if things go wrong this time," he reminded them.

"We'll just have to make sure nothing goes wrong, then," Bonty said happily.

Half an hour later, the doctor had completed the severing of their auditory systems and they had figured out a reasonable way of communicating by typing on their comm pads.

ALRIGHT, Galana wrote. LET'S GO AND GET OUR CAPTAIN BACK.

Scrutarius, Bonty and Wicked Mary's *giela* saluted smartly.

ENTERING COORDINATES, the Fergunakil sent to them. The grey of soft-space settled over the bridge viewscreens. ESTIMATED TIME OF ARRIVAL, THREE AND A HALF WEEKS.

They stood in silence – very, very profound silence – for some seconds.

I PROBABLY DIDN'T NEED TO DEAFEN US ALL SO EARLY, Bonty wrote, DID I?

THE STAR THAT SANG (REPRISE)

In the end Galana, Bonjamin and Devlin decided to leave themselves surgically deaf for the three-and-a-half-week journey back into Gozonaar. It was safer, they agreed, since they had dropped into danger unexpectedly on their previous visit and been caught unawares by the *Cthagnon* and the Sirens' song. There shouldn't be any surprise drop-outs this time, since the Captain's decision was what had landed them in trouble originally … but still, it was better to be safe. And it gave them the chance to get used to operating in text.

For Molranoids, known for their highly sensitive ears, it was a particular challenge. Galana had never realised how dependent she was on hearing. And for a few days immediately following the operation, she and the others were a little clumsy and prone to losing their balance thanks to the disruption to their internal gyroscopes. Bonty said it had brought back a foggy memory of her early life, although *when* exactly remained unclear. She'd had an illness called 'sliding ear' which had left her similarly unsteady on her feet.

By far the most unsettling thing, however, was the gleaming mechanical *giela* of Wicked Mary.

In the newly silent corridors of the *Conch*, the machine would regularly sneak up on Molran, Bonshoon and Blaran. They would look up from their written conversations to find it standing in the bridge doorway behind them, watching them with its bright little collection of sensors. It turned walking anywhere in the ship alone into a deeply creepy experience.

Wicked Mary insisted she wasn't sneaking up on them.

I AM ACTUALLY CLATTERING AROUND QUITE LOUDLY, she wrote on their comm pads, MAKING NO ATTEMPT TO HIDE MY PRESENCE.

WHY WOULD YOU DO THAT? Bonty wrote. YOU KNOW WE CAN'T HEAR.

WELL I AM STILL BEING POLITE, Wicked Mary replied. AND YOU DON'T NEED TO WRITE YOUR ANSWERS TO ME, I CAN STILL HEAR YOU.

It was difficult to know how effective the deafness would be against the Sirens. The *Conch* had recorded the song – some twenty years of it, in fact – but those records were difficult for Scrutarius to pry out of the backup computer, and had seemingly been corrupted in the storage process anyway. They couldn't hear the resultant sounds and weren't enraptured by them, but there was a good chance they bore little resemblance to the mind-altering song that had left them stranded in Gozonaar in the first place.

WHAT I DON'T UNDERSTAND, Galana wrote, IS WHY NOBODY HAS TRIED TO JUST BLOCK THEIR EARS BEFORE. OR WHY MORE SPECIES LIKE THE FERGUNAK HAVEN'T PASSED THROUGH GOZONAAR UNHARMED.

PERHAPS A LOT HAVE, Bonty suggested. BUT THEY CONTINUED ON THEIR WAY WITHOUT LEAVING A NOTE.

AND EVEN IF THEY DID, THE COLD HEARTED WOULDN'T HAVE TOLD US, Devlin added. SEEMS LIKE THEY WANT PEOPLE GETTING CAUGHT IN HERE.

Galana spent several days poring over the full report offered by Wicked Mary. It was unhelpful, mostly because the only reason their Tactical Officer hadn't been bewitched by the Sirens was because she had been so completely cut off from the rest of the ship. Her *giela*, before Hartigan had taken over it, had not picked up the Sirens' song and her access to the ship's backup computer had not included incoming comms signals by default since the computer had not known who she was. It was probably lucky the backup computer *was* stupid, Galana reflected. If it had been more fully aware of what 'one Fergunakil life-sign' meant, it probably never would have cooperated as much as it had.

The rest of Wicked Mary's report was a long and painstaking log of her extended battle to gain control over ships systems one subroutine at a time, outsmart and sedate the bewitched crew, and fly them all to safety. A battle that had taken place over the course of almost twenty years – and even that was a misleading number. Wicked Mary may have been struggling to save them in the *physical* world for twenty years, but in the high-speed realm of her electronic presence, it must have seemed like centuries. Millennia.

There was little more for them to do for the weeks they spent in soft-space, but they were all quite experienced in passing long, boring stretches in the grey anyway, so in the end it wasn't that different from a normal dive. The fact that they were backtracking along their course, going back into Gozonaar – *on top* of already losing twenty years – was demoralising, but there was nothing to be done. Galana resolved never to mention that she'd suggested they go around Gozonaar instead of through, a detour that would have cost them five months instead of two hundred and forty.

Finally, they arrived at the coordinates from which Wicked Mary had fled a couple of months previously, and dropped out into real space.

For a few moments they stood on the bridge, looking out at the strange sight.

Well, Scrutarius broke the figurative silence by writing, Didn't You Say Basil Had Escaped In The *Cthagnon*? Let's Grab Him And Get Out Of Here.

Galana sighed as she looked out across the volume of space. They'd dropped into what looked like a normal solar system, although in this case there didn't seem to be many planets – just a lot of rocks loosely accreted into a ring around the star. A great many of the smaller rocks, however, were identical. And unpleasantly familiar-looking.

She consulted the computer's scans, which Devlin had coaxed into working. In this arc of the system alone, there were upwards of a million alien ships, all of which looked exactly like the *Cthagnon*. There were also, Galana noted, a lot of metals and fragments scattered through the system that could only be the remains of other, non-*Cthagnon* vessels. Alien ships from elsewhere in the galaxy, perhaps, brought here the way the *Conch* had been and then taken apart for their materials.

Whatever Is Happening Here, It Looks Like The Citadel Of Cold Hearts Is Only A Small Part Of It. Bonty summarised, and looked around uneasily.

Galana nodded. Any Hint Of The Captain's Life-Signs? she wrote. Devlin shook his head.

Perhaps We Should Wake Chilly. Bonty suggested. I Could Operate On Her And Then She Could Find Basil's Mind …

Galana shook her head. I Think It Would Be A Risk To Intrude On The Icebox Now, she wrote. I Assume You Would Need To Sedate Her Before Operating On Her Ears, Or At Least Bring Medical Gear Into Her Presence. She Might Think We Are Attacking Her. She Reacted Strongly When I – she stopped writing with a frown as the most important question belatedly occurred to her. Are We Receiving An Audio Signal?

Devlin had stepped over to the comms console where Chillybin usually stood. Yes, he wrote. I'm Not Looking At It In Too Much Detail, But There Is Definitely Something Coming Through On The Comm System.

I Am Once Again Not Hearing Anything, Wicked Mary reported.

Good, Galana replied. We Do Not Seem To Be Experiencing Any Of The Euphoria Or Confusion You Mentioned In Your Report From Our First Encounter. She looked around at the others, who nodded agreement.

No, Wicked Mary concurred, You All Seem To Be Your Usual Boring Little Selves.

Thank You, Mary. Bonty typed.

They continued their research. There did not seem to be any sign of the Sirens that had lured them here and marooned them so long ago. The swarm of alien ships did not appear to be the source of the transmission. Nor could they *cut off* the transmission. Whenever they did, it started up again seemingly by itself. It didn't take long to figure out why this was.

There Are No Sirens, Galana wrote. The Song Is Coming From The Star.

They'd encountered such a sun before, but it hadn't had anywhere near this much power over them. There had been no alien ships, no brainwashing, nothing of the sort.

The backup computer wasn't very good with the various scanners and sensors, but they took some quick measurements. The star was similar in size and shape to the previous one they'd encountered, and perhaps a few hundred million years younger. It was singing in the same weird energy-and-particle way the previous one had. The song had been picked up on the same channel, and when they switched it off the computer simply picked it up again and switched it back on like it was a comm signal.

It Shouldn't Do That, Scrutarius wrote with a frown. I Think The *Cthagnon* Must Have Put Some Glitch In Our System To Make The Comm System Play The Song Automatically. I Might Need The *Conch*'s Main Computer To Track It Down.

We Can't Risk That, Galana sent. Not Until We Are Back Outside Gozonaar. With The Captain.

I Think I Have Found Him, Wicked Mary put in. Galana, Bonty and Devlin turned to look at the *giela*. I Was Scanning The Alien Ships, the Fergunakil continued, And Approximately Three Hundred Of Them Have Heat Signatures. As You Know, We Repaired The *Cthagnon* So It Could Fly Us Here. This Was How Captain Hartigan Could Sneak Away In It, And How (Hopefully) He Has Managed To Stay ~~Fresh~~ Alive All This Time. It Seems Like There Are A Lot Of Ships Out There Which Were Repaired By Other Groups, And Probably Contain Aliens Similarly Entranced By The Sirens' Song. Which Turned Out To Be A Star's Song, she concluded, Only I Did Not Know This, Because I Was Not Allowed To See Through The Ship Viewscreens Or Connect To The Comm System Properly, But I Don't Like To Sound Critical Of AstroCorps Regulations -

Galana sighed and stopped reading. Which One Has Captain Hartigan In It? she asked.

This One, Wicked Mary passed on the coordinates, lighting up one of the multitude of alien ships in the viewscreen. IT IS THE ONLY ACTIVE SHIP IN THE HUMAN-OPTIMAL ZONE, NOT TOO COLD AND NOT TOO HOT. OF COURSE THIS IS ONLY A THEORY.

IT'S WHAT WE HAVE, Galana said with a shrug. TAKE US INTO DOCKING ALIGNMENT.

The *Conch* moved cautiously into the drifting derelict ships, the crew tense for any sign that the enchanting song might be about to affect them despite their precautions. The solar system remained silent and innocent to their disconnected ears.

DOCKING NOW, Wicked Mary reported.

DEVLIN, BONTY, WITH ME. Galana wrote. She looked across at the *giela*, which returned her glance with its usual completely unreadable assortment of sensors and lights. I THINK WE CAN TRUST WICKED MARY TO WAIT FOR US.

THE MOMENT YOU LOOK LIKE FALLING UNDER THE SIRENS' SPELL, I AM BLASTING THE *CTHAGNON* TO PIECES AND CRASH-JUMPING TO SAFETY. Wicked Mary promised. Galana nodded, and followed Devlin and Bonjamin off the bridge. Scrutarius stopped on the way to the docking bay and picked up a large equipment bag in his left hands. Galana gave him a questioning look, but he waved it away with his upper right.

The *Cthagnon*, of course, was as silent and eerie to their deafened ears as the *Conch* had been for the last few weeks. Molran, Bonshoon and Blaran snuck aboard and made their way to the chamber they'd tentatively identified as the main bridge or viewing deck when they'd been studying the ship the first time around. Of course, knowing that it wasn't exactly a *starship* in the usual sense but rather a sort of complicated trap for bringing aliens to this solar system, the *Cthagnon* made a bit more sense now. It was actually quite clever, Galana thought to herself – allowing alien species to 'repair' the derelict allowed them to set it up according to their own living requirements. They built their own cages.

Captain Hartigan was standing silhouetted against the rubble-strewn darkness of space and the bright, fierce glare of the sun in the centre of the system. He turned when he heard his shipmates enter the room, and smiled vaguely. His mouth moved, but of course none of them could make out what he was saying. He appeared at peace, and glad to see them. Galana put a reassuring smile on her own face and hoped the others were doing the same.

Basil had visibly aged. His face was lined. His moustache, and his impressive mane of head-fur, were now almost as much grey as black. He was crisp and tidy, however, his excess fur clean-shaven, and didn't seem in any way malnourished. Whatever had kept his brain occupied during his time here, it had allowed him to go on maintaining himself in reasonable health. Of a sort.

He said something else, his beatific smile faltering slightly.

Bonty stepped up to the human, placed her lower hands reassuringly on his shoulders, and brought her upper hands up quickly to either side of his head. The gleaming medical devices were as silent as everything else had been since Galana had given up her hearing, and the Captain's yelp was as well ... but the operation was only very briefly painful – and Bonty had assured them it would be even easier to fix than their own ears would be.

Hartigan staggered back towards the viewing window, clapping his hands to his ears, his face anguished and twisted with loss. He stumbled, gazed out at the distant star, then turned back to his crew with a pitifully confused expression. His mouth moved again, but Galana could really only recognise that he was asking a question. Demanding to know what they'd done, no doubt.

"It's no good, Captain," she pronounced carefully, the unheard words feeling odd in her mouth after their weeks of written communication. She could *almost* hear them, as a vibration in her skull, but it made speaking difficult. Of course, at the same moment she realised that he couldn't hear her any more than she could hear him, but hopefully her expression and body language did the job. She shook her head and pointed at her ears, then passed him a communication pad.

Hartigan scowled at it, turning it this way and that as if trying to remember what it was or how it worked. Eventually, still frowning mightily, he jabbed at the pad with a thick finger.

WHY DID YOU DO THAT? he sent. I ALMOST HAD IT FIGURED OUT!

MUCH AS I WOULD LOVE TO STAND HERE WRITING LETTERS TO EACH OTHER FOR A WEEK, Devlin cut in with a message he had clearly written in advance, MAYBE WE CAN GET OUT OF HERE AND FIX OUR EARS INSTEAD?

CAPTAIN, Galana wrote formally, reaching out with her lower hands to place them calmly on Basil's wrists as the human scowled again and started to jab at his communicator, WE HAVE BEEN ENTHRALLED BY THIS SONG FOR TWENTY YEARS. WE MUST CONTINUE OUR JOURNEY. YOU ARE AN ASTROCORPS CAPTAIN AND THIS IS YOUR MISSION. THE *CONCH* IS YOUR VESSEL. REMEMBER THE LAST ALICORN.

Hartigan read this, his face clouding with doubt, then surprise, then alarm. His free hand rose to his face, ran over the new lines there. Alarm turning to horror he patted his head-fur, and was evidently relieved to find it was still there.

TWENTY YEARS? he wrote. Galana nodded grimly. YOU MEAN I'M ALMOST *THIRTY* NOW?

IT IS 1048 YM. she typed with a frown. YOU WERE ALREADY PAST THIRTY YEARS OF AGE WHEN WE DEPARTED DECLIVITORION-ON-THE-RIM. BY NOW YOU MUST BE SEVENTY -

She stopped at a touch on her arm, and looked up to see Devlin grinning and shaking his head. She looked from the Blaran to the human, who was also grinning. Sighing, she deleted the message. She couldn't remember the years they had spent in Gozonaar but even if she could, she doubted they would have helped her understand humans any better.

Hartigan's smile faltered, and he pointed at the star. He started to talk again, then stopped with a grimace of frustration and went back to poking at the communicator.

WE CAN'T LEAVE. he wrote. THAT'S WHY I STAYED WHEN WICKED MARY TOOK THE REST OF YOU AWAY THE OTHER DAY. He stopped, grimaced again, and shook his head. OR WHENEVER IT WAS. he continued. I DID IT TO SAVE THE SHIP. He looked up at their puzzled expressions, then bent his head to the pad again and typed for some time. IT'S HAPPENED BEFORE. IF WE LEAVE THE *CTHAGNON* EMPTY AND FLY AWAY IN THE *CONCH*, THE STAR WILL BURN US. THE OTHER SHIPS WILL FIRE ON US. THAT'S THE ONLY REASON YOU GOT AWAY BEFORE. SOMEONE HAS TO STAY IN THIS SHIP AND LISTEN. THIS STAR ISN'T LIKE THE OTHER ONE. IT *MUST* BE LISTENED TO.

YOU'RE NOT LISTENING NOW. Bonty pointed out. Basil looked doubtful.

WAIT. Devlin typed. He carefully opened the bag he'd brought with him, and fiddled with something inside. Almost immediately, as Galana was watching them, lights began to come on in the scattering of *Cthagnon*-vessels visible in the nearby asteroid field.

SEVERAL OF THE DORMANT SHIPS HAVE ACTIVATED, Wicked Mary sent urgently from the *Conch*, AND WHAT APPEARS TO BE SOLAR FLARE ACTIVITY IS BUILDING IN THE SUN. IT WILL NOT BE SAFE TO GO TO RELATIVE SPEED ... Devlin rummaged in the bag again, then closed it with a grim expression on his face. NEVER MIND. Wicked Mary continued. THE SHIPS HAVE GONE COLD AGAIN AND THE STAR IS SETTLING. IF YOU DID SOMETHING, PLEASE KEEP DOING IT.

WHAT DO YOU HAVE THERE? Galana asked.

Devlin shook his head. He crossed the room to the window where Basil had been standing, crouched, and placed the bulky equipment bag on the floor. He opened it, brought out several smaller containers and pieces of equipment, then lifted a larger storage box out with his lower hands and placed it carefully alongside, lifting its padded lid and leaving it standing open. He stood, looked down into the box for a moment, then turned and headed back to the others.

CHIEF ENGINEER SCRUTARIUS. Galana typed sternly.

EARS TO LISTEN. Devlin typed curtly. LET'S GET OUT OF HERE.

Galana took a half-step towards the little collection of packages Scrutarius had left on the floor, but Bonty stopped her with a hand on her arm and a strangely severe expression.

They returned to the *Conch*, and the singing sun of Gozonaar and its mysterious fleet of ships allowed them to leave without further complications. As soon as they were in soft-space and established there was minimal risk of dropping out inside Gozonaar again, Galana went to wake up Chillybin. Then they all reported to the medical bay.

"I am going to expect a *full* report on how exactly you got us out of Gozonaar, Chief Engineer Scrutarius," Galana made a point of saying the moment Bonty finished repairing the Blaran's auditory system. She held up her data pad. "Starting with why the backup computer now reads *two hundred and fifty-six* life-signs on board," she read calmly. "Captain Hartigan; Commander Scrutarius; unknown aki'Drednanth; unknown Molran; unknown Bonshoon; unknown Fergunakil; two hundred and fifty unidentified dumblers," she lowered the pad. "A clear one hundred and seventy-one *fewer* than when we first escaped the so-called Sirens."

"You'll have it just as soon as we get the main computer back up and running, Commander," Devlin promised. "Just keep in mind that the backup computer is so dumb, it thought *that* was the Captain," he pointed at Wicked Mary's *giela*.

"I will do my best to remember that, Chief Engineer," Galana promised. She studied his face for a long moment. The Blaran's expression was a picture of earnest innocence. "I imagine," she went on, "that what you had in that bag was one hundred and seventy-one small electronic devices that would fool the star and its ships into believing there was still somebody listening to the song. And that as a result those devices also fooled the backup computer into believing there was a large number of unidentified dumblers on board."

"You're very perceptive, Commander Fen," Devlin said. "That's *precisely* what happened and my report will make that *very* clear."

She didn't question him further, but headed down to the Aquarium where Wicked Mary was enjoying the reactivation of her full food and environment-cleaning systems. This much, at least, they'd been able to bring back online almost as soon as Basil and Devlin had returned to the *Conch*.

"How are you, Tactical Officer Mary?" Galana asked. The algae had been cleared away and the lights were back up, returning the murky darkness of the aquatic deck to its usual magical undersea cave appearance. The massive shark – *noticeably* larger, Galana thought, than she had been twenty years previously – was swimming lazily back and forth, occasionally ripping a fish from the water and shredding it with great enjoyment.

"Fine thank you, Commander," Wicked Mary replied.

"Thank *you*," Galana insisted. "I am placing an official commendation in your record – for resourcefulness and reliability above and beyond the Six

Species charter and the high standards of AstroCorps."

"I trust," Wicked Mary replied, "you will not put a copy of that commendation in my own cybernetic grid log. The knowledge that I struggled for twenty years to save the lives of the five of you rather than eat you and fly away – it would disgrace me entirely in the eyes of my fellow Fergunak."

"I am sure the situation would have been different had Captain Hartigan not taken your *giela* away," Galana said supportively.

"Yes," Wicked Mary agreed in evident relief. "Yes, that is true. But even so - "

"I will not log a copy of the report," Galana promised with a smile.

"Thank you, Commander," Galana nodded, and turned to go. "Commander?"

"Yes, Tactical Officer Mary?"

"As you know, I made several efforts to break into the *Conch*'s main computer in the course of bringing the backup computer online."

"Yes," Galana said. "The main computer was affected by the song. You had no choice. I'm sure that will not reflect poorly - "

"You do not understand," Wicked Mary said. "I found out something very strange about this ship's computer."

"Oh yes?"

"Yes," the Fergunakil said. "At its maximum operating strength, the computer uses less than two percent of its total capacity."

Galana frowned. "What do you mean?"

"You are aware, of course, of the myth that an organism's brain uses only a fraction of its capacity," Wicked Mary went on. "It *is* a myth – organic brains use *all* of their capacity. Yes, a lot of it is going on under the surface, like breathing and subconscious processes, but it is all accounted for. In the same way, a starship computer might use a small amount of its capacity to form an interface – the clever and interesting personality we communicate with. The part that knows the difference between Captain Hartigan and a small robot that says 'by jingo'," she paused briefly. "Captain Hartigan is the one that wears trousers," she added.

"I am aware."

"When I say our ship's computer uses only two percent of its capacity," Wicked Mary went on, "I mean for *everything*. A lot of processing power goes to the ship systems, with a tiny bit left over for the computer's interface and personality … and all together this adds up to two percent."

"What about the other ninety-eight percent?" Galana asked.

"The rest of it is a wall," Wicked Mary said. "A wall, and a thing behind the wall," Galana frowned and opened her mouth again. "I am a little tired, Commander," the shark went on. "I am not as young as I once was. I hope we will have another chance to speak of this."

Disquieted, Galana left the Aquarium.

Of course, it didn't pay to listen too closely to the things Fergunak said. They enjoyed spreading unsettling rumours and making air-breathers suspicious and afraid. But Wicked Mary was not generally *like* that. And something about what she'd said ... when Galana had heard it, she hadn't been surprised. On the contrary, it had somehow seemed to make sense of a lot of things. Galana just wasn't sure what it meant.

A wall, and a thing behind the wall.

Shaking her head, Galana returned to the bridge.

Soon, in **The Perils of High Elonath:**

Basil didn't remember his stay in Gozonaar any more than Galana, Bonty or Devlin did, but he had taken the emergence and their loss of twenty years a lot harder than they had. A human losing twenty years was a much bigger deal than a Molranoid losing twenty years. Possibly the only one of them with a shorter life expectancy than Hartigan was Wicked Mary, and she was considerably younger than him.

He never quite figured out what the singing star's message had been, although he did remember how tantalisingly close it had felt the moment Bonty had deafened him. They suspected this was just an illusion planted in his mind to keep him there, keep him listening. Galana, Bonty and Devlin didn't have any such recollections, presumably because they'd been sedated rather than being fully conscious when the song was taken away from them.

It was odd, though. Since none of the landbound crewmembers had noticed the passage of time in Gozonaar, it was easy to forget that they had spent twenty years in there. Only the Captain, for whom twenty years was a considerable length of time, even felt any different – and he tended to laugh it off in his usual cavalier manner. *Galana* felt as though they had flown into the strange region, encountered some difficulties, doubled back and then finally departed. The sight of Captain Hartigan and his grey hair, Wicked Mary and her great craggy body that had grown so huge, was occasionally disconcerting.

Chillybin, at least, was mostly unchanged. So much of her existence passed in the dream anyway, it was easy to ignore the aging of her flesh. She didn't speak about the time she had spent waiting for them to make their way to safety. Galana supposed, if the worst had happened and they'd been trapped there, that Chilly's body would have eventually died and she would have returned to the Drednanth between-life with a few interesting stories to tell her sisters.

"Did you know my father was a famous Sojourner?" Basil asked Galana one evening. He spent more time in his private quarters these days, sometimes not even emerging to oversee the brief stops they made at various places. If there wasn't life – and it had to be *interesting* life – in a volume they stopped at, he accepted the reports and waved them impatiently on. And for the past couple of years, as the far side of the galaxy crawled steadily closer, there really hadn't been very much interesting life out there.

"I did not know that," Galana admitted.

"Oh yes," Hartigan was studying himself in a viewer, touching his grey streaks of hair almost absently. "He sang and danced … Darius St. Charles Hartigan. He died when I was a nipper, don't y'know. Ten years old, I was. A lot of famous folks came to his funeral."

"That must have been difficult for you," Galana hazarded.

"Did you know, his grave was paved over with a Ghoan dance square?" Hartigan went on. Galana shook her head, knowing the Captain must be aware that she hadn't known any such thing. "His gravestone read *It will not offend me to dance. To dance is to know joy, and the universe needs more joy*. He had a dance floor installed so people could dance on his grave," he laughed. "I'm older than he was when he died."

Galana was spared the trouble of finding a response to this – *I did not know that* and *That must have been difficult for you* had just about used up her repertoire – by the ship dropping unexpectedly out of relative speed.

"Captain and Commander to the bridge," the *Conch* announced. "We have flown into a relative cancellation field and are being held."

Galana helped Basil up. He was still strong and vital, but the abrupt collapse of the relative field had brought them out of soft-space uncomfortably, and humans didn't walk something like that off the way Molren could. Together they hurried to the bridge. Scrutarius, Bonty and Chillybin were already at their posts.

"What've we got?" Hartigan asked crisply.

"Well, it's some kind of relative field suppressor," Devlin replied, pointing at a huge, grey-domed structure highlighted in the middle of the viewscreen, "and a couple of alien starships on approach," at this, a pair of smaller moving objects were highlighted. There didn't seem to be anything else in the area. No solar system, no other ships … "No comms from any of them yet," the Blaran added. "Right Chilly?"

"The ships are transmitting a signal, but I am not detecting minds inside them," Chillybin amended. "They may just be automated, and the message a greeting signal."

"They don't look like *greeting* ships," Hartigan said, "do they?"

"I am attempting to feed the signal through our translation files," the *Conch* said. "Perhaps there is a match in the data given to us by Captain Pelsworthy of the Boze – ah. Here we are. *Attention unidentified vessel*," it continued in a harsh, booming tone that echoed over the bridge.

"Maybe dial it back a bit, old girl," Hartigan said with a little wince.

"Sorry," the *Conch* said, then carried on in a quieter, yet still blunt and authoritarian voice. "You are in grave danger. For your own safety, accompany the escort ships to the following coordinates and report to the Outpost for more information. You are in grave danger. Do not attempt to re-enter the grey space on your previous course. Accompany the escort ships to Low Elonath Outpost."

Galana turned and looked at Captain Hartigan in surprise.

"Low Elonath Outpost," Devlin said casually. "Now why is that name so familiar … ?"

"Could there be some connection to the mysterious and dangerous *High* Elonath, where the Last Alicorn is said to have been taken?" Bonty added.

"*Finally*," Hartigan said, with eyes shining. "Now we're getting somewhere."

THE PERILS OF HIGH ELONATH

"Well, this is just dreadfully dull."

It was a short distance from where the *Conch* had been picked up to the mysterious Low Elonath Outpost, but made far longer by the fact that they were not allowed to activate their relative drive and jump there in minutes. The suppression field would have prevented them from doing so even if the Low Elonath Outpost ships hadn't made it very clear that they shouldn't make any sudden moves.

The suppressor machine appeared to be casting its shadow over an area the size of a large solar system, preventing relative speed technology from operating. It was just one of a network of suppressors forming a sort of barrier in this part of space. Quite a feat of engineering, Galana noted, but there was nothing much for them to study. They'd briefly discussed the possibility of flying away on their subluminal engines, fighting off the escort ships if they needed to, getting to the edge of the suppression field and continuing on their way. They agreed, however, that this was an unnecessary risk. They had no way of guessing the capabilities of the escort craft, even if they were just automated machines, and there was a very good chance that Low Elonath Outpost would be able to provide them with information about the dangerous region they had almost blundered into – and still *intended* on blundering into.

In the meantime, it was several hours to Low Elonath Outpost and the escort ships weren't talking.

"Well, nothing for it but to wait it out, what?" Captain Hartigan seemed energised and youthful in a way he had not been since emerging from Gozonaar. "How about a game of muzzock?"

"On board ship?" Galana asked. "How?"

"The question isn't *how*, it's *why*?" Devlin added. "Muzzock is the most mind-numbingly tedious game in the universe."

"Bah, you don't understand the subtlety of the game," Basil declared. "You never have. It just so happens the main corridor is exactly the right size and with only a couple of minor alterations to the bounce rules it's perfectly easy to adapt it to indoor playing ... "

Human and Blaran continued to argue the merits of the game even as they headed out and began to set up the beams and arches that Hartigan *just happened* to have in a handy compartment. It felt like an old debate between the two friends, although as far as Galana recalled they had not played the game once in all their long, boring dives through soft-space. For her own part, Galana had never managed to watch all the way to the end of a round of muzzock due to the awareness – that usually kicked in at the start of the second hour – that she only had five thousand precious years of life to live, and she had already wasted an hour of it watching muzzock. It was, she supposed she'd have to agree, a boring game. Or one the subtlety of which she did not understand.

There being little else to do, they waited out the uneventful journey until the *Conch* announced that they were approaching a larger structure.

"Presumably it is Low Elonath Outpost," the computer said as they all filed back onto the bridge.

The space station did not look much different from the heavily armoured grey dome of the relative suppressor device, although it was larger. Several more of the possibly-automated escort ships were flying around it, along with similar-looking but more heavily-armed versions that looked downright formidable. There was still no nearby sun, but Low Elonath Outpost was visible as a grim outline of reinforced viewing ports and weapons placements.

"Are we ... *worried* about all the guns and armour this space station has?" Devlin asked casually.

"Looks like a bally fortress," Hartigan agreed.

"We were warned that High Elonath was a dangerous place," Galana remarked. "Clearly, the neighbouring regions are prepared for that."

"It would probably be a good idea to be nice to these dumblers," Wicked Mary suggested. "We may have prevailed in a battle against the escort ships, but those larger vessels seem far more powerful. And the Outpost itself ... I do not recognise the weapons or armour but I would estimate they would destroy us without difficulty, and we would barely leave a scratch on them."

"Unless of course all of these weapons just *look* impressive, and they're actually completely harmless to our shields," Hartigan put in lightly.

"That is ... very unlikely, but not impossible," Wicked Mary conceded.

"Let's be nice anyway," Galana advised.

"Of course, Commander," Hartigan said.

"We're always nice," Wicked Mary added.

"We are being hailed," Chillybin reported, and tapped her console.

"Attention unidentified vessel," the *Conch* said in its Outpost-administration voice. "You are a guest of Low Elonath Outpost. You will be processed, your information will be recorded, and a safe route to your destination will be mapped for you. Processing is non-invasive and you will not be harmed. If you wish to disembark and enjoy the use of the facilities, you may do so in the habitat area suited to your life-form class. Indicate your peaceful intentions and willingness to cooperate by powering down your weapons and defensive energy sources. Do this now."

Hartigan looked at Galana, then Wicked Mary, and shrugged.

"Do it," he said. "It's not like we had anything much powered up anyway, is it?"

"Deactivating albedo shielding," Scrutarius said doubtfully.

"Shutting down modular rail cannon," Wicked Mary reported. "This will increase the ramp-up time for our primary weapon from a few seconds to almost an hour."

"That shouldn't be a problem though," Scrutarius added, "since without the shields we can basically be obliterated by a handful of poop flung at us at high speed."

"I'm sure the residents of Low Elonath Outpost keep this volume free of high-speed poop," Galana reassured him.

"Some sort of data-scanner is attempting to interface with us," the *Conch* said. "It doesn't look like it's scanning for anything beyond the surface info level."

"Let them take a peek, old girl," Hartigan said with admirable calm. Galana glanced at Devlin and saw a strange look of worry in the Blaran's eyes. He hid it quickly, though. "And let them know that we'd like to actually *talk* to someone if they do that sort of thing," the Captain added.

A few tense seconds passed, but there was no real sign of interference from the data-scanner. It would be able to pick up the basic details of their crew, mission and the Six Species statement of values, but there was nothing in there they would not have put in a greeting package anyway. More sensitive information about their weapons or biomedical histories would remain hidden, but there wasn't very much in there that Galana thought was *compromising*.

The Outpost didn't seem to be interested in digging deeper, as long as the visitors continued to cooperate. "Attention unidentified vessel," the voice said again. "Low Elonath Outpost is a neutral authority. Star-charts marked with territories in which your computer-type is outlawed will be added to your information package. You would be advised to avoid these territories. Low Elonath Outpost takes no action in these cases unless your vessel's processing systems attempt to infiltrate ours."

"I have assured them I will do no such thing," the *Conch* said mildly in its normal voice. "How exciting that SynEsDyne synaptic computer systems are *outlawed* in so many places."

"Yes," Hartigan said casually, "exciting. Do they have anything else to say?"

"Attention unidentified vessel."

"Of course they do," Hartigan sighed.

"Low Elonath Outpost is a neutral authority. Star-charts marked with territories in which your aquatic cybernetic system is outlawed will be added to your information package. You would be advised to avoid these territories. Low Elonath Outpost takes no action in these cases unless your aquatic cybernetic systems attempt to infiltrate ours."

"I do hope the Fergunak are outlawed in more places than SynEsDyne," Wicked Mary said.

"Look, can we have *one* encounter with dumblers that doesn't degenerate into an argument over who's outlawed in more places - " Hartigan said.

"Attention unidentified vessel. Low Elonath Outpost is a neutral authority. Star-charts marked with territories in which your human being is outlawed will be added to your information package. You would be advised to avoid these territories. Low Elonath Outpost takes no action in these cases unless your human attempts to leave your vessel. That is all."

"That was unexpected," Bonty said mildly.

"I say," Basil exclaimed. "How big's *my* outlawed bit?"

"Surprisingly big," the *Conch* replied.

"I do declare I am offended," Wicked Mary remarked.

"Don't be a sore loser, Bloody Mary," Hartigan went on airily. "But look, if that's all they have to say - "

"Hold on," Galana interrupted. "Are we going to address the fact that dumblers on the far side of the galaxy know what a *human* is?"

"Well, I shouldn't be at all surprised if a few of us hadn't wandered out this far, back in the old days when the Fleet was ferrying us off Earth, what?" Basil said. "Back before there was much, y'know, care being taken about the ol' Six Species borders."

"It only takes one," Devlin added.

"Remember the Gunumbans," Bonty remarked. "Although to be fair, they seemed fairly harmless."

"Humans'll fool you," Devlin grinned.

"Attention unidentified vessel."

"Now hang on, you *very* clearly said 'that is all'," Hartigan objected.

"They're giving us some pretty useful information though," Bonty reminded him.

"That's as may be, Bonty, that's as may be," Hartigan raised a finger. "But it's the principle of the thing. Also we're not unidentified anymore, we're the ACS *Conch*. They found that out pretty much straight away."

"Maybe that's not a good enough reason to update their automatic address protocol," Chillybin suggested. "Should I play the message?"

"Oh, go ahead."

"You have a personal communication incoming from the Head of Low Elonath Outpost Operations," the voice continued harshly. "It is up to you whether you wish to engage in two-way communication. You have proved cooperative."

"Oh," Basil said in surprise. "Well, there you go, see? Nice. Alright, put the Head of Operations through then."

The gloomy view on the screens dissolved into an even gloomier silhouette of a bulky, hunched shape. It was impossible to make out what sort of creature the Head of Low Elonath Outpost Operations was, since it was shrouded in shadow against a deep crimson background. It looked like a heap of large, rounded containers under a sheet in front of a lava flow.

"Hewwo," it said.

Galana suppressed a laugh, but sadly she was the only one on the bridge who did. The Head of Low Elonath Outpost Operations spoke in a high, ludicrously squeaky voice and with an infantile tone that seemed almost impossible to imagine was accidental. Even Chillybin gave a deep, hollow *woof* of hilarity from inside her suit.

"*Computer*," Galana hissed.

"I am not responsible for this one, Commander," the *Conch* hastened. "The Head of Low Elonath Outpost Operations is transmitting in Grand Bo of its own formulation."

Galana nodded to Chillybin, who touched her controls. "Greetings, Head of Operations," Galana said while the Captain got control of himself. "Please allow me to greet you on behalf of AstroCorps and the Six Species. This is Captain Basil Hartigan, I am Commander Galana Fen. Our Medical Officer Bonjamin Bont, Tactical Officer Wicked Mary, Chief Engineer Devlin Scrutarius, and Communications Officer Chillybin. But all of this, I assume, you know."

"Yes," the Head of Low Elonath Outpost Operations mercilessly continued in its hysterical baby-voice. "Gweetimgs. I will get imwediumply to the pwoint."

"Please," Basil wheezed, "please, please do."

"Your imtembded course weeds you diweptly fwoo Low and then *High* Elomaff," the Head of Low Elonath Outpost Operations said, "and out the ubber side before comtimnuing a circumnwavigapun of the gawactic dwisp. Yes?"

"Yes," Hartigan finally managed to gather his professionalism. "Yes, that's true. I understand that's something you lot are here to prevent, for the safety of others and all that?"

"Yes," the Head of Low Elonath Outpost Operations replied, "normawy this is twoo. It's usually nobobby's bismess but the twavellers', if they choose to go into danger even after being imfwormed. We pwevemt people fwom entewing by accidumt, you see. But there is also a wisk that some intwooders into Low and High Elomaff would ... pwovoke the beings that live inside, wemimbing them of our existence and semding them out to do harm. So we do twy to pwevemt too much intwuusimum."

"Y – yes," Hartigan said, his voice a little shaky. "Must – must prevent ... intrusimum. Intrusion," he coughed. "So where does that leave us, my old Operations Heading chum?"

"Normawwy your vessel would be of the 'permit them to enter and pewwish, no harm dumn' type," the Head of Low Elonath Outpost Operations explained. "Nwo offwempse."

"None taken," Basil replied.

"However, your wecords showed that you have imtewacted with a Boze by the name of Juddewome Pelswerbie," the Head of Low Elonath Outpost Operations continued.

"We have travelled together and cooperated on several occasions," Galana took over while the Captain came to terms with the way the Head of Low Elonath Outpost Operations had said 'Judderone Pelsworthy'. "Is this a problem?"

"Not at all. Low Elomaff Outpwoast is a mewtwal aufowity," the Head of Low Elonath Outpost Operations assured them once again. "Captum Pelswerbie is a known and twusted ... well, a *known* vwisitor, let us not exaggewape."

"Understood," Galana replied.

"This would usumully pwomope your vessel to a higher wisk wevel. Umber normal cwircumstwampses, we would pwevemp you fwom emptewing the weegion."

"But now?" Galana asked, after a sidelong glance at her Captain told her she would probably be carrying the rest of this conversation.

"Now," the Head of Low Elonath Outpost Operations said, "Captum Pelswerbie has been a pwisomer of the Deep Tewwos for some time. And the last message she mamaged to get out to Low Elomaff Outpwoast was a vewy specific wequest that you be awowed acwoss the border to wescue her."

"Well, that was kind of her," Galana said.

"I'll be fwamk," the Head of Low Elonath Outpost Operations said, and its large shapeless mass moved ponderously in the ruddy shadows. "I don't fimk you have any chance of fweeing Captum Pelswerbie fwom the Deep Tewwos. We have not heard fwom her in almost fifteem years. But I fimk she also mew that we would stop you because of her connection to you, and she mew that you dearwy wamted to enter Elomaff, and this wequest would pwovibe a woophole for us to awow you to do so."

"I don't know how much sense that makes," Galana admitted, "but if you are going to let us through … "

"Yes, it is a pawadox," the Head of Low Elonath Outpost Operations conceded. "Captum Pelswerbie is permitted to pass, yet you would not be awowed on the basis of your assocication with her, yet you are awowed to pass on the basis of a wequest for aid fwom her. Low Elomaff Outpwoast wegulashums were not cweated with the Boze in mind."

"I can certainly sympathise with that," Galana replied.

The charts they were given were vague, marking only their existing and practically useless AstroCorps and Boze maps with the areas where assorted crewmembers and the computer were outlawed in this section of the galaxy. It didn't, at a casual glance, seem as though it would interfere terribly with their continued journey, provided they survived High Elonath. High Elonath itself, and the surrounding ring that was 'Low Elonath', was itself a surprisingly small volume, at least compared to the size of the areas where humans were outlawed. They could cross the area, Galana calculated, in less than a month if they didn't stop. The estimated location of the 'Deep Terrors', and therefore of Captain Pelsworthy, was marked as well. It stood just on the High Elonath side of the boundary between Low and High Elonath.

"What about these Deep Terror chaps?" Hartigan asked. He had the same information they did, but preferred to let the others provide summaries rather than waste time 'double reading'.

"The Deep Terrors appear to be aquatic," the *Conch* said. "They are hostile, territorial but quite advanced, and thought to be descended from a simple life-form that survived the destruction of the Empire of Gold and its collapse into High Elonath fifty million years ago. They may have been corrupted by some weapon or environmental effect that was left behind after the collapse."

"Aquatic?" Basil said with interest.

"Yes. In fact, their ancestors may have survived because they were hidden in a deep ocean on one world or another of the Empire of Gold," the *Conch* continued. "There are some records of encounters with them, some very careful peaceful dealings, and some prisoner-taking as has happened with Captain Pelsworthy. There has been no improvement in relations sufficient for the people of the Outpost to consider calling them anything but 'Deep Terrors' … although that may just be a translation of what they call themselves."

"Anything else?"

"A few notes about their weapons which I believe Wicked Mary is already examining," the computer replied, "and a decidedly sketchy medical and cultural database for Doctor Bont."

The Last Alicorn

"Look like big jellyfish," Basil remarked, looking at his screen.

Galana couldn't help but concur. There had apparently not been many meetings with or even sightings of Deep Terrors since they were so hostile and secretive, but the images showed an almost-spherical globe of translucent jelly with an unpleasant-looking mass of stingers trailing from its underside like strings of fat purple grapes. The main body of the thing was about the size of an aki'Drednanth.

"Actually, they're more complex than the various gelatinous zooplankton we're used to seeing in aquatic environments in Six Species space," Bonty said enthusiastically. "Their bodies seem to be protected by a thicker layer, almost a hide even though it's still quite malleable, and there's evidence here that they might be hive animals, like some types of insect … but yes, I suppose," she concluded, glancing at the Captain, "basically big jellyfish."

"Well," Hartigan said, "it looks like we have almost a week at relative speed to get to this part of Low-or-High Elonath. Plenty of time to study. Of course, no way of saying how much of the way we'll have to go at sublight speed. Might take us a bit longer than that, what?"

"There is a final message from the Head of Low Elonath Outpost Operations," Chillybin reported. "They are going to deactivate the nearest suppressor so we can go to relative speed."

"Is that all Squibby Bubbums has to say?" Basil asked in amusement.

"No," the aki'Drednanth replied. "Would you like me to play the rest of the message?"

"Sure," Basil said. "Might as well go into High Elonath with smiles on our faces."

"High Elomaff is imkwedibwy damgewus, the Deep Tewwos are omwy the bwegimming," the high, childish voice said. "Eevum though you have an aki'Dwebmamf with you, it won't be emuff. You won't survive.

"The magical cweature you seek does not exist. You're chasing a chilbwen's story. There is nuffimg in High Elomaff but deff. You should weave Captum Pelswerbie to her fate and contimue awoumb this weejum."

"Is that all?" Hartigan asked. He wasn't smiling. Not even 'aki'Dwebmamf' had been enough to lighten the severity of the message.

"That's all, Basil," the computer replied in a subdued voice.

"Ah, what do they know?" Devlin said. "Let's get in there, save Roney from the Deep Terrors, and find this stupid Alicorn you haven't shut up about for the past half a century or more."

"Well said," Bonty agreed.

"Yes," Chillybin added.

"Maybe there will be water for me to get into at last," Wicked Mary remarked.

They all turned to look at Galana.

"Oh, was this one of those 'each crewmember has to say something spirited and encouraging' things?" she asked. "I was already running a rescue simulation. Um, yes. Let's go into the dangerous place, *not* get destroyed, and then leave again."

"Very spirited and encouraging, young Fen," Basil congratulated her. "We'll make a human of you yet."

Galana lifted her ears at the familiar threat. "Please don't."

Hartigan grinned and slapped his console, sending them into soft-space.

Of course, nothing much happened very quickly with interstellar travel. The grey settled over the screens and the purposeful moment ended, leaving them all sitting at their consoles in the usual sheepish silence that followed a jump to relative speed. After that, there was a week of nothing much to do before they arrived at their destination.

In this case, there was a slight edge of anxiety to the boredom throughout the jump. If the Low Elonath Outpost mob had suppressors, as the Captain said, there was no reason for the Deep Terrors not to have them. And that meant they could be pulled out of relative speed at any time.

Fortunately, they weren't. A few shipboard days later they arrived at the spot marked on the Low Elonath Outpost charts, shields charged and weapons powered up, as prepared as they could be against the formidable Deep Terrors.

"We have a rather inhospitable looking solar system," the *Conch* reported. "All the planets seem to be gas giants, or else have no atmosphere at all."

"I was rather expecting a water planet or two, for these swimming fellows," Hartigan said.

"There is a lot of ice floating free," the computer said, then paused. "Oh."

"What is it?" Hartigan said, although by then it was visible on the viewscreens. What had at first looked like an asteroid belt turned out to be a huge field of wreckage. Ships, space stations, it was hard to tell what it had been – but all of the structures had clearly been filled with water because now the whole area was surrounded by a great mass of glittering ice fragments. "Any life signs?" he asked without much hope. "Chilly? Any minds out there?"

"Yes," Chillybin replied. "I am picking up the presence of a Boze mind."

"Oh, *jolly good*," Basil said in relief.

"That is not all, though," Chilly went on. "There are also some unfamiliar minds, scattered through this system. It is strange … they may be damaged, or they may not even be *minds* … they are like small, disjointed pieces of minds. I may be able to learn more as I become familiar with them. I do not think they are an immediate danger."

"I agree," Wicked Mary added. "They may be Deep Terror survivors, but there is no sign that any of these vessels are capable of movement. They are adrift. A few have glimmers of power, probably being used to keep the occupants alive, the water inside liquid."

"We should offer our aid," Bonty said. "Hostile or not, they're clearly no threat to us now, and need our help."

"Let's study the situation for a while first," Galana said. "Find out what happened here, and whether we even *can* be of any help."

"Agreed," Hartigan said. "And get Roney out in the meantime. Any idea where she is?"

"I think I've got it," Scrutarius said, tapping and flicking swiftly at his console. A particularly large piece of ice and metal was highlighted on the main viewscreen. "There's power on inside this one," he said, "but doesn't look like a water pocket – the ice is formed up around the outside to seal it, and *this* might be an energy signature from an atmospheric generator," he marked a line in the data. "It's pretty weak, though. I wouldn't be surprised if she's repaired it or put it together out of scrap."

"That is where the Boze mind is located," Chillybin concurred.

Galana pointed. "Also, isn't that her ship?"

They looked again, and the *Conch* obligingly magnified the image on the screens. The chunk of twisted metal and ice turned slowly as they approached and the sun caught a sleek red gleam embedded in the ice on one side of the mass. It did indeed look like the *Splendiferous Bastard*, or at least a part of it. The air pocket, if that's what it was, seemed to be on the far side of the asteroid, almost two miles from the frozen ship.

"Let's get over there and get her out," Hartigan said.

"And tell her Judderone Pelsworthy sent us," Devlin added. "Remember she told us we should say that if we ever found ourselves in the dark ruins of the Empire of Gold?"

"Can't argue with that," Hartigan agreed. "We're unlikely to get a better opportunity, what?"

They manoeuvred the *Conch* in as close as they could to the most intact-looking piece of wreckage. Roney had probably been lucky, Devlin pointed out, to have been in a prison cell when whatever had happened had happened. Whatever the wreckage was, it had been built to last – almost as much as the *Splendiferous Bastard* had been, in fact.

After a few hours of scanning and testing and repositioning, they managed to create a crude docking seal around a stretch of exposed armour plating and finally cut their way into the wreck.

Air swept out of the *Conch*'s docking bay past them even as they were stepping hesitantly into the darkness of the wreck. Fortunately, the pressure equalised quickly. Less fortunately, the interior of the asteroid was chilly and had an unpleasant musty smell. The AstroCorps rescue party crossed the large slab of hull that had fallen into the wreck, crunched through ice crystals and pieces of broken machinery, and raised their lamps over their heads.

A small, tattered shape stood on the far side of the chamber they'd cut into, outlined against the deeper darkness of a doorway. Her fur was dusty and matted, her uniform hanging in shreds, and one of her huge, triangular ears was gone … but then lamplight gleamed off a sharp golden tooth, and Galana realised it was their old friend Captain Judderone Pelsworthy of the Boze, Space Adventurer.

Hartigan cleared his throat. "Judderone Pelsworthy sent - "

"Where the bloody Hell have you been?" Roney demanded.

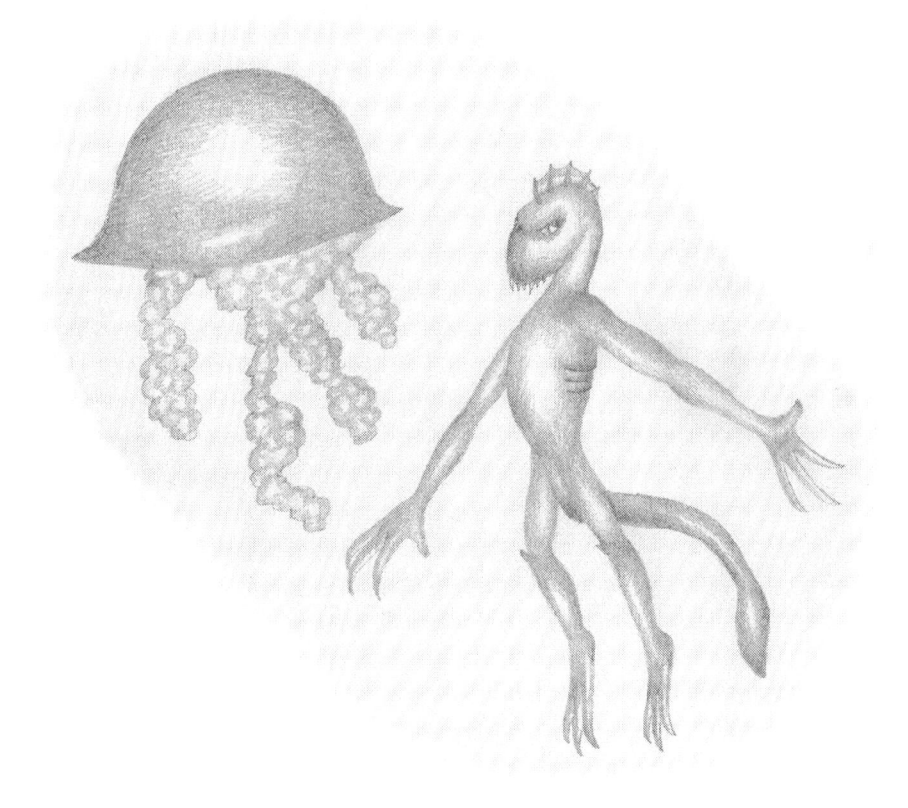

Soon, in <u>The Last Alicorn</u>:

Roney had been trapped in the ruins of the Deep Terror prison for almost five years, although she wasn't absolutely certain of how long it had been precisely.

"It was about half as long as I spent rotting in the cell waiting for you," she said, "but way less fun."

Her ten-year imprisonment had ended abruptly when the Deep Terrors had been attacked and practically wiped out. Only a bit of quick thinking and quicker engineering had allowed her to turn her collapsing prison into a lifeboat, sealing off the holes with ice from the remains of the Deep Terrors' water and using the same machinery that had been giving her air in the first place to *continue* giving her air. Even more fortunately, a large storage chamber of frozen food had been accessible after the dust settled, and she'd been able to melt and filter the ice for drinking water.

Since then, she had been attempting to dig her way through the ice to the part of the prison where her ship had been impounded, but without any equipment it had been slow going.

"Still," she concluded her tale, "it gave me something to do while I was waiting for you to *walk here*."

"I'm sorry, old girl," Hartigan said. "Afraid we fell afoul of the jolly old singing star of Gozonaar and rather got held up."

"The singing *what*?" Roney swivelled her one remaining ear. "Afraid my hearing's not what it once was, biggums."

"Let's get you to the medical bay," Bonty said. "I might be able to grow you a replacement."

"Should be able to if my ship's still intact," Roney said, but let them lead her into the *Conch* and through to the medical bay. "I always went *around* Gozonaar," she added. "Didn't they tell you to go around, at the Citadel?"

"You told us to go around High Elonath," Galana said, since the alternative was breaking her promise never to mention her recommendation that they fly around Gozonaar. "Clearly the reason you were waiting for *us* to come and rescue you was because you knew we were the only people who were likely to fly through anyway."

Roney grunted. "Can't argue with that, I suppose," she admitted. "I knew you'd never go around High Elonath, what with your silly quest to find the humptycorn or whatever it was."

"Alicorn," Basil said. "So what was it that gave the Deep Terrors a good seeing to? Any idea?"

"I know *exactly* what it was," Roney growled. "It was the Stonegillers."

"The what?" Galana frowned.

Roney pulled herself up onto the examination bed and eyed Galana while Bonty scanned and poked and prodded at her. "The Stonegillers," she repeated. "*Ghastly* creatures. The Deep Terrors evolved in this place so they can't help being awful. The Stonegillers were nomads, pirates, until they found High Elonath. They're still nomadic, but they *liked* it here, so they moved in. That's how bad they are. They're aquatic, like the Terrors, so the two groups wreck each other's stuff and steal each other's water generators and things whenever they can. That's what happened here."

"Hold still, I'll prepare your ear for grafting," Bonty said.

"I'll break dock and take us around the wreck," Devlin added. "Let's see if we can get the *Splendiferous Bastard* out of the ice."

"Thanks," Roney said. "Thanks, all of you. I was really getting tired of digging. I'm heartily glad you showed up."

"Not at all, old chum," Hartigan patted the Boze carefully on the back. Now that she was in the warmth and light of the *Conch*'s medical bay, it was clear how skinny and frail she was. Galana had no idea how much of it was her ordeal, and how much was the more-than-twenty years that had passed since they'd last seen her. "I'm just sorry we couldn't have been here sooner."

"There are still some Deep Terrors out in the rubble," Bonty said as she worked. "What's your opinion, Roney? Should we try to make contact?"

"I wouldn't bother," Roney said. "If they haven't regrouped yet, they never will. The Stonegillers probably took their – I don't know what it is exactly, something the Stonegillers take out of the Terrors and use like a – like a drug, or a delicacy. It makes them loopy. The Terrors are pretty hardy, they'd bounce back and rebuild from something like this. I thought they would, until a few months went by and nothing happened. That's when I assumed they were all gone. If there's any left alive out there, they're just … just like pieces. Not intelligent, not able to recover. They just sort of float around. Same thing happens if you get one of them alone and try to take it somewhere, cut it off from the rest."

"Maybe they took away the queen," Hartigan suggested. Galana looked at him in puzzlement, and he pointed at Bonty. "Didn't the doc say they were like hive animals? And Chilly was saying she could feel alien minds out there, but they were like little fragments of minds. Maybe they have a queen that controls their hive, and that's what the Stonegillers took to eat. What?" he said, seeming to become aware that everyone in the medical bay was staring at him. "I listen."

"Judging by how long you've been here," Galana said to Roney, "I would assume these Stonegillers are unlikely to come back?"

"Who knows, frankly," Roney replied. "They're not even the worst thing in here. Not that I'm not grateful, like I said, but I think you're mad for coming. And I don't suppose you're going to choose this moment to become sane, and turn around and fly back out of this place as fast as your not-at-all-fast ship can carry you?"

"Not until we've found the Alicorn," Basil said unwaveringly.

"I was sure it was a humptycorn you were looking for," Roney shook her head. "Well, if you're that determined, and I'm stuck here anyway, I might as well go with you. You'll get into all sorts of trouble without me."

"Anyone would think *we* were the ones *you'd* just pulled out of a ruined space prison," Bonty remarked, "instead of the other way around."

It took almost two days to delicately melt the *Splendiferous Bastard* free of the ice, and another two to get it even close to operational. The hardy red ship was not outwardly damaged, but there were issues with its relative drive and weapons that Roney could not immediately do anything about, and would not permit her AstroCorps allies to poke around with. Hartigan and Scrutarius were a little put out by this, after all the help they'd given the Boze, but Galana was still in agreement. Just as the Six Species had rules about giving advanced technology to dumblers, they had to accept that dumblers were right to keep even more advanced technology to themselves.

Eventually, they docked the ships together – a configuration Roney and Basil had taken to referring to as the *Splendiferous Conch* – and turned their faces towards the dark and forbidding centre of High Elonath.

Another uneventful week in soft-space placed them in the general vicinity of the centre of the forbidden and deadly region that had once been the Empire of Gold. There was no guarantee that what they sought would *be* in the centre of High Elonath, but it seemed as good a place as any to start looking.

"Alright, here we go," Captain Hartigan said, his voice trembling with anticipation as the relative speed jump time trickled away towards zero, and their return to normal space. "You know, I don't see why we always make such a big deal of jumping *into* the grey. It's always such an anticlimax, what? We should make a fuss of coming *out* of soft-space. That's where the excitement is."

"We try to," Devlin said, "but you're always so excited to take off."

"And we normally get pulled out of relative speed unexpectedly so we don't get a chance to look forward to it," Bonty added.

"Well, we haven't bally well been pulled out this time," Captain Hartigan said, "and we're about to arrive, so let's have a bit of enthusiasm, what?"

"Hear hear," Roney agreed.

"Is it another one where we all say something?" Galana asked. "I think I have a good one this time," she paused significantly, then spread her arms in what she hoped was a grand gesture. "In the unlikely event the Last Alicorn exists, there is a slim chance we'll find it here."

"We're halfway around the galaxy," Bonty submitted her own offering, "and *might* get all the way around before any of us die of old age."

"I think everything will probably be fine," Chillybin declared, "and even if it isn't, I will return to the Great Ice to await my next life."

"I may be able to make friends with the aquatic aliens that live here after they kill you all," Wicked Mary said.

"I think our uniforms look *very* smart," Devlin added.

"Try harder," Basil said, "all of you. Take notes from Captum Pelswerbie," the jump timer ran down to zero. "Alright then, here we go."

He leaned forward in his seat, and the grey of relative speed vanished into the starry black of normal space.

THE LAST ALICORN

It was, as far as forbidding planets in the centre of dangerous and mysterious zones went, not a disappointment.

"Golly," Captain Hartigan said, bright-eyed. "That is one *forbidding* planet."

The solar system they'd dropped into was in the middle of the zone marked as 'High Elonath', but was right on the outermost edge of the galactic rim. There wasn't much more than a few rocks and rogue asteroids between them and intergalactic space. The system had a bloated and mottled red-purple star in its centre with – as far as scans showed – only a single planet in orbit around it. It was huge, larger than many gas giants Galana had seen, and shaded in drab monochrome. Its clouds were thick, dark grey and boiling with storms. Its land was darker grey and riddled with chasms and barren mountains. And its vast, churning seas were inky black.

"I am not seeing any sign of spaceborne technology in this system," Chillybin reported.

"Minds down on the surface?" Hartigan asked.

"No," the aki'Drednanth said, then went on, "yes. Not on the surface – beneath the surface. In the water."

"Let me guess," Scrutarius said. "Stonegillers."

"It seems so," Chillybin said. "They are not familiar minds. And the water is filled with heavy metals that are interfering with our sensors."

"I'll have a fiddle with the doodads," Scrutarius said. "Reverse the polarity of something."

"Doesn't that just mean turning it over?" Bonty asked.

"Yes, but *sciencier*," Devlin flicked an ear and crouched by the side of Chillybin's console.

"I gave you my notes about the Stonegillers," Roney said, "didn't I?"

"Yes," Galana said, "but they were a little light on physiological and technological data, and heavy on the different nasty things they smell like and the ghoulish things they enjoy doing to their enemies."

"That's physiological and technological data," the Boze objected.

"I liked the bit where they used their mouths and the gills under their arms as a sort of jet propellant thing," Bonty said. "And how they can fly for short distances in air as well. And hold their breath up on land for some hours. It was all very interesting. Terrifying, of course, but interesting."

Galana called up Captain Pelsworthy's file and studied the images and information again. The Stonegill was roughly humanoid, although from the accompanying notes it seemed to be at least twice the size of a human, closer to three times. It wasn't as big as a Fergunakil, but it was big. Scaly, reptilian, a dark grey colour to go along with the colour scheme of the planet these ones had apparently decided to make their home, with powerful arms and legs and a long serpentine tail, it had a head like a great lizard and a mouth full of long, curved teeth. It did look terrifying.

"They may look like wild beasties, but that's just how they like to play," Roney said. "They have starships and guns and all the toys, but they like getting out in the water and hunting with their wits and their teeth."

"I can understand that," Wicked Mary said.

There was the usual uncomfortable silence at this, before Hartigan cleared his throat. "So, um, Dev, any luck with those scanners?"

"I've been down here for *thirty seconds*," Devlin protested.

"Isn't that enough?"

"I could prepare a landing tank in less than an hour," Wicked Mary offered. "I could go down and attempt to make diplomatic contact, aquatic species to aquatic species. A lot of the problems between air-breathers and real life-forms come from a lack of understanding. And it has been a long time since I left this ship."

"I didn't think this sort of confinement bothered Fergunak," Bonty said. "You've never mentioned it before."

"Did she say 'real life-forms'?" Hartigan added.

"Try it now, Chilly," Devlin stood up.

"There are energy signatures under the water that could be ships," Chillybin confirmed, "or aquatic settlements of some kind. Six distinct signatures."

"If we can see them, they can definitely see us," Roney said grimly.

"They're not powering up their engines or weapons," Wicked Mary reported. "There isn't much sign of life - "

"Aside from the distress call," Chillybin interrupted.

"The *what?*" Hartigan and Pelsworthy said in unison.

"It is hidden in some normal background noise," Chilly replied, "only now I can pick it out through the interference in the water. Feeding it to the computer for translation."

When the *Conch* spoke, its voice had taken on a cold and somehow watery tone. Galana reflected that it was one of the computer's better efforts.

"They are awake. They will not let us leave. Foolish greed led us here. The last vengeange of the Deep Terrors. An unspeakable trap. You would be wise to abandon us to our fate while you still can. It may not be too late for you."

"Did you say this was a *distress* call?" Devlin frowned.

"I think it's the closest Stonegillers can get," Chillybin said.

"It's lousy."

"There are two … no, three more ships, on the land instead of under the water," Wicked Mary reported. "I did not see them before because they've been … flattened into the landscape a bit."

"*Flattened into the landscape a bit?*" Hartigan was turning from one crewmember to the next and was beginning to look a bit dizzy. "But there's no sign of weapons?"

"No, Captain."

"What could have grounded a half-dozen Stonegill ships, and flattened three of them into the landscape a bit?" Basil asked Roney. "What they did to those jellyfish chaps who had you hostage … I say, didn't you tell us that the Stonegillers weren't the worst things in High Elonath?"

"Yes," Roney said with a frown on her narrow, white-furred face, "but all the bigger beasties out there have great big ships and great big guns. Clearly, the Deep Terror delicacy they took made them hyped-up and overconfident, and they were lured here as payback by the Deep Terrors even as they died. Normally even Stonegillers would avoid the middle of High Elonath."

"I am still not seeing any sign of live technology on the surface," Chillybin said. "Just the crushed Stonegiller ships, if that's what they are. Only one of them matches the descriptions Roney has given us, although you do sort of have to … fold it up into three dimensions in your mind. There *is* one intact structure on the surface that might contain some kind of machinery, but it is barely giving off any readings. It may be a relic of the Empire of Gold – we have seen them before."

"'They are awake'," Galana said.

"What's that, Fen?" Hartigan asked.

"The Stonegillers said 'they are awake'," she explained. "What if there was something on this planet, perhaps stored inside this old relic Chilly's found, and the Stonegillers interfered with it and drew them out?"

"Something like a Riddlespawn?" Bonty asked.

"No," Roney said. "If it was a Riddlespawn, we'd all be dead already. But it was *something* alright."

"Should we … save them?" Bonty ventured while they were considering the possibilities.

"*No*," Roney snapped again. "You heard them, we'd be wise to abandon them and get out of here. Isn't it a violation of your daft AstroTeam regulations to go against a message like that?"

"Astro*Corps*," Galana corrected her. "Chilly, are you sure there are no minds on the land? Only the Stonegillers in the ocean?"

"I do not know for certain," Chillybin said. "I can not even confirm they are Stonegillers, since I am unfamiliar - "

"Oh, they're Stonegillers," Roney confirmed. "But what about whatever's got them trapped down there? Assuming we're actually *caring*, and aren't going to just fly on like sane people would ... "

"What about the ruddy *Alicorn*?" Hartigan said. "We need to land. There's no other way."

"There's *so many other ways*," Roney said in exasperation.

"Captain," Galana agreed without much hope, "it is really not advisable - "

"Tish and pish, Fen, we're going down there and that's final," Hartigan said. "We can't find the Alicorn from up here, and this is what the Six Species is meant to be about, and Bloody Mary's long overdue for a swim, and – I say, Mary, how long did you say it would take you to build a landing tank for yourself?"

"Not long, Captain," Wicked Mary said. "I had already done most of the preparation work while we were on our way here. It will be a tight squeeze, but since I only need to be in the tank for a short time ... it is just a matter of filling the central compartment of Captain Pelsworthy's ship with water - "

"Now *hang on*," Roney said sharply.

"I was sure you would not mind, Captain Pelsworthy," Wicked Mary said. "Your ship is still not capable of relative speed but it is able to take off and land. And you were ever so grateful to us for rescuing you from that asteroid, weren't you?"

"How did you manage to prepare a compartment in Roney's ship to hold water?" Devlin asked admiringly.

"I got quite good at sneaking around and making structural changes while we were trapped in Gozonaar," the *giela* replied.

"*Nobody* flies the *Splendiferous Bastard* but me," Roney snapped.

"I would not have it any other way," Wicked Mary said. "I do not have control over your ship's systems. You would need to land it. Or at least get close to the surface of the ocean, and then dump me."

"It's settled then," Hartigan said.

"No it isn't," Galana objected.

"It is, because I just remembered I'm the ruddy Captain," Hartigan declared. He turned to Roney. "And I'm pulling rank on you too, old chum," he added. "I'm the only Captain here with a working ship."

"Alright, biggums," Roney said mildly. "I don't think you'll have a working ship much longer either the way you're going, but alright."

In short order, the *Nella* and the *Splendiferous Bastard* were pulling away from the *Conch* and dropping into the atmosphere of the planet Hartigan had decided would be named Forbidulon. Lamentably, his Captainly decisiveness hadn't quite been expended after giving the order to land.

"It's perfectly ghastly down there, isn't it?" Bonty remarked. None of the crew had wanted to stay behind. Even Wicked Mary had sent her *giela* on the *Nella* while she went with Roney. The *Conch* had been left in orbit under the control of the automatic systems. Even the computer, housed as it was in the detachable shuttle's SynEsDyne synaptic core, was accompanying them.

The *Splendiferous Bastard* peeled off and headed out over the dark ocean towards the Stonegillers in distress. The *Nella* set down near the possible relic Chillybin had found, and they cautiously disembarked.

It was indeed cold, and gloomy. The ground was mostly flat aside from the occasional towering spire of jagged grey stone that thrust up from the surface like teeth. Despite the size of the sun and the fact that it was close to local midday, there was neither light nor heat in any satisfactory amount from the huge red-purple star. In fact, Basil had been forced to don a thermal suit and Chillybin was able to leave her great silver armour plates in the shuttle and crunch along the icy grey ground without refrigeration. She kept her transcription glove on, so she could still communicate directly with her crewmates.

"I'm actually surprised the gravity isn't higher," Galana felt the need to defend Forbidulon's honour a little. "A planet this size … "

"It's pretty bally high, Fen," Hartigan grunted.

"Still - "

"Oh no," Scrutarius said as the relic came into sight. It was a low, blocky structure that might have looked like it had been carved out of the surrounding stone, except it was a slightly different shade of dusty grey. "I recognise this thing."

"What?" Bonty exclaimed. "You do? *How?* We're on the far side of the galaxy."

"*They* still recognised humans," Hartigan pointed out. "Obviously some members of the Six Species have been out here."

"Not Six Species," Devlin said grimly. "This is old, probably from back in the days of the Wild Empire, maybe even earlier. Five Species stuff. This thing is a *Þurshaugr*."

"A what now?" Hartigan frowned.

"*Þurshaugr*," Galana murmured. The AstroCorps Academy taught some ancient Fleet history, but this was practically folklore. "*The burial mound of the*

Ogre."

"Ogre, you say," Hartigan breathed.

"Thought you'd like that part," Devlin said slyly. "Of course it's just a word for these sorts of structures. They didn't actually bury Ogres in them."

"Burying Ogres just made them angry," Chillybin said through their communicators, and gave a low grunt of amusement.

"But the Alicorn originally *belonged* to a pair of Ogres," Devlin insisted. "The stories are just a bit unclear about what brought it all the way out here."

"Fleet Separatists, apparently," Galana said disapprovingly. "Those pirates are the ones who hid their booty in things like this," she glanced at Devlin. "Strange that you would recognise the design."

"Well, you know," he said vaguely. "I *am* a Scrutarius. One of the most skulduggerous families in the criminal subspecies."

They walked up and stood in the shadow of the relic. Its front was cracked, its doorway a gaping black hole with a pair of great broken slabs of grey stone lying just visible inside.

"So what is this thing, and why are you so bally spooked by it?" Hartigan asked. "If it had Ogres buried in it, looks like they weren't ready to stay buried. Maybe Chilly was right."

"They're not really *graves*," Scrutarius repeated.

"And those doors were broken *inwards*," Galana added.

They crept into the smashed doorway. Wicked Mary activated a lamp on her *giela*'s head. The keening wind that had been making the cold of Forbidulon even more biting cut off mercifully as they crossed the threshold. The doorway led into a tunnel that curved downwards into the ground.

"*Þurshaugr* were supposed to be inhabited by terrifying biomechanical monsters constructed by the Separatists to guard their treasures," Galana said to break the silence.

"Thanks, Fen," Hartigan said.

Bonty, who had hurried ahead of them to study something carved into a wall, froze and looked down. Her bulk prevented Galana from seeing what exactly she was looking at. "These guardian monsters," she said faintly over her shoulder. "Were they, oh, large segmented things like an armour-plated worm with a lot of knife-legs and a big barbed hook at one end?"

"That sounds accurate," Galana said, putting a hand on her gun. "Why do you ask?"

"Because the smooshed-up remains of one are pressed into the tunnel floor here," Bonty pointed. "There's also the pulverised remains of a Molran here. Or possibly a Blaran or a Bonshoon. It's all a bit flat to be certain, but at least we can confirm this *was* one of ours. It looks like they were both beaten into the stone using a piece of the door. Look, this slab has some of the knife-legs and an eye tooth stuck in it."

They gathered around the remains.

"That slab must weigh ten tons," Hartigan marvelled.

"Any other signs of life?" Galana asked Chillybin.

The aki'Drednanth shook her great shaggy head, then crouched and snuffled at the remains of the guardian monster and the unfortunate former Molranoid. She moved her gloved hand quickly, forming words for their communicators.

"I cannot sense any minds," she said, "but I can smell something."

"Something big and segmented and knife-leggy?" Devlin asked. "Or possibly Molranic or Blaranish or Bonshoonian?"

"No," she replied. "These creatures have been dead for some hundreds of years, and I cannot smell any more of them."

"Something horsey and feathery and Alicornesque, then?" Basil asked hopefully.

"No," Chilly answered. "Anything else that was in here has long since been overlaid with the smell of Ogre."

"Ogre?" Galana asked. "*Actual* Ogre?"

"That would explain what I saw on the wall here," Bonty hurried back to the wall she'd been examining. "These are old Fleet markers. Or horrible Separatist pirate markers, I suppose. This first part is *very* old, this bottom part is quite a lot fresher. I was expecting it to say something about this being a *Þurshaugr*, but it's far more specific," she turned and beamed at them in the light of Wicked Mary's lamp. "This is the *first* trove. This is where the Ogres' belongings were buried when they were stolen from the Fleet. This is the *reason* all the other treasure holes were called that," she continued in excitement, and turned back to the wall. "It says here that when the pirates took the Ogres' stuff, they didn't realise that it had *actually* belonged to Ogres. And they fled to the far side of the galaxy and left the stuff here in the hopes it was far enough to escape their terrible anger. And … oh."

"'Oh'?" Hartigan prompted.

"Well, apparently it wasn't," Bonty said, "because the thieves were tracked down one by one and stamped on. The very last of them fled back here again, probably in one of those three ships we found flattened nearby, and wrote this last bit," she gestured at the lower part of the carving. "It says that she came back here so she could give the stuff back to the Ogres and apologise when they tracked her down."

"Let me guess what happened next," Scrutarius said cheerfully. Bonty waved a lower hand in invitation. "The Ogres arrived in the *second* of those three ships we found, bashed down the door, beat the guardian beastie to death with the pirate while she was trying to apologise, then flattened them both with a piece of the door. Then the Stonegillers showed up, tried to take the Ogres' stuff, and got one of their ships stamped flat when they tried to escape and they've been hiding underwater ever since."

"That doesn't explain what happened to the Ogres' ship," Galana said.

"I suspect," Chillybin replied, "that when the Stonegillers tried to get away and the Ogres brought down their ship, they also smashed the other two ships just because they were there. Ogres were not known for their subtlety, or the quality of their memories."

"Should we be getting in the *Nella* and getting out of here?" Bonty asked.

"Probably too late," Devlin said, still sounding cheerful. "By now, if they're still around – and I would think they are, judging by the Stonegillers cowering down in the ocean – they'll probably attack us if we try to leave. Our best bet is to meet them and try to make friendly contact. Assuming that's even possible, with Ogres."

"It should be," Chillybin said. She loped past them, deeper into the passage. "They are already aware of us, so it would be safer *not* to flee at this point."

"I thought you said you couldn't sense any minds," Hartigan said, then blinked in the lamplight. "Oh."

"Yes," Chilly's voice said over the comm system. "They do not have a very loud psychic presence."

"What a *nice* way of saying it," Bonty approved.

They descended into the ancient tunnel. Hartigan murmured into his communicator in an attempt to find out how Roney and Wicked Mary were doing, and Roney reported back that she'd delivered the shark to the turbulent ocean and was returning to orbit. Wicked Mary had apparently not been in contact with the Boze since leaving the ship, but Roney admitted her vessel was still in a state of disrepair.

"You could just ask me, Captain," Wicked Mary's *giela* said.

"Oh, right," Basil coughed in embarrassment. "How's it going, old girl?"

"The water is extremely cold, but at least it is still liquid," Wicked Mary reported. "I am getting my bearings but have not yet made contact with the Stonegillers."

The tunnel opened out into a large chamber, and the crew of the *Conch* looked around in surprise.

At first glance, most of the contents of the *þurshaugr* looked like junk from somebody's attic. There were crates and racks, an assortment of objects that could have been weapons or sports equipment, and a surprising collection of small shiny knickknacks, albeit with the shine hidden under a layer of dust. Now even Galana could catch the scent of Ogre. It was fairly similar to thawing aki'Drednanth, but more musk than mildew.

"We probably shouldn't be in here," she murmured. "They have clearly made this into their den and if Ogres are as territorial as aki'Drednanth - "

By then it was too late. The massive shape of an Ogre, which had been curled up comfortably next to a battered old piece of machinery and doing an eerie impersonation of a shaggy armchair, rose up and stretched with a low growl that was more curious than angry. Galana tentatively identified the machinery as an ancient slow-bore atmospheric control station, but that was only because her brain was desperately looking for things to do in what it was convinced would be its final moments. *I am going to continue listing and describing pointless technical details*, her brain insisted stubbornly, *right up to the moment I get spread across the floor.*

The Ogre looked almost exactly like an aki'Drednanth, except possibly a little *more* enormous, and sporting a pair of heavy curled horns on its head just above and behind its glittering crystal eyes. It stumped forward with another rumble, and Chillybin moved smoothly to place herself between the Ogre and the rest of the crew. The two massive creatures snuffled at one another carefully.

"You am'n't Tuesday," the Ogre grunted, surprising Galana. It wasn't wearing any visible equipment to turn its gestures into words, and the voice seemed to be coming directly from its deep barrel chest. The words were gibberish, and Galana wondered if maybe the Ogre had some kind of mechanical transcription implant that had begun to run down after so many years. She realised that her brain was looking for things to do again.

"No," Chillybin said with a movement of her fingers.

"You'se Truck?" the Ogre said after a long moment of reflection.

"Truck sister," Chillybin replied in the same nonsensical way. She raised a hand and thumped her chest. "Chilly."

"Water chillier," the Ogre said, but its posture seemed to relax and its attitude became less hostile. "Tuesday down on beach," before Chillybin could respond to this possible invitation, the Ogre looked past her at the others. It pointed at them. "Hey."

"My friends," Chillybin said, and gestured to each of them in turn. "Basil. Galana. Devlin. Bonjamin. Mary."

"Lotsa names," the Ogre grumbled disapprovingly.

"Sorry."

The Ogre seemed to take this in stride. "Where you come from? What you want?"

"Captain?" Chilly murmured, and shifted aside to allow Hartigan to step forward. He did so, *very* carefully.

"Greetings," Hartigan said with admirable boldness.

The Ogre grunted. "You'se Mary, right?"

"I – no, I'm Basil," the Captain turned and glared at Galana, even though it was *Scrutarius* who was sniggering. "We ... well, we came here to find the Last Alicorn. Just to see it," he added quickly. "Not to – to take it or bother it or anything daft like that."

"Oh," the Ogre said, this time sounding positively pleased. "You wanna see Sparkles? Him's up flyin'. Come on," the huge, hairy brute shouldered gently through the AstroCorps visitors and knuckled away into the tunnel.

Hartigan looked at Galana again. This time his eyes were wide with excitement.

"*It's here*," he whispered.

"It's called 'Sparkles'," Scrutarius muttered.

"It short," the Ogre paused in the tunnel mouth, having heard the Blaran's comment. "It short for Sparklebutt Glitterpoops Whimsyfart Flutterfloof da Third."

"But *our* names were too difficult," Scrutarius said in amusement.

"You'se names not diff'cult," the Ogre disagreed, and pointed a thick, clawed finger at Devlin. "You'se Mary, right?"

"Yes," Devlin agreed solemnly.

"Captain," Wicked Mary spoke up as they followed the Ogre back towards the surface, "I thought you would like to know, I have found the Stonegiller ships. I had been wondering why the Stonegillers did not simply pilot to a safe distance under the water and then take off. Surely the Ogres cannot swim that fast, and they seem to be stranded on the landmass you are currently exploring."

"I wouldn't make any assumptions at this point," Galana warned. "The Ogres are formidable creatures. Remember the Man-Apes, who eradicated the Charad'chai? They were a *lesser* breed of Ogre."

"As my own species is," Chillybin added.

"I don't know if that's fair," Galana said automatically.

"So what about the Stonegillers, Mary?" Hartigan asked.

"It looks like all of their ships were crippled," Wicked Mary reported, "quite neatly. Only one of them made an emergency landing on the ground, however, and that one was destroyed by the Ogres. The rest made relatively safe oceanfall, but they are still damaged beyond repair. Some of their key energy feed components seem to have been ... ripped out, and their hulls breached by some kind of projectile. They have repaired what damage they can but they do not have replacement parts for the rest."

"Could Ogres throw stones that hard?" Galana asked Chillybin.

"Probably," Chilly said, "but I do not think this was the Ogres' doing."

"Have you run into any Stonegillers?" Basil asked.

"Swum," Devlin corrected him. "Have you *swum* into any - "

"Silence in the ranks."

"I have not encountered any Stonegillers yet," Wicked Mary replied. "I will keep you informed."

They marched from the *Þurshaugr* and into the biting wind behind the lumbering form of the Ogre. It led them directly to a cluster of the jagged stone spires that reared into the gloomy deep-purple sky, motioned for them to stop, then loped forward to stand at the base of one of the formations. Gala looked up but could see nothing in the freezing overcast.

The Ogre raised its huge tusked head and sniffed the air, then let out a short, barking roar, shockingly loud, and then shuffled back among the AstroCorps team.

"Watch out," it said, with alarming caution in its gruff voice.

They didn't have much chance to prepare. Sparklebutt Glitterpoops Whimsyfart Flutterfloof the Third landed in front of them with a loud crack of stone on stone a couple of seconds later.

The Alicorn was not beautiful. It was not a colourful fairytale creature. It certainly wasn't anything that Galana would have imagined from the name 'Sparklebutt Glitterpoops Whimsyfart Flutterfloof the Third'. It was a solid block of myth, with all the parts that *weren't* flying unicorn hewn roughly away. From its hard grey-black hooves to its short, chipped obsidian horn to its ragged sweep of brown and black feathered wings, it was heavy and bestial and fierce. Its chest and back bulged and rippled with the muscles required to provide lift to its massive body. Its eyes were wide and dark and quite mad, and situated disturbingly closer to the front of its skull than the eyes of an equine should be. Its teeth were elongated pegs of tarnished chrome. It was a stallion – very, *very* noticeably a stallion – and it smelled overpoweringly of horseshit and ammonia.

To Galana's alarm the Ogre had only *raised* its caution levels, actually hunching over to make itself look smaller and angling its head so at least one of its eyes was fixed on the ground and the other was categorically *not* looking at Sparkles. To her even greater alarm, Captain Hartigan was doing none of these very sensible things. The insane human, his face rapturous in joy and triumph, was stepping *towards* the Alicorn, gazing at its blunt, brutal face in adoration.

"He's beautiful," Basil said in a low, emotion-choked voice. He raised a shaking hand, holding up his communicator pad. "Do you see him? Do you *see* him? *He's real.*"

"I see him, Basil," the *Conch*'s computer replied – possibly, Galana reflected in a moment of terrified clarity, because everyone else was too transfixed to answer.

"We did it," Basil whispered. Tears spilled from his eyes. "We found him, Nella. We - "

He was still moving forward, his other hand coming up to touch Sparkles's great quivering snout, and the Alicorn clearly decided that enough was enough. Wings like antique midnight spread with a creak and a boom to either side, Sparkles rose onto his thick hind legs and curled his forehooves against his chest, and his head lowered to point the thick, uneven spike of his horn directly at the tiny silver-clad human. Galana stared at the short black weapon and realised, *far* later than she should have, what had grounded the Stonegill ships.

Devlin was the only one of them who didn't seem to be frozen. "*Basil!*" he shouted, and launched himself at his friend just as the Alicorn dropped. He tackled Hartigan, throwing him sideways, and there was an appallingly loud, gristly *crunch* as Sparkles's horn punctured the Blaran's back. Blaran and human were driven to the flat stone ground, Hartigan with a grunt and Scrutarius in silence.

Sparkles raised his head, thick red-amber blood drizzling from his horn and down his face. He bared his teeth and let out a high, whinnying growl utterly devoid of sanity.

With another great boom of his wings and a gust of wind that sent Wicked Mary's *giela* tumbling across the ground and staggered even the aki'Drednanth and Ogre, the Last Alicorn took to the sky once more. Galana looked up in time to see him circle the nearest spire of rock, flap his wings once, and then he vanished into the low clouds.

"Dev," Hartigan had pushed himself out from under the motionless Blaran, and was gingerly attempting to get a response from him. Bonty pushed past Galana and crouched by Devlin's side, her upper hands feeling at the awful wound in his back, her lowers fumbling with her medikit. "Devlin, old boy, talk to me."

"He's alive," Bonty said tensely, "but he'll need surgery. I can accelerate the internal damming, but we need to get back to the ship. *Now.*"

The Ogre watched as Bonty worked on Devlin deftly, then picked him up in her arms and straightened while the others hovered around uselessly.

"Sparkles *likes* you," the huge creature declared supportively.

Galana, Hartigan and Wicked Mary returned to the *Þurshaugr* while Bonty and Chillybin took the *Nella* back to reconnect with the *Conch*. While they were waiting to hear back from the doctor, they attempted to learn as much as they could about the Ogres and the Alicorn. Hartigan was shaken by Sparkles's aggression, but still determined to learn everything.

Unfortunately, the Ogre was poorly equipped to teach. It didn't remember coming to the planet and it didn't know anything much about the Alicorn – although it did point out the huge metal crate Sparkles had been stored and transported in. It was still lying, dented and partially dismantled, in a corner of the underground chamber.

"I don't understand how any living thing could survive for so long in a box," Galana shook her head. "Even if it was preserved in a special field like this structure had once."

"Mm, Sparkles is part God," the Ogre said quite positively.

Galana lowered her ears. "Excuse me?"

"Why?" the Ogre said with a suspicious squint, and sniffed the air. "You fart?"

"No, I – did you say Sparkles is part … *God?*" she stammered.

"Yup," the Ogre confirmed. "Him's mum was un'corn, him's dad was God. Or maybe uver way round," it conceded after a moment's consideration.

Any hopes that they were just talking to an unusually *thick* Ogre lasted exactly as long as it took the second Ogre to arrive at the *Þurshaugr*. The second Ogre's name seemed to be Tuesday, which solved one riddle, but the first Ogre was clearly an intellectual in comparison. Together, they managed to *just about* establish that the Ogres and the AstroCorps crew – or 'the lil silver guys' – were on the same side and had all come from more or less the same place, but that was about it. The smarter of the two claimed to have lived in a giant robot once, but that was just enough information to be tantalising.

Sparkles's fondness for the new arrivals at least meant that their ships didn't come under attack, although Galana got the distinct impression that this was not a permanent state of affairs and even the Stonegillers may have been allowed to take off and land once or twice before they'd outstayed their welcome. The Ogres did not remember who the Stonegillers were, although after an extended period of explanation they did finally admit to vaguely recalling eating something out of the ocean that tasted like 'crocodile butt', a positive change from the assortment of small, hardy native land animals that tasted like 'hairy leather butt'. The weird thing about this was, when asked if they would like to return to Six Species space and have proper food, the Ogres perked up and asked if there was 'hairy leather butt' in Six Species space too.

They did not want to return with the *Conch*, and they certainly had no intention of trying to herd Sparkles back into his crate and take him along. Galana was quietly relieved to hear this, and even Basil sighed but nodded in acceptance.

"Captain," Bonty said over the communicator a short while later. "Devlin's stable. I may need to operate one more time but he needs to rest a bit. His insides were pretty mashed. Chilly is on her way down with the *Nella*, and Roney is taking the *Splendiferous Bastard* down to pick up Bloody Mary."

"The Stonegillers?" Hartigan asked, turning to the *giela*.

"They did come out to meet me in the end," Wicked Mary admitted. "Roney was right, they like to play hunter and avoid using their weapons and technology."

"They attacked you?" Hartigan said in outrage. "Did you tell them you were there to help?"

"I tried," Wicked Mary said innocently. "They did not seem interested. Roney was, I must say, right about that as well."

"So much for aquatic-to-aquatic understanding," Galana felt obliged to say, since Scrutarius was unable to comment for himself. "Are you alright?"

"I believe I will recover, yes," Wicked Mary's *giela* nodded at the Ogres. "They do taste rather like crocodile butt, though."

"Bloody Mary, did you *eat* the Stonegillers?" Galana said wearily. "You were supposed to save them."

"Captain Pelsworthy's ship will be a tight enough squeeze without bringing meat back with me, Commander," Wicked Mary replied. "Besides, I have plenty of supplies in the Aquarium."

"What a Bloody Mary?" Tuesday asked.

Galana and Hartigan glanced at one another, wondering how – or indeed *if* – to explain.

"It a drink," the first Ogre, whose name may have been simply 'Big', since that was all Tuesday called it, said in a low rumble. "Burny drink."

"It's my nickname," Wicked Mary said smoothly.

While all of this would only have raised more questions for most species, the Ogres simply nodded and seemed to forget the whole topic. Galana decided, for simplicity's sake, to not bother explaining their Fergunakil crewmate at all.

The *Nella* set down just outside the *Þurshaugr* and Chillybin met them at the entrance. She was carrying several large boxes.

"Big and Tuesday might like the food that's available on Forbidulon," she explained, "but Bonty and I thought they might also like a little taste of home. There's a basic ration synthesiser here, although it will run out of raw materials and battery power eventually ... and a selection of sweets and treats, both from the *Conch* galley and my own Icebox stores. We don't have much information about Ogres, but one thing we do know is that they eat almost anything, and have a soft spot for sweets," she turned to Galana. WE SHOULD PROBABLY RETURN TO ORBIT BEFORE THEY REALISE THE SWEETS WON'T LAST FOREVER, she flashed to her in text form.

And so, with a final round of goodbyes and a last plaintive look up into the sky from their Captain, the crew of the *Conch* took off from the dread planet Forbidulon for the last time. *Nella* and *Splendiferous Bastard* reconnected to the *Conch*, and together AstroCorps and Boze set their sights on the edge of High Elonath.

"Well, Captain Hartigan," Galana said while Basil was programming their next relative jump. "You were right. Your fellow AstroCorps officers scoffed – including myself – but you were absolutely, completely right. The Last Alicorn is real, and you found him."

"He's real," Hartigan agreed. He'd brought down one of his precious cigars and was puffing it in triumph, a rare sight outside his quarters. "And he was everything I'd dreamed of and more."

"I'm sure Chief Engineer Scrutarius will agree once he is out of the medical bay," Galana noted.

Basil laughed. "You joke, Fen, but you wait. Dev's going to boast about taking an Alicorn to the back for me until the stars burn out. I'll never hear the bally end of it," he laughed again, then turned and gazed out of the for'ard viewscreen. They'd already pulled away from Forbidulon and the mottled purple sun was behind them, the velvety black of space ahead. "Right then," he said, "I'm all done here. What say we go home and start handing out I Told You Sos?" he stuck his cigar between his teeth, and grinned.

"Aye aye, Captain," Galana said.

"Home it is, Basil," the *Conch* agreed warmly.

The *Conch*'s armour plates opened and the relative generator field rings unfurled. They fired up in sequence, activating the field around the ship and projecting her into soft-space.

The ACS *Conch* plunged into the grey. Destination: home.

THE END

ABOUT THE AUTHOR

Andrew Hindle was born in Perth, Western Australia, and did some stuff there for a while before moving to Sotunki, Finland.

He now lives happily ever after in Sotunki with his wife Janica, his daughters Elsa and Freja, and a very small and *very* exclusive online community of readers who he frequently considers he does not deserve.

He almost always means that in a positive way.

OTHER BOOKS BY ANDREW HINDLE

Arsebook: My Rear In Status 2011
(The story of one man's short, cowardly and dishonourable battle with cancer, told through the enduring medium of social networking status messages)

THE FINAL FALL OF MAN
Eejit
Drednanth
Bonshoon
Fergunakil
Blaran
Molran
Damorak
Human

TALES OF THE FINAL FALL OF MAN
Deadshepherd: Anthology 1
The First Feast: Anthology 2
Panda Egg (The Cromicles of Theria): Anthology 3

ORÆL RIDES TO WAR
Bad Cow
Greyblade

FOR YOUNGER READERS
Are You My Corpulent Brood Matriarch?

Printed in Poland
by Amazon Fulfillment
Poland Sp. z o.o., Wrocław